# ANDREA KANE

# THE MURDER THAT NEVER WAS

# ANDREA KANE

# THE MURDER THAT NEVER WAS

ISBN-13: 978-1-68232-000-6

THE MURDER THAT NEVER WAS

For questions and comments about the quality of this book, please contact us at CustomerService@bonniemeadowpublishing.com.

www.BonnieMeadowPublishing.com

Printed in USA

### Publisher's Cataloging-in-Publication

Kane, Andrea, author.
    The murder that never was / Andrea Kane.
    pages cm -- (Forensic instincts)
    LCCN 2015954525
    ISBN 978-1-68232-000-6

    1. Serial murderers--Fiction. 2. Murder--Investigation--Fiction. 3. Thrillers (Fiction)
I. Title. II. Series: Kane, Andrea. Forensic Instincts novel.

PS3561.A463M87 2016      813.54
        QBI15-600201

To all foster kids who struggle to overcome the odds and to all foster families who help them do it.

And to

Chuck, Board member, and most of all friend, who brought so much to our lives. You will be deeply missed.

# CHAPTER ONE

*Lincoln Park*
*Chicago, Illinois*
*May 17th*

Lisa Barnes couldn't believe how quickly her luck had changed.

A week ago, she'd been in poverty-stricken hell. Now, she had a job, a place to stay in a nice Chicago neighborhood, and maybe, just maybe, a future.

She strolled around the cozy, two-story rental house that was now her home—at least temporarily—touching a figurine here and a photograph there. She still had to pinch herself to accept her good fortune. Especially after last week's start of another string of failures. How many jobs had she tried to get that week—every day starting at eight a.m.? And then again today? At least fifteen in total, maybe more.

Her doctored resume, complete with skills she didn't have, was a loser. So she'd tweaked it just enough to include her personal background—eighteen years in foster care—hoping to elicit some sympathy.

That hadn't worked, either.

All bullshit and full of unmerited confidence, she'd walked into every business in downtown Chicago, from a bakery to a stationery store, asking for any position they had—a stock person, a cashier—anything. She'd stopped just short of begging.

One look at her work history, plus the gaps it contained, and they'd all tossed her out.

She'd all but given up when she spotted that snotty rich-women's gym tucked away at the end of Michigan Avenue, just past the designer shops.

It was so pink inside that Lisa almost puked. It looked like a giant ball of cotton candy—the walls, the carpeting, even the trim on the trainers' little spandex outfits.

Pink. Pink. Pink.

How could these women stand it?

The clientele dripped money. Lisa hadn't spent so much of her adult life living in shitholes not to be able to recognize über-wealth. Diamonds flashed everywhere, like brilliant spots of light on the women's fingers, wrists, and ears.

Surely a place like this would have the cash to offer her a job.

Lisa approached the marble front desk, combing her fingers through her light brown hair and giving the woman behind it a glowing, fake smile. She knew she looked passable—she'd worn her only silk top and a pair of designer jeans. She was more cute than pretty, but she was also thin and fit, and she knew how to use makeup when she had to.

The woman at the desk was clearly the owner. She emanated a sense of authority. At first, she gave Lisa a familiar glance and then did a double take. Clearly, she'd mistaken her for someone else.

Realizing that Lisa wasn't who she'd thought she was, the owner's whole manner changed. It was marketing time. She eyed Lisa up and down, assessing her from top to bottom. She could afford to be discerning; she herself was petite, toned, and slim, her blonde hair tied back in a ponytail, and her demeanor perky. In fact, all the trainers looked perky. That must be a requirement for the job. That and dazzling white, perfect teeth.

Smiling—also with perfect white teeth—the owner said, "Welcome to Designer Fitness. I'm Kristen. How can I help you today?"

Lisa widened her smile, hoping her teeth didn't scream the words *caffeine-stained*. "Hi, Kristen. I'm Lisa. Actually, I was wondering if you might need a new employee. I'm looking for the right job."

"I see." A complete shift in attitude. No surprise. "Are you a trainer?"

"Unfortunately, no. I, myself, work out every day, but not professionally. I can assist in any other way you need, however."

Kristen's forehead creased. "Such as?"

"Welcoming the clients. Showing prospective ones around. Handling desk duty."

A pause. "Do you have a resume?"

This was the part where it went straight downhill.

As she'd done all day, Lisa pulled out her paperwork. She knew what it said by memory. A spotty education that didn't look good, no matter how much she'd doctored it. Ditto for the odd jobs, although she'd claimed to have been a hostess in the five pricy restaurants she'd worked in, rather than a waitress in three of them and a coat check girl at the others. And then there were those stellar jobs at the supermarkets—jobs she'd upgraded to stock manager rather than the cashier that she'd been.

Upgraded or not, none of the jobs was impressive and none of them had lasted more than six months, at best. So she'd inserted the early childhood stuff—about spending eighteen years in the foster care system, working as a nanny—a stretch from the truth, which was that she'd done lots of babysitting—to become financially independent as soon as she turned eighteen.

So much for the doctoring.

Kristen handed her back the pages with that same incredulous look on her face that Lisa had seen all day.

"I'm sorry," she said. "You have no pertinent work experience, and I don't think you're the right fit for our clientele."

"Please," Lisa replied. "I need a job desperately. I'll do anything you need—mop floors, clean bathrooms—anything."

Kristen was in the process of shaking her head.

That's when the miracle had happened.

"Kristen," a female voice behind Lisa said. "You know, we can use a ladies' lounge assistant. That place is always crowded, and the clients have been complaining that no one's been providing enough towels, toiletries, snacks, bottles of water—you name it. Maybe this young woman could fill that role."

Lisa turned, and her eyes widened for a second. No wonder Kristen had mistaken her for someone else. This woman could be her sister.

Recognizing the same thing, the woman—her attire identifying her as a personal trainer—grinned. "Now there's even more reason to give you a job. Our clientele would love the resemblance. They'd be talking about it for weeks." Seeing her boss wavering, the trainer said, "Why don't you let me interview her and see if she'd fit in. She certainly has the right look," she added in a teasing tone.

Kristen wasn't about to argue with that. "Fine," she agreed, going off to assist one of her clients, who was having trouble learning how to use the new Tread Climber.

"What's your name?" Lisa had blurted out.

"Julie Forman. What's yours?"

"Lisa Barnes."

And that had been the start of a very long and, ultimately, hit-it-big day.

Julie had conducted the interview over lunch at a nearby diner, watching Lisa as she hungrily downed a burger, an order of fries, another of onion rings, and an enormous hunk of cheese-cake. Julie, of course, ate grilled salmon—dry—and a small green salad with balsamic dressing. For dessert, she treated herself to a sorbet.

Lisa knew she must look like some kind of wild animal, but she couldn't seem to help herself. She hadn't had a decent meal in three days.

Julie didn't comment on Lisa's behavior. She did skim her paperwork, however, an expression of compassion flickering across her face as she read the life Lisa had led.

"You were in foster care all your life?" she asked.

"Till I was eighteen, yes." Lisa showed no emotion. "My mother dumped me on the steps of some church. Typical sto-ry, would be my guess. A teenager who was scared to death and didn't know what to do with a baby she didn't want or know how to care for. At least she didn't throw me in the garbage, right?"

Julie hadn't smiled. "You haven't had any breaks in life. Were any of these foster homes happy experiences?"

Lisa shrugged. "They were okay. Some better, some worse. But it wasn't all their fault. I was a handful."

"Why doesn't that surprise me?" Julie said, sounding amused. "It says here that you're twenty-nine. Is that true?"

Lisa nodded.

"Me, too." Julie glanced down. "At least we don't have the

same birthday. I've got three months on you—assuming the date you gave is also real?"

"That's the date the nuns who found me gave to foster care," Lisa responded. "Everything on the page you're reading is as true as I've been told."

"Fair enough." Julie leaned forward, folding her hands on the table in front of her, indicating that the compassionate part of the interview was over. "You fabricated the rest of this resume."

Lisa played the innocent very well. "What do you mean?"

"I watched you when we came in here and were seated. You had no comfort level with that hostess at all. But you were beyond patient with our fairly inept waitress. You practically jumped up and wrote the order down for her. It's not a leap to figure out what you really did at your restaurant jobs."

Lisa knew when she'd been caught. So there was no point in lying. "Mostly, I was a waitress. I was also a coat check girl. And, for the record, I worked my ass off at all those jobs. Oh, and before you cut this interview short, I wasn't a manager of any kind at the supermarkets. I was a cashier."

"And the nanny part?"

"A glorified babysitter—not that I see a difference."

Julie's lips twitched. "As long as you've decided to drop the pretense, I have another important question for you. Do you do drugs?"

"I have in the past," Lisa replied. "Weed. Coke. And, yeah, I've gotten in trouble because of it. But that's over now. I'm clean." All that was true. And there was more—none of which Julie needed to know. She'd been young and stupid and desperate. But she'd managed to slam the door on that chapter of her life.

Julie scrutinized her intently, then said, "I believe you," and continued on. "In your opinion, do you think you can handle the job I suggested?"

Lisa's brows shot up. "Are you still considering hiring me? Even after you know how much I exaggerated my resume?"

"Not all of it," Julie reminded her. "Your personal background is real—and can be verified, I assume?"

"Sure." Lisa shrugged. "Go for it. None of that is fiction or an exaggeration."

"Then I repeat my question—given the very basic jobs you've held, do you think you can handle the one I suggested to Kristen?"

Amusement danced in Lisa's eyes. "Being poor and having those basic jobs, I've been around people who were richer than me all my life—as a child and as an adult. I know how to cater to them. But I'll also read any manual, policies, or instructions you give me and have them memorized overnight. My brain just kind of does that by itself."

"That's impressive. Are you trustworthy?"

It was a legitimate question. Still, Lisa's brows shot up again. "Are you kidding? Do you think I'd steal from the only place that's offered me a job in two weeks? I'd have to be a complete moron to do that."

"Good point." That glint of empathy was back in Julie's eyes. "I'll make you a deal. You need a job. I'll urge Kristen to hire you. In return, I need another pair of hands. I just moved to a new place a few miles from here. It needs some work, and I need some help doing it. I work in two separate, completely different gyms, which means very long hours. I don't have the time to fix the place up myself. You can move in for a while—it's big enough for two people—unless, of course, you're already situated?"

Lisa thought of the dumpy motel she'd been staying in. The decaying walls. The combined stench of sex and sweat. The bugs that Lisa had no desire to identify. The gross, leering pervs outside the place who eyed her up and down every time she came or went, yelling out suggestive, horny remarks.

The place was a shithole. And Lisa had been counting her dollars as she prayed and planned to get out of there.

"No, I'm flexible on that score," she said, probably too quickly.

If Julie sensed her desperation, she didn't let on.

"Good," she replied. "Then you can move in right away. In the meantime, you can borrow some of my clothes. You need the right look—clothes, makeup, etc.—to work at our gym."

"I get it. Time to go classy." Lisa was staring at Julie, stupefied. "You'd really do all that for me?"

"Actually, yes. There's something about you I like. Maybe it's the resemblance, which I get a kick out of. Maybe it's because you're straightforward. You didn't bullshit your way out of it when I confronted you with the truth. Yes, you doctored your resume, but it was out of desperation, not greed. And you did a hell of a job, by the way. You might lack experience, but you're smart. I think you'd be a good addition to the staff. And I think you deserve a chance. Just don't screw it up."

"I won't." Lisa had felt as if the weight of the world had been lifted off her shoulders.

Instead of reveling in her newfound opportunity, she did what she always did—shot off her stupid, impulsive mouth.

"Trusting me at work is one thing, but how do you know I won't steal your money and rob your house?" She wanted to kick herself even as she said the words.

Julie burst out laughing. "Probably because you just asked me that question. But also, I don't have much worth stealing—unless you're into little antique figurines?"

Lisa grimaced, then quickly straightened her expression. "Sorry."

"They're not my thing, either," Julie replied. A tinge of sadness came over her. "But my parents left them to me."

"Do you have brothers and sisters?"

"Nope. Just me."

"You're almost as alone as I am." Lisa felt a wave of kinship. "It sucks, doesn't it?"

"Big-time." Julie cleared her throat. "Anyway, I think we have an understanding." She reached across the table to shake Lisa's hand. "Do you have a cell phone?"

Lisa's brows rose as she met Julie's handshake. "I'm a street kid, not a dinosaur," she replied. "Of course I have a cell phone. I know what to save my lousy salaries for. And a state-of-the-art smartphone was number one on the list."

Julie's lips twitched. "What's your number?"

Lisa gave it to her.

"Good. I'll give you a call tomorrow, after I talk to Kristen."

Lisa finished her stroll around the house and plopped down on the sofa.

She and Julie had made a fair amount of progress this week, getting the place in order. She didn't mind doing it, because Julie was really being great to her. Even the job at the gym wasn't too bad, if you ignored the vapid conversations about wallpaper and vacations. Just as she'd promised Julie, she'd read the rule book, dressed right, and played the part. The reward was acceptance by the clientele and an occasional whopper of a tip.

And finally—a friggin' paycheck.

The only thing that worried her a little was Julie's change in attitude these past couple of days. She'd seemed like such a sunny, bouncy person. Now, she spent longer hours at her other gym. When she came home, she was quieter, more pensive, and clearly deeply bothered by something. Lisa only hoped it wasn't her. She'd really been trying. Sometimes her mind went to the scariest possibility—that by some horrible fluke, Julie had found out the full story of her past. But when that thought popped up, Lisa nipped it in the bud by reminding herself that someone as straightforward as Julie would have confronted her and tossed her out. No, she would not let herself go there.

Thinking about Julie's state of mind, Lisa decided it was time to extend herself a little bit more. She stood up, walked into the kitchen, and checked out the freezer. There was a Styrofoam package of chop meat in there—just enough to make some of her A-plus meatballs. And she knew there were boxes of pasta and cans of tomato sauce in the house, because she'd arranged the pantry last night.

Maybe a good, homemade dinner would make Julie's mood brighten.

Pulling out the chop meat to defrost, Lisa glanced at her watch. Julie had left over an hour ago, saying she had to do some errands and pick up a few things at the corner convenience store. It must have been a lot more than a few things for her to be gone so long.

Lisa opened the front door and peeked down the street. The sun was starting to dip down toward the horizon, and there was still no sign of her benefactor.

The May evening was still warm enough to sit outside, and Lisa needed the air anyway. After a full day of waiting on rich women and a few hours of deep house cleaning, she was ready to relax.

She poured herself a glass of iced tea and went out to the front porch, sitting on the top step to enjoy the evening and wait for Julie to arrive.

About a half hour later, she spotted Julie coming down the street. She was striding angrily, gripping a bag in her hands. Even from a distance, Lisa could see that something was very wrong. As she approached, Lisa could see that she was shaking.

This wasn't a bad mood. This was bad.

Lisa's stomach clenched. She rose and put her iced tea on the small outdoor table.

She was just about to hurry down to see what was wrong when a car sped down the street, stopping right next to Julie. The passenger door flew open, and a barrel-chested man with tattoos on his arms stepped out. He was holding a gun.

Julie turned, startled, and dropped the bag she was carrying to the sidewalk.

She didn't even have time to scream.

It happened in two seconds. Pop. Pop. Two muffled gunshots, straight into her head. The killer grabbed the bag off the sidewalk and jumped back into the car, which then screeched off.

Julie had crumpled to the street, blood gushing from her skull, the contents of her purse spilling out around her. Cosmetics, wallet, cell phone—everything rolled onto the street.

For an instant, Lisa froze, bile rising in her throat.

Then, she raced down the stairs and straight to Julie's lifeless body.

She squatted down. No pulse. No sign of life. Julie was gone.

Had those bullets been meant for her? Had they found her after all these years?

Lisa's head flew up, and she looked all around. The block was deserted. The killer had used a silencer, and no one had heard the shots but her.

It was just her.

What the hell should she do? If the drug ring was after her, they'd come for her again as soon as they realized they'd killed the wrong girl.

Unless they never found out.

Self-preservation took over. Lisa reached over and grabbed Julie's wallet, cell phone, checkbook, keys—anything that could identify her as Julie Forman.

Digging into her own pocket, Lisa pulled out her ID wallet and dropped it next to Julie's purse.

That's all the time she had. She could already hear sirens approaching, which meant that someone had heard the screech of tires, and maybe even seen Julie's body, and called for help. She prayed they hadn't spotted her. She couldn't wait around to find out.

Shaking violently, with tears of sorrow and panic splashing down her cheeks, she glanced one last time at Julie's body.

Then she took off.

## CHAPTER TWO

*Downtown Chicago, Illinois*
*May 14th*
*Three days earlier...*

Julie Forman couldn't believe how quickly her luck had changed.

Just as she was about to fulfill her dream of buying her own gym with the inheritance her parents had left her, just as she had made huge strides in helping sixteen-year-old Shannon Barker move one step closer to realizing her Olympic dream, everything had turned to shit.

Shannon had been counting the days until her birthday—and not for the same reasons most sweet-sixteeners did. She'd wanted to become eligible for the US women's gymnastics team.

Julie was just Shannon's personal trainer, albeit at the hard-core gym Training Elite, which was Julie's second place of employment. Specifically designed for athletes with a purpose, the gym—located just a couple of miles away from Designer Fitness—was the complete antithesis of the latter. No Pilates, aerobics, spin, or yoga classes. Just pushing to the max, sweating, and moving up level by level, working toward a competitive goal. Julie worked with Shannon on comprehensive strength and cardio training, catering her workout to a professional gymnast's needs. Shannon was at Training Elite six days a week religiously, training for three hours in the morning and two in the evening.

In addition to that, Shannon's daily highest-level workouts were conducted at the Apex Olympic Gymnastic Center, which was one step away from officially training at one of the three United States Olympic Training Centers.

Her manager/coach was Yuri Varennikov, who was practically a celebrity in the world of Olympic-training gymnastics. He was all about blistering hard work, discipline, and results. He managed Shannon's upcoming career, pushed her to the limit, and turned her over to Jim Robbins, top-notch trainer to professional athletes. Jim's job was to mold Shannon into the star she wanted to be. He did everything, from stretching her to perfecting her technique on every piece of gymnastics equipment. He seemed to know just how much his pupil could take, because Shannon always rose to the challenge.

In the past few months, Julie had truly started to believe that Shannon had a real shot. Her strength and her endurance had peaked. And, having watched Shannon train with Jim, Julie could see that her form and skill had peaked right along with them.

Julie's star pupil was on the brink of something wonderful.

Until three days ago, when the whole world had shifted.

Shannon had run into Training Elite wearing a shoulder brace, tears streaking her cheeks. She'd begged Julie to talk to her alone.

They'd gone into Julie's small private office and shut the door.

"Honey, what's the matter? What happened?" Julie had been truly alarmed—and not only by the injury. The young girl had been sobbing and shaking and running trembling fingers through her hair again and again. She could barely catch her breath, she was sobbing so hard.

"It's over," she gasped. "My whole life. Everything. It's over."

A chill shot up Julie's spine, and she sucked in her breath. "How did you get hurt, and what did the doctor say?" she forced herself to ask calmly.

"During practice. I tore my rotator cuff."

"Okay. Okay. Let's try to calm down. That's going to set you back. But it'll heal, Shannon. Even if it requires surgery, it will heal."

"No, it won't." Shannon began sobbing anew, dropping into a chair and covering her face with her hands. "The X rays showed that the rotator cuff muscles and tendons are really weak and not likely to repair well. But it's worse than that. They ran more tests and an MRI. They say that my heart muscles are enlarged. They say that whatever is wrong will weaken my heart function over time."

"Cardiomyopathy," Julie murmured, feeling her stomach turn over.

Shannon's head came up. "Julie, I'll never compete. Never. They told me so. It's over. Just like that. It's over forever."

Julie's breath was coming fast, and her mind was racing. She walked around and wrapped an arm around Shannon's good shoulder, holding her while she wept. Her thoughts converged on the most likely cause of this sudden and severe situation. She hated sounding accusatory, but she had no choice.

"Shannon," she asked quietly. "Have you been taking anything? Any performance-enhancing drugs?"

Shannon didn't answer.

Julie squatted down so she could stare directly into her student's eyes. "Tell me the truth. I'm not here to judge you. I want to help you."

Shannon's lips quivered. "There is no help for me. My life is over. I just want to die."

"Did you take something, Shannon?" Julie repeated.

Shannon reached across Julie's desk with her good arm, plucked a tissue from the box, and blew her nose. "He said they weren't drugs. They were all-natural supplements. I Googled the name of them, at least the one he gave me, and it was exactly what he said. They were helping me so much—building up my stamina, building up me. I felt great. I was training great. Julie, I was ready. And now this…"

"He?" Julie repeated. "Who is he?"

Shannon was silent for a moment. Then she whispered, "Jim."

Julie tried to hide her shock. Jim? Jim Robbins? Shannon's Olympic trainer and trainer to so many other professional athletes? "Jim Robbins has been giving you supplements?" *Supplements, my ass,* she thought silently. *They were PEDs.* "For how long?"

"Ages. And they've been working great. I never thought…"

Julie rose and wiped her own tears away. She wanted to beat that man senseless. How in God's name could he have given a young girl PEDs under the guise of supplements, knowing full well what they could do to her? How many other athletes had he done this to? And why the hell didn't someone know about it?

"Shannon," she said gently. "Who else knew about the supplements?"

Shannon shook her head from side to side. "No one. Jim told me to keep it between us, because other people might misunderstand and think I was taking steroids. So I did." Her eyes narrowed on Julie's face. "But they were PEDs, weren't they? They had to be. Supplements don't destroy a person's body like that. Oh my God." A fresh batch of tears. "I'm going to go right back there and confront him. I'm going to tell him that…"

"No, you're not," Julie interrupted. "Jim is a despicable

man. I don't think it's safe to threaten him." Julie took Shannon's hands in hers. "I want you to trust me. I'm going to take care of this. I'll find evidence to bring Jim down without endangering you. You've suffered enough. Just rest your shoulder. Follow the doctor's orders. And call Phyllis Hawke." She grabbed a Post-It and scribbled down her name and number.

"Who's that?" Shannon sounded like a lost child.

"A therapist. She works with young women in situations just like yours." Julie paused. "Wait a day or two until I speak with your parents and get their permission." Julie knew damned well that she would be calling the Barkers the instant Shannon walked out her door.

"They'll give it to you. They're so worried about me. That's why they let me come to you now. They knew you'd understand. This was my dream, my everything. I have nothing left."

"Yes, you do. I know you don't believe me now, but there'll be a new dream one day. I promise you. In the meantime, please, just do as I say. Promise me you won't go to Jim."

"I promise," Shannon said woodenly. Her eyes were filled with disbelief and devoid of hope. "I couldn't face him, or anyone, right now anyway." A pause. "My parents think I should take time off from my schoolwork and just rest."

"I agree," Julie said. Shannon was home-schooled and, in addition, had a personal tutor. It was the only way for her to get an education in between the rigorous hours of training.

"I don't care about school. Honestly, Julie, I don't care about anything."

Julie was fighting with everything in her to stay calm. "That's how you feel now. And it's completely justified. It'll change. I promise." Julie turned her head and glanced out the window. "Is your driver here?"

A nod. "He drove me here. And he's driving me straight home."

"Good." Another squeeze of her hands. "I'll visit you to-morrow. In the meantime, just rest. Don't think. Don't plan. Just let yourself feel what you need to feel. If your parents agree, I'm sure Dr. Hawke will see you right away. She's a compassionate and un-derstanding woman. You can trust her to listen and to help you."

"Okay," Shannon said in a small voice.

"I'll walk you to the car."

Julie led Shannon through the gym and to the waiting chauffeur. She wouldn't let Shannon put herself in harm's way.

But Julie herself was another story. No one was going to hurt this wonderful, joyous young girl, strip her of her hopes and dreams, and get away with it.

She was going to get the proof she needed and lock the bastard away.

Alexei took a final drag of his cigarette and then tossed the butt out his car window. He'd kept the souped-up black Civic idling in neutral so he could take off at a moment's notice if he was ap-proached. Hands on the steering wheel, he leaned forward, peering inside the gym's bay window. His stare was fixed on the glass wall of the small back office, giving him a clear view of the occupants inside. The little gymnast was shaking with sobs and talking to Ju-lie Forman. There was no doubt that she'd told her. The trainer was hugging and consoling her. He couldn't make out much else, but it didn't take a brain surgeon to know what was happening.

Shannon Barker had spilled her guts to Forman. All that mattered now was what that nosy bitch planned to do about it.

He ducked down as the two of them walked to the front door. Another hug, and the teenage girl left the gym and gingerly slid into the backseat of the waiting Town Car. The driver eased out of the parking lot.

Alexei followed close behind. He had to make sure that

the kid was going straight home like a good girl. After that, Slava was expecting a phone call. Alexei would report in while he drove back from the kid's house. But he knew what his boss would say.

Keep a close eye on Julie Forman. And make sure her mouth stays shut.

Julie went through the motions for the next few days, biding her time and planning her course of action. Shannon was in therapy. She'd be okay—eventually. She was an astonishingly strong young woman. And Julie wasn't about to screw up the girl's life—or maybe even threaten it—by giving in to the burning urge to beat the shit out of Jim Robbins. What she had to do was quietly find the evidence she needed, and then use it to destroy his career—and him.

So she waited.

She forced herself to go through her regular days, planning to leave several days between Shannon's meltdown and her own purposeful intervention. Let Jim think he was safe. Let him figure that Shannon had locked herself in her bedroom and was curled up in a small ball of self-pity, sobbing buckets of tears. As long as he believed that she was keeping her mouth shut, he'd relax.

And that's when Julie would act.

On the day in question, Julie worked her regular hours and then headed home. She listened to Lisa's amusing stories of the Rich Ladies' Club, as she called the gym members she catered to each day. Then, as the evening approached, she told Lisa she was going out to the convenience store and running a few other errands.

She didn't take her car. She took the bus. That way, if someone was following her, they'd have trouble picking her out if she exited with a group of people.

The expansive Apex Center—where Shannon did her hard-core Olympic training with Yuri Varennikov—was fairly quiet when Julie arrived. There were, of course, some athletes training, but today was Jim's day off. She'd made sure of that. She walked through the front door, waving at the security guard. He waved back, recognizing her from the many times she'd been here to watch Shannon run through her dizzying workouts.

Once inside, Julie headed down to the hallway to where the business office was located. She didn't have the skills to hack into their computer system, but Jim wasn't exactly a rocket scientist. Hopefully, he would file his records in an old-fashioned file cabinet, rather than scan and save them electronically. There wouldn't be anything overt, obviously, but Julie was willing to bet she could find something incriminating—even the tiniest scrap of paper alluding to "special" transactions he'd made, whether through a doctor, a pharmacist, or some other scummy medical products dealer.

Jim wasn't a professional drug dealer. Dollars to donuts, he'd be sloppy enough to make a mistake. And she was going to find it.

She waited in an alcove until she saw Martha Peele, former Olympian and owner of the Olympic Center, walk out of the office and head down the hall to the ladies' room. Then, she peeked through the pane of glass on the door.

The room was dark. Julie turned the knob.

Unlocked.

She had to work fast—before Martha returned to finish her work and lock up for the night.

Julie yanked open the file drawers, looking only for the ones with labels on them indicating they belonged to Jim. Most of the papers inside were reports on his athletes, recommendations for future training, and injury treatment regimens. Nothing unusual—except that a half dozen of the athletes' reports had little red stickers in the upper right-hand corner.

Weird.

Just in case that was in some way significant, Julie held on to the files that held those stickered-reports. The rest of the files she returned to the drawers.

As she was putting back the last of them, her knuckles brushed up against a raised flat surface way in the back of the drawer—a raised surface that moved at her touch. Gripping it with her fingers, she pulled it out.

It looked to be a small journal.

Julie opened it—and realized she'd found the proof she needed.

The journal was a ledger, documenting all of Jim's transactions with some anonymous company. No reference was made to its name or the distribution of PEDs, but the front of the ledger was labeled with the letter R and the word *supplements*. The ledger itself detailed dates, times, and quantities alongside the initials that corresponded to the stickered athletes' reports.

There were no addresses, phone numbers, or email addresses, and no additional information, not even monetary amounts.

None of that mattered. The evidence was clear: Jim was supplying PEDs to a select number of his star trainees. The lack of dollar amounts, receipts, or paper trail meant that Jim dealt only in cash, obviously to hide the little "side business."

Furthermore, Jim wasn't a genius. Hell, he wasn't even being discreet about his suspicious records. No, there was no way he was doing this on his own. Someone was working with him. Someone smart and seasoned, with a healthy cash flow and the right connections.

But who?

Julie doubted it was Martha. She was known as a crackerjack businesswoman. She made a ton of money owning and running this place. And she wasn't stupid enough to get involved in something as dirty as this, something that could blow up in her face and send her to jail. No. Whoever Jim was reporting to had to be someone on the outside, someone shrewd who was running a more widespread operation bigger than just one dealer, one Olympic hopeful, one state-of-the-art training center.

But Jim was Julie's starting point.

She took the ledger and the stickered reports from Jim's cabinet.

Nudging the copy machine out of sleep mode, she scanned page after page, in rapid fire, until she'd compiled a ton of information. Then, she put the ledger and the files back where she'd found them and shut the file cabinet drawers. She pulled out the plastic supermarket bag she'd stuffed in her tote, putting the stack of copies she'd made inside.

Slipping out of the office, she peeked up and down the hall to make sure she was alone.

All clear.

She left the same way she'd come in.


"There she is," Vitaliy said, poking Alexei.

"Yeah, I see her." Alexei lit up another cigarette, watching Julie Forman wave to the guard and head out. "I also see the bag she's carrying. She didn't have it going in."

"Nope." Vitaliy watched Julie's progress. She'd reached the sidewalk and turned left. "She's going back to the bus stop." Vitaliy, who was behind the wheel, turned over the ignition.

"Slava's going to want whatever's in that bag." Alexei pulled out his gun and snapped a magazine into it. "Drive to her house. We'll get her near there. The bus stop's too public."

Vitaliy gave a quick nod and then steered the car, turning onto the main street.

He drove right past Julie as she walked straight to her own execution.

# CHAPTER THREE

*Tribeca, New York*
*Offices of Forensic Instincts*
*May 18th*

Emma Stirling couldn't believe how quickly her luck had changed.

She was staring at her pink-and-purple Forensic Instincts business cards—the complete antithesis of the navy-and-white traditional cards that the rest of the investigative team had. They'd given in to her on this one request, just because they got her and because they were great. These cards were awesome, and they made her feel the same.

It had only been six months since she'd conned her way into this job. Now, she was not only a receptionist, she was a real and recognized part of the FI team.

Many people had started their careers in the mailroom and made it to the boardroom. Emma planned on that happening to her. After all, she was only twenty-two. Plenty of time to get there.

Forensic Instincts was the private investigation firm with the reputation that brought clients in by the droves. Most of their clients were affluent and dubious about law enforcement's abilities to help them. But some of them were just average people with anything but average problems. Casey Woods—the president and founder of FI—never turned someone away because of financial circumstances. The company was successful enough to adjust their fees according to the client's ability to pay. It was always a team decision as to whether or not a client was taken on, and they always got it right.

Emma regarded the FI team as her family, especially since she had no other. They were brilliant, they were diverse, and they were the best. The media couldn't get enough of them. And Emma was lucky enough to be here, especially since her life before FI had been shit.

This morning had started out quietly, giving Emma time to get everything in order for the workday and to catch up on her own social media network. Maybe today she'd take a look at what was going on in Chicago, where she'd been born and lived until she was seven. Chicago held her only happy childhood memories, along with being the only real home she'd had before FI.

When she was seven, her parents had relocated to New York. A year later, they'd died in a plane crash, and she'd been turned over to foster care, being bounced from one home to another. But she remembered Chicago—especially the deep-dish pizza. And it was always cool to see who had been voted the best pizzeria of the week. New York had great Sicilian, but it wasn't the same.

Rather than hopping on Twitter and scrolling through her usual feed of the people she followed—from friends to celebrities to cool magazines to fashion trends—she went straight to the *Chicago Sun-Times* web page. She was just about to navigate to the food and dining section when a news clip caught her eye: "*Tragic End to a Tragic Life.*"

She clicked on the article, feeling sick as she read:

*Lisa Barnes, a twenty-nine-year-old woman, was found shot to death in the middle of a residential street in Chicago's Lincoln Park neighborhood. Currently, she'd been working as a gal Friday at Designer Fitness, a high-end gym five miles from the shooting. As she was a former foster child with a police record, no one has come forward to ID her body. Police believe the murder to be a drug crime.*

End of article.

End of a life.

Emma felt a surge of anger. A former foster child with a criminal record—probably for stealing a pack of gum that could have dated back ten or even fifteen years. But that didn't matter. They had to call it drug-related. Foster kids were always druggies, even as adults, right? No one claimed her, so she was discarded like the trash they assumed she was.

Nothing in life. Nothing in death.

The whole thing made Emma furious.

She was still seething when the front door of Forensic Instincts swung open, and Ryan McKay—the team's techno-whiz and the hottest hunk going—walked in. Too bad he'd just celebrated the big three-oh and was way too old for Emma's tastes. To her, Ryan was a smartass big brother. To the rest of the female population? He was a Peter Luger steak waiting to be devoured. Those smoldering Black-Irish good looks and rock-hard body combined with his air of casual deference was the magic combination.

Too bad all those drooling women were shit outta luck. Whether or not Ryan admitted it to himself, he was pretty much taken, and by one of Forensic Instincts' very own: Claire Hedgleigh. Claire was the FI team's claircognizant—or, to quote the vernacular, their psychic. She and Ryan were polar opposites, so the sparks flew like crazy when they were around each other. That applied at the office and, as the whole team knew, in the bedroom.

Now Ryan marched up to Emma's desk, clearly in a whole different mindset than Emma.

"Hey, brat," he greeted her. "I just came from the gym. Look what I bought." He pulled open a bag and flourished what looked to be a complicated set of yellow bands, with straps and handles and God knew what else.

"Uh… that's cool—I think," Emma said, her attention temporarily diverted from the article she'd been reading. "What is it? Some kind of sex toy?"

Ryan frowned. "No, and you're way too young to know what those are."

"I'm twenty-two."

"Barely out of diapers. Anyway, this is a TRX Suspension Trainer—a portable performance training tool. You can use it anywhere. It leverages gravity and body weight—in this case, mine—so I can do hundreds of exercises right here at the brownstone."

"Why were you shopping at the gym? I thought you and Aidan were planning Marc's bachelor party?"

Marc Devereaux, Casey's right-hand guy at FI—former Navy SEAL, former agent for the FBI's Behavioral Analysis Unit—had reunited with the love of his life, and they were tying the knot. Love? Marc? No one ever thought it would happen.

But it had. And now, Ryan and Aidan, Marc's older brother, couldn't get enough shots in ribbing him about it.

"We're planning the rager, don't worry," Ryan replied with a grin. "We bought Marc a TRX, too. He'll be thrilled. It was invented by a Navy SEAL. He'll immediately think it's a superior device."

"And the party?" Emma prompted.

"Oh, yeah, that. It's all set. It'll be me, Aidan, and three of Marc's buddies. We're hitting the gym for a hard-core circuit training competition. After that, we'll be drinking ourselves into oblivion at that new bar one block over."

"That's a bachelor party?"

Ryan's grin widened. "In Marc's eyes, yes. He specifically said no strippers."

"And you listened?"

"Sure we did." Ryan winked. "But we never promised anything about lap dancers. See you later." He scooped up his new exercise equipment and headed downstairs to his man cave, or his lair, as everyone called it, to try out the TRX.

Emma's smile vanished as her gaze drifted back to her computer screen. There was something about this murder that just got to her. Maybe because it was so unfair. Maybe because it hit too damn close to home.

But it was going to take time for her to put it out of her mind.

*Amtrak Lake Shore Limited, somewhere between Chicago and New York*
*May 19th*

Lisa leaned back in her seat, staring blankly out the window as the train sped along to its destination.

It had been two days since Julie was killed, and she was still a trembling wreck. She'd never get that image out of her head—Julie lying on the ground, crumpled, blood pouring out of her head.

Dead.

"Concentrate on the book for a while, and turn your nightmares off." Miles Parker, who was sitting across from Lisa, clicking away on his laptop, leaned forward and tapped on the textbook. "You've got to get that whole ACE Personal Trainer Manual down pat and be ready to take the test by the time we hit Manhattan and jump on that train to Upper Montclair."

"You know I can do it, no problem." Lisa turned her head to look at her oldest and closest friend with tortured eyes. "We've both seen a lot of stuff, Milo, but seeing someone murdered right in front of me? That was something I'll never get over."

"Shh," Milo said, glancing quickly around. "I know. And you will get through it. I'm here now to make sure of that. But we can't talk about this in public, remember?"

"I remember." Lisa glanced down at the manual on her lap.

"Good girl…Julie."

Julie.

Milo had worked fast and hard to transform Lisa's identity in a mere forty-eight hours.

He'd waited until the crime scene had been cleared away. Then, he'd taken the house key that Julie had given to Lisa and casually let himself in. He'd brought a cardboard box with him and gathered only the things he needed—Julie's laptop, checkbook, a bunch of photos and personal papers, the ACE manual, some personal trainer books, and a few personal items, such as costume jewelry and three new Lycra workout outfits to start Lisa out.

Beforehand, he'd rifled through the stuff Lisa had taken off Julie's body. Her cell phone had all her contacts in it. Her wallet was pay dirt. It contained her driver's license, social security card, credit cards, and ATM card. As a lucky bonus, Julie had kept a cheat sheet with all of her passwords to every account. Milo could have found a way to get that information—eventually—but this way it meant they could get away faster and without tedious hacking work.

God bless Milo. He'd been Lisa's protector since they were kids in the foster care system. They'd always been close, whether or not they were living in the same home. Although being separated didn't happen often. They'd always fought to be a "package deal" as they'd moved from foster home to foster home—and more times than not they were successful. Lisa was a brat, and Milo was always her sidekick, not to mention intervening whenever she was being punished, so he was far from a favored child. Letting him go was a no-brainer if it meant getting rid of Lisa.

As an adult, Milo still was a loner. Most people thought he was odd, and maybe he was. With a genius mentality that translated into being socially awkward, and interests in advanced scientific theory and children's cartoons, he walked to the beat of his own drum. Add to that a mop of unruly light brown hair that always looked unbrushed and a perpetual attire of jeans and oversized graphic T-shirts that swallowed up his lanky frame— well, let's say he never really fit in.

Except with Lisa.

She'd always recognized how gentle and kindhearted Milo was, understood him on a level no one else seemed able to, and fully got how brilliant he was. He'd find the right answer to every problem. He'd certainly found one to this catastrophe.

He had a computer brain from the get-go.

He'd always found part-time jobs throughout high school, helping people troubleshoot and fix their laptops. He also could hack into anything to get whatever information he needed.

And now, as an adult, he had a good, solid job with Dell computers as an online tech support guy—where he could deal with people without actually being in their presence.

Even though both Lisa and Milo had agreed to test their independence by renting separate places to live in, Lisa had run straight to Milo after the shooting, and he'd stashed her away in

his tiny studio apartment. He'd held her while she sobbed, made
her something to eat even when she wasn't hungry, and given her
his bed while he camped out in his sleeping bag. He knew what
was at stake, who Lisa was afraid of and why. And he knew that
she had good reason to be.

When she was calm enough, he'd given her instructions,
which she'd followed to a tee. She'd taken the cash that was in
Julie's wallet and gone to a salon on the other side of town, where
she'd gotten a haircut and highlights. She'd then picked up colored
contacts to change her eye color from hazel to golden brown.

It was enough. She looked startlingly like Julie.

Milo had done the rest. He'd searched the Internet, ex-
ploring dozens of cities and towns across the country, until he'd
found exactly what they needed: a small local gym that was rent-
to-buy in Upper Montclair, New Jersey.

The woman who needed to unload it was moving to Europe and required an instant transaction. So she'd settled for a
modest monthly rental with the hopes that Julie would be pur-
chasing the popular gym in no time. It was in the heart of a yup-
pie area, near mass transit to Manhattan, and included in the
deal all the newest and most extensive array of training equipment.

So Milo and Lisa were on their way to a new life.

"Thank you," Lisa murmured now. "For everything."

"I'll take some home-cooking as my payback." Milo
winked, his gaze returning to his computer. "Plus, it's a cool opportunity for me. I've never been to the Big Apple or to New
Jersey. And my job is certainly transportable—as am I."

"Where are we living?"

"Right on Bellevue Avenue in Upper Montclair, one
block from your gym. I rented us an apartment with one and a
half bedrooms, a living room, a bathroom, and a galley kitchen.

I'll use the half bedroom as a combo bedroom and computer station. We'll be fine."

"Wasn't that expensive?"

"Not too bad. Plus, we have my income, your inheritance, and the gold mine of a gym you're about to launch."

"Does the landlord allow pets?"

Milo grinned. "Still dead set on getting that dog, I see. Well, you'll have your wish. Pets are allowed. But I'm not cleaning up turds, so the training's on you."

"Fair enough." Lisa glanced at Milo's keyboard, which he was now pounding on again. "What are you doing?"

"A whole bunch of things, Julie." He kept using her new name so it would sink in and become her own. "I logged on as you. I'm now emailing your landlord, telling him you got a sudden out-of-town job and had to relocate ASAP. I told him to charge your credit card for the duration of your lease so he's appeased and doesn't raise any red flags. I know the rental house was furnished, but I'm letting him know that he can sell everything else, donate it to charity, whatever, and to keep the proceeds for his trouble."

"Oh." Lisa was trying to process everything Milo was saying.

"I'm also emailing your two gym bosses, Kristen and Nora, and explaining that you're leaving town. I scanned an article from the *Sun-Times* reporting Lisa's death, and I'm attaching it to the emails. I'm saying that, after living with someone who was shot to death right in front of your house, you're too freaked out to work. That you've got to get out of Chicago. I'm sending your apologies for the lack of notice and any inconvenience it causes them, and asking them to email any unemployment paperwork. Blah, blah, blah."

Milo paused and gave a baffled shrug. "Kristen and Nora

are both females. Statistics say that females are far more moti-vated by feelings than males are; I've read that in several reliable sources. So, they'll understand where you're coming from and forgive you. I don't get it, but that's how it will go down."

"I guess." Lisa tucked her hair behind her ear. She was still getting used to this new angled style, although she'd really admired it on Julie.

The old Julie. The dead Julie.

She shuddered. "Milo, do you really think we'll be able to pull this off? I mean, I can memorize anything and pass any test. But becoming another person..." She broke off, glancing quickly around as she recalled what Milo had said about talking about this among people.

"Not a doubt, Julie," he replied. "You're going to create a gym that everyone will want to join. Just read your book, do your magic memorizing thing, and the suburban women will be breaking down your doors to sign up for the diamond package."

His brow creased as he began pounding into the comput-er again. "In the meantime, I'm getting us a backdoor exit, a way to vanish if something unforeseen blows up in our face."

"What do you mean?"

Milo leaned forward and stabbed at her book with his forefinger. "Read. Do what you do best. Leave the rest to me."

"All right." The new Julie Forman turned to the next page in the manual and began to absorb the required information.

Milo was never one to let grass grow under his feet. He'd seen sure things turn to shit way too often. He'd mentioned the backdoor plan offhandedly to the new Julie, but his task was very real, very difficult, and very imperative. He had to make sure they could vanish on a dime if need be.

With that in mind, he fired up Freenet and went to

the Nerdageddon index. He appreciated the anonymity that the darknet offered, although he hated how it had become a haven for child pornography. At least Nerdageddon tried to filter out that crap, and Freenet would keep his activity hidden from others.

What he needed now was a link to a discussion board of security experts who understood how people could be tracked. Some of it was obvious, like social security numbers, driver's licenses, bank accounts. But even frequent shopper cards, patterns of Amazon purchases, etc. could be linked to individuals, even their cell phones. These were the avatars in the know. Disappearing off the grid was not easy in today's digitally linked world. He needed advice and he needed it fast.

It took him a while. Then—success. He found the right link. A chat room called Kerberos. The double entendre was fitting. Kerberos was a computer authentication protocol developed at MIT and widely used on the Internet to prove one's identity. It also referred to the three-headed dog guarding the entrance of the Underworld, making sure no one got in or out. Milo added himself to the chat room, adding the screen name "ScoobyDoo" and an appropriate picture. Milo grinned at the irony of ScoobyDoo and Kerberos—two diametrically opposed personalities in the world of fictional canines.

He posted his question: "How can someone leave his prior identity behind and become a totally new person?" He turned on the notification so as answers were posted to his question, he would receive a notification to return to the Kerberos chat room and read them.

Now all he could do was wait and hope that the right geniuses would answer.

"Are you fucking kidding me?" Slava Petrovich—or Slava

the Slayer, as he was known for his cold and brutal executions—slammed down the newspaper clipping and rose menacingly from behind his desk. He was an odd contradiction—he looked like a cross between a bulldog and a prizefighter, yet he dressed in expensive Italian suits and had an office befitting the high-level business executive that he was—sometimes.

Now his voice—speaking entirely in Russian—reverberated around the room, and his eyes were blazing. "You killed the wrong goddamn woman."

Alexei swallowed. "It looked just like her. She went to Apex, pulled all this shit, and copied it." He gestured at the bag he'd dumped on Slava's desk, with all the file pages and receipts that Julie had confiscated and photocopied.

"You fucking idiot, that wasn't her," Slava snapped. "That was the bitch who was staying with her, the one she got the job for. Julie Forman must have paid her to do her dirty work, so you assholes would follow her and blow her away. Which is exactly what you did. Now the useless whore is dead, and Julie Forman is God knows where. She ditched her apartment and took off."

"If that's true, we got the bag off of the dead woman before she could do anything with it," Vitaliy said.

"Maybe that's true. But we don't know what proof she already got from that stupid little gymnast. Julie Forman is a potential loose end. Jim Robbins is a definite one. He's a prison sentence—or worse—waiting to happen. And I'm the lucky one who has to deliver all this news and get my head handed to me." He flung an arm toward the door. "Get the fuck out of my sight."

Slava rubbed his temples as Dumb and Dumber left the room. He had a huge fucking migraine, and it was about to get worse.

Sliding open his drawer, he took out two aspirin and popped them into his mouth, washing them down with a shot of vodka.

He dreaded the phone call he was about to make. This would not go over well.

Like a prisoner being marched off to his execution, Slava picked up the phone and entered the number.

# CHAPTER FOUR

*Tribeca, New York*
*Offices of Forensic Instincts*

Ryan was waiting for some online feedback on the team's current case. The info would be coming soon, so there wasn't enough time to tinker with his current robotic project. As a result, he took a quicker, alternative route to passing the time—he conducted his routine check-in on the few darknet chat rooms he frequented.

Kerberos was one of his favorites. It was interesting on many levels. Technically, he enjoyed the expert banter about Internet security. For pure entertainment value, he was always amazed by individuals trying to escape detection—everyone from cheating spouses to tax cheats screwing the US government to dirty business partners screwing each other. What he couldn't stomach was the child predators posing as First Amendment advocates. He made sure to give them what appeared to be the right advice, except for the one or two "errors" that he knew law enforcement would be monitoring. A few months later, the avatar would grow silent. Other members would speculate, and Ryan would just grin at the thought of another scumbag in jail. Lady Justice could be a fickle mistress at times.

One new post caught his attention. Someone named ScoobyDoo was asking how to disappear. The brevity of the question was concerning. Usually, cheaters of one kind or another would pose hypothetical situations, such as: "My friend wants to keep an affair secret from his wife and has asked for my advice. What should I tell him?" But this post had none of that. Straight and to the point.

Ryan needed more information, but the code of conduct prohibited asking why. This needed finesse.

Ryan posted a simple response, using his own screen name, AdrenoJunkie: "To answer your question, I would need to know some specifics about your situation. How old are you? Are you disappearing alone or with others? How will you support your future lifestyle? In what country and type of community— urban/suburban/rural/remote—do you want to live? Are you willing to forgo all forms of communication with friends and family, as well as digital commerce using all forms of payment? There are more questions to be answered, but this will start a meaningful dialogue."

Most people would give up right after reading his questions. They would realize what they'd have to leave behind and what they would have to give up in the future.

Ryan wondered whether ScoobyDoo would even respond.

Two hours later he had his answer.

And it rapidly triggered his own response.

*Julie. Julie. Julie.*

Lisa had drilled that name into her head every day of the past three weeks. She'd been called that by Milo to the point of Chinese torture, and she'd been addressed as that by every job applicant she'd interviewed. She'd literally and totally started thinking of herself that way.

Lisa was dead. Julie was alive and opening a new gym in

Upper Montclair, New Jersey.

Lisa was now Julie. And the gym—*her* gym—now proudly called Excalibur—was just ten days away from its grand opening.

She'd always loved working out, running, and staying fit. Well, this was a big step beyond that. She'd learned a hell of a lot about her profession in the past few weeks. Her ACE exam was behind her, passed with flying colors. She was officially a certified personal trainer. Along with passing the ACE exam, she'd done a ton of hands-on work. She'd studied and become proficient at the machines, taken a half dozen workshops, and watched as many YouTube videos as she could find, along with exercise DVDs to familiarize herself with the latest moves. Most of all, she'd worked out nonstop, gaining stamina, muscle development, and core strength.

She might lack experience, but she'd made it her business to know her stuff.

In addition to that, she'd hired two highly qualified PTs to work with her clients. They'd both been recently unemployed, thanks to the economic climate. So they were grateful for the job offers and had come to her at reasonable rates. She was watching her budget carefully. As for the gym itself, she and Milo were prepping it for its grand opening, totally revamping and refreshing it for the big day.

Now, she stood in front of the floor-to-ceiling mirrors that lined the back wall of Excalibur and admired the results of the hard work that she and Milo had invested. Through the reflection of the mirrors, Julie could get a panoramic view of the entire gym—including the sprawling front desk, the spacious main workout room, the two smaller rooms in either corner, plus a third turf room off to the side.

She'd worked her ass off to make sure the gym was both male and female friendly. No estrogen overkill colors or bullshit smoothie bar. This was the real deal, with equipment, space, and instructors to satisfy everyone.

They'd paid a ton of money for the brand new rubber floor in the weight area, but it was worth every penny. Industrial strength, the floor was thick, tough, and texturized—the best there was. Situated on the heavy-duty floor were five adjustable benches, perfect for lifting weights, bench-pressing, and doing leg squats.

In the small turf room off the weight area were three TRX suspension systems. Julie was still reading up on all the core-building aspects of the TRX, but she couldn't wait to try it.

The machine circuit was the nucleus of the gym. The previous owner had chosen Cybex machines to make sure her members were safe and able to get the most out of their work-outs—shoulder flies, chin-ups, ab crunches, leg presses, triceps extensions, and bicep curls. That was a great plus for Julie.

She'd made sure all her bases were covered: ellipticals, treadmills, bicycles, stair climbers, and row trainers complete with flat-screen TVs, courtesy of Milo, to entertain the members. Spin bikes. A small, dedicated room for aerobics, yoga, and Pilates classes was equipped with blue, moveable mats, exercise balls of various sizes, resistance bands, yoga mats, step stools, and jump ropes.

The final section of the gym was dedicated to locker rooms for men and women, a vending machine with bottled water, Gatorade, and energy drinks, and Julie's personal office—a private space she'd never dreamed of having but now did.

She took in the total effect and smiled.

Thanks to the previous owner and a ton of grunt work, Excalibur was now a cutting-edge gym. Julie was confident that her membership would soar as soon as she opened the doors.

And the cash would come rolling in.

*Chicago, Illinois*
*Nineteenth Police District*

Police Detective Frank Bogart was closing out his evening shift by plowing through his low-priority pile. He scanned the skinny file on top and swiveled around in his desk chair to face his partner.

"Hey, Paula." He waved the file in the air. "Are we pursuing this or labeling it as closed?"

"What's this?" Detective Paula Kline asked, barely looking up. She was preoccupied with moving in high gear, thanks to the not-happy phone call she'd just received from her husband, informing her of the now-burnt dinner he'd cooked for her. She was in deep shit.

"The murder of that woman Lisa Barnes." Frank had opened the file and was skimming it. "Remember? We talked to Ethel Simmons, that elderly woman with the walker in the next building who heard the car and got a quick glimpse of the body. Because of her handicap, she didn't wait around to see if anyone else showed up. She just shuffled as fast as she could over to her landline to call 911. So that's it from her end. We've got nothing else—no witnesses, no motive other than pure speculation, no friends or family—zip. We've also got no time or resources. So do we close the case?"

"Yeah, I guess." Paula leaned back in her chair and crossed her arms over her breasts. "Although it still niggles at me that the woman she was staying with..." She paused, searching for the name.

"Julie Forman," Frank supplied.

"Right. That Julie Forman disappeared into thin air right after the murder."

"She was scared shitless, according to the emails she sent to her employers."

"Don't blame her. But the story she gave her landlord was that she got a better job elsewhere and had to take off ASAP."

"Okay, so she made that up. Any way you slice it, it sounds like a woman who was taking off out of fear." A pause. "Unless you think she's the killer?"

"Honestly? I don't know what to think. I think it would be really stupid for Julie Forman to kill a woman in cold blood right outside her house—especially since that woman was her boarder. And nothing we've heard about Julie indicates she's stupid. So my gut instinct is to say no, she didn't kill her. But that doesn't mean she didn't catch a glimpse of the real killer. Or that she doesn't know something."

"You're right." Frank grew thoughtful. "Problem is, we really don't have the financial resources to launch a full-scale investigation. And we don't have a clue where Julie Forman is. That having been said, do you think we should call in the homicide detectives at Area North and try to track her down?"

Paula blew out a breath. "I think that's too over-the-top. I think we should just keep the case open a little while longer. Let's see if we can find Julie Forman with a minimal amount of digging. If we do, we'll run a few questions by her. If those come up empty, I'll be comfortable closing the case."

"Sounds like a plan."

*Tribeca, New York*
*Forensic Instincts*

Ryan's back-and-forth communications with ScoobyDoo told him that, for whatever reasons, the guy was in deep shit. Either he desperately needed Forensic Instincts' help or he deserved their intervention to bring him down. He'd never agree to a face-to-face meeting. Ryan would have to surprise him. But in order to do that, he would need to know exactly where Scooby-Doo was hiding. Ryan's instincts told him the guy had serious tech skills, but Ryan operated at a much higher level of expertise. To be able to triangulate an IP address, which would tell Ryan approximately where his target was physically located, he would need to set a series of well-hidden traps that he hoped Scooby-Doo would miss, so as to allow Ryan to figure out the information he needed. It would only be a matter of time.

Not willing to waste that time, Ryan proceeded to gather as much data on ScoobyDoo as possible—data that extended beyond their chat room interactions re vanishing into thin air. In Ryan's experience, those who frequented the darknet usually posted other offerings via their screen names—a manifesto, a game, fervent opinions on a chosen topic.

Ryan's next round of digging commenced.

What he came up with was fascinating.

ScoobyDoo had posted some kind of first-person survival game, called *The House*. There was no introduction, so Ryan pushed forward, bringing up the first level: Level One—Mrs. Higgins.

His gamer instinct told him that the specificity of giving the level a person's name was significant. So he took a screenshot just before a cutscene activated.

The scene revealed that the protagonist was a young boy being driven to a house. The boy got out of the car and walked up the steps to the front doors, opening them and walking inside.

As the scene finished, the doors to the formidable house closed behind him. An equally formidable woman, presumably Mrs. Higgins, locked those doors and walked upstairs with the key, threatening severe consequences for misbehaving...and worse for trying to find the key. It seemed the point of this game was to escape the house and avoid punishment.

Ryan rolled his eyes. This was a typical point-and-click survival adventure with no real threat and little challenge. It was like playing with a preschool block set—not worth this adrenaline-junkie's time. But, hey, Ryan was trying to track down leads about this ScoobyDoo, so he followed the simplistic game along anyway.

Since this character was a young boy, Ryan figured he should move him to the kitchen for a snack. The boy reached into the fridge, grabbed a PB and J sandwich, and swallowed it whole. As soon as he swallowed, a health meter popped up in the top left-hand corner of the screen.

*That's weird,* Ryan thought to himself. *What's the purpose of the health meter? Those don't exist in typical point-and-click adventure games.*

His curiosity aroused, Ryan checked out the floor plan, now visible as a tiny thumbnail icon in the upper right-hand corner. There was a tiny green dot to indicate where he was located. Gamer instinct told Ryan he should explore the downstairs before going up. He walked into the living room, right off the kitchen. Excellent, a TV. This could be useful. He switched the TV on, turning up the volume. Suddenly, the map icon started flashing, a moving red dot appeared, and there was the sound of thundering footsteps. Once again, gamer instinct told Ryan that an enemy was headed his way, but he didn't yet know who or why. Two seconds later, Mrs. Higgins appeared, face red and eyes flashing. A dialog box popped up, saying: *Turn off the goddamned TV! It's too loud. It's giving me a migraine. You know I hate it when you do bad things like this!*

In a split second, before Ryan could even process what was happening, the woman smacked his character across the face with a closed fist. The boy's health meter dropped to seventy-five percent. The bitchy woman kept screaming, threatening to hit the kid again if he didn't turn off the TV. So Ryan had him turn off the TV and scramble away, hiding behind a couch.

A cutscene now revealed Mrs. Higgins storming off to the kitchen. Ryan heard the sound of ice in a glass, followed by the distinctive splash of liquor. Then more footsteps leading upstairs, and a slamming door.

As the scene finished, Ryan pieced some things together. For any "bad behavior," the boy would be attacked by this woman with no means of defending himself except running away or hiding. And her attacks were strong enough to take chunks out of his health. The only way to beat the level was to find the key and escape, but if he got caught, something worse than that attack would happen. The questions for Ryan were: What constituted bad behavior? Where were the hiding places? And where were some clues to help him find the key?

The story continued to unfold, and Ryan soon learned that bad behavior was something totally subjective, hiding places were tough to come by, and clues to find the key were well hidden. At one point, the boy got caught checking the medicine cabinet in the bathroom, and Mrs. Higgins came screaming at him with a bat. Luckily he found a closet to hide in.

This game was way more challenging than Ryan had initially thought. And more twisted. The villain was an alcoholic psycho with a violent temper. And there was no strategic way to appease her. So the boy took a beating.

Plowing expertly through the game, Ryan finally got the boy to find the key in Mrs. Higgins' wallet, which was no easy feat. The boy tried to make a break for it, but as he got to the top of the staircase, the crazed woman jumped from out of nowhere to block him. At this point she was half woman, half monster, puffed face like Ursula the Sea Witch, except red with anger and drunkenness. A huge vein was popping out of the side of her head, no doubt a manifestation of her "migraines." It was time for the Boss Battle...

Wailing with rage and insanity, Mrs. Higgins whipped out an empty bottle of vodka and raised it over the boy's head, preparing for a kill move. Gamer instinct told Ryan to aim for his enemy's weak spot. He made the boy jump as high as he could while aiming his fist right for that throbbing vein...

Queue a cutscene. Totally stunned, Mrs. Higgins' head snapped back, causing her to stumble and fall backwards down the staircase. She collapsed at the bottom in an unconscious heap. Camera angle shifted, and it was suddenly clear that she was dead—impaled by the jagged edges of her own liquor bottle.

A fitting end.

Ryan moved the boy forward at a breakneck pace, headed for Level Two. There were ten levels in total. The premise behind each level was the same as the first: there was an evil captor—each with a different persona and a different name: Mrs. Higgins. Mrs. Kaminski. Mrs. Gillman. Mr. Hilltop. Mrs. Korman. Mrs. Bridges. Mr. Todd. Mrs. Flanders. Mrs. Wilkins. Mr. Engels. As with the first level, Ryan took screenshots of all the captors' names.

Each of these ten captors unleashed punishment on the terrified boy, who grew older, stronger, and smarter with each level. He continued to hide when necessary, looking for clues that would help him escape. The escape plans got more challenging with each level, as did the captors. Each Boss Battle got harder, too, with more shots needed to destroy the captor in various ways.

*The House* ended with the boy—now a teenager—walking off into the sunshine. Inconclusive but hinting at the positive. Typical gamer melancholy for dramatic effect.

Ryan sat back in his chair and folded his arms behind his head. He had to take a minute to congratulate himself for not losing his gamer edge. He could still complete a complex game faster than any pro.

Okay, enough ego for now. Time to analyze the scenario. ScoobyDoo's game was very unusual and very specific in the way of details. No doubt he'd had the whole game scripted before he'd started coding. Something made him choose this setup when no other survival games were like it—and whatever that something was, was personal to him.

Ryan was willing to bet that he'd lived this life.

So what had he become as a result—a stronger, more compassionate man or a dangerous monster?

The answer to that would tell Ryan who he was potentially helping to vanish off the grid.

*Upper Montclair, New Jersey*

Julie and Milo were settled into their new apartment—as settled as vagabonds on high alert ever were.

For the time being, life seemed to be holding its own.

Home from the gym, Julie sat on her bed, cross-legged. She opened her laptop and signed in. In the smaller bedroom, she could hear Milo on his headset, calmly but expertly answering the questions of a Dell customer.

Calling up her Facebook page, she settled herself to read the newsfeed and see what was going on.

She never expected to find a personal message waiting for her. But she did.

Nervously, she clicked on it. It was from Shannon Barker—the sixteen-year-old gymnast who the dead Julie had been training at the gym and who was destined to be an Olympic contender.

With pains in her chest, she read:

*Please call me, Julie. I understand why you ran. It was probably you they were after. We need to talk. I'm completely unhinged. I don't know what to do. Should I go to the police? What did you find out about Jim Robbins? Who else is he working with? Is it someone at the Olympic training center? Call me on my new cell at 312-555-4929.*

Julie's throat was so tight she could barely speak. She shoved the laptop aside and ran into Milo's doorway, waving for him to cut his call short.

"Come in here," she begged, a tremor in her voice. "*Now.*"

Three minutes later, Milo was reading the PM, his forehead creased in a frown.

"Okay," he said. "Let's stay calm. We knew that the old Julie was killed for a reason. We just didn't know why. Clearly, this kid has some idea. She's looking for advice on what to do. Give it to her."

"What?" Julie stared. "What the hell am I supposed to tell her? I have no idea what's going on or why the murder happened."

"Interesting." Milo was off in his own little world of thought. "It looks like the killers weren't targeting Lisa after all. I wonder who this Jim Robbins is. He obviously works at an Olympic training center. If Shannon trained there regularly, the place must be in the Chicago area. Should take about three minutes to find out everything there is to know about him."

"Maybe this kid Shannon is a drama queen," Julie muttered. "Maybe she just rents too many thriller movies and has conjured up this whole thing."

"Yeah, except that we have a dead body to back her up," Milo reminded her.

"You're right." Julie dragged a hand through her hair. "What do we do?"

"You message her back ASAP," Milo instructed in his usual pragmatic way. "Calm her down. Use Jim Robbins' name to coax out whatever info you can without arousing her suspicions. Most of all, keep her from going to the cops."

"What do I tell her about me?" Julie spread her hands wide in question. "Do I tell her where I am? Do I ask her to keep it a secret? I can't very well lie to her. Clearly, she and dead Julie had a personal relationship. I saw Julie training her once or twice. She acted kind of big sisterly toward her."

"Then that's what you'll be. Tell her you're in New Jersey, opening a gym. Ask her to keep that information quiet, since you're scared that the killers will come after you. Tell her you didn't find out anything, even though you tried. Let her do most of the talking," Milo ended by advising. "You do the listening. You'll learn more and give away less."

"And where do I call her from? Julie's cell?"

"Julie's cell hasn't existed since the day we left Chicago. I downloaded all the contents and got rid of the thing. You've been using a new iPhone." A grin. "A newly-released one, too. I upgraded."

"Great." Julie wasn't in a humorous mood. "I'm a lousy actress, Milo. How do I pull this off?"

"By remembering that you're a scared woman who witnessed a murder. Shannon is more than aware of that. So she won't be surprised by the new cell number, or any jumpiness in your tone. Obviously, Julie is in some kind of a hot mess—one that Shannon's also involved in. Remember, she got a new cell, too. She clearly doesn't want to be called by the wrong person. She's probably scared to death that she's next on the hit list."

"Who's doing this?"

"That's what we have to find out."

Milo headed back to the computer in his room. He'd made it his business to sound calm and reassuring. But, given Julie's level of agitation, he had work to do.

He logged out of all his programs and fired up his Tor browser to ensure anonymity from this point forward. He was hoping he'd find the answers he'd been looking for about how to create brand-new untraceable identities. He wasn't ready to push the panic button yet, but he knew that having all the bases covered would settle Julie down. Even when they were in foster care together, she was okay as long as she had a way out. It was up to Milo to provide that escape route.

He entered his user name and password. Instantly, he perked up.

ScoobyDoo had a new subscriber to *The House* and a private message of his own.

## CHAPTER FIVE

Shannon had been gripped by a constant state of panic ever since Julie's disappearance. It was so severe that it eclipsed the mourning of her lost life as a gymnast, her recent arthroscopic surgery to repair her torn rotator cuff, and her now-impossible goals as an Olympic hopeful.

What if Jim and the killer who had shot that Lisa girl were after her, too? What if they planned to kill her? What could she do to hide? To stop them?

She couldn't run away, not without her parents calling everyone up to the National Guard until they found her. And she couldn't talk to anyone, including the police. Not without proof.

She'd tried so hard to get it. She'd had both her blood and her urine checked, hoping there'd be evidence of the drugs in her system. But it had been too late. Whatever Jim had given her clearly had a short half-life and had already dispersed. It had been a long shot anyway. Jim wouldn't have chosen a steroid that could be detected in the bloodstream for months, maybe even longer. So that possibility was out. And now Julie had vanished along with whatever she might have found out. So Shannon had nothing.

She'd considered going to the cops anyway, to tell them

everything she knew and to see if they could help her. Not only to protect her, but to find Julie and determine what she knew and if she, too, was in danger. But she couldn't. The risk was too great. Not only could the killers be following her, but she herself might be in legal trouble, no matter how hard she'd try to make the police understand that she'd thought the pills she was taking were healthy supplements. Why would they believe her? She was an Olympic hopeful who'd do almost anything to get the gold.

God, she'd been such an asshole.

In the meantime, she couldn't disguise her state of mind. Her parents were frantic, her psychiatrist was deeply troubled, and her tutors were well out of their league and afraid to say or do the wrong thing. So Shannon shut down like a clam, distancing herself from everyone and going so far as to end her psychiatric sessions after an intensive two-week regimen of daily visits.

Everyone attributed it to the devastation she was enduring about the shattering loss of her career. She let them think that. It was partly true anyway. As for the rest—if she wasn't going to the police, she certainly wasn't telling anyone else about Julie's investigation and the PEDs Jim Robbins had been giving her.

Shannon hadn't seen Jim since the day she'd spilled her guts to Julie. It wasn't a reach to guess that he believed—with a great sense of relief—that Shannon had just fallen to pieces and was avoiding anyone connected to her old life. Obviously, the last thing he wanted was to be found out. Shannon might have no proof that the supplements she'd been taking had been performance enhancing drugs, but that didn't mean she couldn't make a big stink about it and ruin his career—not to mention get him investigated and possibly arrested.

Despite her fear, she was half tempted to take that step and blow open Pandora's box.

But she didn't. She was too scared. And she was so alone.

Then she got Julie's Facebook message.

And everything changed.

Julie had finally reconnected. According to her private message, she'd fled to the East Coast after the murder, to some town in New Jersey called Upper Montclair. She'd sworn Shannon to secrecy about her location, and about the fact that she was opening her own gym in a week. She seemed really stoked about the gym. Normally, Shannon would have been thrilled for her. But now, all she could think about was danger and death. Julie really hadn't addressed either or answered any of her questions. She'd just expressed concern for Shannon's state of mind, and asked her where things stood in every aspect of her life.

Was she too scared to even broach the subject?

Shannon hadn't wasted a second. She'd typed in a response, blurting out everything that had been crowding her mind these past weeks. How she'd withdrawn from the world and stopped seeing her therapist. How she was sure she was still a target for Lisa's killers. How she was more than certain that the PEDs Jim Robbins had been giving her were part of something bigger. She'd concluded by begging Julie to tell her anything she'd found out before disappearing, since Shannon had no place else to turn.

Julie was all over the response the instant it arrived. The information it contained was invaluable toward handling the potential crisis at hand.

Milo did his job pronto. He researched Jim Robbins and the Apex Olympic Gymnastic Center. He revisited all of dead Julie's emails, concentrating on those to Shannon, which were rife with sympathy and compassion. And he put together a list of professionals, such as Shannon's manager, who were closest to her, so he could concoct a viable dialogue for the new Julie to have with Shannon. Once he'd compiled everything, he prepped Julie for her Facebook Messenger response.

In that response, Julie made sure to be soothing as she tried to calm Shannon down. This time, she'd addressed the subject head on. She'd echoed Shannon's fears but said that, unfortunately, she'd learned nothing—so far—other than what they already knew. She wasn't giving up her efforts, she assured Shannon, even though, at this point, she had nothing to take to the police. But she was still digging into Jim's background, along with the background of the Apex Olympic Gymnastic Center. She was even delving into the history of Shannon's trainer, Yuri Varennikov, covering all bases to see who might be involved. Given that her investigation was delicate and potentially danger-ous, she made Shannon promise not to go to the cops, not until they had real evidence. She concluded by telling Shannon to pri-vate message her anytime, and they could have a good, long cell phone talk right after the chaos of her gym's grand opening was behind them.

The reply from Shannon came instantly: *Thank God I'm not alone.*

Milo read the last of Julie's return message over her shoul-der, along with Shannon's instantaneous response.

"Nice work," he praised with a nod. "You used all the research I got you and added a warm, personal touch. That should keep Shannon's hopes up and her impulse to go to the cops at bay."

"I hope so," Julie replied. "But I'd better keep the lines of communication open. She's a scared teenager. They're not known for their impulse control. Remember?"

"Yeah, I remember. And I agree. Stay in touch with her. Feed her little snippets of things as I find them." Milo paused. "And if she happens to be right, we're all in deep shit."

*Manhattan, New York*

Emma hated the subway. It was one of the evil necessities of living in the city. Normally, she walked the mile from FI's Tribeca brownstone to her apartment on Mulberry Street. But she'd met some friends for drinks uptown, and now she was relegated to this miserable form of transportation.

Luckily, she'd gotten a seat, albeit a slimy one next to some weird woman who was staring straight ahead, swaying back and forth, and talking to herself. She had a large canvas bag sitting on the floor in the aisle—not a sharp idea. But it was none of Emma's business.

She returned to her iPad and the follow-up news tidbits she could find about that girl, Lisa Barnes, who'd been shot to death in Chicago. There was little to nothing to dig up, only an obituary and a throwaway commentary that the Nineteenth district of the Chicago Police Department was still looking for the killer.

Bullshit on that. They'd shut the investigative door five minutes after they'd determined that Lisa was a loser who'd been in the system and who had had a sketchy youth.

Emma slapped her iPad closed on her lap with a frustrated sound. She didn't know why she couldn't shake her preoccupation with this murder, but she couldn't. It just hit too close to home.

She was half tempted to take her thoughts to Casey and see if Forensic Instincts could do anything with them. But Lisa Barnes hadn't been a client, and they had no right to step into a case halfway across the country without a reason.

Emma was still lost in thought when, out of the corner of her eye, she spotted a twenty-something guy in a sweater and jeans weaving his way through the subway aisle. Up went her antenna when he slowed down an aisle or two ahead of her and quickly eyeballed the tote bag lying on the floor in front of him.

Emma sized this jerk up in a New York minute. It took one pickpocket to recognize another.

Calmly, she waited.

Sure enough, the guy lurched forward as if he'd lost his balance from the motion of the train. He grabbed hold of the seat rail in front of him and allegedly tripped over the bag. While struggling to regain his footing, he reached down and, in one swift motion, scooped out the weird woman's wallet. Just as swiftly, he straightened, excused himself, and continued along his way.

Emma bolted to her feet, careful to take her own belongings with her. She wriggled her way past the woman who was an unknowing victim, and marched up behind the asshole who'd just stolen her wallet.

She tapped him on the shoulder. He startled and turned around, obviously expecting to see a cop. Instead, he found himself facing an angelic young blonde with a body to die for.

"Hey," he greeted her with a charming smile. "Can I help you—in any way?"

"Yup." Emma nodded. She extended her hand, palm up. "You can either give me back the wallet you just lifted or I can kick you in the balls so hard they'll come out of your mouth." A shrug. "Your choice."

The guy's jaw dropped.

"Like I said, your choice," Emma reiterated. "But I think you'll prefer option one. I'm a hell of a balls kicker."

He opened and closed his mouth several times, resembling an unappealing guppy. Then, he reached into his pocket and pulled out the well-worn wallet, placing it in Emma's extended hand. "Bitch," he muttered.

"I've been called worse. Now get lost. And if you're thinking of making any more trouble, think again. Option two is still available."

With that, she pivoted and went back to her seat. Vaguely, she found herself wondering how much cash was in the wallet. She immediately dismissed that thought. She was a different person now. But, hell, once an addict, always an addict. The important thing was that she didn't act on her impulses—unless they were for the benefit of Forensic Instincts.

She didn't even bother sitting down, just grabbed hold of the nearest handle to brace herself for the remainder of the ride. She glanced down at the humming, oblivious woman.

"Excuse me, ma'am," she said. "I think this fell out of your tote bag." She passed her the wallet.

The weird woman blinked, seemingly coming out of her reverie for a moment. "Oh, thanks." She stuffed the wallet in her coat pocket. "Never saw it fall."

"No problem." Just to be sure no further threat existed, Emma slanted her gaze quickly in the direction of where she'd accosted the pickpocket. He was nowhere to be found. She doubted she'd be seeing him again. And if she did, her knee was ready and able.

"Stupid bag," the weird woman was muttering under her breath as she glared down at the offensive tote bag. "You're supposed to have enough room to hold everything. You're an asshole."

Emma bit her lip and averted her gaze. No need to respond. The woman had resumed her under-the-breath monologue.

The train whistled and Emma glanced up. The next stop was hers. Thank God. Man, did she hate subways.

## CHAPTER SIX

Casey rolled over in her bed, blinking away the ear-ly-morning sunlight. She wished she shared an iota of the sun's energy and perseverance. But this morning? Not a chance. She was too exhausted to even think of moving, much less rising. And the chest wall of the hard, muscular man pressed against her was the reason.

She buried her face in her pillow, determined to eclipse the day for just a few short hours.

"Morning, lazy." Hutch clearly had different ideas. His deep voice came from just above her head. And it sounded very much awake.

"Lazy?" If Casey weren't so wiped out, she'd laugh. "You kept me up until almost four a.m. I can tell it's barely dawn. Be-sides, don't sound so smug. I topped you in stamina last night."

A chuckle. "That's a pipe dream, sweetheart. It'll never happen. And you're certainly not helping your case now. Where's that stamina you're boasting about?"

"Recouping."

"You've had two hours to recoup. Time to resume."

Casey groaned. Hutch was a twenty-four seven kickass guy—mentally, physically, psychologically. He'd shone in his years as a DC cop, blown through his FBI new agent training at the top of his class, excelled throughout his career at the Bureau, and was now the unspoken leader of his team at the FBI's Behavioral Analysis Unit in Quantico.

It was disgusting how productive one human being could be. People called her a dynamo who could survive on little sleep. Well then, Supervisory Special Agent Kyle "Hutch" Hutchinson was one step away from superhuman.

He was already kissing the side of her neck. "Wake up, beautiful."

"I can't." But Casey could already feel her body responding. When it came to Hutch, it always did.

"Try."

She did, and with great success. It wasn't a surprise; she was as starved for him as he was for her.

The problem was, with Hutch stationed in Quantico, Virginia, and Forensic Instincts deeply entrenched in Manhattan—not to mention both hers and Hutch's insane schedules—they only got to see each other once a month, if they were lucky. And that was just too damned long to be apart.

The tension over this tough obstacle in their relationship was intensifying. They were both feeling the strain.

Neither of them was a child. They'd been together a long time, close to two years. Casey was thirty-two, and Hutch was coming up on thirty-five. This wasn't the story of two teenagers going to two separate colleges. They were two adults, very much in love, very committed to each other, and struggling with a virtually insurmountable situation.

It wasn't as if they didn't discuss it. They did—a lot.

This visit's conversations were even more difficult, and more raw, than most.

Maybe it was Marc's upcoming wedding that was making

them feel more sentimental. Maybe it was their growing feelings for each other. And maybe it was whatever was on Hutch's mind these days—some new, unspoken preoccupation. It was personal, yes, but it was primarily work related, which confused Casey about how their relationship factored into it. But she knew the drill. She couldn't and wouldn't pry. If it was BU business, it was classified and unable to be shared.

But it was taking things to a whole new level of emotional strain.

"A penny for your thoughts." Hutch leaned over and kissed Casey gently on the lips.

"Nothing exciting. I'm just tired."

"Uh-huh." Disbelief laced Hutch's tone. "Let's get up, take a shower, and have a meaningful talk. No bullshit and no interruptions."

Casey tensed. It wasn't that it was unusual for Hutch to read her mind. It was just that his words told her that this wasn't going to be an average I-miss-you conversation. This was going to be some indiscernible moment of truth.

God, was she ready for whatever was about to come?

Only one way to find out.

"Okay, I'll get up," Casey agreed. Her heart was slamming nervously against her ribs. At the same time, her legs were still wobbly from their lovemaking. Quite the contrast.

She struggled for levity. "But forget any ideas you have about us showering together. If we do, it'll be noon before we have our talk."

"I wasn't going to suggest it—not this time." Hutch didn't sound teasing. He sounded very serious.

Casey swallowed hard.

Gingerly, she slid to the edge of the bed and swung her legs over the side.

THE MURDER THAT NEVER WAS

A handsome red bloodhound rose from his dog bed and plodded over, nuzzling Casey's hand with his jowls.

"Morning, Hero." Casey smiled, stroking his head and silently thanking him for giving her a moment to compose herself. "Hutch will take you out while I shower."

Hero was a full-fledged member of the Forensic Instincts team. A retired FBI human scent evidence dog, Hero could sniff out anything for miles and miles and help the team track down anyone. He'd only left the BU because he wasn't a good traveler, which made it impossible for him to continue on in the Canine Unit. But he was smart, he was expertly trained, and he was loving—and, since the day Hutch had brought him to Casey as a gift, he'd become not only her teammate but her beloved pet.

"C'mon, boy." Hutch was already out of bed, pulling on his sweats. "Let's do our business, and then I'll get you some breakfast while I put up coffee." Hutch met Casey's gaze. "Go ahead. I've got this."

Hutch took Hero on a productive jaunt around the block. He didn't belabor the walk—not this time. They were back at the brownstone and up on the fourth floor, where Casey's apartment was, in fifteen minutes. The coffee was brewing, and all the ingredients for vegetable omelets were laid out beside the carton of eggs when Casey emerged. She'd thrown on sweats and was towel-drying her hair.

"I was going to make breakfast while you showered," she said.

Hutch's brows rose. "Burnt Eggo waffles again?"

She made a face. "You don't have much faith in my culinary skills. Then again, you're right. I can't even crack an egg without getting pieces of shell in it. So I'll just blow-dry my hair and wait for you to shower. Then you can whip up one of your amazing omelets for us."

"Grab a cup of coffee. I won't be long."

Hutch let the hot water beat down on his body as he quickly and methodically showered. Despite how straightforward and sure he was coming across to Casey, he was uncharacteristically unsettled about how this conversation would go. The pride and excitement she'd feel about his accomplishment and its subsequent reward were a given. But that's where the certainty ended. The reality would sink in. And how would it be received? As an opportunity for them? The opening of a door? Or the shutting of one, based on her perception of this as an invasion of space?

Hutch just didn't know. And that was an anomaly for him. Reading people was his forte and his job. And Casey? He knew her better than anyone else did, partly from what she offered him and partly from what he deduced.

She was a very complex person. Raised in a reserved family of sky-high achievers, she was used to sharing her mind and her convictions but never her emotions. Her innermost self was a mystery—except to him—and her deepest feelings were well hidden, even to the FI team. It often amazed Hutch how little of herself Casey shared with co-workers who were truly family. Yes, she was always there for them and demonstrated loyalty, caring, and compassion. But asking for that caring and compassion in return? No way.

She never allowed her soul to surface, not really. She was determined to always be a strong leader for her team. She never forgot for a minute that she was the boss. So she made sure to always be a take-charge woman who was at the top of her game. Displaying indecision or uncertainty meant signs of weakness.

And caring too deeply was taboo.

Hutch had shot that last part to hell. It had taken more than a year of tirelessly breaking down those walls, getting her to lower her guard, to trust him, and to finally admit that she loved him.

It had been worth every ball-breaking moment.

And for months it had been enough.

Now it wasn't.

Hutch turned off the shower water and grabbed a towel, vigorously drying himself so he could get out there and address this eight-hundred-pound gorilla soon to be in the room.

Funny how life played out. The biggest personal crossroads of his life was dovetailing with the biggest professional crossroads of his life. He'd been a key player for the Bureau's Counterterrorism Department as they foiled a major plot against the US. That victory had led to an extraordinary offer. And the implications of that offer would affect the course of his future.

He knew what he wanted.

It was time to find out if Casey wanted the same thing.

*Chicago, Illinois*

Shannon couldn't take it anymore. Her fear was too great, her patience too limited.

Sequestered in her bedroom, she curled up on her bed, pulling her favorite blanket over her. It was times like this that she felt as if she were a helpless little girl again.

Sometimes she wished she were a regular kid who'd gone the regular teenage route. But the path she'd chosen—not to mention the horrors of what was going on these past few weeks—extinguished any childhood she had. Innocence and naivety were things of the past.

Now, tears slid down her cheeks. She'd promised Julie she wouldn't go to the police. And she recognized that Julie was right. They had nothing to offer in terms of proof.

Julie was hunting for it. But Shannon couldn't wait. She had to find it.

So, yes, she'd promised Julie that she wouldn't go to the cops. And, yes, when she'd first found out the truth about Jim, she'd promised Julie she wouldn't confront him, either. But that was then. This was now. Circumstances had changed—and a life had been lost.

Jim might be the weakest link. Maybe he'd blurt out something. Maybe just the fact that Shannon would surprise him by getting in his face would be enough to trip him into giving up a name or a piece of pertinent information. Maybe. But maybe was enough. Shannon couldn't survive on Julie's Facebook messages alone. She was unraveling. She had to stop the pain.

The decision was made. She was going to see Jim. Now.

*Forensic Instincts*
*Fourth Floor*

Seated at her cozy kitchen nook, Casey curled her hands around her coffee cup and studied Hutch. He'd adjusted his stool so he was angled across from her, rather than beside her. Clearly, he wanted to take in her physical cues as well as her verbal ones. And clearly, he intended to facilitate what they were about to discuss. Casey would have her say. But right now, this was Hutch's show.

Those omelets were going to have to wait.

Hutch's expression was sober as he stared into his coffee mug, lifting it to his lips for a brief swallow before putting it down.

"You're making me very nervous," Casey said. "I feel like I'm one of your profiling targets."

Hutch didn't smile. But he did meet her gaze. "This isn't a profiling session. But it is a significant conversation. And it's time we had it."

His tone and choice of words made Casey's thoughts take a frightened detour. She'd assumed this talk was going to be about them and their relationship. But Hutch sounded like it went far deeper than that. "You're okay, right? You're not sick."

"I'm fine, sweetheart." Hutch reached over and squeezed her hand. "In perfect health. It's nothing like that."

Casey felt a surge of relief. "Thank God. In that case, would you stop scaring me and get to it?"

A hard nod. "You're right. Okay, here it is in a nutshell. I've been working a bunch of high-profile cases lately, with both the counterterrorism and the cybercrime squads. Our team was the one who cracked the cases wide open. Most recently, I worked a counterterrorism case for which I was in the forefront. I tracked down the subjects and ended the threat. That's all I'm at liberty to say."

"In other words, you were a hero," Casey said. "I know you. You're one of a kind and an asset to the Bureau."

Hutch's lips curved slightly. "An unbiased opinion. But thanks." He cleared his throat. "My contributions caught the eye of several ASACs. One of them controls all the Violent Crimes Programs in his field office. We have a history. He mentored me when I was a newbie."

ASAC. Assistant Special Agent in Charge. Casey knew the acronym. She also knew its importance and where this might be heading, even before the next words came out of Hutch's mouth.

"Thanks to his recommendation, I'm being offered a huge opportunity in a different location," Hutch continued. "A lateral move but a job that's in high demand, and a field office to work out of. Obviously, that means I'd be moving away from Quantico. My new role would be squad supervisor of the field office's NCAVC. I'd be the BAU coordinator and head of all the

Violent Crimes squads."

Casey was trying to absorb all this. "The NCAVC?" she asked, searching her mind for the meaning of that acronym.

"Sorry. The National Center for the Analysis of Violent Crime. It's comprised of all five BAU units, including the one I'm transferring from."

"Wow." Casey's eyes widened.

"It's a pretty big deal," Hutch continued. "The competition for this job is fierce. It's in major high demand, sought after by a long list of qualified agents. I caught a lucky break."

"Lucky break, my ass." Casey jumped up and went over to hug him. "You earned this promotion, and you deserve it." She planted a lingering kiss on his lips. "I'm so proud of you."

"Thanks." Hutch returned the kiss. "I'm pretty stoked about this."

Abruptly, Casey's mind focused on the carefully omitted details.

"A field office." Her brows drew together. "I'm assuming it's a major one, but I notice you didn't mention the city. Are you about to drop the bomb that you'll be moving to LA?"

"No." Hutch held her gaze. "I'm about to drop the bomb that I'll be moving to New York."

Casey's jaw dropped. "As in Manhattan? Are you serious?"

"Do I look like I'm joking?"

Blindly, she shook her head, sinking back down onto her stool. Her head was spinning.

"I haven't accepted the position yet," Hutch added, studying her reaction.

Her chin shot up. "Why the hell not? This is the opportunity of a lifetime. You'll be able to utilize everything you learned at the FBI, the BAU included, plus everything you learned—and loved doing—as a cop."

"That's all true," Hutch replied. "But that opportunity of a lifetime includes being with the woman I love, having a real relationship, not a long-distance affair. It's a major commitment, and it's one I want. Do you?"

"Yes," Casey answered, tears filling her eyes. "That's all I've been thinking about every night when I'm alone in my bed— how we can be together. *Really together*. It's what I prayed this talk would be about. That somehow, miraculously, you'd found a way. And, yes, I was prepared to make a real commitment. I was dying to make a real commitment. I just couldn't figure out how it could happen, given the obstacles. Well, those obstacles are gone now. No more five weeks in between seeing each other. No more seven-hour commutes. No more trying to coordinate our work schedules. This is the best present you could give me. I want to pinch myself to make sure it's real."

"It's real." Hutch jumped up, closed the gap to Casey's stool, and pulled her into his arms. "I want this—and you."

"I want you, too," Casey murmured, her voice still choked with emotion. "When will this transfer happen?"

"Within weeks—once I accept the job."

"Which you'll be accepting in half an hour."

"Really." There was a smile in Hutch's voice. "And what will I be doing during that half hour?"

"Making love to me."

*Chicago, Illinois*

It was getting dark.

Shannon had planned it that way. That would be the time when Jim would be leaving the Apex facility.

She'd slipped out the back door of her house—the muffled noises of her departure drowned out by the TV show her parents were watching as they relaxed in the family room.

Quickly, she'd headed for the bus stop. And now she was at her destination.

The light sensors in the Apex Center's parking lot had done their job, so the area was illuminated. There was no sign of Jim. But his car was parked in its usual spot. And Shannon wasn't going anywhere until she confronted her former trainer. During her bus ride, she'd thought through her strategy. She wouldn't go right for the jugular, because Jim would shut down and she'd accomplish zip. She'd keep him off guard. And then she'd go for it. It was time this meek little kitten grew some claws.

Sure enough, twenty minutes later, Jim exited the building, whistling as he slung his gym bag over his shoulder and headed for his car.

Shannon stepped out of the shadows, shoving her fists deep into the pockets of her jeans for courage—and to turn on the voice recording app on her cell phone. Then, she headed directly over, reaching Jim just as he dug out his car keys.

"Hi, Jim." A gentle hello. No venom. No cause to get him riled up—yet.

He started when he saw her. He was definitely surprised and not at all happy.

"Shannon. What are you doing here? I thought you were home recouping."

"I was. I have been. I'm going crazy. Besides, I really needed to talk to you."

"About?"

Shannon feigned hurt. "And here I thought you'd be all sympathetic about my crashing and burning. Guess I was wrong. I was just a business investment to you."

Jim's expression softened. He'd obviously reminded himself that Shannon was just a young girl whose life had been blown to bits and who couldn't do anything damaging to him except cry on his shoulder.

"That's never been true," he said in a tone filled with compassion. "You know how much care and effort I put into my trainees. You were amazing—a true contender for Olympic gold. What happened to you is a tragedy. I'm sorry if I didn't visit you or send flowers or something. I got the feeling you needed your space."

"I did." Shannon raised her gaze. "And I've used that time to think about how something like this could have happened." A blip of a pause. "Jim, what was really in those *natural* supplements you gave me?"

Exit compassion. Enter wariness. "You know what was in them."

"Do I? I only know what you told me, all of which I checked out on the Internet and which came back with glowing reviews."

"So? What's the problem?"

"The problem is you lied. They weren't natural supplements. They were PEDs."

"*What*?" The attempted denial was pathetic. The blotches of color that darkened Jim's face spoke the truth.

That was all Shannon needed.

"Admit it, Jim—admit it to my face." Shannon dropped all pretense of being the teenager in distress. "You killed my future and screwed up my heart so I'll never be normal or healthy again."

"I don't know who you've been talking to," he said, visibly restraining himself. "But like I said from the beginning, there were no PEDs—"

"You lied." Shannon's eyes were blazing now. "I'm young,

not stupid. There's only one thing that could have done this to me—your phony supplements. And you. You did this. And I'm on my way to proving it."

"Proving it?" There was the straw that broke the camel's back.

Jim closed in on her, any fear he might have had suddenly overshadowed by aggression. "To who—the cops? You have no proof."

"I was drug tested. There were tiny traces of whatever the hell you gave me," Shannon lied. "Not a lot. But enough for them to keep the investigation alive."

"Then why haven't I heard from them?"

This was Shannon's ace. "Because they follow protocol. I don't. They're digging around, even trying to figure out if there's a tie between what happened to me and that shooting outside Julie's apartment. I told them you were too stupid to plan something like this on your own, that we should forget you and get to whoever you're working for. Who's the brains, Jim? You're just a dumb runner."

"You little bitch…" He backhanded her across the face.

Shannon lurched backwards but grabbed hold of the hood of Jim's car and steadied herself. The physical assault would aid her cause. But she needed something verbal. Something she could take to the police.

"I don't hear any denials. So save your ass. Who are you working for? Or do you want to be put away for murder, too?"

"Fuck you, little girl. Now get the hell out of my face. And don't come back unless you bring the cops with you." Jim unlocked his car, jumped in, and paused to lower the window. "If I see your face around here again, I'll make sure the people you're so worried about shut you up for good."

He grabbed the steering wheel and sped off.

Shannon just had time to leap out of his path to keep

from being run down.

What he'd said was evidence. It had to be.

She'd send Julie a message, attaching a copy of the audio. Julie would know what to do.

## CHAPTER SEVEN

Dr. Maxim Lubinov walked to the podium at the front of the Marriott Marquis ballroom, his steps punctuated by the applause of his colleagues. So many colleagues that even the most expansive conference rooms—dividers removed—wouldn't hold them. They eagerly awaited Dr. Lubinov's presentation. He was a foremost expert in microbiology, and his topic today was on scientific advances in increasing cell energy production.

In his midfifties, Dr. Lubinov was tall and lean, his blond hair and goatee specked with gray. Years ago, he'd studied as both a Harvard undergraduate and a medical school student, and had been a resident of the US ever since. So, he was very much Americanized, despite his obvious Russian roots—light blue eyes, craggy features, straight nose, and pale complexion, plus the slightest of accents.

He was a formidable man, and he glanced neither right nor left as he climbed the steps to the podium. Dmitry Gorev, his assistant, was waiting for him there, ready to support his efforts as needed.

Lubinov began with his customary air of professionalism. Polite but with a superior undertone. No one objected. He was more accomplished than everyone in the room combined.

He knew it and they knew it. So a touch of arrogance was more than acceptable.

He began to speak. Notes were furiously typed into iPads as he presented thirty slides and the explanations that went with them. Cutting edge. Fascinating.

Forty-five minutes later, at the conclusion of the presentation, the audience was eager to probe Lubinov's genius. He answered one question after another, until the moderator brought the Q&A portion of the presentation to a close. Several people rushed the stage, hoping to get one of their follow-up questions answered, but Dr. Lubinov had already gathered up his material, and he and Dmitry were heading toward the exit.

The limo was waiting directly outside, just as requested. The two men got in. Once safely inside the limo, Max let his true persona show.

Visibly irked, he turned in his seat. "Dmitry, what you just witnessed was a room full of idiots. Not one of them truly understood the significance of my research and how it would change human existence."

Dmitry nodded his agreement—an agreement that was as genuine as his understanding of his employer's intolerance. Why wouldn't he be intolerant? He was a bona fide genius. Dmitry felt incredibly lucky to have been chosen as his assistant. There had been a long line of interviewees. Few of them had survived even the preliminary screening, much less the intensive two-hour interview that followed. Dmitry knew that his own Harvard pedigree and background in microbiology and stem cell research had weighed heavily in his favor. So had his sheer intellect. But there was something even more intrinsic that had gotten him this job.

He was the only one who could handle Maxim Lubinov.

Max was off the charts when it came to mood swings, extreme actions, and irrational behavior that bordered on frightening. At the same time, he was like the sun—the center of his own solar system, beaming out brilliant rays of knowledge, discovery, research, and expectations. Dmitry not only took all this in his stride, he knew how to filter it, to absorb what the end goal was, and to turn it into the reality Max demanded.

Dmitry wasn't foolish enough to believe he'd ever fully understand his boss, nor was he unaware that he was always walking a fine line with danger. But he got Max, comprehended who he was and what he wanted to bring to this world.

So it was all worth it. Dmitry's job was twenty-four seven. He worked like a well-compensated slave. But he loved what he did, even when fear crept into the picture.

As if on cue, Max's private cell phone rang. He reached into the pocket of his jacket and pulled it out.

"Yes?"

"It's me." Slava's voice echoed from the other end—that cell phone echo that made it possible for Dmitry to hear. Slava was speaking in Russian. Dmitry was fluent in that, even though he was born in the US. His parents had emigrated from Russia and often spoke in their native tongue.

Slava continued. "The situation we were keeping an eye on just kicked us in the ass." He proceeded to elaborate on what had transpired between Jim and Shannon at the training center.

"You're sure?" Max also spoke in Russian.

"Alexei called me a few minutes ago. He and Vitaliy were at the Apex Center when it happened. Separate cars, like you asked. Alexei was following the kid, and Vitaliy was following Robbins. The kid and Robbins had it out. He slapped her—hard—then took off. He didn't look like a man who had nothing to hide. The guys stayed on them. She took the bus, and Robbins took his car. They both went directly home."

"Fucking asshole." Max's eyes narrowed, anger blazing in them. "Let's talk about the girl first. Is she a real threat?"

"She's a little girl throwing empty accusations around. She doesn't know anything except that Jim was feeding her PEDs. She did go on a fishing expedition, demanding to know who he was working with. And he all but admitted he was working for someone, the stupid fool. But he didn't give her any details. She's suspicious but has nothing to go on." A pause. "I'll take care of her if you want me to."

"No." Max cut him off. "We can't kill both of them without raising red flags to the cops. And Robbins is the real problem. Bring him to the manor. Friday night. Seven o'clock. Tell him it's time we met, that we're having a drink to celebrate our growing success. Egocentric assholes like him will buy into that, no questions asked. He'll probably buy a new suit for the occasion."

Slava chuckled. "Consider it done."

Dmitry shifted in his seat. He'd be expected to attend this supposed celebration.

It was going to be deadly.

*Tribeca, New York*
*Forensic Instincts*

Emma fidgeted in her chair, typing a few idle notes in the margins of their client's latest interview.

"You're not being very productive, Emma," a voice that seemed to come from nowhere and everywhere said.

She pulled her hands off the keyboard and rolled her eyes. "I'm not in the mood for a lecture today, Yoda. Besides, you're not my Jiminy Cricket anymore, remember?"

"I recognize that it's been three months, two weeks, and six days since your three-month probationary period—cut short by Casey—ended. But I remain responsible for making sure every team member is working up to his or her full potential. Today you're not."

Emma groaned, wishing that Yoda—Forensic Instincts' extraordinary artificial intelligence system, created, of course, by Ryan—would go away and torture someone else. Not that he was wrong about her lack of productivity. Then again, Yoda wasn't wrong about anything. He was a hundred percent brilliant, and so human-like it was startling. No surprise, given his inventor. As the team openly acknowledged, Ryan was a genius, and Yoda was omniscient.

Ignoring Yoda's admonishment, Emma picked up the four pages she'd printed on the murder of that Lisa Barnes girl in Chicago. Two of them were chat room bullshit from people who clearly didn't know what—or who—they were talking about. She tore those up now and chucked them into her wastebasket. The other two pages were all that mattered—a pathetically naked obit and an equally sparse article below which was a driver's license photo—probably the only picture of Lisa Barnes that was available. Emma had expanded the photo before printing it. She wasn't sure why. She just felt a kinship with this woman, one that wouldn't go away.

Inexplicably, Emma's eyes filled with tears. How weird. She never cried. This murder—the woman who reminded her of herself, the city it had happened in—all that had just hit her hard. She'd get over it. She just had to keep busy.

She turned back to the computer and began working before Yoda could chastise her again.

"Honey, what's wrong?" Claire was shrugging out of her jacket as she approached Emma's desk. Clearly, she'd spotted Emma's watery eyes. And, hey, if it had to be someone who caught a glimpse of the tiny crack in Emma's emotional armor, it was okay that it was Claire. Nurturing, kind, compassionate Claire. If Emma wanted to confide in someone, Claire would be it.

"I'm okay," she said. "Just a little…" She wasn't sure exactly how to elaborate. She wasn't used to this kind of sharing. And how could she explain her connection to a dead stranger?

She didn't have to. Claire was already touching the pages Emma had just put down, almost as if she'd been drawn to them. "May I?" she asked.

Emma nodded.

"So much negative energy," Claire murmured before she even read what she was picking up. "I feel chilled just touching these." She scanned the article, absorbing all the details as she read them. Then she looked at Emma, understanding in her eyes. "That poor woman. First, a tragic life. Then, a tragic death. The foster care, the time on the streets—her background is similar to yours."

"Yes." Emma acknowledged that without hesitation. Then her chin came up, and her expression grew defensive. "And people like us are always judged. This article says nothing except that she was a foster care kid turned street scum, with a juvie record. That, of course, meant she had to be a useless junkie who had this coming to her."

"I agree. What I just read was biased and unfeeling."

"Lisa Barnes didn't have a family, but maybe she had friends, other people who cared about her," Emma said. "Given how tiny this obit article is, half of them probably don't know she's dead—especially if they don't live in Chicago. Just because I stay plugged into my roots doesn't mean everyone does." Emma bit her lip. "I almost brought this murder to the team and asked them to investigate. But I'm not a client, and no one has approached us, nor will they. So this can't be an FI case. I've been trying to find out more about Lisa Barnes on my own. And I've come up with zip. Then again, I'm a rank amateur when it comes to investigative digging."

Before Claire could reply, Ryan blew by, en route to the stairs and his lair.

He stopped when he saw the drawn expressions on both women's faces.

"Who died?" he asked, unfortunately saying the absolute worst wrong thing.

"A twenty-nine-year-old woman with her whole life ahead of her," Emma snapped. "That's who."

Ryan startled. "What…?" He saw the warning in Claire's eyes. "I'm so sorry. I had no idea. Was she a friend of yours?"

"No. A kindred spirit."

Nipping this in the bud, Claire explained the situation to Ryan, showing him the obit, the article, and the photo.

"Pretty girl. Shitty break. I'm sorry, Emma." Ryan was never at ease when it came to sentiment. "Is there anything I can do?"

"Yeah. Figure out who did this and why." Emma waved away her own request. "Sorry. That was ridiculous. I'll get over it. It just hit too close to home, I guess."

Ryan glanced at the two pages again. "I'm in the middle of the case we're working on. But you know I'm too restless to do just one thing at a time. Do you want me to poke around and see what I can find out about this Lisa Barnes and why she might have been murdered?"

Emma's eyes widened. "You'd do that for me?"

"We're a team, remember?" Ryan reminded her. "I've bailed you out of worse binds than this." He was referring to a near-sexual assault that had happened during their last case, one in which he'd played the hero. "This job is a piece of cake compared to that."

Emma's lips curved, and she smiled for the first time in days. "Thank you very much."

"Thank me when I come up with something." He held up the pages. "Can I take these to make copies?"

"Of course."

"I'll return yours later." He loped off, descending the stairs to his techno-hideaway.

# CHAPTER EIGHT

*Upper Montclair, New Jersey*

The gym looked spectacular—helium balloons and streamers placed in strategic positions in the main room, hors d'oeuvres being passed around to the crowd of people coming in, a rented smoothie bar whose server was preparing free all-natural drinks for the occasion, and a huge *Grand Opening* sign hanging right outside the door. All this had cost Julie and Milo a pretty penny, but it would be worth it. One thing they'd learned: If you acted like you were rich, people bought into the idea that you were rich.

The local media was there, too, taking pictures of Excalibur, chatting with Julie and her staff, and typing into their iPads about the excitement of a new, upscale gym in town. It wouldn't exactly make national headlines, but it would be well-received by the residents of Upper Montclair.

The day was everything Julie could have dreamed of and more. She was a little uneasy about the audio file Shannon had sent her. But, as Milo had pointed out, it did nothing but confirm what he'd already dug up—that Jim Robbins was a scumbag who was handing out PEDs and probably working for someone to do it. Milo and Julie would continue to keep the door open between Julie and Shannon, just to keep tabs on the situation. But, so far, they were all right.

And Julie wasn't letting anything detract from this big day.

Her phone buzzed, and she glanced down at the screen.

*Having fun, superstar?* the text read.

Julie smiled. Milo might be stashed away at the apartment, maintaining his usual solitude, but he was by her side in spirit.

*You know very well how awesome everything here is,* she typed back. *You're watching this on your computer.*

*Busted*, he admitted.

Julie's smile widened. Milo had done so much for her. He was every bit as much a part of this day as she was.

*Why don't you come over?* she texted.

The reply was typical Milo. *I will...when the crowds die down. In the meantime, enjoy.*

*I will.*

Julie slipped her iPhone back into the pocket of her designer jeans. The trendy jeans, combined with her embroidered silk blouse, completed the look of an understated but successful businesswoman. She was a hit, and so was Excalibur. Clients were signing up at the front desk—both for trial sessions and for full memberships. Every time she saw a signature added, Julie's mind said ka-ching. She and Milo were going to make a shitload of money from this venture. And she was going to enjoy her work in the process.

The next step was getting that puppy she'd always wanted. He'd belong to her, raising her count of true, loving friends to two.

Between Milo, the pup, the apartment, and Excalibur, maybe, for the first time, this Julie Forman would have a real home.

*Tribeca, New York*
*Offices of Forensic Instincts*

Ryan had been closeted in his lair for endless hours. Emma had been through a lot as a child, and if Ryan could help her find peace about why someone had killed Lisa, then so be it. Hacking into some state agency was no big deal. At the Linux bash shell prompt, Ryan typed in deminotaur www.state.il.us/dcfs.

Deminotaur was the name of the custom script he had written to unravel the layers of security between him and the prize. Minotaur referred to the infamous maze and monster from Greek mythology. The URL belonged to the Illinois Department of Children and Family Services.

Ryan sat back and waited as the hacking script performed its magic. In a matter of minutes, the outer firewall was penetrated. The next phase could take hours or days. Ryan hoped for the former as he initiated the second part of Deminotaur.

Eight hours later, Ryan had secured access to the ID-CFS. He delved into the IDCFS's database of closed cases. It was tedious work, but he managed to finally dig up "Lisa Barnes," the name that was pinned to her basket when her birth mother dumped her on the steps of the Chicago church. From there he switched screens and obtained Lisa's social security number via the Cook County Medical Examiner's Office.

He pulled up Lisa's foster care records.

Emma wasn't wrong to feel for this girl. She'd lived one shitty life. After the church did its initial job of placing her, she'd been bounced in and out of foster care homes all her life. At eighteen, she'd taken off after having done some drug running that Ryan doubted she truly understood or recognized the full scope of or the danger it put her in.

He went for the iffiest part first—the part that could, most likely, have gotten her killed. Drug running, no matter how naïve the runner was, could be a small, bullshit operation, or it could be part of something bigger.

After poring over the info, Ryan was convinced that, in Lisa's case, it was the latter. The drugs she was delivering were part of a stash run by a huge Mexican drug cartel. If they suspected she knew anything more than a dumb street runner should, they'd take her out in a heartbeat.

Ryan would have to piece together the dozen years in between her drug involvement and when she was killed, figure out why the cartel would suddenly place Lisa on their radar after this long passage of time. Had she been into other serious shit for them in between then and now? Had she accidentally dug up something or seen someone she recognized from the past?

Force of habit made him delve deeper into Lisa's specific foster care family placements. Get a feel for the person's roots. Was she kicked out of these places for a reason? Were those reasons because the family she was living with simply couldn't care for her anymore? Or was she a huge problem—one they were eager to get rid of? Were her overall experiences good or bad, and how did they shape who she'd become? Could anyone—kid or adult—whom she'd lived with have started her on the path to drugs, either using or selling?

If emotional analysis was needed, he'd call on Claire-voyant. He grinned, as always, thinking about the jab of a nickname he'd come up with for Claire, and about how much she did *not* like it. But watching her get all pissed off was just too much fun to avoid.

His concentration returning to the task at hand, Ryan read through Lisa's case file history, covering the ten foster homes she'd lived in. There was a consistent theme: Difficult to discipline and a blatant disregarder of rules. Your basic brat.

Various transgressions spanning the eighteen years of foster care. Starting with little girl antics:  Painted the living room walls piss yellow. Dumped the cat litter box all over the living room. Poured Jell-O in foster mother's jewelry box. Overturned potted plants and taught the dogs to pee in the resulting dirt. Removed dirty dishes from the dishwasher and put them on the kitchen shelves. Put a garden snake in the master bedroom bed as a greeting to her foster parents.

Ryan choked back laughter. Creative little tyrant, wasn't she?

Fast-forward to Lisa's glorious teenage years. Thirteen years old: smoked cartons of her foster parents' cigarettes and passed them around to the other kids on a regular basis, one time resulting in a basement fire—and in her being expelled from that home. But not before the foster parents had pressed charges for the considerable damage that had been done.

Checking out those charges, Ryan made a side-trip to the Archives of the Clerk of the Circuit Court of Cook County and did the necessary hacking. Finally finding what he needed, he opened Lisa's sealed file. Yup. That's what her juvie record was for. Not for the drug running, which clearly no one was aware of, but for property damage. It was obviously just an angry, punitive act on the part of the foster parents, since Lisa didn't have a penny to compensate the couple for their property loss.

Ryan rolled his eyes and went back to his original research of Lisa's foster homes.

Next house. Fourteen years old: Lisa stole the keys to the family car and drove around the neighborhood. Fifteen years old: caught trying to hook up with a new foster kid the first night he'd moved in—a new kid who was described as being sixteen and mature, which meant hot and experienced.

And the list went on and on.

One interesting data point jumped out at Ryan. Seemed that Lisa had a tight childhood-to-adulthood friendship with another foster kid. Miles Parker. The two of them tried staying together throughout the transfers. Obviously, they were pretty successful, given that they were both fostered by eight of the ten houses Lisa had lived in.

Ryan would have to hack into Miles Parker's file next.

But before that came a background check on all the foster parents. Ryan called up the names, ready to begin. The data came up on the screen, and Ryan did a double take.

Higgins. Kaminski. Gillman. Korman. Bridges. Todd. Flanders. Wilkins.

Just to be a hundred percent sure, Ryan checked out all the screenshots he'd taken of ScoobyDoo's survival game.

The only names missing were Engels and Hilltop. Add those two and you'd have every psycho-villain in there.

"Holy shit." Ryan's hand was already moving his mouse around.

"Is there a problem, Ryan?" Yoda inquired.

"Not a problem. A crossover between two of my projects. One that really shocked the hell out of me. I've got to hack into a file. Now."

He did that in record time.

Miles Parker's file confirmed what Ryan already knew. The guy had been a foster child. There was a list of his foster parents' names. The other two that Ryan was looking for sprang out at him—Engels and Hilltop. Those, plus the eight in Lisa's file, confirmed the obvious.

Miles Parker was ScoobyDoo. The only unanswered question was why ScoobyDoo wanted to disappear. Was it because he had killed Lisa or was it because whoever had killed Lisa was coming after him next? There was only one way to find out. He had to find Miles.

Ryan still needed more information to go on.

With that in mind, he hacked into the Chicago Police Department's Nineteenth District's files to get the full lowdown on Lisa Barnes' murder. He skimmed through the closed cases. Nothing. Puzzled, he moved on to the open ones.

His brows rose when he discovered that Lisa's case was still open, although the file was a skinny two-page folder. It contained the same obit and article that Ryan already had, plus the police report stating the date, time, and cause of death. It mentioned Ethel Simmons, the elderly woman who'd heard a car screech off, looked out the window and saw the body and the blood, and called the police. It also mentioned Julie Forman, who Lisa had been staying with for the past week.

Evidently, Julie Forman was the reason the case was being kept open. Seemed she'd packed up, quit her jobs, and taken off right after the murder. The reason she'd given her employers and landlord was that she was too freaked out to continue living in a place where a guest in her home had been killed right outside the front door. She'd even gone so far as to tell the landlord he could sell whatever of hers he wanted to. She just wanted out. She'd never even talked to the police—she was gone by the time they'd tried to contact her.

*We're talking one extreme reaction,* Ryan thought. *Not only that, but it all happened at the exact same time that Scooby-Doo was desperate to disappear, as well.*

That was two too many coincidences for Ryan.

Somehow either one or both of them had been involved in Lisa's death—either directly or indirectly.

He'd go back to Miles Parker's foster care files now, see if he had any violent tendencies. But, after that, Ryan had one goal in mind.

He had to find not only Miles Parker but Julie Forman.

## CHAPTER NINE

Dr. Maxim Lubinov's Vermont estate was large yet incredibly well hidden.

Located high in the Green Mountains of Burlington, Vermont, it covered twenty-five vast private acres. The manor itself was set far, far back from the country road, swallowed up by thick-treed terrain, where no passerby could see it.

Exactly how Max wanted it.

He'd spared no expense in the building and decorating of the manor itself, specifically because he'd be the main occupant enjoying it. Oh, there were many others living on the premises— everyone from Dmitry to his medical staff to his technicians. But they were there at his bidding and could be dismissed at any time he chose.

Max's living and sleeping quarters were appointed with oriental rugs, exquisite upholsteries, and polished teak furniture. The furnishings originated in the Far East, Scandinavia, and Europe, particularly Paris—a myriad of differing cultures and manufacturers, producing a combination of contrasting colors and styles that somehow worked when they were integrated. The vaulted ceilings were so high that they gave the impression the place was a castle. And the panoramic view of the exquisite

Green Mountains was visible from every corner of the house, along with the beauty of Lake Champlain at its feet.

In addition, Max had had an entire extension wing built for the cerebral testing center and the high-tech workout rooms that were trials for his research, and which were always in use. Trainers, doctors, psychologists—his entire staff was usually on duty and *always* on call. The well-oiled machine needed little supervision, but Max was in every room every day to get updates.

Still, none of that was the heart and soul of Max's work. That jewel was located behind the house, where he spent most of his time and where he was headed now.

He strode through the house, glancing at his watch as he did. Slava had called in an hour ago to report their location. In forty more minutes, Jim Robbins would arrive, escorted by Slava, Alexei, and Vitaliy. That moron Robbins thought he was being invited to the home of his never-before-met brilliant employer for social niceties. He had no idea that he was being invited to his own execution.

He'd find out soon enough.

Grabbing a jacket from the coat closet as he walked by, Max left the manor through the rear patio doors. He headed directly to the barn complex, which had been built by the finest craftsmen—with the tightest lips—to his specifications.

Situated five hundred feet from the rear of the manor itself, it was a master architectural achievement and an equally master camouflage.

The exterior looked like a series of beautiful stone and heavy wood-beam buildings, ostensibly part offices, part stables, part veterinary clinic, and part garage. But appearances were deceiving. The complex appeared to be just like any other stables that a rich man would have on his estate. But hidden inside, where prying eyes couldn't see, were extensive medical and laboratory facilities, where Max's genius was coming to life.

In this annex was his life's work. His gateway to the future.

He punched the key code into the Hirsch pad and stepped inside.

It was like a busy ant colony before him. His technicians were moving quickly about a room that was lined with metal chemical storage cabinets and complete with the highest-tech equipment possible. The desks and counters were filled with scientific equipment, including two Leitz microscopes, microscope slides and slide covers to prepare biological samples, Bunsen burners to heat material as necessary, three deep sinks, ethanol and distilled water stations for sample prep, and a plethora of flasks, beakers, pipettes, and test tubes, along with tweezers soaking in alcohol.

The techs were dropping stains—grams and methyl blue—on tissue samples to enhance the contrast of certain cell structures.

This facility was the central nervous system of his whole operation. This was where the medications were manufactured that enhanced the human mind and the human body of those worthy individuals who qualified for his program.

He'd recently told Dmitry that just a five percent increase in cell energy production would transform a top athlete with superior brainpower into a record-setting Olympian and genius. And he was right. They were just on the threshold of a breakthrough. Max had consistently achieved a four percent increase in energy output and mental capabilities of the physical and mental prodigies under his training regimen. Five percent was imminent. Max was confident. Which was why he wouldn't tolerate a single blip—not from anyone. And certainly not from a destructive moron like Jim Robbins, who'd tainted Max's entire process.

The situation with Shannon Barker had not been an unfortunate accident. It was the result of his underling's ill-qualified attempt to accelerate what wasn't meant to be accelerated. Before that, Shannon had been blossoming into a warrior, ready to take on the Olympic challenge and walk away with the gold. Not to mention her grades were greatly improving, despite her rigorous training schedule, and much to the surprise and pleasure of her parents and trainer. Her diminished health, which had annihilated any future Max could have assured her, was a tragedy that never should have occurred.

And now she was on the warpath. She should be. But that didn't change the fact that Max couldn't allow her to prove anything more than an annoying gnat. If she went too far, she'd have to be swatted away.

But Shannon wasn't Max's immediate threat. That honor belonged to the son of a bitch who'd done this to her: Jim Robbins.

Well, Max would be rid of him tonight.

Putting that thought aside, Max walked through his biochemical facility, peering over shoulders, studying his techs' progress. He'd handpicked each of them. They were all at the top of their classes at the University of Vermont Medical School. They'd all signed contracts with stringent confidentiality clauses. And they all had a pretty good idea that a mere lawsuit wasn't the punishment for breaking their contracts.

Now, they all felt Max's presence behind them. They were nervous as hell when he inspected their work, but that only made them try harder, work longer and more productively.

Max glanced to his right. A long aisle down from the biochemical stations were the actual stables themselves. Max owned three exquisite horses—two mares and a stallion—all of which were the initial candidates for his research. At the moment, two of his most trusted and noted veterinarians were in the stalls, monitoring the horses' vitals after an early-evening workout. One of the vets glanced up and, spying Max, gave a pleased nod about what he was finding. Max nodded back. Lab work had been done earlier today, and the results had been excellent. In addition, the horses' speed and pacing during the races held on Max's private track showed increased energy and stamina, and their mental acuity showed just how much their intelligence had been enhanced.

Thanks to Max's work, these horses could win the Triple Crown.

Satisfied, he left the barn complex and headed back to the manor. He had just enough time to change before dinner.

Seated in the backseat of the limo, Jim Robbins was both excited and nervous. As directed, he'd arranged to take off three days from work. That meant his trip would be a busy one, and big business would be discussed—business that could propel his career forward big-time.

The drive from Chicago had been endless—almost fifteen hours, heading east. But it was worth it. He'd been waiting for this invitation for ages. And after all his successes with top athletes, he believed he'd earned it.

Meeting Dr. Lubinov was an honor.

He leaned back in the luxurious leather vehicle, comfortable despite being blindfolded. The two Russian employees of Dr. Lubinov who were driving him had waited until the last leg of the trip to put the blindfold in place. Jim hadn't been surprised. He'd heard that everyone who visited the estate was subject to the same procedure. Dr. Lubinov valued his privacy. He had no intention of allowing people to know where he lived or where he worked. And he wasn't about to make an exception with Jim. No problem. Jim got that.

But a toast to his numerous successes wasn't the only purpose of this meeting. Jim would have to be an idiot to think otherwise. And, dear God, he'd have to tread carefully.

With a hard swallow, he mentally walked through the dark side of what to expect. He'd be sternly reamed out for what happened to Shannon Barker. That was a given. But Lubinov didn't know the whole truth, and Jim could never let him find out. Not if he wanted to live.

The truth was that he'd taken it upon himself to increase Shannon's PED dosage over the past several weeks, just to get her to that about-to-be-attainable next level of achievement. He'd stockpiled just enough pills to get her through a month. Yeah, his plan had backfired big-time. But he'd covered his tracks well, so no one was privy to any of this. Consequently, the task at hand would be to attribute what had happened to a one-time fluke occurrence, probably based on Shannon's body chemistry and perhaps Yuri pushing her too hard.

Jim would keep the subject on his many success stories and suck up whatever mental beating he had to. He'd shift the focus from himself to Shannon, elaborating on the trouble she'd been causing since her accident, and expressing concern that she was a threat to their entire project.

It wasn't all that off-base. Since Shannon's medical condition had been diagnosed, Jim had been browbeaten numerous times by Yuri and by Shannon's parents. They weren't about to let this drop. Then Shannon had confronted him herself. The little brat had actually come at him like a clawing cat, spewing all kinds of accusations. He'd leave out the part about smacking her. He should have controlled his reaction better. But none of that mattered, since no one had been around to witness it. Jim would simply lay out the facts to Dr. Lubinov. He was confident that his boss would have his associates pay Shannon a little visit—to do what, Jim didn't want to know. But the problem would be solved, in whatever way Dr. Lubinov deemed necessary.

The ride became bumpy, and Jim could feel the sharp incline the limo was now traveling. He straightened in his seat.

They were on a mountainous path. That was new. And that had to mean they were almost there.

Jim couldn't wait.

## CHAPTER TEN

*Offices of Forensic Instincts*
*6:30 p.m.*

The entire FI team—Casey, Marc, Ryan, Claire, Patrick, and Emma—walked into the office's main conference room on the second floor and took their seats at the sweeping oval table. It was a surprise to no one that Casey had gotten them all together; it had been a couple of days since they'd had a full-scale meeting to discuss the Worster case—which was moving along at a rapid clip—together with whatever else was pending or up for discussion.

The fact that this meeting was called for a Friday evening didn't cause anyone to bat an eye. This was status quo—it was Casey's expectation that everyone be available whenever necessary.

Casey seated herself at the head of the table, Hero stretched out at her feet, his body language conveying that he was aware and alert. She leaned over to scratch his ears, then turned back to sip at her cup of coffee.

Marc and Ryan exchanged glances. So did the rest of the team. Casey was super Type A. She never procrastinated; their

meetings always began with a bang. This time was pronounced-
ly different. She was definitely distracted, or maybe preoccupied
was a better word. Whichever it was, it was oddly out of character for her.

"Case?" Given Marc's role as Casey's right-hand, and the
longest-standing member of Forensic Instincts, it was a given
that he'd be the one to speak up. "You okay?"

Casey's head came up, and her faraway look disappeared.
"Fine. I just wanted to catch us all up on the Worster case and to
fill you in on another matter." She glanced quizzically from Marc
to Patrick Lynch, FI's top-notch investigator.

A retired FBI agent, Patrick was the team's father figure,
and, all too often, its voice of reason. The team had a tendency
to walk a fine line between legal and illegal and usually ended up
toppling onto the side of the latter. Patrick inserted himself to
keep them on the straight and narrow—most of the time. There
were occasions when even he broke the rules, particularly when
a life was in danger.

Now he waited for what he knew Casey was about to ask
him.

Sure enough, her next question was: "How many of the
investors on Ryan's list did you two catch up with?"

Patrick passed over his handwritten list of names and
notes to Casey. Even though he'd adapted beautifully to the computer age, he still preferred to scribble down certain details. "I've
interviewed eight."

"And I've interviewed seven," Marc replied, handing over
his printed list.

"Only seven? You're slowing down, guy," Ryan noted with
his usual good-natured sarcasm. "Too much prenuptial bliss."

Marc shot him a look. So did Casey.

"Don't start, Ryan," she said, although her tone was gentler than her expression. "At least wait until the meeting is over before you give Marc a hard time."

"You got it, boss." Ryan snapped off a salute.

With that, both Marc and Patrick reported their conversations with the potential criminal still threatening Mr. Worster.

"Patrick and I have already reviewed our combined lists," Marc said. "In my opinion, two of my suspects and one of Patrick's don't ring true."

Patrick nodded. "I agree."

"Then let's isolate those three and have Claire get involved," Casey replied. "We'll arrange for three separate circumstantial meetings. We'll see what her instincts tell her." A questioning look at Claire. "Does that work for you?"

Claire gave a half nod. "Yes, but I want to read the interviews first. That will help me get a basic feel for what I'm dealing with."

"In the meantime, give me whatever you've got on those specific three subjects," Ryan inserted. "I'll dig into every facet of their lives and see what I turn up."

"Good." Casey gave the immediate go-ahead. "Because I had another meeting with Mr. Worster this afternoon. He's still very jittery, and rightfully so. The threats keep coming. If the offender is serious about carrying out these threats, then he or she is a killer and must be stopped now. If he or she is a bullshit artist who gets off on issuing death threats, that's a criminal offense, as well, albeit a less serious one. Either way, we're dealing with someone who belongs behind bars."

Pausing, Casey glanced around the table. "Any other updates?"

Emma averted her gaze, visibly uneasy.

It didn't take Casey's level of behavioral expertise to spot that cue. "Okay, Emma, spit it out," she said. "What's going on?"

"We're trying to stop a potential murder." Ryan jumped in before Emma could get herself into trouble by coming across as an immature girl who was less than a team player.

From there, Ryan—with Claire's help—described the full situation with Miles Parker, Julie Forman, and the shooting death of Lisa Barnes. He explained what he had dug up and where he was going with it.

"I've got to find this Miles guy. He could be a killer."

Casey's brow was creased as she listened. "The problem is, we have no client. No one has approached us on this."

"I know," Ryan responded. "But I feel responsible at this point. I'm not neglecting my work on the Worster case—that comes first. However, this has gone way further than Emma's emotional connection to the dead woman. Whatever's going on, Miles and/or Julie could be in danger themselves. Or they could be planning something more. Or they could just be plain old getting away with murder. I don't think we should turn our backs on that—not when all I'm doing is some online research."

"Online research?" Casey's lips twitched. "I shudder to think how many systems you've hacked your way into to get your data." She waved away his oncoming protest. "Go for it. I agree with your approach and your goals." She turned to Emma. "I'm sorry for the pain this has caused you. I wish you felt you could have come to me to talk it out and see if there was anything the team could do to help. However, in the future, I expect to be filled in on what's going on before any actions are taken. This is a team, and I'm the team leader."

"You're right," Emma said with hesitation. "I'm sorry, Casey. I just didn't think of it as an FI case possibility—not when there was no client. But I should have told you about it and asked if there was anything we could do. I'm so grateful to Ryan and Claire for caring enough to jump in. I know that the rest of you would have done the same. My bad."

"We'll figure this out," Casey told her. "Don't worry."

"I know we will."

Casey turned back to her cup of coffee. She took another sip, that distracted expression back on her face.

"Okay, boss, what's up?" Marc demanded. "You've clearly got something else on your mind. Let's have it."

No one was taken aback by Marc's bluntness. Not at this point in the meeting. Still, they were relieved that he was the one who'd said it like it was. Any of the rest of them might be cleaning out their desks right now. Casey didn't tolerate insubordination, unless it was being done one-on-one and in private.

Casey put aside her coffee—again. "Nothing is bugging me. I just have some news. It's predominantly going to affect me, but I have a strong feeling that the team will benefit from it, as well." A hint of a pause. "Hutch got an unbelievable opportunity from the Bureau. He's leaving Quantico for a job in the field. He'll now be squad supervisor of his new field office's NCAVC. He'll also be the BAU coordinator there, as well as the head of all the Violent Crimes squads."

Marc's brows shot up. "Impressive. It couldn't happen to a more deserving guy."

It was no secret that Marc thought the world of Hutch. They'd been friends at the BU, and Marc had been the one to introduce him to Casey—a success story that he took great pride in rubbing in.

"Which field office is he going to?" Patrick asked. "It must be one of the biggies for him to leave the BAU in Quantico."

"I'd say so." Casey glanced around the table, responding to the sea of curious expressions. "In two weeks, he'll be working at the New York Field Office."

"Yes!" Marc leaned forward to give Casey a high-five.

"That's awesome all ways around—personally, professionally— you name it. Hell, he can even come to my bachelor party."

Claire stood up, walked around the table, and gave Casey a huge hug. "I'm so happy for you. I know you're not planning out your and Hutch's future—at least not yet—but I also know how much this long-distance relationship has taken out of you. All that stress will be eliminated. And good for Hutch—he'll be doing all the things he loves best."

"Including—" Ryan began with a lecherous grin.

"Don't even think of going there," Claire interrupted in a tone that made him stop mid-quip.

"You can thank Claire," Casey informed Ryan. "She just saved your ass." An innocent look. "Unless you'd rather thank her later? In your own personal way?"

"Oooh, snap," Emma said with a grin. "Ryan, you've just been shot down by our brilliant leader."

Ryan threw his hands up. "I surrender." He grew serious. Brows drawn together, he gave Casey a cautious look. "Don't rip me a new one, boss, but, since this will impact the team and our entire confidentiality system, I have to ask—will Hutch be moving in here?"

"It's a fair question," Casey replied, and it was clear she'd been prepared for someone to ask it. "I'll be as honest as I can. Hutch is aware of the possible conflict of interest. Plus, he and I are taking it a step at a time. So he'll be getting his own place, as soon as he can actually find one. Affordable housing in the City is next to nil. Hutch might have to stay here for a bit. Is that a problem for anyone?" She glanced around the table. "Seriously, I want you to be honest."

The whole team shook their heads.

"Hutch is always a welcome addition," Patrick said. "Plus it's very refreshing to spend time with a law enforcement agent who actually follows the rules."

A group chuckle ensued.

"Hey," Marc said. "Why doesn't Hutch take my place? Bensonhurst is pretty convenient to Federal Plaza."

"Convenient isn't an adjective I'd use to describe any Manhattan commutes," Patrick muttered. "Give me my place in Hoboken anytime. One train ride and I'm home."

"Okay, as convenient as possible," Marc amended. "The point is, I'm virtually living at Maddy's, moving my stuff in a little at a time. I never use my place." A corner of his mouth lifted. "And I'd sublet it to Hutch at a great price."

Casey was nodding enthusiastically. "I think Hutch will love that idea. Run it by him."

"Are you kidding? I'm calling him the minute we walk out of here. Heavy-duty congratulations are in order."

*7:30 p.m.*

Jim sat nervously at the long, polished teak dining room table, listening to the silence and toying with his food. Dr. Lubinov had welcomed him to his home, said he hoped Jim liked fish, and then led the way to the dining room. That had been the last word spoken.

Conversation was obviously not going to take place while they ate. That would come later. Okay, he could live with that.

He turned back to his meal, pretending to be fascinated by it.

Dr. Lubinov sat at the head of the table, calmly chewing each bite of salmon, pausing only to neatly cut and eat his asparagus. Jim had seen photos of his employer, so there was no major surprise with his appearance. His formal attire wasn't a surprise, either. Everything about Dr. Lubinov—his public persona and his way of doing business—was sophisticated and formal. He wore a custom-made suit that probably cost more than Jim made in a month. His silk tie was perfectly knotted, and his white dress shirt was crisply pressed.

The only other person present was Dmitry Gorev, a young guy who'd been introduced as Dr. Lubinov's assistant, and who looked very serious and just as intent on his dinner as Jim was.

The men who had driven Jim here had vanished the instant they'd escorted him into the foyer and removed his blindfold. Just as he'd remembered from before the blindfold, they looked like thugs. Well, Dr. Lubinov needed protection, given the significance and secrecy of his work. But Jim had to admit that he'd heaved a sigh of relief when it'd become clear that they were not going to be dinner guests.

The meal seemed to go on forever.

Finally, Dr. Lubinov folded his napkin and placed it on the table in front of him. As if on cue, an efficient maid entered the room and cleared the dishes away.

It was only then that Dr. Lubinov interlaced his fingers on the table, looked directly at Jim, and spoke. "Well, Mr. Robbins, I hope you enjoyed your meal." The man's English was perfect, with only a hint of an accent. "It isn't often that I invite one of my employees to my home."

"Your home is beautiful, and dinner was delicious." Jim felt as if he had marbles in his mouth. The truth was, he hadn't even glanced around the parts of the house he'd walked through, and he'd barely tasted his salmon. All he wanted was to hear what Dr. Lubinov had to say. "I feel honored to be here."

"Good." The doctor nodded, as if that was the expected answer. "It's been brought to my attention that you've trained a half dozen of my finest subjects and done an excellent job of increasing their physical potential. I wanted to commend you for that, and to show my appreciation."

"Thank you." Jim felt a wave of gratitude. "That means a lot, coming from you. I so admire your work and all you're trying to accomplish."

Dr. Lubinov smiled, a patronizing smile, as if Jim didn't have a clue what the potential of his work was. Well, he probably didn't. But what he did know was all that mattered. He enjoyed his work. Even more, he enjoyed the money and notoriety he was getting for his "added" assignments. And getting praise like this from the master himself? Jim's world was complete.

"Of course, there was that incident with the young gymnast, Shannon Barker," Dr. Lubinov said, never changing expressions. "That was a very unfortunate event. It was the first and only black mark on my research."

Jim swallowed, hard. He took the exact tactic that he'd planned.

"I was devastated by that," he said. "Shannon was one of my shining stars. I don't know if her physical constitution wasn't up for our trials or if her manager was pushing her too hard."

"Yuri Varennikov," Dr. Lubinov supplied. "He's known to be very hard on his Olympic trainees."

"Exactly." Jim's relief was intensifying by the minute. He leaned forward, a conspiratorial look in his eyes. "I think you should know that both Yuri and Shannon's parents, not to mention Shannon herself, have all been harassing me. They blame me for what happened. I've tried to appease them, but they've been relentless. Shannon actually confronted me in the parking lot the other day, spewing nonsense about my working for someone who's supplying me with PEDs. I, of course, denied everything."

"That was wise," Dr. Lubinov said. "Their reaction is to be expected. Shannon's life is effectively over."

That caused Jim pause. What did that mean? Was Dr. Lubinov going to have Shannon killed?

He felt a pang of guilt and remorse.

He fought the pang off. It was either Shannon or him. And he wasn't planning on dying, not even if it meant throwing an innocent teenager under the bus.

"She has no proof," Jim said, at least trying to save Shannon's life. "The police wouldn't take her seriously, believe me. I just think that maybe you should keep an eye on her—just in case."

"Indeed. I completely agree with that assessment." Dr. Lubinov signaled to the maid, who hurried in with a bottle of Stolichnaya—a classic Russian vodka that Jim knew cost a pretty penny—and three shot glasses, already filled. She placed the bottle in front of Dr. Lubinov, then carefully placed the shot glasses on the table, one in front of each man, deferring first to her employer and last to their guest.

"Let's put aside the past and toast to the future," Dr. Lubinov said. Raising his glass, he nodded in Jim's direction. "To you, Mr. Robbins. For all you've done. *Na Zdorovie.*"

With that, he put the glass to his lips, threw back his head, and drained the glass. Dmitry followed suit.

Quickly, Jim did the same, trying not to react to the burn of the pure alcohol as it blasted down his throat. He wasn't a big drinker, and when he did have vodka, it was mixed with orange or cranberry juice. Still, he wasn't about to insult his boss.

He set down the shot glass, wondering how he was going to turn down a refill without pissing off Dr. Lubinov.

To his surprise, the doctor didn't offer him another.

That was good. Because the burning sensation in his throat began to spread through his body. It hurt—badly. And he felt lightheaded and sick. He unknotted his tie. He was so hot he couldn't breathe. His heart began pounding, faster and faster... reaching the point where it felt like it was exploding out of his chest. He fought for air, ultimately sliding off the chair and onto the floor, gasping for air, pain searing through his body.

"The poison is slow-acting enough so I can say what I need to," Dr. Lubinov said, pouring himself another shot with utter calm. "But don't be fooled. Ultimately, your death will be horribly painful. As it should be."

The reality of what Dr. Lubinov was saying sank in. "*You poisoned me?*" Jim was barely able to speak.

"Of course. Did you really think I would let you get away with tainting my life's work with your filthy ambition and greed? Did you think I didn't know that you doubled Shannon Barker's dosage in the hopes of building a superstar overnight, rather than be prudent and move ahead on schedule? Did you think I didn't know that you made a public spectacle of yourself in the parking lot, jeopardizing my work with your violent outburst? You're a stupid, useless fool who I'm going to enjoy watching die."

Jim was beginning to drool and foam at the mouth. The pain was agonizing and growing worse by the minute. His insides were burning...disintegrating. What an idiot he'd been. Oh, God...

Dmitry ran out of the room, barely making it to the bathroom before he vomited.

Max remained, rising from his chair to closely watch every dying moment. With a total lack of emotion, he nursed his vodka, studying Jim as he twisted and writhed on the floor.

It was only when Jim contorted and then went deadly still that Max nodded in satisfaction, put down his shot glass, and left the room.

Slava would dispose of the body later.

## CHAPTER ELEVEN

Once again, Ryan had lost track of the time. Part of that was Claire's fault. She'd come into his lair a little after midnight, locked the door, and pulled him down onto the small rug in the corner of the hard-floored room. She'd seduced him shamelessly—what choice did he have but to give in?

His lips curved, remembering. For such a soft-spoken, perfect lady, Claire was anything but that in bed. Or on the floor. Or anywhere they happened to be when they tore each other's clothes off. So, frankly, he didn't care that it was three a.m. The half-hour interruption had been well worth the time spent away from his efforts to locate Miles and Julie.

But now it was serious business time. His progress had been moving along at a breakneck pace since Claire's visit. Maybe she'd gotten his juices flowing. Maybe he was just so close he could taste it. Maybe...

Success.

Leaping to his feet, Ryan pumped the air with his fist, filled with self-congratulations and the taste of excitement to come.

Miles had been a worthy adversary, but the pupil had a lot to learn from the master. Ryan had set multiple traps for

ScoobyDoo—traps that would triangulate and reveal the digital footprint of ScoobyDoo's Internet activity. Any one trap would be insufficient to break the anonymity afforded by the darknet, but working in concert, Ryan could narrow the list down to a couple of IP addresses, and from that, to the most likely location.

The winner was Upper Montclair, New Jersey, which had turned up a seventy-three percent probability. Awesome that it was that close to Manhattan. No unrealistic time commitments, plane flights, or convincing Casey—which would never happen—to close in on his quarry.

It was field trip time. And he wasn't going there alone, not when he had a badass Navy SEAL to ride shotgun.

Marc Devereaux's cell phone rang.

Groaning, he untangled his limbs from Madeline's and groped for the offensive object that was ringing on the night table beside his head. It had to be close to friggin' four in the morning, and he and his beautiful fiancée had just fallen asleep—something they didn't do much of when they were in bed together. The last thing he wanted was a conversation.

"You'd better answer that," Maddy murmured, nestling her face against Marc's shoulder. With great difficulty, she raised her head and glanced at her nightstand clock. "It's after three thirty. It's got to be work."

"Yeah. Lucky me." Marc took a quick look at the Caller ID. "It's Ryan."

"What a surprise."

"Not a welcome one." Marc punched on his phone. "This had better be good," he said to his teammate.

A chuckle. "Are you and Madeline still burning up the sheets? Damn, you're getting married in a month. The good stuff should be over by now."

"Sorry to disappoint you." Marc was in no mood for chit-chat. "What's going on?"

"I know you're interviewing suspects in the Worster case." Ryan got down to business, referring to the current FI case. "But Claire-voyant has to do her thing with the suspect list anyway before you start interrogating people. Can you disappear for a while tomorrow?"

"Does Casey know about this?"

"Not yet. But don't worry. I'll run it by her as we drive."

"When we're already halfway where we're going, and she can't say no." Marc rubbed his eyes. "By tomorrow, I assume you mean today."

"Yeah." Ryan sounded a little sheepish. "I guess it's late."

"Only if you keep normal hours." Marc folded his free arm behind his head. "Is this about those people you're hunting down for Emma?"

"Uh-huh. I think I found Miles—or at least the town he's in."

"I'm not flying to Hawaii."

"You don't have to. He's right here in the tri-state area—Upper Montclair, New Jersey."

"Convenient," Marc replied. "Okay, I'm in." He closed his eyes. "Can you fill me in on the details when I show up at the brownstone—which will be late?"

"Sure. Go do your encore. We'll talk in my lair whenever you show up."

Marc pressed the end button and put down the phone.

"I'm awake now," Maddy announced, propping herself up on one elbow. "What do you intend to do about it?"

With smoky eyes, Marc rolled her under him. "Get inside you and stay there."

*Chicago, Illinois*
*Nineteenth Police District*

Detective Paula Kline juggled her cup of coffee as she sat down at her desk—a desk so cluttered she couldn't find a spot for her cup. She'd promised herself a dozen times that she'd organize her file pile. It had never happened. And it wasn't looking too good for the near future. Not with the caseload she had.

Her computer binged for the dozenth time in the past half hour. Yet another email, hopefully one that wouldn't require more than ten minutes of the time she didn't have.

She sat down and took a look.

Interesting. The Google alert she'd set up on Julie Forman had found something: a web page with her name on it. Paula followed the link in the email message, which took her to a newspaper called *The Montclair Times*. She scrolled down on the page and stopped when she saw the snippet on the opening of a new gym called Excalibur, owned and managed by none other than a Julie Forman. There was a small color photo of her, smiling and holding up a free weight.

"Hey, Frank?" Paula called out to her partner.

Detective Frank Bogart swiveled around in his chair. "If it's a new case, forget it. I'm drowning as it is."

"No, it's actually a low-profile existing case." Paula proceeded to tell him what she'd found. "We need a photo of Julie Forman to make sure it's the same person we're looking for." She accomplished that the quickest way possible, signing on to Facebook and searching for Julie Forman.

There were several, but only one whose photo came close to what Paula was looking for. She clicked on that entry.

A page, photo, and brief bio came up.

"Yup," Paula confirmed. "Same woman."

"Well, what do you know." Now, even Frank looked intrigued. "How do you want to handle it—the locals?"

"Uh-huh. Now we call the Montclair PD and ask them to pay a visit to Ms. Forman. Maybe she can help us close the Barnes case."

*Jersey City, New Jersey*

Ryan exited the Holland Tunnel on the Jersey side of the Hudson River, just ten minutes from FI's Tribeca office.

"Great, no traffic," he said cheerfully, steering the Sprinter Van onto the highway.

"Not a surprise. It's ten o'clock on a Saturday morning." Marc was talking to Ryan but eyeing the odd-looking contraption in the console cup holder between them. It looked like a combination of a bumblebee and a helicopter—palm-sized, yellow with black stripes, bee's wings, and helicopter rotor blades. The damn thing even had a face, complete with a shit-eating grin.

"At this rate, we should be in Upper Montclair in less than forty minutes," Ryan continued.

"Uh-huh." Marc was trying to figure out the weird little gizmo on his own, so he wouldn't have to ask Ryan and listen to a long-winded, egocentric speech about his new, brilliant creation.

"I'm glad that Casey was cool with our doing this—although I think she was kind of pissed that I didn't ask her first."

"Did you doubt that?" Marc gave Ryan a you're-kidding-me look. "But not to worry; she'll get over it. Casey's got a heart of gold. If we can help Emma, and potentially solve a murder, she'll forgive you for playing hooky for half a day."

"Yeah. Besides, this is gonna be a cool and productive trip." Ryan glanced down at his new drone, after which his gaze shifted to the dashboard, where his gadget's batteries were charging in a power pack plugged into the 12V outlet.

"Okay, I give up. What the hell is that?" Marc demanded, pointing at the insect contraption.

"That's Bee."

"Yeah, that much I figured. What is Bee? And don't tell me it's a flying pollinating insect."

A chuckle. "Don't you first want to know *who* is Bee? That's as cool as what he does."

Marc groaned and slid down in his seat. "I'm never going to get the short version of this. So go ahead. Hit me with an explanation of your toy and the brilliance of its creator."

"Okay, I will." Ryan looked as exuberant as a child talking about his first Hot Wheels. "Bee is Bumblebee the Autobot."

When Ryan saw Marc's blank expression, his own jaw dropped. "Autobots? The Transformers? The comic books, the TV series, the movies? Hello?"

"Okay, it's some sci-fi thing. I get it."

"Are you bullshitting me?" Ryan almost drove off the road. "The Transformers go way back—they're even older than you are. What did you *do* as a kid?"

"You mean before TV was invented?" Marc sounded amused now. He was only eight years older than Ryan. "I played with GI Joe and dreamt of being a Navy SEAL."

Ryan shook his head in utter disbelief. "I'm actually talking to someone who's never heard of the Transformers. I'm in shock. Okay, I'll sum it up for you. The Autobots are a faction of sentient robots from the planet Cybertron. Their leader is Optimus Prime, who, as an aside, Bumblebee hero-worships. The Autobots are the good guys; the Decepticons are the bad guys. Good versus evil, and all that neat stuff.

"Anyway, all the Autobots can transform themselves into different vehicles. Bee can become an awesome yellow

Chevy Camaro with black stripes. He's one of the youngest and fastest Autobots. He's small, but he's full of energy and compassion for humans. He gets things done, and he's a little whirlwind while he's doing his job. Is that a perfect prototype for my drone, or what?"

Marc's shoulders were shaking with laughter. "Every time I think you've outdone yourself, you prove me wrong. Where it comes to this stuff, you're the most creative ten-year-old I've ever met."

"A *genius* ten-year-old," Ryan amended, not the least bit offended by the description. "Bee is going to kick some serious ass when we're close to Miles Parker's location. He can only cover about a five-hundred-foot radius. But once he's in the zone, his speed, flight ability, and video-recording potential are going to find our guy for us. Wait till you see Bee in action. You're not going to be able to hide how impressed you are."

"I don't doubt it." The truth was, Marc was impressed. He always was by Ryan's brilliant ability with robots and gadgets. With a twinkle in his eye, he looked down at the grinning bumblebee. "Welcome to the team, Bee."

## CHAPTER TWELVE

Once the FI van reached Upper Montclair, Ryan spent a fair amount of time driving around the numerous smaller business districts looking for the Wi-Fi SSD that was linked to ScoobyDoo's IP address: TheMysteryMachine—a fitting name, since that's what the Scooby Doo van was called.

No luck.

That changed in a hurry.

As he headed east on Bellevue Avenue, a block past the intersection with Valley Road and almost where the business district turned residential, the signal strength meter in his Wi-Fi sniffer came alive.

"What does that mean?" Marc asked instantly.

"It means that TheMysteryMachine, a.k.a. Miles Parker, is nearby." He made a turn, following the signal strength.

"I get your strategy up to this point," Marc said. "But once your signal strength reaches maximum potential, how exactly do you plan on finding some faceless guy in a thriving town?"

"Easy. He isn't faceless." Ryan pulled into the last remaining metered parking spot on the street. "I hacked into the DMV records when I was digging up information on Miles Parker. Got the photo of him on file."

"Of course you did. Why did I ask such a stupid question?"

Ryan smiled, shifting the van into park and facing Marc. "So, are you ready for some human reconnaissance?"

"My specialty." Marc tucked his pistol into the waistband of his pants. "I doubt I'll need this. But just in case Parker is violent, I'll be ready."

Glancing in his side-view mirror to make sure he could hop out, Ryan turned off the ignition. "I've seen you bring a murderous hulk to tears with your Special Ops training alone. A gun is overkill for you."

"I've needed it in the past—and used it. So, let's say I'm prepared." Marc opened the passenger-side door. "Let's go."

Ryan got out, locked up, and took care of the parking meter. He switched to the Wi-Fi app on his iPhone, keying in on TheMysteryMachine's signal strength as he began walking around. Marc strode along beside him. None of the passersby seemed to notice what Ryan was doing. They assumed he was texting someone, just like everyone else.

They approached a narrow alley nestled between a line of low-level apartments and a cluster of stores—a coffee shop, a jewelry shop, a trendy clothing store, and a gym. The gym was closest to them, directly facing Bellevue Avenue, and Marc and Ryan could hear the *thump-thump* of music emanating from inside.

"The signal seems strongest here," Ryan said. "It's coming either from the apartments or the stores. An alley is good. It gives us some privacy. We won't have a crowd of people staring at Bee." Ryan glanced up at the sky. "It's also overcast. That'll work in our favor. Even so, we'll only have a few chances for Bee to do his thing before we become a spectacle."

"That sucks. Then we'll have to come back another time."

"Exactly. And we don't want that. C'mon."

Ryan led Marc back to the van. Opening the door, he

picked up Bee from the front-seat console, detached the charging cable, and then grabbed the control he'd built to maneuver Bee in his flight.

"All set. Back we go," he told Marc.

They returned to the alley, where Ryan placed Bee on the ground.

"It's time for you to see Bee in action," he announced to Marc.

He activated the drone with a touch of the controls and watched proudly as his homemade gizmo whirred to life. With it hovering five feet off the ground, Ryan checked the video feed on his iPhone. All good. Then he deftly moved the controls, sending Bee skyward, aiming the camera toward the row of apartment windows that faced the alley and then in and out between the stores.

"Very cool," Marc noted.

"Watch." Ryan pressed another button, and colored neon lights began flashing on Bee. Red. Blue. Green. "Now *that's* cool. You should see the display at night."

"Right now it's going to alert half of Upper Montclair to Bee's presence," Marc said, grabbing Ryan's arm. "We're keeping a low profile, remember? Now turn those damned lights off."

Ryan scowled but did as Marc demanded, knowing he was right. "Another minute wouldn't have made a difference. But fine." He manipulated the controls again. "Time for Bee to make a return trip, just to make sure he captured everything we need on video."

As Bee doubled back, sending video that covered as much territory as possible, Marc frowned. "How are we going to make out anything specific? There are dozens of people in these buildings."

"Oh, ye of little faith. I'll blow up all the images when we're back in the van with my laptop, and we can study the video scenes. Right now, I have to pay attention to maneuvering Bee, or else he'll crash into one of the buildings."

"Hey, cool toy." A little kid of about seven was standing at the alleyway opening, licking an ice cream cone and staring up at Bee. "Can he do tricks? Can he fly upside down? Does he have a pilot? Can you talk to him? Does he answer?"

"Handle this," Ryan muttered to Marc, scrutinizing Bee as he maneuvered the drone toward them.

"We want him to do all kinds of cool tricks, but he's still not working right," Marc told the little boy. "We're taking him home to fix him up."

The little boy's face fell, just as his mother rushed over and took his hand. "I'm sorry if he's bothering you," she apologized to Marc. "But he ran off as soon as he saw your little helicopter." She gave her son's hand a tug. "C'mon, Robbie. It's time to go home."

"Can I buy one of those in the toy store?" the boy asked, pointing down the street, ice cream dripping down the cone and onto his jacket sleeve.

"Hopefully, someday, once we get him working right," Marc said. He gave the child's mother a friendly smile. "No problem. I have a niece who's younger and more inquisitive than your son. It's a sign of intelligence."

"It's also the reason I need midafternoon naps." Laughing, Robbie's mother took some napkins out of her purse and wiped up her son's face and jacket sleeve. She then wrapped another napkin around the now-soggy ice cream cone and put the cone back into her son's hand.

"Go hang out with your mom, Robbie," Marc told him. "I'll bet if you check the toy store in a few months, you'll see a cool surprise there." He gave the boy a wink.

Brightening up, the little boy nodded. "Okay!"

With that, he trotted off with his mother.

"I'm glad you can handle kids," Ryan said. "I suck at it. Bee's my idea of a play pal."

"Well, I'm going to have a lot more than one curious kid to give explanations to if you don't get that thing back here and out of sight."

"Consider it done." With a few more maneuvers and a slight increase in speed, Ryan brought Bee home to rest. The little drone landed at his feet, that shit-eating grin on its yellow face. The rotors went still as Ryan turned off the controls.

He snatched Bee up and followed Marc, who was already headed back to the van.

Sitting in back of the van, Ryan popped out the micro SD card from Bee's abdomen and inserted it into the slot on his laptop so that he and Marc could review the video footage that Bee had captured on his flight. Most of the apartments he'd scanned were vacant or showed people sleeping in their beds.

"Doesn't anyone work?" Marc muttered.

"Not on Saturdays, they don't. Saturday is sleep-in day for the nine-to-fivers."

"That sure as hell doesn't include us," Marc replied.

"Nope."

Next, they viewed the insides of the stores. Most of the stores were geared toward and occupied by women. The coffee shop was a maze of people, sitting down at the tables or waiting for takeout.

"When it comes to the coffee shop, we'll have to go in and check the place out by foot," Ryan murmured. "It's a zoo." He continued to view the footage.

Next came the gym, which had a scripted sign outside, labeled *Excalibur*.

Ryan intently studied the gym's interior, moving from machine to machine, person to person. Abruptly, he stopped, his spine going rigid. "That's him," he said, pointing to a guy in his late-twenties with a mop of light brown hair, who was sitting at a wide steel desk, working on a computer that was catty-cornered in the gym's rear area.

"You're sure?"

"Positive." Ryan gave Marc a high five.

"Let's get moving." Marc was already opening the van's rear door. "After all this, we're interrogating the hell out of this guy."

Excalibur was hopping when Ryan and Marc walked in. Cycling, weight lifting, cardio work—it was all in full swing.

"Wow, look at this place." Ryan's gym-rat eye was roving the room. "High tech. Great stuff." His gaze found the lanky, rumpled-haired guy who was leaning forward, his stare fixed on the computer. His brows were knit in an expression that Ryan recognized all too well. Something was stumping him. And he wasn't going to walk away until he figured it out.

"I hope Miles Parker's not a killer," Ryan murmured to Marc. "He's pretty talented on that baby."

"Coming from the master, that's quite a compliment." Marc ambled along beside Ryan, simultaneously looking around as if he were a potential customer. No point in going all military and scaring off their suspect.

They reached the back of the gym and walked up to the steel desk.

"Hey," Marc greeted Miles as they reached the desk. "I don't see anyone up front. Are you in charge?"

Milo tore his gaze away from the screen and looked up at them, his eyes faraway in techno-land. "What?"

"Do you run this place?"

"Oh." Miles finally caught on and snapped into regular-person mode. "No. That would be Julie, the owner. She just ran out to the coffee shop to get me a caffeine fix. She'll be back in a minute."

As always, Marc kept his game face on. But that wasn't Ryan's forte.

He did a double take. "Who did you say owns this place?"

"Julie. Julie Forman." Miles sounded cautious. "Why?"

"We've heard her name from friends who said she's an amazing trainer." Marc jumped in to lie—and to give his teammate time to compose himself. "We knew she worked somewhere in New Jersey. We just didn't know it was here."

Time for a question to shift things in a different direction—one that would take Miles out of guard-dog status.

"So she not only works here, she owns the place?" Marc asked.

"Yeah." Relief flooded Miles' face. "And your friends were right. Julie's the best." He gestured around the room. "Help yourself to a tour. She'll explain the machines, the membership, everything, to you when she gets back. It's an awesome gym."

"It looks that way." By now, Ryan had gotten himself in check. Not to mention he'd spotted the TRX suspension systems in the small turf room. Very cool. And the gym had tons of space, plus all the machines were state-of-the-art. Maybe they should have Marc's bachelor party here. There were plenty of cool clubs in Montclair—which was an essential, since Ryan was determined for Marc to get that lap dance, like it or not—and they could hire a limo for the night, since they'd all be wasted on the way home.

By now, Miles was shifting impatiently in his chair. "Is there anything else? Because I really need to get this backup server working, or Julie's going to be in deep shit."

"I hear you." Ryan snapped back to the matter at hand. He was about to make Miles' server problem look like a walk in the park compared to his exposed identity problem.

Walking around behind the desk, Ryan leaned forward to gaze over a startled Miles' shoulder. "Yup." Ryan gave a sage nod. "I can see you have your work cut out for you."

"You know computers?"

"Better than you can imagine. For example, I just finished playing a long game of 'Scooby-Dooby-Doo, where are you?', and I've finally reached my end goal. Success. Nice to meet you, Scooby."

Miles nearly shot up off the chair. He scrambled to his feet, whipping around to face Ryan. His face was white as a sheet.

"Who are you?"

"AdrenoJunkie," Ryan answered without batting a lash. "Or, in real life, Ryan McKay." Ryan extended his hand. "Great to finally match a screen name to a person, Miles."

Miles stared at Ryan's hand as if it were an alien. "How did you find me?"

"Pure genius. And now I need to talk to you."

Wildly, Miles looked around, searching for somewhere to run even as he clearly realized there was no way to get to the door and escape—especially given the "make-my-day"-looking guy who AdrenoJunkie had brought with him.

At that exact frozen second in time, a feminine voice sounded from the front of the gym, accompanied by footsteps that said she was headed their way.

"I'm back, Milo." A breathless young woman hurried over, carrying two cups of steaming coffee. "Sorry I was gone so long. The place was a madhouse. But the good news is that I brought you renewed energy."

As she spoke, Ryan and Marc turned in her direction, ready to take on their second quarry.

"Hi," the woman said. "Can I help you?"

Ryan did his second double take of the day. He stared, his eyes narrowing on her face as his mind searched, found, and connected the unexpected dots.

"Shit." He exhaled sharply, still staring at her, an incredulous expression on his face. "Julie Forman, my ass. You're Lisa Barnes."

## CHAPTER THIRTEEN

With a soft cry, Julie dropped the two cups of coffee on the floor and took a step backward, fear filling her eyes. Hot, black liquid shot out everywhere, but she was oblivious to it, even as it splattered her workout gear, doubtlessly burning her. She looked like a terrified bird, and, instinctively, her gaze darted to Milo.

She saw the ashen expression on his face and fell apart.

"I don't… I never meant… It's not what you think…"

"Julie, shut up." Realizing she was about to spill her guts, Miles snapped into survival mode. Surviving, and protecting his best friend, trumped all else—just as it always had.

His jaw tightened, and he repressed any signs of upset or fear. "Are you cops?" he asked Ryan and Marc.

"Nope," Marc replied. "Just concerned citizens helping out a friend."

"A friend? What friend?"

"That's irrelevant. Your elaborate pretense is what's relevant." Marc took a few menacing steps forward. "Care to share?"

"Nothing to share." Milo jammed his hands into his pockets. "I don't know who you're working for or what you're after, but we have nothing to say to you. If you're looking for someone named Lisa Barnes, we don't know her. She doesn't work here. So you've reached a dead end. Now I suggest you go back where you came from. And tell your *friend* to leave us alone."

Ryan arched a brow. "After all the time I took figuring out why you needed a permanent escape plan? I don't think so. In my experience, the only people who want to fall off the map are either scared or guilty. Which is it, Scooby?"

Before Miles could reply, Julie jumped to his aid. "Miles did nothing. As for me, I'm not Lisa…"

Ryan waved his arm, cutting her off at the pass. "You can forget taking the Fifth. I enhanced photos of Lisa Barnes myself. I also checked out photos of Julie Forman. You sure as hell resemble each other. And I see you made a few decent changes to your appearance to play that up. But not enough to hide your real identity. So skip the denials."

Julie—Lisa—began trembling from head to toe. Tears started streaming down her cheeks. Clearly, she'd reached her breaking point.

"Please leave us alone," she begged. "We're just living our lives. We're not hurting anyone."

"But have you hurt anyone?" Marc demanded. "That's what we're really interested in hearing about." He pressed on, capitalizing on her current emotional weakness. "We originally thought that Julie Forman might have joined forces with your friend Miles here to do away with Lisa. Now it turns out that it's Julie Forman who's dead. That opens up a whole new realm of whys."

"It also makes a lot more sense," Ryan added. "Given how close Lisa and Miles were through eighteen years of shared foster care, why would he ever kill her? But Julie Forman, a relative stranger who might have had something on them? Or maybe someone with an inheritance that was ripe for the taking? That's another story entirely."

Spotting Miles' start of surprise, Ryan said, "Oh, did you

think I hadn't done my homework on Julie Forman? You should know better. I know all the details of the real Julie's life, including that tidy little inheritance her parents left her." A quick scan of the gym. "I can see you've put it to good use."

"Stop it!" Julie—Lisa—was bordering on hysteria. "Please, I don't know what you plan to do to us, but can we at least go into my office and talk first?"

"No talking," Milo responded, a warning gleam in his eye. "We have nothing to say."

"Please, Milo." The woman standing there, shaking, had obviously taken all she could. "I have to know who's after us. I'm scared."

"There's nothing to be scared about. We've done nothing wrong. And no one is going to hurt us. So just go clean up and teach your next class. I'll show these guys out."

After a long moment of hesitation, Julie turned away, numbly heading for the ladies' room.

Miles swallowed, looking at the floor as he spoke, much of his bravado gone. "I'm not stupid. You busted your ass to find me—to find us. That means whoever you're working for wants us pretty badly. We don't know anything. We're not a threat. Please make sure they know that." He raised his head. "And please, tell them to leave *Julie* and me alone."

Marc shot Ryan a sidelong look. Murderers? These were no offenders. These were victims—two frightened children with nowhere to turn.

Somewhere out there was a killer. And Miles and Lisa were right in the line of fire.

Ryan returned Marc's look with a quick nod of agreement and then reached into his pocket and pulled out a business card.

"Like I said, my name is Ryan McKay," he told Miles, handing over the card. "This is Marc Devereaux. We work for an investigative firm called Forensic Instincts. Look it up. We're the good guys. With an awesome track record. Clearly, there are bad guys out there who you think are looking for you. Talk to Lisa. Then give us a call. We can help."

"We don't need help," Miles replied, even as he took Ryan's card, scanning the information on it.

"Yeah," Ryan said, making direct eye contact. "You do."

Lisa would always be Lisa. In every way that mattered, Julie was dead.

Those words kept drumming and drumming inside Lisa's head. They were followed by: Would she and Milo be the next to die?

Sitting up on the bed, back against the headboard and knees drawn up to her chest, she waved away Milo's attempts to calm her down.

"This whole charade is over," she said. "All the endless work you put into recreating us, relocating us, cutting off ties—it was all for nothing. They found us. They know who we are."

"Who are they?" Milo countered. "Yeah, Forensic Instincts knows who and where we are. But they're not in the killing business. So who's after us? And which person are they after—Lisa or Julie?" Milo shook his head in frustration as he paced the room. "It could be someone from Lisa's past who's coming out of the woodwork after all these years. Or it could be someone who saw Julie as a threat, based on those Facebook messages you're getting from that kid, Shannon. Added to that, do they even know who they killed and who's still alive?"

"Does it matter? Whether I'm Lisa or Julie, someone is after me."

"Of course it matters. I get it that we're in trouble. But we have to figure out the whos and whys, Lis." It was the first time Milo had abandoned the use of Julie as her name. "I looked up Forensic Instincts. They're a pretty big deal. And Ryan McKay borders on genius. He definitely knows everything there is to know about us, including our entire life history."

"Great. And he's working for a client who's after us."

"Is he?" Milo frowned, his brain trying to untangle the pieces. "Then why did he give us his card instead of a bullet to the head? That doesn't fit."

"I guess not." Julie couldn't deny that one.

"I'm leaning toward calling them," Miles said. "The longer we do nothing, the greater the chances are of us getting hurt." He purposely omitted the "kill" word.

"We could just take off, start over somewhere else." Julie's eyes were desperate. She hated that she was even saying this. The home she'd thought she'd found was disintegrating before her eyes. But staying alive trumped nesting.

Milo scowled. "That wouldn't be my first choice, not given the situation. But if we have to, we will."

"You do have that backdoor plan, right?"

"Of course."

But Milo's gut twisted. He couldn't tell his best friend, who trusted him with her life, that his backdoor plan had evaporated the minute Ryan McKay had walked into Excalibur.

Now they were on their own.

Ryan called a team meeting at the brownstone the minute he and Marc got back to Tribeca.

He explained everything that had happened in Upper Montclair, concluding with the fact that Miles and Lisa were in deep trouble—the kind of trouble that ended with dead bodies.

"*She's alive?*" Emma's eyes were wide as saucers. "This is so creepy. I never thought…" She broke off, looking at Casey.

"We're not going to let this go, are we?"

Casey blew out a breath. "It's not a matter of letting it go, Emma. It was never ours to begin with. In order to have a case, Lisa and Miles have to come to us. They have to want our help. We can't force it down their throats."

"They will come to us," Ryan assured her. "They're scared shitless. Give them some time to sort it out. Miles Parker is a smart guy. And Lisa is over the edge. Between the two, we'll be hearing from them soon." A pause. "Casey, I've got to be honest. I don't think I can let it go, either. I met them. They're younger than I am. And we're talking about murder. I couldn't live with myself if they were killed because I backed off."

Casey nodded. "I can't disagree with you. Just promise me that you won't compromise the Worster case. His life's in danger, too. And he's already our client."

"I won't," Ryan promised. "I can handle both. You know that. I never do just one thing at a time; it bores me to death. I've gotta keep my mind in a bunch of places to keep it sharp. Don't worry. We'll get the son of a bitch who's threatening Mr. Worster. And we'll rescue our soon-to-be clients, too."


Emma grabbed Ryan's arm on the other side of the conference room door. "Once Lisa calls, I want to help," she said adamantly, but quietly so it stayed between them. "Remember, I'm the one who brought her case to FI."

Ryan's lips twitched. "Jumping the gun a little, aren't you, Feisty? What case?"

"The one you just told Casey was a phone call away." Emma's chin came up. She wasn't backing down an inch. "I know that you don't plan on waiting for them to call. I know you're on your way to your lair, ready to burn up your computer so you can get information on whoever might be after them."

"Busted," Ryan admitted. Emma's gutsy nature was some-thing he admired. She might be young, but she was as worldly as they came. "You want to get your feet wet. I get it. Okay, I'll keep you in the loop. And I'll put in a good word with Casey about you working this with me *if*—and it's still an *if*—Lisa and Miles contact us."

"Okay." Emma's stance relaxed a bit. "I'll wait to hear what you find out. It should take you about an hour."

"An hour?" Ryan shook his head. "You have way too much faith. It's going to take a lot longer than that. This is hard, detailed work." A grin. "I just make it look easy because I'm that good."

"Yeah, well, go downstairs and be that good. And I don't mean with Claire. You two can burn up the rug in your lair later. Now it's work time."

Ryan blinked. "How the hell did you know...?"

"I know everything that goes on here," Emma informed him. "I'm the human equivalent of Yoda. And remember, he taught me everything I know."

"Subject dropped." Ryan was already descending the staircase. "And I wouldn't share your theories with Claire-voyant. She's not as uninhibited as I am."

"No one is."

Emma waited until Ryan had disappeared before she headed down to her first-floor desk.

So much for part one—getting Ryan to agree to share his findings with her.

Part two was something Ryan hadn't considered.

She was FI's executive assistant—the very person who answered the phones.

So bring on Lisa and Miles. She'd be waiting.

## CHAPTER FOURTEEN

Shannon sat cross-legged on her bed, clutching her iPad and rereading the highlighted section of the Apex Olympic Gymnastic Center's newsletter for the dozenth time. Her heart pounded harder and faster with each reading.

Jim Robbins had been officially declared missing. He'd last been seen on Friday afternoon at Apex, leaving for a few days' vacation. It was now Wednesday, five days later. He hadn't reported to work, hadn't contacted his friends or colleagues, and hadn't shown up at his apartment—according to his live-in girl-friend, who'd been told by Jim that his trip was going to be all business. All attempts had been made to reach him, and they'd all come up empty. The police were now involved, and, as of yet, there were no clues, much less results.

Shannon whimpered and fell back on her pillows.

What was she going to do? Were the cops going to in-terview her? Did they know that she and Jim had argued right in the middle of the Apex parking lot last week? Would she be a suspect? Would she be forced to tell them what she knew?

And, even scarier, was Jim dead? Had whoever he was working for killed him? Had he become a liability rather than an asset?

How would that impact her? Was she next on the hit list? She had to get out of here.

Grabbing her iPad, she opened up Facebook and began composing a private message to Julie.

Julie was dealing with her own fears, and the last thing on her mind was checking her Facebook messages.

She was at the gym, trying to go about her business, trying to distract herself. It worked pretty well when she was giving aerobics classes or working with individual clients. Not so well when she was in her office, lost in thought and imagining the worst. Milo was back in the apartment, locked away in his bedroom, pounding on his keyboard. When he was in that mode, he didn't talk. He just worked. And Julie didn't push him. She just prayed that, whatever he was doing, it pertained to their back-door escape route. Because her nightmares were becoming vivid, and every time the front door of the gym jingled, she was terrified that killers were on their way in.

A little after three o'clock that Monday, her fears were realized—but in a completely different way.

The door did jingle, and, as she had for the past three days, she jumped in her office chair, her head shooting up so she could peer out front and see who had entered.

Two men in suits were showing ID to the receptionist at the desk. And, based on instinct and experience, Julie knew they were cops.

She whipped out her cell phone and called Milo.

"I'm working," he answered.

"Two detectives are here," Julie hissed into the phone.

"Where are they and where are you?" Milo demanded.

"They're at the front desk. I'm in my office."

"Get into your private ladies' room—*now*. Stay there as

long as a woman can pull it off. I'm on my way."

Thank God they'd installed a small bathroom attached to Julie's office.

She rushed inside and locked the door behind her. Going straight to the sink, she turned on the faucet and splashed cold water on her face. Dragging air into her lungs, she looked up at the mirror over the sink. Her eyes were wide and terrified. And she was pale as a ghost.

She couldn't face the police looking like this.

Carefully, she dried her face, trying not to wipe off her makeup. Her handbag was in her office, so she didn't have access to anything replenishing. Time to improvise.

She pumped a little body lotion onto her palm and smoothed it over her hands and lips. Close enough to lip gloss— at least her mouth looked full and soft rather than drawn and naked. And her hands looked as smooth as her manicured nails.

That done, she combed her fingers through her hair and played with it until it looked stylish and put-together. She adjusted her Lycra workout outfit, which was form-fitting and needed little help to look good. Then, she pinched her cheeks, bringing some much-needed color into them.

Last and most important, she forced the terrified look from her eyes and replaced it with calm professionalism. She'd done enough acting in her life. It was time to do some more.

A tentative knock at the bathroom door. "Julie?"

"Yes, Marti?"

Her receptionist made an audible swallow. "I'm really sorry to bother you, but there are two detectives up front who want to speak to you. What should I do?"

The poor girl was in total freak-out mode. Not that Julie could blame her.

"I'll be right out to handle it," Julie called back. "It's probably about the robbery attempt in the jewelry store down the street."

"Oh. Oh, yeah. Of course."

No wonder Marti sounded as if she'd never heard about any robbery attempt. There hadn't been any.

"Also, Miles just walked in," Marti added. "He's not at the computer, so I guess he wants to talk to you, too."

With a deep breath, Julie unlocked the door and stepped out. "Sounds like I'm very popular today," she said with a smile.

Marti had clearly calmed down. Seeing her boss look and act so natural calmed her down even more.

"Please send the detectives to my office. And just tell Milo I'm in here with them."

"Okay." The teenage girl trotted off, her ponytail swinging as she gestured to Milo and headed up to the front desk.

Julie sat down at her desk, thumbing through some paperwork.

A minute later, the two detectives appeared, one of them knocking on her open door.

"Ms. Forman?" he asked.

"Yes." Julie rose. "Come in, Detective...?"

"Atkins," he supplied. "And this is Detective Brown."

Detective Brown acknowledged her, as well. He was tall and lanky with salt-and-pepper hair. Atkins was shorter and paunchier, and probably a few years older than his partner. Neither of them looked like they were about to go in for the kill and arrest her. They just looked like they were here to do their job.

"Nice to meet you both." Julie rose and shook their hands, wishing Milo would get his ass in here. "What can I do for you?"

"We just have a few questions," Atkins said.

"About?"

"What happened in Chicago. Lisa Barnes' murder, to be specific."

Julie nearly wept with relief. They might think she knew something, but they didn't know she was Lisa Barnes.

She sank down in her chair, genuine tears filling her eyes as she thought back to that day, something she desperately tried to block out. "It was the most horrifying thing I've ever seen. I freaked out in a way I've never done before."

"Indeed," Detective Brown said. "The thing is, you grabbed a few things, left your apartment, your places of employment, your entire life in Chicago, and you ran. You didn't even stay long enough to call 911. Why is that? Did it ever occur to you that Lisa Barnes might still be alive? That the EMTs could have gotten her to the hospital and saved her?"

Julie shook her head, grabbing a tissue to wipe her eyes. "I'm ashamed to say it, but no. Nothing occurred to me. I acted out of blind panic. Looking back, I was incredibly selfish. But I just knew in my gut she was dead. All that blood, and she was all contorted and so very still…" A shuddering breath. "Maybe I'm just trying to justify my unforgivable actions. The truth? I don't remember the hours right after that. One minute I was staring down the street at what I believed was a dead body, and the next minute I was on a train heading here."

Atkins was writing things down on a pad, taking notes the old-fashioned way. "Why Upper Montclair?" he asked. "And how did you manage to settle in so quickly, both personally and professionally? It's almost as if you knew you'd have to start over somewhere far away."

Julie turned sheet white. "Wait—do you think I had something to do with Lisa's murder?"

"Frankly, we don't know what to think. But the Chicago detectives asked us to pay you a visit."

They thought she was a killer? She felt that surge of panic and hysteria bubble up inside her again.

Abruptly, Milo poked his head into her office, coming to her rescue once more.

"Hey, Julie," he greeted her. "The server is back up and…" He broke off, seeing the two men standing in front of Julie's desk. "Excuse me. I thought you were alone."

"It's fine, Miles. Come in." She beckoned him, trying not to look like she was grasping on to her life preserver. "These are Detectives Atkins and Brown. They have questions about Lisa's death."

Atkins turned to look at Miles in surprise. "You knew Lisa Barnes?"

Miles' jaw tightened. "She was my best friend from the time we were kids. We were in foster care together."

"And your name is?"

"Miles Parker." He turned up his palms quizzically. "Why are the Montclair police investigating her death? She was killed in Chicago. And I had no idea there was an investigation at all. Why didn't the police call me?"

"I'm not understanding this," Detective Brown said. "Lisa Barnes was your best friend, yet you never spoke to the Chicago detectives, and you took off with her landlord right after she died?"

Miles looked appalled. "Took off with her landlord? Lisa put me in touch with Julie a week or so earlier. She said that Julie wanted to start her own gym and not work for anyone else. I'm a tech for Dell Computer, and I talk to people everywhere. I'd heard about this place. I knew it needed major work, but I also knew that all the equipment was in place. Julie wanted to own her own gym and was willing to relocate."

His voice grew low and shaky. "Then Lisa was killed. Julie

showed up at my doorstep, a complete wreck about what she'd seen. My only tie to Chicago was Lisa. I needed to get out of there. Julie needed a computer tech. So I went; we left together." He swallowed hard. "As for the police, no one ever contacted me. Maybe they didn't even know I existed. Lisa and I had agreed to each find our own place to live, after a lifetime of depending on each other. So I guess the cops assumed she was alone. I don't know what they assumed. But I didn't hear from anyone—not then, and not since."

Atkins and Brown looked at each other.

Julie went the next step, turning teary eyes toward Milo. "The detectives seem to think I had something to do with Lisa's murder. Or at least, that's what I'm inferring from their line of questioning."

"*What*?" Milo's reaction was perfect. "Why the hell would you kill Lisa? You barely knew her. You gave her a job when no one else would. And you let her stay with you, borrow your clothes, learn about personal training and dealing with rich, snobby people. You were more of a friend to her in a week than anyone except me had been to her in years, maybe ever."

His head snapped back to face the police. "What's the motivation? Why are you dredging up Lisa's murder? Are you just using Julie as a starting point? Do you plan to drag Lisa's name through the mud?"

That perked up the detectives' ears, just as Milo had planned.

Create a diversion. He was a master at that.

Sure enough, Brown asked, "Why? Is there something to dredge up?"

Milo pretended to look as if he wished he could recall those words. "Nothing that would make someone kill her."

He sounded less than convincing, and Atkins took over. "Let us be the judge of that. What was she involved in? Drugs?"

Again, Milo looked less than forthcoming. "She lived a shitty life. So, yeah, she did a little drug running when she was young."

"And when she wasn't young?"

"Look, she didn't share all the details with me. She was probably trying to protect me. But I know it turned out the gang she was dealing with back in the day were part of a bigger cartel. I think she met with a few bigwigs once or twice. That means she saw their faces and could identify them. Maybe that became a problem. I don't know. But it's the only thing I can think of."

"Please, detectives." Julie didn't have to feign her anguish. "Please don't harass us. Like Miles said, he was Lisa's best friend. As for me, I just want to go on with my life and try to forget what I saw."

"I'll never forget losing Lisa," Milo added. "If I knew who did this, I'd have to be restrained from killing them myself."

Again, the two detectives exchanged glances.

"I take it you two don't plan on leaving Montclair?" Brown asked.

"Of course not," Julie replied. "I just bought a gym here and rented an apartment. Miles and I are splitting the rent and the space. Excalibur is my baby. I plan on making Upper Montclair my home."

"So we can find you either here or at your apartment?"

"Yes. And you can call me anytime." Julie handed them her business card. "My cell number is on there."

Milo dug in his pocket and produced a rather wrinkled business card of his own. "Sorry. I don't carry too many of these around with me. But my cell number's on it. Use it, and share it with the Chicago cops. Like I said, I'd love to face the bastards who killed my friend so I could beat the crap out of them. Just give me the chance and it's done."

Atkins closed his notepad. "I think we have enough." He shot Brown a let's-go look. "We'll be in touch."

## CHAPTER FIFTEEN

Emma was at her desk, electronically storing Marc's interview with the wack job who was now Suspect Number One in the Worster case, when the phone rang.

She hit the save button on her keyboard and scooped up the phone.

"Forensic Instincts. May I help you?"

There was a long pause at the other end of the phone, and Emma's antennae went up. It was either Lisa or Miles. She knew it.

Sure enough, a guy cleared his throat and said, "Is Ryan McKay there?"

Emma would find Ryan if she had to pull him out from under Claire or smash all his gadgets. "Yes, he is. May I ask who's calling?"

"Miles Parker."

Yes. Emma pumped the air with her fist, while she kept her voice steady and professional. "Just a moment, Mr. Parker, while I track him down."

The instant she put Miles on hold, Emma raced for the stairs, nearly tripping on her way down to the lair. Sending Ryan a text wouldn't work, not if he was working.

"Ryan!" She flung open the door to his man cave and

burst inside. Big surprise. He was leaning over his computer.

"Nothing yet, Emma," he informed her. "And, in the future, please knock. I know you're jumping out of your skin, but…"

"Miles Parker is on the phone," she interrupted, practically vibrating as she spoke. "He's asking to talk to you. And I'm sitting in on the call when you take it. So put it on speaker."

Ryan's head shot up. He looked like a kid in a candy store.

"Line three," Emma instructed, planting herself on a chair next to his workstation. "The phone's under there." She pointed at a slew of papers that were strewn everywhere. "And remember, put it on speaker."

Ryan was already clearing the pile, groping for the phone. "Only if you keep that mouth of yours shut," he replied. "Miles is calling *me*. He doesn't even know you exist."

"*Yet.*"

"Right. Yet. But he's scared shitless. Don't make him run before we even get him through the door."

"I won't say a word. I won't even breathe. I promise. Just please, take the call before he changes his mind and hangs up."

With a nod, Ryan punched line three's blinking light. "Hi, Miles," he said calmly. "It's Ryan."

"Julie and I need to talk to you." Miles wasted no time on niceties. "Things have happened since you were here. We're in real trouble."

Ryan leaned forward, frowning. "Are either of you hurt?"

"Not yet. Not in the way you mean." Another pause. "Look, I didn't want to make this call. I don't even trust you. But our backs are up against the wall. And we've got nowhere to turn. So you're it—at least if we can come close to meeting your fee. We invested everything in the gym. We can scrape together a few thousand dollars left from the trust, but we…"

"Don't worry about it," Ryan assured him. "We'll work

out a fair price later—one that won't wipe you out. Right now, we need to hear your story and take whatever action we need to keep you safe."

"Can you come back to the gym?"

"Bad idea." Ryan shook his head at the phone. "From what you're saying, I'd be willing to bet you're under scrutiny. Let's not give them something to scrutinize—like a big meeting in Julie's office. All our resources are here at Forensic Instincts. That's where you need to be. Take the train into Penn. I'll give you directions from there."

"I don't need directions," Miles responded. "I know where you are."

"Sorry, Scooby." Ryan tried to lighten up the conversation, since Miles sounded as if he were about to implode. "I forgot who I was talking to."

Miles didn't laugh. "Can you see us today?"

"Catch the next train. We'll be waiting."

"One more thing. I want your assurance that this isn't a conflict of interest, that you're not representing someone who's potentially after us."

"You have my word," Ryan replied. "You're it."

"Okay. We'll be there soon."

Ryan disconnected the call and looked at Emma. "Seems we have a new case, huh?"

"Damn straight." Emma high-fived Ryan. "And this one's mine."


Julie was practically twitching in the train.

"I hope we're doing the right thing. I hope this isn't some kind of trap."

"It isn't." Milo shook his head. "I did enough research on Forensic Instincts. Not only are they phenomenally successful, they're the real deal. We might not want to trust them, but we're going to have to. And, for what it's worth, I believe Ryan McKay."

"Why? Because he's AdrenoJunkie?"

Milo had filled Julie in on pieces of his escape plan. He'd left out the part about not having a second backup.

"No, because he's been straight with me from the beginning—even when he was trying to figure out my motives for wanting to disappear."

"We could have run, again," Julie muttered, knowing she was being utterly ridiculous.

"With the cops on our tail? Great idea."

"Okay, you're right." She dragged her fingers through her hair. "We're up against the wall. So we'll talk to Ryan McKay and that other guy—Marc something."

"Devereaux," Milo filled in. "I'll give you a full rundown now on all the team members and what to expect."

"Good idea." Julie frowned as her iPad made a binging sound. "The damn thing won't shut up."

Milo's brows shot up. "And you've ignored it? Check it right away. It could be that Shannon kid."

"Yes. I know. Why do you think I've been avoiding it?"

"You can't run away from this one. The only way I can keep us protected is if I know what's going on." He pointed at the iPad. "Read."

Nodding, Julie opened her iPad and saw she had three Facebook messages—all from Shannon Barker. "Don't you ever get tired of being right?" she asked Milo.

"I don't want to be right. I want us to be safe. What does she say?"

"Checking now." Julie opened the Facebook Messenger app, seeing that the second and third messages were begging her to read and answer the first one.

Her chest tightened.

Quickly, she read the contents of the first message, shooting up in her seat. "Oh, no."

"What is it?" Now Milo looked concerned.

"Apparently, that trainer, Jim Robbins, disappeared off the face of the earth five days ago. Shannon is hysterical. She thinks he's dead and she'll be next." Julie lifted frightened eyes to Milo. "With me close behind."

"Given the timing? It's possible," Milo responded, speaking as calmly as he could so as to minimize Julie's panic. "What else does she say?"

Julie's eyes returned to the lengthy message, and the fear in her eyes turned to panic. "Milo—we're out of time. She's coming here. She's not going to be put off, not this time. She's too young, too afraid, and too alone. She's already packed, taken a few hundred dollars from her parents' emergency cash drawer, and written a note to them saying she's heard from me. She told them I'm running a gym in New Jersey, and that she's heading over here to stay and work with me for a while to heal."

Milo's wheels were turning. "Okay, the New Jersey slip-up isn't a big deal. Even the cops know we're here. Does she say when she's coming?"

"Now. She bought a ticket from Union Station to Penn Station. She plans on leaving tonight and getting in around six tomorrow evening. She wants to know what time I can pick her up. Oh my God…what am I going to do?"

"You're going to message her back ASAP." Milo leaned forward, elbows on his closed laptop. "You're going to tell her to take the train from Penn to Upper Montclair. You're going to instruct her to message you as soon as she gets in so that you can pick her up and get her to your place. Don't mention any landmarks or street addresses, and especially not Excalibur's name. I don't want her knowing any of that until she's here, far away from her friends and parents, where she can't blurt it out. The police are one thing. A chattering sixteen-year-old is another. We want to keep this quiet."

"*What are you talking about?*" Julie demanded. "*You're telling me to welcome her here with open arms? Are you crazy?*"

Milo looked up, meeting her flabbergasted eyes over his computer screen. "I'm practical," he replied. "She's coming whether we like it or not. She's reached the out-of-control point. Not good. We have a much better shot at keeping her in check here than we do if she's in Chicago. We still don't know the full extent of this nightmare we walked into, and we've got to find out. Most of all, we need to keep a lid on the whole situation."

"You do realize that the second Shannon lays eyes on me she's going to know I'm not Julie."

"Of course I know. But given the circumstances, that's inevitable. Like I said, we can control her reactions once she's with us." Milo leaned forward, squeezed his friend's hand. "Remember where we're headed now. We're meeting with Forensic Instincts. This is yet another thing to talk over with them. It's going to be okay."

Julie knew what Milo was doing. Trying to calm her down. And, as always, it worked.

She drew in a sharp breath. "I'll message Shannon back right now. After that, you'd better brief me on Ryan McKay and his whole team. I want to be in the driver's seat, right along with you."

Milo grinned. "That's my girl."

## CHAPTER SIXTEEN

Claire was in her yoga room on the third floor of Forensic Instincts.

Sitting in lotus position, she breathed deeply, holding Marc's report on Suspect Number One in the Worster case, along with the fountain pen that Marc had stealthily managed to swipe from the scumbag's office. She finished glancing through the report, then curved her fingers around the fountain pen, focusing on the feelings it evoked.

They were ugly. Dark. Rife with anger and hatred toward Mr. Worster. He was capable not only of sending those emails but of acting on them. Marc needed to know.

Claire was just rising to her feet when the door blew open, and Emma burst in.

She blinked in the dimly lit room, glanced at the pen and file folder Claire had gathered up, and then realized what she'd interrupted.

"Oh, Claire, I'm so sorry," she said. "I thought you were doing your yoga. I had no idea you were working on the Worster case."

Claire waved away Emma's apology. "No problem. All done here. I've just got to find Marc."

"He's in the conference room, talking on the phone with Hutch and making arrangements to sublet his apartment to him."

"Thanks." Claire shook her head in amazement. Emma was an emotional, reactive carbon copy of their calm and factual Yoda. The two of them always knew exactly what was going on at FI. The extent of their awareness was somewhat unnerving—especially when it came to her sex life.

"I have a huge favor to ask," Emma broke in to Claire's thoughts to ask.

Cautiously, Claire said, "Go ahead."

"Miles Parker called Ryan. He and Lisa Barnes are on their way over to meet with him, and then probably the whole team. Ryan's alerting Casey now."

"That's good." Claire said it with the knowledge that it was so. "Now we can help them."

Emma chewed on her lip. "The thing is, this feels like my case. You know all the reasons why."

"Yes, I do, and it's completely understandable," Claire replied gently. "You know Casey will make you a part of it."

"I know. But first impressions matter. A lot."

Claire's lips twitched. "Yes, I do know. I remember Alice in Wonderland walking into our office six months ago to apply for a job."

A grin. "Yeah, I pulled that one off well. I was like a bouncy little cheerleader, gushing on and on about all of you."

"Right. And then picking all our pockets without us feeling a thing."

"That part's irrelevant—at least to what I'm saying." Emma shook her head in frustration. "I'm just talking about your reaction to me when I first walked in. You know what I mean."

"You mean that you want our potentially new clients to respect you."

"Exactly. And they won't do that if I'm sitting at the front desk like…"

"Like an assistant and a receptionist?" Claire supplied. Tucking a strand of blonde hair behind her ear, she started to laugh. "You want me to switch places with you and greet our guests?"

Emma grimaced. "It wouldn't exactly be switching places with me. You don't have to say you're the team's assistant. You could go ahead and tell them who you are, and say you're looking for something at the desk. I just need you to man the position so I don't look so…so…low level."

"I think our little pickpocket has become a snob," Claire said, still laughing.

"I'm not a snob; I'm a realist. I look like a combination of Barbie and Skipper. That usually works in my favor, but not in this case. I want to look like a professional; like this isn't my first case." Emma turned pleading eyes to Claire. "Please help me."

"Help me, Obi Wan, you're my only hope," Ryan said in a high falsetto. He was leaning against the door jam, arms folded across his chest, an exasperated expression on his face. "You're still the most convincing little con artist going. You picked the softest-hearted target here and went there like a homing device."

His gaze shifted to Claire. "You don't have to do this, Claire-voyant. I told Emma she could assist. I didn't tell her she was taking Casey's job—or mine, for that matter."

Claire raised her brows at him. "Just because I'm kind doesn't mean I'm naive. I know Emma. And, believe me, I could hear the violins playing a mile away. The thing is, she's right. First impressions are everything. So I don't mind participating in this two-minute charade. Frankly, I'd love to see what Emma could do with this case if she were given a chance. She's inside Lisa Barnes' head, Ryan. She understands what foster kids like Lisa and Miles go through. We'd be stupid to waste that connection because of my ego—or yours."

Ryan heard her, loud and clear. "You're right," he surprised her by saying. "I might be the brains behind this case, but Emma has the heart to pull it off."

"That's what teams are for." Claire walked to the door. "Let's grab Casey now and run all this by her. If Lisa and Miles are already on their way, we'd better get things moving."

Twenty minutes later, Casey, Marc, Patrick, and Emma were seated in the smaller, less intimidating conference room— less intimidating but with no less of Ryan's tech-tools—and Yoda on standby. Ryan was downstairs in his lair, waiting to be summoned by Claire, who was gathering together some fictitious material at the front desk.

During the ten minutes she'd been there, the phone had rung five times—calls from potential clients to law enforcement to the media. She'd answered questions, taken messages, and then finally sent everything to voice mail, simultaneously buzzing Casey in the conference room.

"Give Emma a raise," she said. "I can't handle this job."

Casey began to laugh, even as Emma pumped her fist in the air and hissed, "Yes."

"No raise," Casey told them both. "Maybe a few high fives, but no raise. Besides, Emma is getting her reward right now. She's about to make her investigative debut."

"I was a big part of the last investigation," Emma reminded Casey, referring to the near murder of Madeline Westfield, Marc's incredible fiancée.

"Yes, you were," Casey agreed. "But this time you're getting a turn at the driver's seat. So shift cautiously."

Emma knew what that meant. She was getting her first

chance to prove herself as a full-fledged team member. She'd better not blow it.

The front doorbell sounded.

"We're on," Claire said, disconnecting the line. She walked to the front door, punched in the security code, and opened it.

She recognized Miles and Lisa from the photos Ryan had showed her.

So did Yoda. But that didn't stop him.

"Miles Parker and Lisa Barnes, who currently goes by the name of Julie Forman, have arrived," he announced.

"Thank you, Yoda." Claire kept her smile in place, fighting the urge to roll her eyes at how very Ryan Yoda was. She extended her hand, first to Lisa and then to Miles. "Hi. I'm Claire Hedgleigh. Welcome to Forensic Instincts."

Miles was looking around as he met her handshake. "Hi. Great AI system. Yoda. Great name, too. I'm guessing Ryan designed it."

"He did," Claire replied. "And we've come to believe that Yoda is human and omniscient."

"Nice combo."

Claire turned to Lisa, who shook Claire's hand but who looked completely out of her league—and a hell of a lot more like Julie Forman than she'd looked in her original photo.

"Are you all right?" Claire asked gently, seeing—and sensing—the fear and uncertainty emanating from the poor young woman.

"Not really." Lisa was blunt. "I'm not sure we should be here. I'm not sure we can trust you. But Milo feels otherwise. And I do trust him. So we're here."

"Fair enough." Claire pressed the intercom button that connected with the lair. "Ryan? Our clients are here."

"I'm on my way up," he replied.

Claire gestured toward the stairs leading to the second floor, where all the conference rooms were located. "The team is all gathered together. We've got coffee, tea, and water inside. Is there anything else I can get you?"

"No, that's good," Lisa said. Again, she looked nervously around. "The whole team? Shouldn't we just talk to Ryan?"

It didn't take a psychic to sense Lisa's trepidation. She wasn't being dismissive; she was being self-protective.

"We always work as a full team," Claire explained. "We're most effective that way. But not to worry. There are only six of us, seven counting Yoda. With the exception of him, we're all nice, regular people." A smile. "We won't overwhelm you, I promise."

"You're far from regular people, from what I've read." Miles was as blunt as Lisa. He took his friend's arm and urged her to the stairs. "But I know how you work. Your method is fine with us—as long as you're working with us."

They reached the landing just as Ryan bounded up the stairs and joined them.

"I'm glad you decided to take us up on our offer," he said. "Let's go inside and have a seat."

He and Claire showed them into the conference room that was diagonally across from their main conference room. It was more compact, and the decorum was completely different. This room was more eye-popping—done in sharp blacks, whites, and reds. In contrast to the more traditional main conference room, this room was very contemporary, and, at the same time, very appealing. The table was black oak, the chairs were red leather, and the walls were white with thin red and black lines running horizontally across where the wall right-angled with the ceiling. A combination of classy and trendy—perfect for certain clients, including the ones who'd just walked in.

Sure enough, Lisa eyed the room and said, "Nice. Whoever designed it has good taste."

"That would be me, and thanks." Casey stood, extending her hand to each of them. "I'm Casey Woods. Ryan's told me a lot about you and your situation. I'm glad to finally meet you."

"Ah, the boss lady." Milo shook her hand. "Your credentials are impressive, but you won't need to read my body language. I say everything I think."

"Thanks for the heads-up," Casey replied. "That's a refreshing trait." She indicated the team members seated at the table. "You've already met most of us—Ryan, Marc, Claire, and now me."

"And Yoda," Milo added. He shot Ryan an appreciative look. "Very cool. Well done."

Ryan shot off a salute. "I aim to please."

"This is Patrick Lynch," Casey introduced, waiting as Patrick shook hands with each of them. "The magnificent bloodhound lying over there and staring at you is Hero. And over here is the team member who's responsible for getting you here—Emma Stirling."

## CHAPTER SEVENTEEN

Emma's head shot up. Casey was giving her full credit and opening the door for her to lead the way. Emma couldn't, wouldn't, let her down.

Composure in place, Emma rose to shake their hands. "I'm so glad you're here," she said. "I know we can help you."

Miles and Lisa both looked puzzled by this turn of events and taken aback by Casey's announcement.

"I thought Ryan was our ticket in," Milo stated bluntly.

"Nope." Ryan shook his head. "I was second on board with this case. Emma zeroed in on you, did all the initial research, and brought the case to me—to us. She's a very tenacious and loyal investigator. You're very lucky; she came to your rescue before you even knew you needed rescuing."

"You lost us," Lisa said.

"Not completely," Milo corrected her. "I did a background check on each of you. Emma's past bore a striking similarity to ours, Lis. Foster care and all."

"Oh." Lisa was clearly surprised.

"I'll fill in the blanks," Emma offered. "Let's all sit." She paused, then figured what the hell. She didn't have to be a receptionist to be cordial. "Can I get you some coffee or something?"

"We're fine." Lisa was already settling herself at the conference table, sitting next to Emma and directly across from Ryan and leaving the empty seat beside her for Milo.

Once they were seated, Emma explained everything, touching briefly on her own previous life but concentrating mostly on how she'd stayed connected to Chicago, and how, as a result, she'd found Lisa's obit.

"The rest was obsessive on my part," she said in her endearingly shoot-from-the-hip manner. "I was so pissed that Lisa Barnes was being dismissed like a strung-out junkie because of a juvie record and a life in foster care that I couldn't leave it alone. I didn't know about Miles—all the detailed discovery was on Ryan's part—but I knew that Lisa deserved better than what she got. I had so many questions, and I felt such a strong connection to her—to you," she amended, addressing Lisa, "that I couldn't let it go. Thankfully, my team is exactly that—a team. They all jumped in to help me. Which is how Ryan found the connection between ScoobyDoo and Miles, and between Miles and Lisa. When he and Marc visited you in Upper Montclair, they saw you were freaked out and in trouble."

"Wow," Lisa said. "That's nothing like the story I was expecting to hear. We thought you were working for whoever's after us. And all along this was happening because you felt like we were kindred spirits." She swallowed. "Thank you."

"No problem."

"A lot has happened since we saw you, and before we saw you," Milo told Ryan and Marc. "But I want you to sign a confidentiality agreement. And we'll sign whatever contract you need us to."

"They've been prepared." Casey slid several sheets of paper across the table. "Ours are already signed. The contract is waiting for your signature."

Milo took the pages and scanned them, passing them to Lisa. "Just so you know, this whole situation found us. We're innocent of any wrongdoing."

"That's not quite true," Marc said. "You're guilty of identity theft. But we're not the police. So that information stays in this room."

"I appreciate that," Lisa said, signing the documents and passing them back to Milo. "And, for the record, the identity swapping was completely spontaneous and all me. Milo wasn't involved. I saw Julie Forman shot dead. Given some of the things I've done—"

"Your drug running," Ryan supplied.

A brief pause. "Yes. Anyway, I assumed it was my past coming back to haunt me. So I was desperate to have the people I'd worked for think I was dead. I took Julie's wallet and cell phone, and planted mine on her. I was too freaked out to function. I ran to Milo." She gave a small, self-deprecating laugh. "I always have and I always do."

"And Miles did the rest," Emma murmured. "He cleaned up after you and created new identities and new lives for you."

"Exactly."

"How did you meet Julie Forman? You were obviously close if you were living in her apartment."

"Not at all. We only knew each other for a week." Lisa went on to explain Julie's part in getting her a job at the gym and giving her a temporary place to live. "Our resemblance to each other was a fluke."

"So you think the cartel figured out the truth and they're now after you?" Patrick asked.

"That's what we thought at first," Milo replied, sliding the fully-executed agreements across the table to Casey. "And it's still possible. But there's a hell of a lot more going on here than we knew. We walked right into a completely separate but potentially explosive situation."

"Which is?" Casey asked.

Milo hesitated. He glanced at Lisa, seeking her permission to fully confide in the Forensic Instincts team. "I trust them, Lis," he stated frankly. "But you have to also."

Lisa chewed her lip and then nodded. "Emma sealed the deal. Knowing who set the wheels in motion—and why—convinces me that she and her team are in our corner. So, yes, I trust them. Go ahead."

Emma was practically glowing. "Thank you," she said. "We'll come through for you, I promise."

"I believe you."

With that, Milo told the team everything, from the private messages sent by Shannon—including the audio tape she'd attached of her argument with Jim Robbins—to her impending runaway trip to Upper Montclair, to their visit from the Montclair police.

"Now we're leaning toward the fact that it really was Julie they wanted to kill, not Lisa," Miles concluded.

Casey leaned forward. "Let's dismiss the audio tape. From what you've told us, there's nothing solidly incriminating on it. Lisa, tell us what you remember about the shooting. You obviously were up close at some point if you swapped IDs with Julie. Did you see her approaching the apartment? Did you see the vehicle or its occupants? Anything you can remember could help."

Lisa dragged nervous hands through her hair and stared down at the table. "I haven't wanted to relive that day, that moment. It was the most horrifying thing I've ever seen."

"Try. You're in a safe place now."

Swallowing, Lisa forced the memories to resurface. "I

was sitting outside on the front steps of the apartment. I saw Julie coming. But she wasn't herself. She was furious, shaking, striding to the apartment like she was about to punch someone. I remember that, because I was scared to death that she'd found out about my past. She was gripping a bag and her purse. In a nanosecond, a dark car came speeding down the street and right up to her. The passenger door opened, and a big, creepy guy with tattoos on his arms got out. He was holding a gun. Before Julie even had time to react, he put two bullets straight into her head."

"Two gunshots and no one came running?"

"I guess he used a silencer. He had to, because the shots were like muffled pops. Julie crumpled. Everything in her purse flew out. Blood was splattered everywhere. The guy jumped back into the car, and they took off."

"You're sure no one else was around?"

"Very sure." Lisa's eyes were damp. "I double-checked before I ran to the body. There was blood pooling all around her head. She wasn't breathing. I checked her pulse. I had to make sure…but she was dead. That's when I took what I needed from the stuff that had been in her purse—her wallet, her cell phone, her keys, her checkbook—anything tied to her identity. I planted my ID on her body and bolted."

"Did you take the bag?" Marc asked.

Lisa blinked, processing his question.

"You just said she was gripping a bag," he reminded her in a quiet tone that pressed her just enough to get answers without flipping her out. "It must have fallen out of her arms. Did anything spill out? Did you do a quick check to see if there was anything in it you should have? Did you take it? Leave it?"

Prodded into remembering, Lisa shook her head from side to side. "It wasn't there." She paused. "The guy who shot her took it."

"So you have no idea what was in it?"

"No."

"Which is probably why you're still alive," Marc said. "They figured that nobody else knew anything."

"I didn't—not then."

"Okay," Ryan interrupted. "So Julie must have, unfortunately, walked into a situation involving a dangerous PED distribution ring—the one that that young gymnast, Shannon Barker, was PMing you about."

As Ryan spoke, he was already thinking about the next steps he had to take. "Yoda," he said. "Do a cursory search on Shannon Barker and Jim Robbins…"

"Yoda doesn't need to waste his time," Milo interrupted. "I've done an in-depth search on both Shannon and Robbins, as well as on the Apex Olympic Gymnastic Center, where Shannon trained, and on Yuri Varennikov, who was Shannon's manager." Milo pulled out his laptop, flipped it open, and turned it on. While it booted up, he glanced quickly at Ryan's business card to verify his email address. "I'll send you everything I have right now." A corner of his mouth lifted. "Should I cc Yoda?"

"Was that humor, Ryan?" Yoda inquired. "Or is a response in order?"

"It was humor, Yoda," Ryan replied. "Not to worry. I've got this." He frowned thoughtfully as Milo began to email material to him. "You hit a brick wall so far on who Robbins could have been working for?"

Milo nodded. "But, like you and Marc said, whoever it is, Julie must have found out more than she should have."

"Agreed." Ryan was still frowning. "But how did Julie get involved in the first place? For Shannon?"

"Her actions were a part of who she was." Claire had that faraway look in her eyes. "Julie Forman was a nurturer.

She took Lisa in and got her a job, and Lisa is a grown woman. Shannon, on the other hand, is a teenager and one of Julie's charges. Julie felt committed to finding out the full scope
of who was responsible for harming Shannon—and to doing
something to stop them."

"All of which spells trouble," Marc said, rolling his coffee mug between his palms. "Julie must have found some paper
trail—physical evidence that was in that bag she was carrying.
The big guns had to get that bag and shut Julie up before she had
a chance to share what she'd found with anyone else."

"Where do the Montclair police fit in?" Lisa asked, her
palms upturned in question. "Why did they show up at my door?
Do they really think I'm a murderer?  And who tipped them off
to me?  I can't imagine it was Shannon—that doesn't fit."

Ryan shook his head. "Shannon's all about being under
Julie's protective wing. She's her only ally. The last thing she'd
want is to turn her over to the cops. No, the police were just doing their job. I hacked into the Chicago Police Department records, specifically to read the Lisa Barnes homicide file. It was
being kept open pending finding Julie Forman and eliminating
her as a suspect or a witness. My guess is that they found out
where Julie was and asked the Montclair police to pay her a visit.
Their energy on this seems pretty low, so I'm guessing they're not
really investigating hard-core."

"We'll coach you on what to say if they show up again,"
Marc added. "But I agree with Ryan. I think they'll give Chicago
their report, and they'll all call it a day."

"Of course," Emma muttered. "Why bother with a thorough investigation of a piece of trash like Lisa Barnes?"

"Hey, kid, don't knock it," Ryan said. "I know how passionate about this you are, but the best thing for Lisa is if the cops
go away. There's enough of a tangled web here for us to sort out,

and enough enemies we have to find and expose."

Casey rose and poured herself another cup of coffee. "Let's get to your next hurdle," she said to Lisa and Milo. "Shannon Barker. She's showing up on your doorstep tomorrow. She's going to see that you're not Julie. She's going to have a million questions and be completely freaked out. We need to coach you on how to handle her so that you keep her contained and on your side. It's more than doable; you just need the right method to do it. That's where I come in."

Milo nodded. "I guess I was wrong. I do need a behavioral specialist, maybe not to read my body language but to teach me how to read somebody else's."

"This isn't just about body language," Casey corrected. "You're going to have to guide her in her thinking, as well as her actions."

"I wish we knew more about Julie's thought process when she was killed—what she found, what she planned on doing with it—things like that. It would help a lot in handling Shannon's insecurities. As it is, we're kind of shooting blind," Milo said.

"That's where I come in," Claire responded. "Hopefully, I can give you some of those answers so you know more about what you're dealing with. How many of Julie Forman's personal items do you have? And I don't mean her ID, cell phone, and computer. That's the tech stuff, Ryan's department. I mean truly personal items—clothing, family photos, jewelry, even her perfume. Those are the tools I need."

Lisa stared at her, fascinated. "Milo says you're a psychic."

"I actually said she was a claircognizant," Milo corrected. "It's a more precise definition, one that doesn't conjure up images of crystal balls and séances."

Claire's smile reached her eyes. "Thank you for that. Very few people make that distinction. Claircognizance—clear knowing—is a metaphysical sense in which I simply know something to be true, even though I can't back any of it up with fact or provide an explanation as to how I know it. It's not that the term psychic is wrong, it's just that it's so overused and in all the wrong ways."

"And handling Julie's things can trigger your awareness?" Lisa asked.

"I can't promise you results, but, yes, that's usually what happens."

"Well, producing a bunch of Julie's personal items is no problem. I have some of her photos, books, costume jewelry, and workout clothes. We wanted to make the identity switch as real as possible. So Milo collected the most significant things he could find from her apartment—along with all the tech stuff Ryan needs—right before we took off."

"Good. Can you get all that to me with time to spare before Shannon's arrival tomorrow evening?" Claire asked.

"Sure," Milo said. "As soon as we get home, I'll pack up everything I took from Julie's apartment. Then I'll hop an early train here first thing tomorrow morning and bring it to you while Lis is running the gym."

"That's not happening," Casey replied. "We're going to be here most of the night prepping you, not only for when Shannon shows up but for what you should do to stay safe and below the radar. No more media coverage for your gym, for example. Nothing that puts you in the public eye. I'd be willing to bet that whoever killed Julie knows exactly where you are. They'll be keeping an eye on you, making sure you're a good girl who started a new life far away that's of no threat to them."

"Do you think they know they killed the wrong woman?" Milo asked.

"It's a definite possibility. Either way, they're going to be vigilant."

"Are you going to help keep us safe?" Lisa's eyes were wide with fear.

"Absolutely. That's part of what we need to discuss. Marc and Patrick are the go-to people for that. They'll need to know every moment of your schedules so they can work out a system to protect you. So you'll need to spend a chunk of tonight meeting with them. While that's happening, Ryan will be reviewing all the material Miles just emailed him and digging even deeper. He'll come up with more, believe me, and some of what he finds might impact how we instruct you."

Casey turned to Emma, letting her know that she hadn't been sidelined. "And Emma's going to have her own agenda. She has the tightest personal connection with the two of you. She'll think of tactics we won't. I'll leave that in her hands. But, any way you look at it, you're not leaving until you're ready for what you're about to face and how to manage it—and extract what you need to from it. That kind of prep could mean you'll be here till dawn. So we'll have to find another way for Claire to get what she needs—which, incidentally is of vital importance, just like everything else I just specified."

"I'll go to Upper Montclair now," Claire offered. "Just give me your address, your keys, a list of what I'm looking for, and where I can find everything."

"That's not happening." Patrick was shaking his head adamantly. "I'm sure their apartment is being watched. And you have no training in this area, Claire. We have to get in and out without being spotted. I'll drive to Upper Montclair. It'll be faster than the train. I'll be back in two hours. Marc can brief me on whatever I miss."

"Okay." Lisa handed him her apartment keys and took a pad and pen out of her handbag. "Give me two minutes. I'll compile the list and locations of what you'll be looking for." She was already scribbling, with Milo peering over her shoulder and muttering add-ons.

Five minutes later, Patrick was out the door and on his way.

"Okay, you two," Casey said to Lisa and Milo. "You're up first with me."

## CHAPTER EIGHTEEN

*Burlington, Vermont*

It was a cool May night in the breathtaking Green Mountains.

Max's focus wasn't on the panoramic view. It was on the taste of success.

He sat in his study, sipping his Hennessy Privilege V.S.O.P. He was savoring not only his cognac but the promising weekly status report he'd received, summarizing the progress of all his prospects.

Max knew exactly how to get the most out of people. He had learned from the master—his father. A military instructor in the Russian army, his father's job was to break men's will and turn them into soldiers. By day, the battle-hardened man would terrorize hundreds of soldiers. At night, he would terrify his children with his mere presence—all save Max. Max learned and grew from his father's dominance, his demands for mental and physical superiority. His father loved his work and was excellent at his job. The military decoration, The Order "For Military Merit," conferred to him by the Russian Federation, said so. Whenever Max challenged his father, his father would simply point at the coveted medal and say: "When you have a more impressive one of these, then I will listen to what you have to say."

Max respected that immensely. And he knew his father would soon respect what he was doing here in the United States.

On that thought, he made his decision.

It was time to summon all his handpicked trainers and, from the most accomplished members of their applicant pools, to select the next wave of champions.

Leaning forward, Max pressed the intercom button to awaken all phones in the complex.

"Dmitry," he commanded. "Report to my private study immediately."

Five minutes later, an out-of-breath Dmitry knocked on the door of Max's study.

Max's clipped response came from within. "Enter."

Swiftly, Dmitry stepped inside, sat down in his assigned seat in Max's office, and awaited his employer's orders.

Max set down his cognac, then steepled his fingers in front of him on the desk.

"Dmitry, the results this week are extraordinary," he said. "It's time. Arrange for our usual meeting in St. Thomas one week from tomorrow."

"Will that give everyone enough time to prepare?" Dmitry asked.

"If they want to win, they'll make it enough time."

"True." Dmitry didn't challenge his boss on that one—although he often expressed his opinion to Max in ways no one else was permitted to. Max trusted Dmitry, thought highly of his intellectual capabilities, and regularly elicited his thoughts. It was one of the best perks Dmitry enjoyed as the assistant to this brilliant, terrifying man.

"Tell Oskar I expect him to personally oversee all aspects

of our meeting," Max continued. "Tell him I want Maine lob-
sters this time—not the crap he tried to pawn off on us last time.
Also, tell him I expect him to double the number of servers. They
move at half the speed of normal people. I expect twice as many
to make up for their shortcomings."

Dmitry nodded. He didn't need to write things down. He
had a photographic memory, particularly when it came to Max.

"I'll take care of it," he assured his boss.

"Good." Max picked up his cognac. "That will be all."


As the door closed behind Dmitry, Max's private cell
phone rang.

"Yes?" he said in Russian.

"The Barker girl is on the move," Slava reported, also in
Russian. "She bought a train ticket and is on her way to Upper
Montclair."

"Obviously headed for Julie Forman." Max considered
that fact thoughtfully. "She probably read about Robbins' disappearance and lost control. Speaking of which, I'm assuming you
took care of all his pertinent files at the Apex Center."

"Those files are now gone."

"Good. Then Shannon Barker's mecca to New Jersey
doesn't concern me, as long as it's comfort she's seeking. We'll
have to keep a close eye on her. She could become a loose can-
non, if getting together with her mentor results in either one of
them deciding to do some more digging. But with Robbins out
of the picture, there's really nothing for them to pursue. And Forman's computer friend knows nothing. So they'll all share one
big dead end together."

"And if they decide to push past that dead end and search
for what's beyond it?"

"Then they'll all share a grave next to Mr. Robbins."

*Upper Montclair, New Jersey*
*Train Station*

*Are you here???*

Shannon was frantically messaging Julie even before the train came to a stop. The twenty-one-hour ride had given her way too much time to think. She'd checked the online Chicago newspaper sites a dozen times to see if Jim had resurfaced. He hadn't.

Her worst fears were bubbling up inside her, and she somehow knew they were a reality.

Furtively, she checked her private messages as she walked down the platform.

She nearly sagged with relief when she saw she had a reply from Julie.

Clicking on the response, her face fell.

*I was held up at the gym and am now picking up food for us. My friend, Miles Parker, who's the best guy in the world and completely trustworthy, will be standing at the foot of the platform, waiting for you. He's wearing an Excalibur (that's my gym's name) T-shirt and holding up a sign with your name on it. He'll get you safely to my place, where we can get you settled in and talk. It'll be okay, Shannon. And I can't wait to see you!*

The last part brightened Shannon's mood a bit. She raised her head, scanning the area as she walked.

There.

A tall, scruffy-looking guy with a lopsided grin, wearing a chocolate-brown T-shirt with a gold-embossed logo of crossed swords and the word "Excalibur" on it, was posted in a direct path of the descending passengers. The sign he held up said, *Shannon Barker.*

Milo watched Shannon walk in his direction, wearing jeans and a zip-up hoodie, her wavy, light brown hair tied back in a hairband. As she slipped her iPhone into her pocket, her expression seemed to change from fearful disappointment to reluctant acceptance. Good. This was the way it had to be. Forensic Instincts was right. Whenever Lisa and Shannon had their first face-to-face, the girl's illusions would shatter. And the fallout from that sure as hell couldn't happen here.

"It's going to be a traumatic and emotional event," Casey had explained. "You want it to occur in a controlled environment—like your apartment. Not in the middle of a bustling train station. You have no idea how Shannon will react. She might freak out and try to run, or start crying and carrying on. You can't let that happen in public, and you certainly can't let her bolt. Keep the leverage in your hands. There's no way Lisa can risk walking over and picking Shannon up herself. So Miles, you pick her up. Emma will be waiting in the apartment with Lisa to help defuse the situation and ease Shannon into the truth."

Casey had gone on to outline the steps Lisa and Milo should take to pull it off.

They'd followed FI's instructions to a tee.

Milo's grin widened as Shannon shyly approached him, her backpack slung over one arm. "Shannon?" he verified.

She nodded.

"I'm Miles Parker." He stuck out his hand to shake hers. "I'm Julie's right-hand guy, and her best friend. She's said such great stuff about you. I'm glad to meet you."

A smile lit Shannon's eyes. "She did?"

"Yup." Milo took her backpack. "She's grocery shopping now. She wants you to have a home-cooked meal on your first night here." A pause, and Milo groped in his pocket, pulling out his wallet and flipping it open. "There's my Excalibur photo ID badge—just so you won't worry that I'm not who I say I am."

Shannon glanced at it, and Milo felt a wave of pity for the poor kid. She was trembling. "I'm an idiot," she said. "I should have asked to see that right away. I'm just not used to..." She broke off, chewing her lip in a nervous gesture.

"Hey, you're sixteen. Cut yourself some slack. Coming all this way by yourself was a huge deal—and a brave one." Milo gestured toward the street. "Let's go. Julie's probably on her way home by now. We'll meet her there."

Just as FI had predicted, the walk to the apartment contained some nervous questions about Milo.

"How long have you and Julie known each other?" she asked. "Do you text all the time, or have you always lived close enough to get to see each other?"

If you tell the truth, you don't have to remember anything. Casey had drilled Mark Twain's quote into Milo and Lisa over and over again.

"We've been friends since we were kids," Milo supplied. "Until a few weeks ago, I lived in Chicago, too. I came to New Jersey with Julie when she ran."

"Oh." Shannon looked surprised. "You just quit your job and took off? Are you guys in some serious relationship or something?"

"Nope." Milo hid his grin. Her youthful openness was kind of refreshing. "We're very close, but it's more like brother and sister. And I didn't have to quit my job. I'm an online tech support guy for Dell computers, so my job is transportable. Give me an Internet connection and my laptop, and I'm in business."

"Cool." Shannon fell silent, obviously deep in thought as she fiddled with the zipper of her hoodie. "Did Julie tell you what's going on?" she blurted out.

"Yes, she did." Milo kept his demeanor calm. "She's scared, just like you are. And she's worried about you. But I'm the only one she's confided in."

Shannon nodded, looking almost relieved that someone else—a much-needed ally—was clued in.

Milo led Shannon across the street, simultaneously easing her into the next reveal: their living arrangements.

"Julie's a better cook than I am, so you're lucky she's in the kitchen tonight. I'm usually holed up in my room with my computer."

The implication registered, and Shannon angled her head toward him. She looked more concerned about where that left her than she did about a guy staying with them. "You and Julie are roommates?"

"Yup." Milo kept it light, grateful that Shannon wasn't so sheltered that the very thought of this would send her running. "It keeps the cost of living down. And given the circumstances, I'm glad to be around for you ladies."

Shannon started fiddling with her zipper again. "Uh… how many rooms… I mean, how big is the apartment… I mean…"

Milo saved her from further embarrassment. "Big enough," he assured her. "Julie's got the master bedroom, and I've got the small one. But I usually camp out in the living area; it's bigger and I can do my work there. So it was no sweat to turn the second bedroom over to you."

"That's great." Shannon exhaled with visible relief. "I just feel bad that I'm putting you out."

Milo gave a dismissive shrug. "I'm a guy. Put me anywhere and I'm happy. Just as long as my tech gear is with me, there's no problem."

"Thank you," Shannon said. Seeing Miles slow down, she

glanced up at the apartment building they were approaching. "Is that where you guys live?"

"Uh-huh."

He led her up the path, swinging her backpack onto his shoulder. He wasn't usually into the gentleman stuff—his mind just didn't work that way—but he felt a tremendous amount of sympathy for what Shannon was about to go through. She was a naïve kid—more naïve than most sixteen-year-olds, because she'd spent her life on balance beams and parallel bars rather than experiencing a normal socialization process with other kids her age, growing and maturing because of it. She'd also just lost her entire Olympic future as well as her health, and had been dragged into a majorly perilous situation. As if that wasn't enough, she was about to find out that her only trusted ally was dead, with a virtual stranger taking her place.

Not only did Milo know how essential it was to get Shannon on their side, he truly wanted to get her on their side, to make her feel like she still had friends who were there to help. Friends who, thanks to Forensic Instincts, were in a much better position to keep her safe than Julie Forman had ever been. He was relieved as hell that Emma was waiting in their apartment, ready to convince her of that.

Leading the way inside the building, Milo gestured toward the stairs, and he and Shannon trudged up the two flights to the apartment.

"Here we are," he announced, pulling out his keys and fitting one in the lock. With one quick turn, the door opened, and they were inside.

The wonderful smell of homemade cooking wafted to their nostrils, telling them that Julie was already home.

"We're here!" Miles called out, waiting until Shannon preceded him inside before he shut the door and turned the bolt behind him, ensuring the closed quarters they required.

"Julie?" Shannon called out in excitement.

"Hi, Shannon." Lisa emerged from the galley kitchen, Emma coming up quietly behind her. "I'm so relieved that you're safe."

At first, Shannon broke into smiles. She rushed toward the person she thought was Julie, arms open and ready to give her a big hug.

Then she abruptly halted in her tracks.

"You're not Julie." All the blood drained from her face. "Who are you? Where's Julie?" Shannon's gaze darted from Lisa to Emma. "And who are you?" She didn't wait for an answer. She whipped around, saw Milo standing with his back against the door. "Oh my God, are you kidnapping me?"

"No, nothing like that, I promise." Lisa was shaking her head, feeling the weight of the world was on her shoulders. Even though Emma was right by her side, she felt as if this crucial part was hers and hers alone.

Emma proved her wrong. "It's okay, Shannon," she said with a reassuring smile. "My name's Emma Stirling. I know you're in trouble. But you're safe here. Really. You won't believe it yet, but all three of us are on your side. We're here to help you, not hurt you."

"I don't know you," Shannon whimpered.

"But you do know me." Lisa followed Casey's advice and made no move to step closer or make Shannon feel cornered in any way. "I'm not a stranger. You're just not putting me in context."

Shannon stared, her breath coming in hard, frightened pants. Recognition dawned but did nothing to abate her fear. "You worked at one of the gyms where I trained with Julie. Designer Fitness. You did all sorts of odd jobs. I remember thinking how much you and Julie looked alike."

Fear transformed to terror, widening the pupils of Shannon's eyes. "You're the one who got shot outside Julie's apartment. You're supposed to be dead. But if you're not…if you're here… what happened to Julie?  Is she… Oh my God…"

Wildly, Shannon turned to flee, only to find Milo still standing in front of the doorway. The girl stood there, cringing like a caged animal, and then slowly sank to the floor, her entire body quaking with tears.

"You killed her," Shannon whimpered. "You killed Julie. And now you're going to kill me. You work for them. Jim's dead. Julie's dead. Now it'll be me. And I walked right into it. Oh my God…"

"Shannon, stop." Emma knew it was time to toss the rule book out the window, thinking of what Claire had taught her about following her instincts. She gestured for Lisa to go to Shannon.

Following Emma's direction, Lisa walked over, squatting in front of Shannon and gently gripping her forearms. "We're in the same boat you are—scared and in danger. And, no, I didn't kill Julie. But I did see her get killed. And it was too much for me. I ran and came here to set up my gym, pretending I was Julie so that no one would look for me."

Shannon didn't respond. But the tremors running through her body seemed to subside a little.

"My name is Lisa Barnes," Lisa continued, speaking as calmly and frankly as Casey had advised. "I met Julie at the gym, about a week before she died. She offered me a job and a place to stay—both of which I desperately needed. She was incredibly kind and generous, and I owe her a lot—and that includes taking care of you, who I know she cared about. Whatever illegal activities are going on, I walked straight into the gunfire, just as you did. We need to stick together to stay alive."

This time, Shannon lifted her head and gazed at Lisa with questioning tear-filled eyes. "I don't understand. Why did you run away to New Jersey? Why didn't you talk to the police? They could've helped us. Why did you switch identities with Julie? Now they have no idea that she's the one who's dead."

"I know. Shannon, I have my own baggage. I thought it was me the killers were after. Selfishly, I was afraid for my own life. As long as the cops and the killers thought Lisa was dead, and that Julie knew nothing about their drug dealing, I'd be safe. As for New Jersey, buying the gym came along at the right place at the right time. I've always wanted to do this. So I grabbed my chance to get out of Chicago and start over."

"So it's been you I've been messaging with all this time?"

"Yes."

"And who is he?" Shannon pointed to Milo. "Where does he fit into all this?"

Lisa let out a breath. "He's exactly what I said he was—my best and most trusted friend. He's also a computer genius. Once I started getting your PMs and realized what was going on, I got Milo involved. He's done a ton of research and found out a lot—all of which I'll share with you if you come in and eat. Please, Shannon..." Lisa squeezed her hands. "I know how scared and confused you must be. But we can help keep you safe and make sure these criminals are caught. Just have some dinner, hear us out, and then, if you still want to take off, we won't stop you." *Please don't let that be the outcome*, Lisa thought, even though she knew that Patrick was on security detail, ready and waiting to follow Shannon if she ran.

Shannon still looked reticent. "What kind of baggage would make you a target for murder?"

Lisa exchanged a quick look with Milo. Reveal as little

as you can without losing her, Casey had said. Don't overwhelm her with details that aren't her concern and that will only freak her out.

"I was a street kid, a reject from the foster care system," she explained briefly. "I had to work for creepy people to survive. I still feel vulnerable when I think someone's after me. Julie knew all that when she took me in—but she did it anyway."

"Oh." That affected Shannon, compassion flashing across her face. "That's terrible. I get it. Okay." Her gaze shifted to Emma. "Are you a policewoman? You look too young."

"That's kind of what I am. But I'm one of the good guys. You have my word on that."

Shannon studied her, clearly not sure what to think. But Emma's Alice in Wonderland appearance had a way of doing the trick.

"Okay," the girl said. "I'll eat. And I'll listen." She rose. "Can I use the bathroom first?"

"Of course." Lisa gestured toward it, fully aware that the tiny window in there wouldn't provide access for escape. "And Milo will put your backpack in your room. Then we'll eat and talk."

## CHAPTER NINETEEN

Once alone, Lisa and Milo exchanged a worried look and then turned to Emma.

"What do you think?" Lisa whispered.

"You did great," Emma replied. "She's on the fence, but she's not running. Let's take that as a positive and move on from here." Emma gestured for Milo to move away from the door. Then she headed for the kitchen. "I'll help you serve. Miles, you set the table. I don't want Shannon to think you're standing guard. Patrick is ready for action if he's needed. You both need to take it down a notch and relax. It's the only way to get Shannon to relax."

"Easier said than done," Lisa muttered, following Emma into the kitchen. She pulled on some mitts, opened the oven, and slid out a large Pyrex dish. "Put out four plates and four sets of silverware," she instructed Milo. "Tonight we're going to eat like human beings—on a table, not the sofa." A quick gesture toward the small table in the equally small dining area. "There are even paper napkins and glasses, all ready for you to arrange."

"Wow. Martha Stewart." Milo gave an appreciative sniff. "I don't get it. You were never into cooking, except for your famous meatballs."

"Well, there's a first time for everything," Lisa replied, setting the dish on a coaster. "I follow recipes well. And the Internet's full of them. You're getting lemon chicken, rice pilaf, and a small Greek salad. Pretty good, huh?"

"I'll let you know after I taste it."

Lisa stuck her tongue out at him, feeling a great deal more relaxed by the normalcy it elicited. Between that and Emma's presence, she was beginning to think she could pull this off. She felt even more relaxed when Shannon reappeared in the kitchen entranceway, the tears washed off her face, her hair brushed and retied, and her expression wary but not terrified.

It was a huge step.

"Let's eat." Lisa gestured for Shannon to join Emma and Milo in the dining area. "I'm sure you've never touched a drop of soda, so I put a pitcher of water with lemon on the table. Is that okay?"

"Yes, thank you." Shannon hovered by the table, torn between sitting down and helping Milo arrange things.

"Sit," Lisa instructed her. "Dinner's all ready. So there's nothing to do but eat."

"And talk," Shannon added.

"Of course. And talk," Emma assured her.

Lisa started carrying in food, intent on making Shannon feel okay in their company. "I hope you like chicken."

Another tentative nod, almost as if Shannon were suddenly realizing how hungry she was.

"I didn't think I'd be able to eat," she murmured.

"Well, you can, and you have to." Lisa used a spatula to place a boneless chicken breast on Shannon's plate, after which she drizzled some lemon sauce over the top. "You, of all people, know how important it is to take care of your health and your body."

The girl lowered her gaze.

"I know you can't compete anymore, Shannon," Lisa said softly. "And I know what it feels like to have your whole life ripped out from under you. But you will have a future—maybe a different one than you expected, but a happy future just the same."

Swallowing hard, Shannon said, "That's what Julie told me."

"She was right. But first we have to get you—and us—out of this nightmare we just found ourselves in." Lisa finished serving the food, and they all sat down around the table. "Now let's eat and we'll all fill you in on what we know."

*Bensonhurt, Brooklyn, New York City*

Hutch carried the last of his boxes into Marc's—now his—second-floor apartment. The place was great: high ceilings, lots of windows, two bedrooms, an updated kitchen, a spacious living and dining room, which opened to a huge private deck. Not only that, the apartment was in move-in condition, thanks to Marc leaving all his furniture and to being former military all the way—fastidiously neat. There wasn't even a damned scuff mark on the gleaming brown-and-tan tile floor.

"This place looks even more meticulous than I remember," Hutch commented, looking around. "I never understood how Marc managed to live in an apartment for years without leaving so much as a scratch on the walls."

"Me, either. But that's Marc—a SEAL to the core." Casey used a box cutter to slice open some boxes and, seeing what they contained, she carried them into the master bedroom. "All clothes," she called out. "I'll do these. You can do the kitchen stuff."

"How about we forget both and do the sheets?" Hutch

called back, a suggestive note in his voice. "I can think of all kinds of ways to put them to good use."

"Can you?" Casey stood in the doorway, arms folded across her breasts, regarding him with a coy expression she rarely wore but found herself liking. In fact, she liked everything about Hutch's move to NYC. "So can I. But work comes before play. Besides, heightened anticipation is exciting."

"Heightened anticipation?" Hutch's brows shot up. "We've spent two years going months at a time without seeing each other. I've taken more cold showers than I can count. How about some throw-you-on-the-bed, impulsive sex for a change?"

The image made Casey draw in a breath. Refusing Hutch's offer was definitely costing her. All she wanted to do was to drag him into that bed, welcome him to NYC, and not come up for air for two weeks. But this easy banter, where time was on their side, was new, and it was fun. It was bringing out a playful side of her she never knew she had.

Not to mention, she knew they wouldn't be alone for long.

She gave Hutch a mouth-watering look. "Nope. I want to see those hot muscles of yours at work—and, after you've lifted and emptied all those boxes, to make sure your stamina hasn't lost its mojo."

"My stamina is going to ensure you pay for making me wait, Ms. Woods." Hutch gave her a very sexy, very pointed look before he returned to his tasks. "I doubt you'll be able to make it to work tomorrow."

"I doubt I'll want to."

Their exchange was interrupted when the buzzer from downstairs sounded.

"Don't look so crestfallen," Casey said, going over to find out who it was. "There's another perk to waiting until we have all night. Leisurely diversity. I just took a quick peek, and there's a huge stall shower and a sunken tub in that awesome master bathroom. So think about that while you're unpacking. I promise to make waiting worth your while."

"I'm going to hold you to that."

"Please do." Pressing the intercom button, Casey asked, "Yes?"

"It's the welcoming committee," Marc responded. "Maddy and I brought a bottle of wine, dessert from the best bakery in Brooklyn—plus two extra pairs of hands to unpack."

"Now that's an offer we can't refuse." Casey buzzed them up immediately.

Two minutes later, Hutch opened the door to Marc and his fiancée, Madeline Westfield—a lovely, dark-haired, totally put-together class act. The Marc who stood by her side was a completely different Marc than the one who showed up at FI every day. This was head-over-heels-in-love Marc, who kept a possessive arm looped around Maddy's waist, even as he handed over a large box of pastries.

"Just inhale them," Maddy said. "Marc was practically drooling from the minute we parked—which was a full block down on Eighteenth Avenue." She smiled up at him, and it was obvious that the head-over-heels thing was reciprocated. The two of them had waited ten years to be together, and, now that it had finally happened, they weren't about to take it for granted.

"They're worth drooling over," Marc informed Casey and Hutch. "Villabate has been here in Brooklyn for over three decades. They make Sicilian bread, cakes, cookies, pastries—you name it—that bring crowds of people in there to stand in line."

"It really is like Disney World in there," Maddy agreed. "The artistry of their creations." She gestured toward the box. "We bought a variety, from cannoli to chocolate mousse to cream puffs—and a few others I can't even pronounce but love to eat—and a bottle of Chianti to go with them." She handed Casey the bottle of wine. "So let's get to it."

She slipped out of her jacket, sizing up the amount of work to be done. She was very familiar with Marc's apartment, so she glanced down the hall toward the bedroom.

"Oh, good. You organized which boxes go where. That'll make it easy. Hutch, you and Casey can do the bedrooms and master bath, and Marc and I will do the kitchen and the powder room." Her forehead creased in thought. "Do you have any paintings you want hung? Marc is a pro at that."

Hutch scanned the walls ruefully. "I made this move and transfer happen fast, so I'm severely lacking in personal touches. Plus, interior decorating is definitely not my forte."

"Well, it is mine." Maddy was an ER nurse, but she also had an uncanny eye for design. "I'd be happy to pick out some things for you. Casey knows your taste. We can do it together."

"Done," Casey said.

"Great, thanks." Hutch gazed from one of them to the other. "Who opts for dessert first and unpacking second?"

Four hands went up.

"I'll get the plastic plates and cups," Casey said, heading for the kitchen. "We'll have great friends, great food, and mediocre place settings. Sounds like the perfect compromise to me."

The buzzer sounded again.

"We're very popular tonight," Hutch said, walking over and pressing the intercom. "Who else is coming to our rescue?" he teased.

"We are." It was Claire's voice at the other end, followed by Ryan calling out, "It depends on why you need rescuing. Should we go away?"

Hutch began to laugh. "No, Mr. One-Track-Mind. Come

on up. Marc and Maddy are here."

"So are we." This time it was Patrick's voice coming through the intercom. "And Adele cooked all day, so we'll be stocking your fridge."

"I'm not going away no matter what you're doing," Emma chimed in. "I brought flowers and homemade banana bread."

Hutch blinked, although he was clearly touched. "Come on up and join the party," he said.

The entire team—plus Patrick's charming wife, Adele, trudged in, carrying everything a newly moved-in person could want. Ryan even brought a leashed-up Hero, together with toys to keep him busy.

Hero had spent many a night in this apartment with Marc, so, the instant he was unleashed, he found his favorite spot near the kitchen and plunked down.

"Hero might not be working, but we are." Adele walked over and gave Hutch a peck on the cheek. "Welcome. I made all your favorite meals, as per Casey's list."

Hutch shot Casey a quick look. So this was why she'd put off their own private welcome. She knew they'd be having visitors.

Casey smiled at him from the kitchen and then went back to work. She arranged the mouthwatering pastries on a big plastic serving plate and gathered up a small box of plastic plates, utensils, and glasses. Stopping only to scoop up some napkins, she returned to the living room, where everyone had congregated—all except Adele, who passed Casey on her way to the kitchen as she hurried to stock Hutch's fridge.

"Don't be long, Adele," Casey called back over her shoulder. "Or I'm afraid the crowd will have devoured your share of the pastries."

"Not to worry," Patrick assured his wife. "I won't let them."

With that, everybody got up, taking things from Casey and setting up the coffee table for a celebratory dessert. Emma went into the kitchen to assist Adele so that she could more swiftly join in the fun. And, in no time at all, everyone was toasting Hutch's arrival, ooh-ing and aah-ing as they dived into the Villabate pastries.

They were well sated, and busily unpacking boxes, when Marc's cell phone rang.

He glanced at it. "Work," he said, setting down the pots and pans he was holding, and striding off to the smaller bedroom for some privacy.

Ryan, who'd been in the living room programing Hutch's TV, walked out and shot Casey a quizzical look. "Anything I should know?"

"I'm not sure." Casey, too, had left her unpacking to exit the master bedroom and gaze into the second bedroom, watching Marc. "We'll find out soon enough."

She narrowed her eyes, trying to interpret Marc's body language. Marc wasn't an easy read. But whatever he was discussing, it was intense.

A few minutes later, he hung up, stepping out into the hallway—where, by this time, the entire FI team was waiting for him—and giving Casey a triumphant look. A look she knew and appreciated only too well.

"That was my buddy at Midtown North," he told her. "You can call Mr. Worster and tell him he's safe. Turns out that Ryan—and Yoda—were right. Number one suspect, Lee Jarvis, is our man. The cops followed up on the anonymous tip they received. They entered the scumbag's apartment and confiscated his computer. Sure enough, they found all the threatening emails that Jarvis sent to Worster, which he sent through a proxy server."

"Which is why I couldn't track his IP address," Ryan said with a nod.

"Exactly. And talk about a disgruntled investor. Jarvis thinks Worster screwed him out of millions, so he planned on tormenting and then killing him. Nice."

"So Jarvis has been arrested? He's at Midtown North now?" Casey asked.

"Being booked as we speak." Marc nodded. "The detectives are calling Worster now, but I'm sure he'd rather hear from us."

"Agreed." Casey rose. "Excuse me for a minute."

Hutch eyed the group as Casey walked away, cell phone in hand. "And what was the tip that this anonymous caller provided?" he asked. While he might not know the details of the case, he did know FI.

Marc shrugged. "Something about a home office full of slashed photos of Mr. Worster. And an unregistered gun, which was apparently just sitting out on our suspect's desk."

"And who would have the access needed to supply this timely anonymous tip?"

"The 'who' is a mystery. That's why they call it anonymous," Marc replied dryly. "My money is on the maid. She works there six days a week."

"The maid."

"Yup."

"Right. And the convenient timing of this incriminating and oh-so-visible evidence that elicited the anonymous tip—do I want to know your ideas on how it got there?"

Marc took a deep swallow of Chianti. "Nope."

Hutch rolled his eyes. "I didn't think so." He was no stranger to the unorthodox methods of this amazing team. Still, he was a federal agent. He couldn't know about illegal activities, no matter how altruistic. So the Forensic Instincts team did their best not to put him in any untenable positions, and Hutch did his best to not ask questions he didn't want the answers to.

Although they all knew he'd walked the finest of lines in the past, especially when it came to Casey's safety.

"This is excellent news," Ryan declared. With great enthusiasm, he refilled his glass. "Now we'll be able to put all our resources into our new case." He glanced from Adele to Hutch. "Sorry, I can't talk about it, because it's ongoing. But it's a really interesting one."

Hutch pursed his lips, glancing into the kitchen in time to see Casey punch off her phone.

"Well, since we can't talk about your new case, and since we've worked up a sweat from unpacking and pretty much polished off every speck of food on this table, not to mention an extra bottle of wine courtesy of Claire and Ryan, I'm thinking we should call it a night." He rose. "I can't thank you enough for the welcome, the food, and the help."

"Aren't you subtle?" Ryan muttered. "I just poured myself another glass of Chianti. Can I at least drink that?"

"Take it on the road," Claire said. "Let's let Casey and Hutch have some privacy."

Everyone hastily stood up, tossing their plates and utensils into a giant trash bag and gathering up their things.

"We really thank you guys," Casey said, returning to the living room. "Sorry for Hutch's bluntness. I think he's exhausted from the long drive and the whole settling in thing."

"Tired, my ass," Ryan commented wryly. "He looks like a hungry wolf about to pounce on you and—"

"Good night, Ryan," Casey interrupted him. "You know the way out." She glanced over her shoulder at Hero, who was snoring in his favorite spot. "Hero can spend the night here, since that's where I'll be." She yawned—a yawn that was about as convincing as a criminal's not guilty plea. "I guess I'm pretty beat, too."

Adele began to laugh. "Shoo, everyone. Casey and Hutch want to share some intimacy." Her eyes twinkled as they met Casey's. "I may be sixty, but sixty is the new thirty. I know when it's time to let a couple have their space."

With that, she scooted everyone out the door, then slipped her arm through Patrick's and followed suit. She turned to give Casey a quick wink.

Casey grinned. "See you all tomorrow, and thanks again," she called after them.

Having locked the door, she turned to find Hutch shrugging off his shirt. "Payoff time, Ms. Woods," he said in a low, sexy tone. "You've got thirty seconds to get into that bed. It's ready and waiting—I made it myself."

With a soft laugh, Casey scooted past him into the bedroom, pulling her sweater over her head and tossing it out into the hall. "Make that twenty seconds, Agent Hutchinson."

## CHAPTER TWENTY

*Tribeca, NYC*
*Office of Forensic Instincts*

Patrick led the way around the back of the brownstone, gesturing for Lisa, Milo, and Shannon to follow him up to the second-story terrace. Once there, he punched the security code into the Hirsch pad and opened the double doors, waiting until everyone was in before shutting the doors behind them and re-entering the code.

Casey walked out of the main conference room. "Did everything go as planned?" she asked Patrick, smiling a hello at the trio of clients.

"Like clockwork," he replied. "These three left Upper Montclair for a shopping spree in the city. They walked up and down Fifth Avenue, buying a few things to make Shannon feel less afraid and more at home." He grinned, pointing to the giant stuffed koala bear in Shannon's arms. "They were very convincing. From there, they headed to Times Square for a movie matinee."

"Which they never saw," Casey supplied.

"Right. I met them in the alley and drove them here. I

parked around the corner, and, as you saw, we came up the back way. No one followed us. We're secure."

"I never doubted it." Casey gave Patrick a thank-you nod, then gazed past him and the koala to the nervous, wide-eyed teenager holding it. "Hi, Shannon. I'm Casey Woods."

"Hi," Shannon said in a small voice.

"Come in and meet everyone." Casey walked over and squeezed her arm. "We're here to help you. Don't be nervous." She took the koala from Shannon's arms and placed it on a nearby table. "I think your new friend will be better off out here. Our bloodhound, Hero, has a tendency to think every toy belongs to him. And I doubt you want to bring home a tattered, slobbered-on stuffed animal."

Shannon's tension eased a bit. "Your dog is in there?" She pointed at the conference room.

"Yes. Not to worry, he's extremely friendly and obedient."

"I love dogs," Shannon said.

"And Hero loves attention," Casey told her. "So if you want to sit in a beanbag chair and pet him while we talk, he'll be your friend for life."

"I'd like that."

"One beanbag chair coming up." Patrick headed upstairs to Claire's yoga room—the ideal place to find a more comfortable alternative to a conference room chair.

Casey escorted their three visitors into the main conference room. She could feel Shannon stiffen up again, and she couldn't blame her. The room would be overwhelming to a sixteen-year-old. All rich wood and high-tech equipment, the room's focal point was a huge oval table surrounded by a dozen presidential-looking chairs—chairs that were now occupied by the entire FI team.

Hero, lying on the floor beside Casey's chair, lifted his

head and gazed intently at Shannon, waiting for his cue.

"A friend, Hero. Stay." Casey gave him a hand signal. Instantly, the tension left his body, and he put his head back down, still watching them with a keen expression on his face.

Simultaneously, Yoda announced: "Three visitors have arrived. As per my programming, they are Miles Parker, Lisa Barnes, and Shannon Barker."

Shannon nearly jumped out of her skin.

"That's just FI's virtual assistant, Yoda," Milo explained to her. "Ryan created him. He's mind-blowing."

"Thank you, Mr. Parker," Yoda replied politely.

"Sure." Milo looked around. "Wow, this room is a lot different than the one we met in yesterday."

"This is our main conference room," Casey replied. "It seems intimidating, but it'll grow on you." She ran her hand over the mahogany credenza, where refreshments were laid out. "I love this place. It's my work sanctuary."

"Well, naturally you love it. You designed it." Ryan's response was pure Ryan. He wasn't being flippant; he was just stating a fact. Casey usually let it go. So did the team, although occasionally one of them shot Ryan a withering look—usually eliciting a clueless expression in response. He was cutting-edge brilliant when it came to technology and naïvely oblivious when it came to emotional awareness.

"That is Ryan McKay," Casey introduced him to Shannon.

"He's the genius who found us and made sure we came here." Milo was already quite the Ryan fan.

"Hey, Shannon." Ryan's easy grin was infectious.

"Hi." Shannon was not only female but she was a teenager—the perfect age for crushes. She stared at Ryan—his chiseled features, his well-honed muscles, his rumpled black hair and dark blue eyes—and she was head over heels.

She blushed, dropping her gaze.

Quickly, Casey came to her aid, introducing all the other team members and sighing with relief when Patrick came back with the beanbag chair. He plunked it on the floor next to Hero.

"You're getting some company, boy," he informed the bloodhound, who raised his head again, this time in interest. His tail began thudding against the floor when he saw Casey bring Shannon over, hopeful awareness dawning in his soulful eyes. His tail-thudding motion sped up when Shannon lowered herself to the chair, and hope was confirmed: she was there to play with him.

After one stroke of his ears, Hero rolled over to have Shannon scratch his belly.

"From human scent evidence dog to lap dog," Marc said dryly. "Rough adaptation, Hero."

The bloodhound responded by snorting loudly in contentment.

Shannon gave a small smile, distracted, at least for the time being. "He's beautiful," she said.

In one fluid motion, Claire came to her feet. She'd already been seated at the table when Casey came in, and Casey had been totally focused on the upcoming client interview. So for the first time, she noticed that Claire was dressed in Lycra capris, a tank top, and a hoodie—her yoga clothes—rather than the business casual she wore to work.

"I'm a yoga fanatic, Shannon," Claire said, before Casey had time to process things. "That beanbag chair came from my workout room. Would you mind if I grabbed another one and joined you on the floor? I work better when I'm comfortable." She gave Shannon one of her warm, enveloping smiles.

"That would be cool," Shannon admitted. "I feel kind of lame being the only one down here—except for Hero, of course."

She stroked Hero's glossy head.

"Great. I'll go grab one and be back in a sec." Claire didn't make eye contact with anyone else. She just walked out of the room, all grace and serenity.

And visionary instinct.

*Smart, Claire, very smart,* Casey thought as she gestured for Lisa and Milo to join everyone at the conference table, which they did. *The more at ease Shannon is, and the more flashes of insight you can pick up from being beside her, the better.*

Casey lowered herself into her chair, positioned just a few feet above Shannon and Hero. She took an extra minute to settle herself, giving Claire more time to return.

"Can we get the three of you anything?" Emma piped up, correctly interpreting the dynamics that were going on. "Coffee? Tea? Water? And we've got blueberry and corn muffins, too."

"Water would be great," Lisa said.

"Coming right up." Emma walked over to the credenza and opened the built-in fridge, pulling out three bottles of water. "Here you go." She handed one each to Lisa, Milo, and Shannon. "We'll eat the muffins later." She grinned. "At least I will."

By that time, Claire had returned and planted a beanbag chair on the other side of Shannon and Hero. She flopped down into it, stroking a hand down Hero's back. "I'm all set," she said. "Sorry to hold things up."

"No problem," Casey assured her. Keeping her posture relaxed and comfortable, she looked down at Shannon, choosing her words carefully. "Shannon," she began. "I know that Lisa and Miles explained to you that we're here to protect the three of you. I hope you feel you can trust us."

"I'll try." Shannon swallowed. "I have nowhere else to turn now that Julie's dead."

Casey nodded her understanding. "I can't even imagine

what a shock it was for you to find out that Julie is…gone. What we don't know is why. We're going to need you to fill in whatever blanks you can."

Shannon looked up, her eyes bleak. "It has something to do with the PEDs Jim Robbins was giving me." A pause. "He's dead, isn't he? They killed him?"

"I don't know," Casey replied honestly. "He may have been harmed. Or he may have taken off by himself, out of fear. Either way, we can't wait around for him to turn up with answers. We have to act right away—find out who they are." She waited while Shannon took a nervous gulp of water.

"After your injury and your realization that Jim's 'supplements' were really PEDs, did you tell anyone other than Julie?"

Shannon shook her head. "Julie told me not to. She wanted me to stay out of it, just to go home, see a therapist, and let her do the digging." Tears clogged Shannon's throat, and the pain in her voice was heartbreaking. "She was protecting me. And it got her killed."

"It's not your fault, Shannon." Claire put a soothing hand on Shannon's arm. "You had no way of knowing this went any deeper than drug distribution, or any further than Jim Robbins and the PEDs he was giving you."

Shannon shoved a strand of hair behind her ear. "Julie must have found something out. But I don't know what." Shannon paused. "I know that Jim worked for someone else—someone bigger. He pretty much admitted that to me when I confronted him in the Apex parking lot. And whoever those someones are, they not only deal drugs but kill people."

"You're not going to be next, Shannon." Casey's voice was firm. "Neither is Lisa or Miles. We're going to make sure of that."

"My guess is that Julie somehow got into Jim Robbins' office at Apex," Marc said. "Whatever she found was there.

Maybe documents, maybe something on his computer, maybe something else. But that material implicated not only him but higher-ups. And they had to get it before someone could use it against them."

"Then why didn't they come after Julie? Or Lisa, if they knew they killed the wrong woman?" Shannon asked.

"Because the papers never reached her." Patrick was thoughtful. "They're definitely keeping an eye on her—and on Miles. But to kill Lisa randomly, when the Chicago police believe she's Julie, would be too much of a coincidence to ignore. It would raise eyebrows and cause the cops to more thoroughly investigate the two murders. That's a big risk for criminals who want to fly under the radar."

"Jim was giving those PEDs to more athletes than just Shannon," Claire murmured. "I'm getting flashes of two others. They weren't at Shannon's level but close." Brows drawn in question, she looked at Shannon. "Do you have any idea who those two gymnasts were?"

Shannon's jaw dropped. "You really are a psychic, aren't you?"

Claire didn't bother plunging into a whole explanation of her gift. She merely waited for Shannon's response.

"Billy Carver and Jessica Majors," Shannon supplied. "They're both awesome. Jim called us the Thriving Three. Billy can't qualify for another year; he's only fifteen. And Jessica is working on perfecting her timing."

Casey was taking all this in. "Are you friendly enough with them to give them a call without arousing suspicion?"

"Sure." Shannon turned her palms up in puzzlement. "Why? What do you want me to ask them?"

"How they're doing at practice since Jim took off. It's very important that you don't use words like *disappeared* or *vanished*.

Keep it casual. I just want to figure out how the drug withdrawal is affecting them."

"It's affected me a lot." Shannon looked sad. "And not only my heart, or even the arthroscopic surgery I had to fix my rotator cuff, but my energy, my endurance, even just taking a walk. I'm so tired. Plus, I have all these daily medications I have to take now."

Claire placed her hand on Shannon's arm again. "Tell that to them. Gush over the wonderful health supplements Jim was giving you, and how much you miss them. Then, ask how many supplements Jim had been recommending they take per day."

"I was taking four—two in the morning and two at night." Shannon was looking nervous again. "Why do you want to know that?"

Claire was gentle but honest. "Because I think Jim was giving you more than the others. Probably because you were closest to bringing him the Olympic gold. If so, that would explain a lot, including your weakened rotator cuff, your accident, and your resulting cardiomyopathy."

"Oh my God." Shannon blanched. "Is that why I got hurt when no one else did?"

"I believe so, yes."

"Shannon," Ryan interrupted. "Do you have Jim Robbins' cell phone number?" He was itching for the right answer. This would be a crucial, first solid lead on Robbins. The background checks that both he and Miles had run had come up empty. On paper, the guy read like a Boy Scout. And his emails, which Ryan had hacked into, were boring and ordinary—completely devoid of incriminating information.

To Ryan's relief, Shannon nodded. "It's programmed into my cell phone."

Ryan grabbed a pad. "Give it to me." He was clearly urgent. "Given the sophistication of this organization, my guess is it's going to turn out to be a burner phone, which would keep his calls anonymous—except from me."

Turning to face Casey, Ryan said, "The phone company won't have records. I've got to find out Robbins' service provider and find a way into their system. That could take a while." Ryan purposely avoided the word *hack*. No need for TMI, not with a teenager. "The provider won't have a name—I'm sure Robbins paid by cash—but they will have records for that phone number. But I've got to act fast. They tend to delete records pretty quickly. I might have days, maybe a week if I'm lucky. And I want to know who Robbins called and who called him. That's imperative to solving this case."

"Do it," Casey replied.

Seeing Ryan's pen poised and waiting, along with his questioning gaze, Shannon gave him the number.

"Unless you need me, I'm on this now." Ryan looked at Casey, who shook her head, gesturing for him to go.

"I'll see you guys later," he told their clients, then took off to do what he did best.

"Can you call your athlete friends now?" Claire asked Shannon.

"Sure." Shannon scrolled through the contacts on her phone.

"Express concern for Jim," Claire advised her. "That'll be your easiest in."

Nodding, Shannon called Billy first.

"Hey," she said when he answered. "It's Shannon… Yeah, I'm a mess, pretty much what you'd expect. I'm in New Jersey visiting a friend. I need to take my mind off things." She drew in a breath. "I wanted to know if you'd heard any news about Jim. I'm worried about him." She looked like she wanted to gag. "Nothing?" No surprise there. "How are you holding up?"

She paused, listening. "I'm feeling tired, too, and my energy level sucks. I miss the supplements Jim gave me—they gave me stamina, which would help me recover faster... You, too? How many were you taking—one or two a day? Yeah, same with me." She gazed at Claire and mouthed the word: *two.* "And Jess? How's she holding up?" Shannon nodded. "I thought I'd give her a call. Maybe I can cheer her up. I know I'm not really part of the Thriving Three anymore, but I still care.

"Thanks for saying that. And you know I'll be cheering you and Jess on." Billy's next words brought an aching sadness to her eyes. "Okay, you go to practice. Text when you can."

Shannon disconnected the call, bringing herself under control. "He feels depleted, but at least Jim didn't bump up his dosage like he did mine. Billy didn't say anything about Jessica, other than the fact that she's depressed without Jim to train her. I'll give her a call now."

The call to Jessica yielded the same results. Although the other gymnast attributed her lethargy to Jim's sudden disappearance, she did confirm that she'd been taking one supplement at night and one in the morning. She wished Shannon a speedy recovery and said they'd get together when Shannon got back to Chicago. Then she, too, ran off to meet the athlete's ubiquitous call to practice.

Tears glistened on Shannon's lashes, and she brushed them away with trembling fingers. "This makes me sick," she said. "Jim was giving me four pills a day for the past month. He was using me as a guinea pig for his...employer. He screwed up my health and my whole life." She took the tissue Casey handed her and blew her nose. "I still don't understand why he chose me. He has so many trainees."

"Because you showed the most promise," Casey answered

her. "I know it's bittersweet to hear, but you were obviously Jim's star pupil. He believed you'd be the one to bring home Olympic gold—soon, with the right PED boost. He gambled and he failed. And you're the one who paid the price." Casey's lips thinned into a grim line.

Shannon wiped her eyes with the tissue. "How am I going to get past this? And now, I might be a murder target..."

"It's okay, honey." With deep compassion, Claire stroked Shannon's arm. "I'm so sorry. I wish we could undo the damage Jim did to you. But I do know you will get past this and thrive. I can sense it just from touching you. It's going to be all right."

"Really?" Shannon asked hopefully.

"Really. As for being a target, our team's not letting that happen. So put it out of your mind." With that, Claire rose. "Let me help move this case along in my own way. I'll be back shortly. Lisa provided me with Julie's personal items—some of her clothes and things like family photos and a few pieces of jewelry. We also have her cell phone, checkbook, and several other things. I spent a good portion of last night using them to see if I picked up any of Julie's feelings or discoveries. I got some fuzzy images. I want to see if I can crystalize them in my mind. But I'll come back before you leave."

Claire's reassurance was purposeful. It was obvious that Shannon was attached to her. If it weren't for time being of the essence, she would have put off her work until after Shannon left, just so she could be there for her. But if she could get anything to share with Shannon that would trigger some additional memories, it would be worth it.

Surprisingly, Shannon perked up, rather than looking crestfallen. "Would what you're doing work with my stuff, too?"

Quizzically, Claire gazed at her, shaking her head in non-comprehension. "What stuff? I'm not following."

"If you can hold Julie's things and get visions about her and who she was dealing with, maybe you could do the same thing with me. I've got something that was once very meaningful to me. And if you could tap into its energy…" Shannon dug around in her backpack and pulled out a stopwatch. "I was thinking of this."

Claire gazed at it thoughtfully, sensing that it was significant—and was about to become more so. "You used it when you trained?"

"Yes." Shannon pressed it into Claire's hand.

Claire sucked in her breath. "Julie didn't give this to you, did she?"

"No." Slowly, Shannon shook her head. "Jim Robbins did."

# CHAPTER TWENTY-ONE

*St. Thomas, Virgin Islands*

The Living Room was Max's favorite meeting room at the luxurious Ritz Carlton. The room had a breathtaking ocean view and looked out over the hotel's exquisite courtyard. It was a vacationer's dream.

Today, however, The Living Room had been transformed from a warmly decorated, crystal-chandeliered meeting area into something resembling the stage on *American Idol*. Inside the room, a raised dais of three people, with Max in the center, was situated way up front, below which sat an empty horseshoe-shaped table. Outside in the hallway was a stream of eager, nervous contestants.

The contestants—Max's nationwide web of athletic trainers—were shifting or pacing anxiously, each one sizing up the competition and convincing themselves that he or she, along with one of their trainees, would be the winner. The prize: a primo position in Max's elite cadre of trainers, accompanied by his or her chosen trainee, who'd be expected to be one of the next Olympians or future Einsteins. The two-person team would be transferred from the members' individual homes to

Max's private, secret estate. Nondisclosure agreements would be signed. The trainers' salaries and expense allowances would double, and if Max's projections were to be believed, they would be part of the team that achieved what evolution had failed to do in two hundred thousand years: create a smarter, faster, stronger human being.

Each trainer had the chance to present three of their finest athletes. Their sales pitch would be punctuated by evaluative comments from the other two occupants of the dais: Dr. Leonid Eltsin, Max's head physiologist, who would provide physical and medical assessments, and Dr. Galina Petrova, Max's head psychologist in charge of the administration of the scathing battery of mental tests used to gauge each candidate's progress, all of which helped her comprise the ultimate character and intelligence evaluations.

It normally took over a week to make this size evaluative meeting happen. Dmitry had trimmed the process down to five days—five days to summon all the nationwide trainers, to inform them to choose their three top contenders and book all their flights for this trip, to make the necessary hotel accommodations, and to have everything set up precisely as Max expected.

That was part of why Dmitry was where he was in Max's hierarchy. There was little or nothing he couldn't accomplish for his employer.

Now, he stepped inside the room and gave Max a questioning look.

Max nodded.

Holding open The Living Room door, Dmitry turned to speak to the first trainer—Dave Perkins—asking him to join them.

Dave wasn't new to this process. He'd been here once before, at which time he and his athletes were not selected. That had really gotten him pissed off, not at Max but at himself, igniting his competitive spirit. Dave liked winning and had been training winning teams and individual athletes for over twenty years. Failure only drove him harder.

For the past few months, he had brutally and ruthlessly driven his athletes to the point of breaking while still adhering to Max's strict limitations on the supplements provided. But Dave's relentless pushing had paid off. Each candidate had improved his physical score from an average of ninety-one to an impressive ninety-five. Mental test scores had gone from eighty-nine to ninety-four.

He walked up to the lectern and nodded in deference to Max, and then to Doctors Leonid Eltsin and Galina Petrova. He steeled himself to look Max in the eye during his presentation. Even though he'd met his employer once before—on his first trip to St. Thomas—he was no less intimidated by the scientific genius's mere presence.

Sucking in his breath, Dave presented his first, and most impressive, candidate, Daniel McCurd—a college junior who was head of the swim team, a track and field superstar, and a four-point-oh student. Dave described all of Daniel's attributes in great detail and then motioned for the AV person to start the video. The visuals were quite impressive. Daniel was on a path to compete in the Ironman triathlon series and someday to win the Ford Ironman World Championship in Kona, Hawaii.

Max calmly turned to Dr. Eltsin and asked for his opinion. The physiologist pulled out a report and confirmed both the test results and the improvement over the past few months. Next it was Dr. Petrova's turn. She pointed out that the candidate's extreme stress levels had reduced his mental score from ninety-five to ninety-four. Dave grimaced. He knew that he was to blame for that drop in Daniel's mental score. He'd been pushing him relentlessly on the physical front.

Max's expression was completely unreadable. He looked at Dave, uttered a perfunctory "Thank you," and then proceeded to turn his attention to the score sheet in front of him.

In the upper right-hand corner was a blank box. Max took his pen and made a simple mark—a large check. Dave and his candidate Daniel had made it to the next round.

Eight other trainers entered the room, one by one, and made similar presentations about their own candidates. Once the entire process was complete, everyone was dismissed, and the painstaking, time-consuming assessment and elimination process began.

A day and a half later, the decisions had been made.

Everyone re-congregated, this time in one of the larger meeting rooms that would accommodate everyone. It was black, white, and austere. No beachfront views, no terrace, all business.

It was the first time all the attendees had been amassed as one. They scrutinized each other, wondering who might possibly have edged them out and who they themselves might have bested. And they were all wondering about Jim Robbins. Word travelled rapidly through their circuit. They'd all heard about Shannon Barker—about how close she was to becoming a champion and about what had happened to her. Whispered words had been exchanged about Jim's potential misuse of the drugs. But no one dared speak their questions aloud—especially the one about what had happened to their fellow trainer.

The nervous tension in the room was palpable.

At the dais, Max cleared his throat, and the whole room snapped to attention. The announcements were about to be made.

"Before I begin, let me express my keen disappointment over the incident in Chicago and the gross misuse of my life's work." Max cut straight to the chase. He paused, his icy stare sweeping the room. "The situation has been dealt with. Jim Robbins is no longer with us."

The underlying message hung in the air like a toxic gas.

"On to the business at hand," Max continued, ignoring the terrified expressions on everyone's faces. "We've seen some outstanding candidates. I'm extremely pleased. Here are my decisions."

With that, Dave and two other trainers were asked to stand up and be recognized—which they did, beaming ear to ear amidst a round of polite but forced clapping. These three trainers would become part of the elite set of trainer-trainees working closely with Max and his scientists. The rest would go back to their respective cities and try their best to do better. Some athletes would be asked to find other trainers—and a few trainers who had tried and failed several times to join the elite ranks would be asked to find employment elsewhere.

Max felt his familiar rush at the meeting's outcome. He was singularly responsible for honing the skills and maximizing the potential of all his candidates. And, someday, those candidates—and the rest of the world—would reward him for his success. He'd receive the Nobel Prize, his greatest dream. And he'd have the respect of every renowned scientist as he surpassed all their achievements.

He could see himself in Stockholm, receiving the gold medallion…

But not yet. Not until Max had a time-tested product and method, along with a long list of success stories. Then he'd be ready to publish and accept the accolades he deserved. And, oh, how the world would prosper from his work.

His formula would be sought after by every significant entity, both national and international. The militaries of the

world. Corporations. Pharmaceutical and nutraceutical companies. They'd all be vying for it, even trying to steal it. He, and he
alone, would dictate the terms. He'd retain ultimate control over
the formula. Initially, the product would be in limited supply.
He'd decide which endeavors and who were worthy enough to
receive it. The quality, distribution, and pricing would all be under his control. No investors. No licensees. No one to tell him
what to do. Only the needy and the greedy begging for his product.

A slow smile curved his lips.

Very soon, all this would be his.

*Chicago, Illinois*
*Nineteenth Police District*

Detective Paula Kline frowned in concentration as, yet
again, she scanned the report the Montclair PD had emailed
her after they'd met with Julie Forman. Something about the
interview didn't sit right. Julie Forman's extreme agitation. The
sudden appearance of Miles Parker, Lisa Barnes' never-before-
heard-from best friend. Stories so smoothly told. Actions that
were questionable.

Added to that now was the disappearance of that Apex
Center trainer, Jim Robbins, whose Olympic hopeful had also
been training under Julie Forman.

All Paula's professional warning bells were going off.

"Are you reading that Montclair PD interview again?"
her partner, Detective Frank Bogart, asked. "Boy, you're really
fixated on this one, aren't you? You're like a dog with a bone."

She shrugged. "I guess. I'm just not getting a good feeling
about the whole thing. Doesn't the series of coincidences raise
any red flags to you?"

"Of course," Frank said. "I'm not saying I disagree with you. This definitely feels off."

"And is it tied to the Jim Robbins disappearance?" Paula asked. "Was he killed like Lisa, or did he take off like Julie? Either way, why?"

"We could ask the Montclair guys to check in on the Forman woman again and ask some questions about her teenage trainee—as well as if she herself had any personal contact with Jim Robbins."

"I think that's asking for more than just a favor. It's asking the Montclair PD to do our job." Paula was fiddling with her pen. "A cursory drop-by was one thing. But these cases are ours. Lisa Barnes was killed here in Chicago, and Robbins vanished from here, as well."

"Yup," Frank agreed thoughtfully. "So it's you and me who need to interview Julie Forman. Problem is, the only way we're going to get permission from the district commander to travel to New Jersey is if we can positively tie the two cases together."

"Then that's what we have to do."

## CHAPTER TWENTY-TWO

Dawn was casting its first hazy light through the windows of the FI brownstone.

Upstairs on the fourth floor, Casey was sick of tossing and turning. She sat upright, raked a hand through her tangled red hair, and scooted up on the bed. She glanced to her side, smiling faintly as she saw that Hutch was still sleeping deeply beside her.

Good to know that she'd tired him out.

With that, she reached over to her computer stand and picked up her laptop, simultaneously switching on the nightstand lamp. She propped her back against the headboard and began reading through the reports her team had been inputting on a daily basis.

It had been a grueling week for them all. They'd been working their butts off as they raced the clock to get a solid lead on this damned PED case. During this time, they hadn't risked another meeting with their clients; it was simply too dangerous. Casey had no doubt that Lisa's gym, her apartment, and her excursions were being monitored. Ditto for Miles and Shannon. The three of them were still alive only because they'd done nothing to indicate to the killers that they were a real threat. Bad enough that Shannon had raced halfway across the country to be with "Julie"—an action that Casey was certain had raised a few red flags, not to mention causing a tightening of surveillance. But that wasn't cause for three messy murders. However, if "Julie" and crew met up with a high-profile investigative team?

That would be suicide.

So it was imperative that distance be maintained.

Ryan had supplied enough burner phones to everyone to keep the lines of communication open between FI and its clients. Since then, he'd been sequestered in his lair, hacking into delicate systems and trying to compile intricate information. Casey could hear an occasional bang, clang, or swear word coming from down there, but she only smiled, knowing that Ryan was working on some contraption that would ultimately help them.

The key word there was ultimately. Not as soon as Casey wanted.

For her part, Emma had truly stepped up to the plate. She'd been talking to Lisa and Shannon several times a day, strengthening her bond with Lisa, and creating one with Shannon. Their chats kept Lisa focused and calm, and Shannon diverted and amused. Emma related really well to teenagers—partly because she was a master at endearing herself to people and partly because she was barely out of her teenage years herself. By making herself the emotional go-to, she was allowing the rest of the team to do their jobs without interruption.

Claire was the most frustrated of the bunch. She'd been spending hours in her yoga room, trying desperately to pick up some helpful energy from Julie's personal items and, most of all, from Shannon's stopwatch.

The watch was cold. Icy cold. That's all she'd gotten, and that's all she'd given to Casey.

But they both knew what that probably meant.

Seeing Claire's intensifying frustration, Casey had curbed her own impatience. She knew that Claire had no control over her gift. Sometimes things came quickly, other times not. Unfortunately, this was one of those "not" times.

Patrick was keeping a watchful, if invisible, eye over their clients.

And Casey and Marc were strategizing over how to best use their skills to gain buried information out of their clients, given the limitations of phone contact, which made body language impossible to read. Even videoconferencing didn't convey enough.

So as of now? They'd basically gained no ground.

Casey sighed, chewing her lip in irked frustration.

"Hey." Hutch's voice was gravelly with sleep. "I think I'm insulted. A night like last night and you're awake, working, and irritable?"

"Hey back, and don't be insulted." Casey shut her laptop and set it aside. "I'm irritable a lot these days—other than when you're casting your sexy spell over me. Our case is spinning in neutral. And you know how impatient I can get."

"You? Impatient?" Hutch grinned. "Gee, I've never noticed." His smile faded, and he propped himself up on one elbow. "Do you want to talk about it—even theoretically? Maybe I can toss in a helpful suggestion or two?"

Casey's shoulders lifted and fell in a shrug. "I'm not sure what I can say, and not just because the case is confidential. Because we're dealing with a dangerous and volatile situation, and the bad guys aren't showing enough of their hands for us to play, much less to win."

Hutch digested that quietly. "I've been there. My suggestion? Sit down with Marc and start from Ground Zero. Lay out the facts and personalities from the beginning. You'll find a thread that you missed when you were dealing with the case as a whole. And, even if that doesn't happen, it'll get your juices flowing. That'll break through the wall you're banging your heads against."

"Good idea." Casey couldn't go into any more detail, so she dropped the subject, instead wriggling over and reaching for Hutch. "Let's say good morning the right way," she murmured, wrapping her arms around his neck. "That'll get my juices flowing, too."

A low chuckle vibrated in Hutch's chest. "Your wish is my command." He pulled Casey over him, and all thoughts of work were silenced for a while.

Marc was in before eight. That wasn't an accident.

After giving Maddy a quick see-you-later kiss, he'd gratefully left her alone, pausing only to grab an energy bar before he'd hurried out of the duplex.

So much for making love to his beautiful bride-to-be. He was heading for the gym to lift weights and work off some stress, and then to the office.

For Maddy's mother was in town.

Maddy and Constance weren't close—in fact, Maddy hadn't even contacted her during those terrifying months when her life was in danger. But since she'd called to tell Connie she was marrying Marc, her mother had been like a kid in a candy store.

Maddy and her first husband, Conrad, had been married for several years and hadn't been the kind of passionate love couple her mother wanted for her daughter. Therefore, all wedding plans had been tepid, at best. But now that she knew Maddy was marrying the love of her life? She was in wedding heaven.

She was also an early riser, and Maddy had spent the

past hour on the phone with her, rolling her eyes and listening to the elaborate floral arrangements her mother had in mind for the reception.

Marc had listened until he couldn't take it anymore. Thank heavens Maddy had talked that exclusive wedding planner into coming on board at the last minute, to manage the wedding and Maddy's mother. A professional like that was worth every penny she got. Let her run the show. All Marc wanted was his ring on Maddy's finger and hers on his. He wasn't sure why flowers and table settings seemed to be dominating the process. And he wasn't hanging around the duplex to find out.

He'd arrived at the brownstone to hear banging, clattering, and an enthusiastic "Yes!" echoing upstairs from Ryan's lair. Okay, now his curiosity was piqued. He walked downstairs and knocked.

"It's me," he said.

"Door's open," Ryan called back.

Marc stepped inside and was immediately whacked in the face by a TRX that was anchored to and hanging from the door. He ducked and then grimaced at the clutter that dominated the room.

All the desk and computer surfaces were filled—printouts scattered all over them. Papers were strewn on the chairs and had overflowed onto the floor, where they remained, untouched. And another TRX was swinging from a post in the back of the lair. Ryan had clearly skipped the gym and done his workout in here.

Taking up the most space of all were the mechanical gizmo parts thrown everywhere, literally swallowing up the rest of the room.

"You're working on something," Marc said, weaving his way through the clutter to where Ryan was seated on a workbench.

"Not just something," Ryan replied. He stopped tinkering with his latest contraption and looked up with a broad grin, holding it up for Marc to admire.

Marc eyed the thing. It was a ten-inch-long brown cylinder with two wires coming out of it.

"Meet Otter," Ryan said.

"Okay, I give." Marc took the bait. "What does this new invention do, and why is it called Otter? I don't see any tail, fur, or feet."

Ryan gave an exasperated sigh, although he still looked both proud and smug. "Otter is my latest and greatest way to gather intelligence. As for his name, he's modeled after a North American river otter pup—same size and body build. More importantly, otters are intelligent, highly curious, and handsome animals. We have a lot in common."

Rolling his eyes, Marc snorted. "Humble as ever."

"Just speaking the truth."

"Right. Go on."

"Anyway, Otter is brilliant in his intelligence gathering." Ryan leaned forward in excitement. "Here's the deal. We plant him in a company that has information we want to find out, especially when we need to sift through large amounts of data contained in a database."

"Like a cell phone company."

"Exactly." Ryan pointed at the two wires. "This plug goes into a network connection, and this one goes into an outlet. The key is to find a place behind a desk or cabinet where no one will look. Otter will slowly but surely gather information, encrypt it, and relay it back to Yoda through a zigzag path across the Internet. No one will be able to connect the information leak to us. Amazing, huh?"

"Wrong, Kemosabe." It was Marc's turn. "How did you

plan on getting Otter inside the targeted company? I don't see any legs, wheels, or tank treads."

A scowl. "I haven't worked that part out yet."

"Well, you won't work it out, because it can't be done. That's where the skills of a clandestine operative can't be replaced by an electromechanical contraption. You need human skills to get past security. Human skills to scan the environment for an opportunistic place to locate...uh, Otter." Marc bit back a smile as he said the name. "Human skills to improvise in real time, making split-second decisions that turn defeat into victory."

"I assume you're referring to yourself?"

"Of course."

"You're not a whole lot humbler than I am," Ryan pointed out. A gleam came into his eyes. "On the other hand, we do make a great team. We've pulled this kind of thing off together more than once."

"Sure have." Marc's brows drew together in thought. "I take it we'll have to go to Chicago to plant Otter in the appropriate place?"

"Yeah, and we can't fly, not with all this electronic equipment that Homeland Security will not understand."

"Then we'll drive. It should only take about twelve hours." Marc was already heading for the door. "I'll run this by Casey. How soon can you be ready to leave?"

"As soon as the boss says yes."

Sitting in lotus position in her living room, eyes closed, Claire cradled Julie's locket between her palms. Cradling. That was always the word that came to mind when she held this delicate piece of Julie's past. The locket was a gift from her parents. She'd lost them three years ago in a car crash. A drunken driver had taken them away. She would have given anything to have

them back. They'd been a close, loving family. The locket emanated tenderness and sadness. With their deaths, Julie felt very
much alone.

Claire sighed. In some ways, Julie was as lost as Lisa.

Putting down the locket, Claire picked up a pair of small
diamond studs. Again, a birthday gift from Julie's parents. Julie
had worn them now more than ever; she felt closer to them when
she did.

Abruptly, an image flashed through Claire's mind, and
she clutched the earrings more firmly, shut her eyes more tightly.
Julie. At the gym. Wearing these. Sitting at her desk. Livid with
anger. Claire was inside Julie's head, feeling her turmoil, knowing
its cause. Shannon's health. The reason for its deterioration. The
consequential demise of her hopes and dreams.

Jim Robbins.

All Julie's thoughts converged into one. She wouldn't let
this go. She'd get into the Apex Center. She'd find a way past security. She'd dig up evidence on the son of a bitch, evidence that
would get him thrown in jail, where he couldn't do this again.
Maybe he was already doing it with his other trainees. How many
of them had he laced with this stuff? Son of a bitch. No one else
could suffer like Shannon.

Poor Shannon. Poor Shannon. Poor Shannon…

Claire felt tears seep from beneath her closed eyelids,
trickle down her cheeks. The emotions were intense—rage at
Jim, compassion and protectiveness for Shannon.

A modern building with several stories and large rooms
of sophisticated equipment.

The Apex Center.

Claire could see it, walk inside it.

Quickly, she snatched up another of Julie's possessions,
this time one that was all business. Her wallet. She'd had it on her

when she'd gone to the Apex Center.

She was inside the building. Claire could sense her presence. Closeted in Jim Robbins' office. Rifling through his files. Finding papers of some kind—papers incriminating enough for her to make copies. She took them. She had them with her in a bag. Hurry home. Hurry home.

Flashes of activity. A car. A tattooed man. A gun. Oh, God—the searing pain in her head as the bullet penetrated her skull. Life oozing out of her body. Pain. Blinding pain. Blackness. The coldness of death.

Claire's eyes flew open. She was gasping for air. Her entire body was in a cold sweat, and she was shaking uncontrollably.

She could still see the scene playing out. The tattooed man snatched up the bag of papers. The killers drove off as rapidly as they'd arrived.

Russian. That realization came to Claire in a flash of insight. They were Russian.

She couldn't see the shooter clearly, not yet. Nor could she make out his tattoos to the point where she could draw them.

But she wasn't letting go of this wallet until she could give Casey descriptions of both.

# CHAPTER TWENTY-THREE

It had been only a few hours since they'd left New York, but Marc and Ryan were like two little boys as they fought over which radio station to play. Marc preferred classic rock like Whitesnake. Ryan preferred hard rock like Nickelback. If SiriusXM were tracking their station changes, the company would be afraid the satellite signal would crash, and they'd automatically terminate the account.

"I'm the one at the wheel; I should have final say," Marc pointed out.

"Well, I'm the one doing the technical research…" Ryan held up his laptop. "So I need the right inspiration."

"Fine." Marc turned the dial once more and was happy to hear Bon Jovi playing. "Good compromise?"

"I can live with it. On a prayer." Ryan grinned at his own cleverness.

Marc rolled his eyes. "Done." Happy to be finished with this bullshit battle, he turned the radio down a notch and switched his attention to the mission ahead of them.

"I'm clear on my role once we get to Chicago, but how is Otter supposed to tell us the necessary information about cell phone calls?"

"So glad you asked," Ryan replied. "As you know, Shannon was able to provide me with Jim's cell phone number. I checked. Jim used U.S. Cellular for cell phone service. I was able to grab the last month of cell phone records before their intrusion detection systems shut me down. From there, I found a few phone numbers of interest. Some of them were to other trainers in the area. Those guys generally had regular cell phones. Maybe they were friends, colleagues, or maybe they were drug dealers like Jim. That's part of what your investigative skills will need to determine when we interview them. But one number in particular kept popping up—and with greater frequency right before Julie was murdered. I traced the number to a TracPhone. Nontechnical types and some senior citizens prefer TracPhones, but a disposable cell phone—a burner phone—is the communication tool of choice for criminals. Phones are purchased with cash and tossed when the minutes run out."

"Boy Genius, I was with the FBI, remember?  I know what a burner phone is and how it's purchased. In fact, I'm pretty sure everyone who watches TV crime shows knows that."

"Sorry."  Ryan had the decency to look sheepish.

"Forget it. Let's get back to your analysis. So Jim called his distributor's TracPhone. How are we going to find out who this guy is?"

"Otter."

Once again, Marc rolled his eyes. "So Otter is clairvoyant like your girlfriend?"

Ryan shot him an irritated look. "Careful with your choice of words. Claire and I are…well, Claire and I. No label's been assigned to it."

"Fine. Whatever. Go on."

"Otter's not psychic, just curious."  Ryan stopped talking to glance out the window, his attention temporarily focused elsewhere. "Before I give you more than you can absorb in one shot, I need an Egg McMuffin and a large cup of coffee. Pull off at the next exit. The golden arches I just saw made me hungry."

"No health food today?"

"Not unless you know of a health food restaurant right off the highway with a drive-through window. I'll have to make do." A grin. "Plus, your body needs an Egg McMuffin every once in a while."

"You don't have to twist my arm. I'm starving. And I need some coffee, too." Marc pulled into the right-hand lane, cruising until the exit ramp appeared and those familiar golden arches rose through the trees, beckoning hungry travelers.

They zipped through the drive-through, grabbing their food and getting right back on the road, this time with Ryan at the wheel. He was the king of eating, talking, and driving, all at the same time.

"To continue. Otter will navigate the digital rivers of Verizon's Chicago network operations center, which TracPhone uses to handle its customers' calls. He'll find every cell tower that was ever involved in handling a call to or from that TracPhone number and send all the detailed information stealthily back to Yoda. Yoda will align the cell phone call information with cell tower log files using time stamps recorded down to microseconds."

"So how is this going to tell us who Mr. Anonymous is?" Marc interrupted to ask.

Ryan raised a hand. "I'm getting to that part. Yoda will be able to triangulate a geographic 'red zone' from the cell tower data. You see, when a cell phone places a call, it contacts cell towers in the area. The idea is to use the one with the best signal strength. Usually, it's the closest one to the subscriber. Sometimes it's not, because of some natural or man-made obstacles—like a hill or a building that impacts the signal strength. By doing a 'mashup' of the cell tower locations—Google Earth for the terrain assessment and signal strength data on the TracPhone calls—Yoda should be able to narrow the location of the distributor to within a block or so."

He took a belt of coffee. "People are creatures of habit. They place the bulk of their cell phone calls from home, their office, or their favorite Starbucks. When the same tower handles cell phone calls at the same time of day, that can give us a clue as to where this guy hangs out. For example, if Yoda comes up with a location during the day in a business district, then we can guess that the distributor has an office in the area. At night, especially late at night, he's probably home. I suspect this guy will be doing business out of his car and his apartment."

"Okay," Marc said, processing all this information. "So we know that this scumbag lives within a block or two of some address. We can't go door to door interviewing people. I don't have my FBI credentials anymore, remember?"

"No worries on that score," Ryan assured him. "We won't have to. Once Yoda figures out the area we're interested in, Otter will switch gears and head in the opposite direction. He'll focus on calls made using the same geographic pattern of cell towers but from another cell phone. In my experience analyzing communications in criminal networks, bad guys will protect themselves from discovery by using a burner phone to talk to people on the street. In this case, that's what the distributor did with Jim. So if Jim were arrested, the cops would only have a disposable cell phone number and no leads back to the distributor."

"Dead end."

"Yup. But a distributor has multiple business relationships and, at some point, would be talking to someone higher up in the food chain. That person wouldn't want the hassle of dealing with revolving phone numbers for all his distributors. He might have thirty people he needs to talk to on a regular basis, spread out all over the US. Imagine the chaos. The person above the distributor would only accept phone calls from known phone numbers."

"Got it."

"So, in a long-winded way, we'll use the burner phone to find a location. We'll use that location to find a regular cell phone number that is being used by the same person. Then we'll go on to use that info to find who the distributor called. My hope is that someone at the top is not concerned about cell phone anonymity, but if they are, we can track them to within another block or two radius. Otter will keep plying the digital rivers of cell phone data and, with Yoda's help and computation resources, build a map of the criminal network using their communications to uncover the players."

Marc snorted. "Between the government listening in to our cell phone conversations, surveillance cameras everywhere, people capturing conversations, pictures, and videos using smartphones, and tech prodigies like you designing, integrating, and hacking all this, there really is no place to hide any longer."

"That's right. If you've got any secrets I don't know about, I will soon."

Marc chuckled. "No such luck. You'll have to play spy somewhere else. I'm as clean as a whistle—other than my work at FI, which is no secret to you. But it does sound like I underestimated Otter."

"You did. But I don't expect you to get my level of genius."

"Just drive, Ryan," Marc said and turned up the radio. "The sooner we get there, the better."

"Casey?" Claire poked her head around the conference room door. Even though Casey had her own office, the whole team knew that this was her favorite place to work.

Sure enough, she was sitting at the oval table, typing information into her laptop, Hero relaxing at her feet.

She and Hero both looked up at the sound of Claire's voice. Hero wagged his tail, and Casey beckoned Claire in, a hopeful glint in her eyes. She knew that look on Claire's face—and what it usually yielded.

"You made some kind of sensory connection?"

"More than one," Claire replied. "You have time?"

"Are you kidding? I'm losing my mind because of how slowly we're moving forward. Sit."

Claire complied. "By the way, where's Ryan? He's not in his lair. And I need his input on a couple of drawings I made." She indicated the pieces of paper in her hand, which she now placed on the desk in front of her.

"He and Marc are on their way to Chicago. They're going to be there for a few days. Ryan's got a new gadget that he says will yield detailed call information all stemming from Jim Robbins' burner phone." Casey gave Claire a wry grin. "As usual, I only half understood Ryan's explanation, but you and I both know that he and Marc will come back with something significant."

Claire nodded. "Fine. Then we'll muddle through my stuff without him."

She spread out the three sheets of paper, angling them toward Casey. "These are fairly accurate depictions of Julie's killer's tattoos. It took me a while to be able to visualize them, but I finally did. This one"—she pointed at the first sheet, which was a sketch of a bull—"is etched on the killer's upper right arm. Next"—she pointed at the second drawing, which was birds flying over the horizon—"is on his upper left arm. And the last one"—she pushed the third drawing, a sketch of a sailing ship, toward Casey—"is on his right forearm."

"Wow." Casey studied each drawing carefully, marveling at Claire's detail. "Wow. That was quite a connection you made. And obviously, these particular symbols stand for specific things. I wish we knew what nationality we're dealing with. That might narrow down our research."

"The killers are Russian. The symbols are, too. I was hoping Ryan could dig up a tie between whatever basic information we come up with to an actual gang or sect who wore this combination." Claire blew out a breath, tucking a strand of hair behind her ear. "On the other hand, it could be a random combination of symbols, not tied to any one group."

"We've got to find out." Casey was picking up her burner phone. "Only I'm not sure Ryan is our best source on this one. I'll let him know what you picked up on when he checks in, but we need inside info—crime families, gangs."

"Hutch?" Claire guessed.

"Yup." Casey punched in a number. "I'm calling Lisa and getting her permission to bring Hutch in, at least on this peripheral level. He doesn't need to know the case details. He just needs to offer us his expertise. And Hutch has seen everything."

She paused as Lisa answered, and then tersely explained that they had an FBI contact who might be able help them out without knowing names or case specifics. Sure enough, Lisa agreed.

Casey hung up and used her own cell to call Hutch. She knew she'd probably get his voice mail, since he was busy orienting himself to his new job.

"Hey," he surprised her by answering, although his head was definitely elsewhere. "Everything okay?"

"Fine. Sorry to bother you," Casey replied. "Can I borrow you for a few minutes after work?"

This time, he chuckled. "Sweetheart, you can borrow me for a lot longer than a few minutes."

Casey's lips tugged into a smile. "Get your mind out of the gutter, SSA Hutchinson. What I need you for is work related."

An exaggerated sigh. "You sure know how to hurt a man's ego."

"Your ego and your libido are in excellent shape. No worries on either score. And I do promise to give you as much time to address the latter as you—we—want. But first…"

"I know. Help on a case. I'll come by the brownstone around six thirty."

"Thank you," she said gratefully. "Now go back to work. Make them wonder how they ever lived without you."

She hung up and turned to Claire. "He'll be here. And he'll zero in on what we need fast."

Quietly, Claire added, "I can also give you descriptions of the killer and the guy driving the car. The descriptions aren't as detailed as the drawings, but I jotted down every physical characteristic that came to me."

Hearing the shaky note in her teammate's voice, Casey looked up.

"There's something else," Claire stated.

It wasn't a question. She could tell that some revelation had profoundly affected Claire.

"It's Julie," Claire managed, her throat clogged with unshed tears. "I was inside her head. It's like I was her. I know what she was thinking, what she did, and where she did it. And then…I felt her die. Every second of it."

"Oh, Claire, I'm sorry." Casey covered Claire's hand with hers. She knew how traumatic these kinds of connections were to her claircognizant teammate, how severely they impacted her. And how could they not? She'd lived inside other victims while they were being brutally raped, assaulted, or murdered. Casey couldn't imagine the emotional toll that would take on a person, especially one as gentle as Claire.

"Thank you," Claire replied, swallowing hard and then shoving back her emotions in lieu of the facts. She told Casey about Julie's distress over Shannon's condition, her rage at Jim, and her determination to get evidence on him—leading to what she'd done.

"So she was at Apex," Casey murmured thoughtfully.

A nod. "She easily got through security, since they'd seen her there before and they knew she was also Shannon's trainer. She broke into Jim's office and found the evidence she needed—a bunch of papers that she photocopied and took with her."

"The bag she was carrying when she got shot," Casey said. "The one that Lisa said the killers took. The papers were inside there. That makes sense. Could you see exactly what the papers were? What was on them?"

Claire pursed her lips in frustration. "Only glimpses. Athletes' records. I keep getting flashes of dates and columns of information. Nothing I can bring into clear focus—yet. I need something of Jim Robbins'. That might help crystalize things for me."

"I know just the person to get that for us." Casey was already pressing Marc's number on her cell phone. "Hey," she said a moment later. "As long as you're en route to Chicago, can you make a brief stop at Robbins' place and collect a couple of personal items for Claire to use?" A pause. "Yes, I know it's a potential crime scene. You've got my go-ahead to do whatever's necessary to get around that. Uh-huh. Great. Thanks."

Casey hung up, frowning when she saw the downcast expression on Claire's face. "What's wrong? I thought that having possessions belonging to Jim was your goal. Now you'll have them."

Claire gave an offhanded shrug. "I'm sorry. I don't mean to sound ungrateful. I appreciate what Marc's doing. It's just that my connections to the people involved seem to be strong today. I wish I had what I need now. I'm afraid that by the time Marc and Ryan get back, the visions will be gone."

"What about Shannon's timer? Can you try again to get something off of that?"

Claire reached into her pocket and extracted the timer. "I keep it with me. I haven't tried connecting with it today, because I've been caught up with my images of Julie and my work on the tattoos. But, believe me, I've held this a dozen times. I just sense coldness. Stillness. My instincts tell me Jim Robbins is dead. But that's my reasoning talking, not my sensory awareness. If I actually saw something, felt something... It's like there's something blocking me from him. I know there's a wealth of information tied to the bastard, but I just can't get at it."

"Don't force it." Casey spoke from the experience of having worked with Claire through several big cases. "Let it go for now. You're exhausted as it is. Maybe your psyche needs a break."

"What it needs is immediate gratification." Sighing, Claire pushed the timer deep into her pocket. Her fingers lingered, and her breath caught in her throat. Inhaling and exhaling became nearly impossible. Sweat beaded up on her forehead, slid down her face.

"What is it?" Casey asked in alarm.

"Jim. Dead. Buried deep underground. Mounds of dirt separating us. He's in a ditch. On the outskirts of some large piece of property. I can't see him. Feel him. Black spots. I...can't... breathe." Claire swayed in her chair, falling back against it.

Leaping up, Casey reached into Claire's pocket and pulled out her hand, snatching the timer from her perspiring fingers. She then bolted for the fridge and grabbed an ice-cold bottle of water. She uncapped it as she ran back and then pressed it to Claire's lips.

"Drink."

By this time, Claire's shallow breathing was starting to return to normal. She gripped the bottled water and took a few thirsty gulps. She then put it down on the table and leaned back in her seat again, trying to regain her equilibrium.

"Are you okay?" Casey was gripping Claire's hands, anxiety etched on her face.

Claire nodded, squeezing her eyes shut and then opening them. "I'll be fine. That was…very intense." She reached for a nearby box of tissues and plucked one out. Pouring a bit of water on it, she pressed the tissue to her forehead, then dabbed at the rest of her face.

Exhaling, she drank some more water, feeling as if she'd run a marathon.

"Now I know why I couldn't get past that barrier," she said weakly. "Whoever killed Jim buried him so deep underground that I couldn't penetrate it. And there was no human being to connect with, since all that's under there is a dead body." An agonized pause. "My God, I was connecting with a dead body."

"You visualized it?"

"I was inside it. It was soulless. But if you mean the scene—yes, I visualized it. A bottomless grave. Acres of land. A big house—a manor."

"Do you know where this manor is?"

Slowly, Claire shook her head. "It was very rural. I could hear water nearby—a lake or another small body of water. There's probably more. But I'm not getting it now."

"That's enough anyway." Casey was shaking her head. "You came close to passing out. You're done for today. Go home. Take a bath. Do some yoga. Drink tea and go to bed."

"It's the middle of the day," Claire protested.

"That's irrelevant." Casey pressed the intercom button. "Emma, could you get Claire an Uber? She's not feeling well. She's going home."

"Of course." Emma didn't ask any questions, not when she heard the anxious note in Casey's voice.

"Casey," Claire murmured, "I can take the subway."

"And pass out on the floor of it? I don't think so." Casey came around to help Claire to her feet. "We'll finish this tomorrow. And I'll check up on you later. No work—rest."

As she guided Claire to the door, Casey glanced back at the table, where the three drawings were sitting.

Claire had done her job.

Now Casey had her work cut out for her.

## CHAPTER TWENTY-FOUR

It was after nine p.m., and darkness enveloped the greater Chicago area.

Dressed as a janitor, Marc calmly lit a cigarette and leaned back against the outer brick wall of the U.S. Cellular office building. He appeared to be taking a long-awaited smoke break.

Twenty minutes later, the steel door opened, revealing a disinterested-looking man pushing a large plastic cart filled with garbage bags. Marc glanced over and nodded at him, as if acknowledging the janitorial plight. The real janitor didn't nod back. He steered his cart over to a large trash compactor and began to lazily empty bags of garbage into it.

Marc waited until he had clear access and the other man's back was to him. Then, he extinguished his cigarette and moved slowly forward, not making the slightest sound. Pulling on his gloves, Marc reached into his pocket for the chloroform-soaked rag that he'd placed inside a gallon-size Ziploc.

In a heartbeat, he clasped the rag over the man's mouth and nose, rendering him unconscious before the poor guy even knew what hit him. Rag secured back in the Ziploc, Marc dragged the limp janitor along, depositing him behind the trash compactor. He then reached inside his own jacket pocket and pulled out a flask. He opened the cap and spilled a small amount of booze on the man's clothing.

The odor of cheap whiskey permeated the air. Marc shoved the flask inside the guy's pocket to complete the setup. If someone found him sleeping, they would smell the whiskey, find the flask, and never suspect an intrusion—just an intoxicated employee.

Still in motion, Marc finished emptying the cart and then grabbed the ID card attached to the janitor's breast pocket. He glanced down at the name. Okay, for the next thirty minutes, Marc would be Bill Hubert, janitor.

With that, Marc pushed the trash cart over to the building entrance and retrieved the small gym bag he'd jammed against the building. He tossed it into the cart. He then held the ID card near the sensor and waited for the telltale *click* as the door unlocked, permitting him to enter the secure facility.

Ryan's instructions were clear. It didn't matter where Otter was placed. The little drone just needed to have access to power and to the computer network. The ideal spot would be behind some heavy desk or credenza that no one would ever want to move.

Marc pushed his cart from floor to floor and from office to office, looking for the perfect spot, stopping only to fill his cart with trash.

He knew he'd struck pay dirt when he entered the office of one Henry Marley and was immediately accosted by a funky odor. A quick scan of the office told him that the décor matched the smell.

The small room was littered with paper, files, unfinished food substances, and aging half-filled cups of coffee with cream that had started to turn. This guy was beyond a pig. He hadn't cleaned this place up in a millennium—and the cleaning crew probably wouldn't touch it, either. And who the hell blamed them? This shithole made Ryan's lair look like something out of *Good Housekeeping*.

On the back credenza was piled a career's worth of files, magazines, and paper plates stained with pizza sauce. Fighting back a wave of nausea, Marc grabbed his gym bag and extracted his flashlight. He bent over, turning on his flashlight and peering around the corner. Bingo. Both a power outlet and a network connection.

Carefully, Marc eased the credenza away from the wall, leaving enough space for his muscular arms to get behind it. His fingers maneuvered the special power and network cables Ryan had crafted securely into place. Both required only three-quarters inch clearance, making them break-resistant and stealthy. On the left-hand side of the credenza, with only a few inches of space between the end of the furniture and the side wall, was a gap big enough for his purposes. He pulled Otter out of his gym bag, plugged the cables from the wall into it, and then slid the peculiar device into place in the corner.

He sent Ryan a text and waited.

Thirty seconds later, Ryan responded: *Otter is swimming.*

With that, Marc went on to complete the task. He pulled out a spray can of faux spider web. He squirted the stuff in the space between the furniture and the wall. If anyone bothered to venture near Otter, they would be greeted with the sensation of spider webs all over their hands. They'd take off like a bat out of hell while desperately trying to shake the nasty stuff off.

Packing up his gear, Marc made his way back to the elevator and down to the service ramp, where he exited the building. He headed over to the trash compactor, grabbed his gym bag, and then emptied the garbage from the cart into the large receptacle. Checking in on the real Bill Hubert, he saw the man was still sleeping off his "binge." Marc removed the flask from the janitor's pocket and tossed it into the compactor. It wouldn't be long before the poor man woke up with a vicious headache, remembering little and talking about nothing, lest he get fired for sleeping on the job or, worse, for drinking or doing drugs.

Marc joined Ryan in the van. Sitting behind the wheel, Ryan barely glanced Marc's way. He was already engrossed in studying what Otter was finding.

As one would to a child playing with a toy at midnight, Marc took away Ryan's iPad. "Drive back to the hotel," he instructed, ignoring Ryan's yelp of protest. "Once we're off-site and safe in our room, you can have your precious tablet back."

Shooting Marc a nasty look, Ryan shoved the van into gear and eased away from the building and down the street.

*Burlington, Vermont*

Max was still feeling the surges of exhilaration from the outcome of the St. Thomas meeting. He now had a new crop of students who would study under his tutelage and who, one day, would represent the results of his scientific genius to the world.

Striding through the cerebral testing center of his manor, Dmitry by his side, he paused outside one door, easing it open so the two of them could look inside.

This evening, two of Max's staff psychologists were administering tightly timed, high-level verbal, nonverbal, and cognitive abilities tests to Carolyn Rynebrook, a truly exceptional addition to Max's program. She'd come to Max from Ithaca, New York, where she'd been attending Cornell as a premed student with sky-high grades. She was also an expert fencer and tennis player, with untapped levels of visual perception and precision. Max's program and supplements would ensure that she'd combine those gifts and fulfill her potential—perhaps someday becoming the world-class surgeon she'd always dreamed of being.

Max stood in the doorway and observed her for a while. Totally focused on her work. Cool under pressure. No hesitation in her answers. Excellent.

He met the administering psychologist's eye and nodded. Then, he left as quietly as he had arrived.

"She's nearly there," Max told Dmitry with a self-satisfied nod.

"Yes, you're right," his assistant concurred, awed, as always, by Max's keen insight at choosing just the right candidates for just the right futures. "Your abilities are uncanny."

Max gave Dmitry one of his rare, if stiff, smiles. "I appreciate your awareness of what I'm accomplishing."

That rare smile vanished the minute his cell phone rang and he glanced down at the number. Slava. Max frowned. If the man who was his eyes and his cleaner was calling, it wasn't for anything good.

"A problem?" he asked in Russian.

"Yes." Slava also reverted to his native language. His English was merely passable. He could get by on it, but not comfortably. "We've got those two cops back in the mix now. They were looking for the Barker girl. They talked to her parents."

"So they know she took off for New Jersey—and to Julie Forman."

"Yeah. And they followed her out there."

Max's head shot up. "When? And by plane or by car?"

Slava barked out a laugh. "The PD doesn't pay for airline travel. They drove. A dark blue Toyota RAV4. They left a few hours ago. But not before they interviewed the entire staff at Apex—for the second time. Then, they poked around Robbins' apartment. And they weren't the only ones. I saw another guy go in there, maybe for ten minutes. He looked more like a Fed than a cop."

"A Fed?" Max's eyes narrowed. "How do you know? Did you see his ID?"

"No, I wasn't that close. But I've seen enough Feds in my time. The way he moved, the way he carried himself—I can't swear to it. But there's too much activity going on in general. It's time for me to do something."

"I agree." Max's wheels were turning. "Fly Alexei and Vitaliy out to New Jersey and send them straight to Upper Montclair. Have them keep an eye on the Forman woman's apartment and her gym. After the detectives show up and question the Barker girl, it's time to act. Have them grab the kid. Instruct them not to kill her—yet. Have them take her to a warehouse, tied up and blindfolded. We need to know what she told the cops and how much she told Julie Forman. Once we know what we're dealing with, we'll know who you need to eliminate."

He turned to see Dmitry staring at him, visibly upset.

"Something wrong, Dmitry?"

"Is all that necessary?" Dmitry was probably the only person allowed to question Max's actions, much less to speak up to him. "The Barker girl's just a kid."

"She's a kid with the potential to destroy everything. I won't let that happen." Max stared directly at Dmitry, his gaze brittle. "You saw me kill a man who used my supplements for his own selfish reasons. He destroyed a young girl's career, her entire life, in the process."

"And now you're threatening to take that life," Dmitry said.

"Kidnapping is not murder. And neither of them would be my ideal choice. However, I will protect what I'm doing at all costs. Ultimately, it will benefit the world. A few casualties are a small price to pay." A long pause. "I assume you can live with that?"

Dmitry couldn't help but nod. It might be ugly, but somehow it all made sense. "I can and I will."

"Good. Then we're on the same page. Let's go check on my stallion."

Hours later, on the bed in his room, Dmitry flung an arm across his eyes, as if that motion alone could block out the darkness of what might be. He admitted to himself what he was agreeing to, what he'd already tacitly agreed to—and witnessed firsthand as Jim Robbins lay writhing on the floor, dying before his eyes.

It was called aiding and abetting. Dmitry could go to jail. But his loyalty to Max ran deeper than his fear. He knew this man, knew that he was driven by the promise of his work. Given the enormity of what he was going to accomplish, did that justify his actions?

Dmitry had to believe that it did.

Death was no stranger to Max, not with a father who was a high-ranking officer in the Russian Federation. Nor was it something to fear or avoid in lieu of the greater good. Max had learned that at his father's knee.

Dmitry was as close to a confidant as Max had. He'd felt honored when, over a drink, Max had shared his background with him.

Max was the oldest of eight children, and the only one who burned with his father's drive and sense of purpose. At a young age, he'd been accepted to an elite European boarding school in Switzerland, after which he'd graduated and come to the US on a student visa to Harvard. There, he'd further developed his scientific aptitude, concentrating in microbiology. Next came Harvard Medical School and then on to becoming a cutting-edge research scientist.

Dmitry swallowed, remembering how Max had told him that, in his first and only job working for someone else, he'd pushed the boundaries beyond what the plebian world could tolerate and, subsequently, been fired. Dmitry had never questioned him about what those boundaries were and how far Max had pushed them. He'd just absorbed whatever information Max was willing to share, kept it to himself, and done his job.

Of one thing Dmitry was certain, and that was that, once Max had been fired, he'd taken the route that he should have taken from the start: gone out on his own. It'd taken only a short period of time for him to develop a series of new and progressive health supplement formulations. There'd been a bidding war, and he'd sold his formulas to one of the world's largest supplement companies for seven figures each, in addition to an ongoing stream of royalties.

It was those financial gains plus the steady stream of income that had allowed him to start and flourish in his new and grandiose endeavor—to better the entire human race and to, one day, win a Nobel Prize.

The scientific community knew him as a microbiology and stem cell genius.

But Dmitry knew he was so much more. And, as a ray of Max's powerful sun, he would do whatever he had to to be the right arm of this extraordinary man.

Including being an accessory to murder.

## CHAPTER TWENTY-FIVE

*Upper Montclair, New Jersey*

Miles was sprawled on the living room sofa, talking on the phone with a Dell customer who didn't know her ass from her elbow, and trying to troubleshoot her problem on his laptop.

Same shit, different day.

The doorbell rang. He ignored the sound, only to have it repeated an instant later.

"Please hold for a second," he said to the shrieking woman at the other end of the line. Muting the conversation from his side, he called out, "Working. Leave the package at the door."

Deliverymen were the closest thing to visitors he and Lisa ever got. Of course, that was by design.

"Chicago Police," a female voice replied with authority.

Milo froze, obviously for too long, because the doorbell sounded again.

The female cop kept her voice down, obviously so the neighbors wouldn't hear. "We just want to ask you a few questions. That's all."

They weren't going away, that was for sure.

Quickly, Milo pulled himself together, his mind racing a mile a minute. "Be right there," he answered.

He returned to his call only long enough to end it, first getting the customer's number and promising her a same-day callback. Unfolding himself from the sofa, he rose and glanced over at the second bedroom, where Shannon's music was playing as she dutifully did the homework her teachers had emailed her.

In a few long strides, Milo was in her doorway.

"Shannon," he said, his tone causing her to snap up and stare at him.

"What's wrong?" she asked, frightened even before she had her answer. She was skittish all the time, which wasn't going to help their cause when answering to the cops.

"The Chicago police are at the door." Milo didn't have time to ease into it or to soothe her fears—or his own. Conversation and personal interactions weren't exactly his strong suits. How was he going to pull off an interrogation?

"Listen to me," he said over Shannon's terrified gasp. "Stay in here unless I come and get you. If you have to talk to them, stick to basic, publically known facts. And, remember, it's Julie who's here, and Lisa who's dead. Stick to that story no matter what. Don't slip up."

"Oh my God." All the color drained from Shannon's face. "No wonder I have two missed calls and a voice mail from my parents. What do the police want? What do they know?"

"I'm about to find out." Milo glanced over his shoulder, expecting loud pounding at the front door to ensue. "I've got to let them in. Remember, stay put. Take deep breaths, and please, just don't freak out on me."

He left the room, knowing full well that Shannon wasn't about to keep it together. He could only pray the cops didn't know she was there.

He blew out a text to Lisa as he walked, letting her know what was going on and telling her to stay at the gym unless it was absolutely necessary.

Sucking in his breath and then exhaling it, he opened the front door.

"Detectives Kline and Bogart," the female detective said, flashing her ID, which showed she was the Kline half of the partnership. She was around fortyish, tall and lean, with chin-length, light brown hair and sharp dark eyes. Her partner, Detective Bogart, was middle-aged, with thinning hair, a hard, solid build, and a more laid-back stance.

Milo could definitely see who played good cop and who played bad.

"May we come in?" Kline asked.

"Of course." Milo, doing what he hoped was a convincing job of looking puzzled, moved aside so they could step into the apartment.

"I'm assuming you're Miles Parker?" Bogart asked, taking a small pad and pen out of the inside pocket of his herringbone sports coat.

The implication of that question registered. The Chicago and the Montclair police had obviously had a nice long talk about the interrogation that had taken place at Excalibur. Which begged the questions: what had they uncovered about him, and what conclusions had they drawn?

Only one way to find out.

"That's me," Milo replied.

Kline's gaze swept the apartment. "Are you here alone?"

"Are you looking for Julie?" he answered, purposely sidestepping the question.

"Both of you, actually. Oh, and Shannon Barker, too. According to her parents, she's staying here with Ms. Forman."

Shit. Milo hadn't expected them to have spoken with Shannon's folks. So any attempt to keep her hidden had just gone up in smoke.

Clearly, these two had done their homework. He'd have to wing this and cross his fingers that Shannon didn't fall apart, and that he didn't contradict himself or look guilty.

"Julie's teaching a class at her gym." Milo then jerked his thumb toward the rear of the apartment. "And Shannon's in there, studying." The best defense was a good offense. "She's kind of a mess. But I'm guessing you know that."

Kline's brows rose slightly. "Why would you assume that?"

Milo went for it. "Because you came all the way here to question us, even though the local police already did. Maybe because Shannon followed Julie here, or maybe because, according to Shannon, her former Olympic trainer is missing. Maybe both."

Both detectives looked kind of surprised at his directness. Good. He'd actually surprised himself.

"You forgot one thing on that list you just ticked off," Kline said. "You. We didn't even know you existed, and yet not only were you and Lisa Barnes joined at the hip, she introduced you to Julie Forman, for whom you researched and found Excalibur. Then, you travelled here with her as her pal and computer guy. That's a long string of coincidences."

Milo forced himself to hide his discomfort. "Truth is stranger than fiction, I guess."

Kline didn't look convinced enough to ease Milo's worry. "We did thorough background checks on both you and Lisa Barnes," she said in a tone that was a warning not to lie.

Milo didn't have to—not about this. "So you know that Lisa was the only real family I ever had. I couldn't stay in Chicago, not without her."

"So you chose to join Julie Forman and start over."

"Why not? I'm sure you know what I do for a living—no roots required. Coming here as Julie's tech guy was a no-brainer."

"Are you two involved?" Bogart interrupted to ask.

"W-what?" Milo started. "No. Not like that."

"Then like what?"

"I told you. I'm her tech guy. We set up the gym together. We share the apartment to save money. She's got her room and I've got mine."

"Evidently not at the moment." Kline swept her arm across the living room area. The guy's clothes strewn around, the blankets crumpled up on the sofa cushions, the pillow with the indent shoved against them—all those things screamed the fact that Milo was using this as a bedroom.

"Shannon's staying in my room," Milo replied. "So, yeah, I'm camping out here for now. But Julie's in the master bedroom." He indicated where that was. "And I'm not."

About that, Kline looked convinced. "Speaking of Julie, we'll be heading over to Excalibur to chat with her after we leave here."

Milo couldn't do anything but nod. "Fine. I'm just not sure either of us can tell you more than we've already told the Montclair police."

"Actually, we have some questions for your friend Julie about Jim Robbins. The same goes for Shannon. So could you please tell her we're here?"

Okay, so that was their angle. Not just to unnerve him and "Julie" but to dig into Jim Robbins' disappearance. Well, the three of them were safe on that score. None of them knew anything about where Robbins was or if he was alive. As long as Shannon steered clear of the PED distribution, they'd be fine.

"Sure." Milo took a step in the opposite direction, then hesitated and turned back to the detectives. "Please go easy on

Shannon. The poor kid just lost her whole future."

"Don't worry, Mr. Parker," Kline replied, shoving her hands into the pockets of her navy pantsuit. "We're not here to upset her. We just want to ask her a few questions."

Nodding, Milo turned and walked to the back room. "Shannon?" Pausing in the doorway, he gave her a firm, keep-it-together stare. "The Chicago police are here. They want to talk to you."

Shannon was curled up on the bed, still wearing that deer-in-the-headlights look. Then again, what sixteen-year-old wouldn't look scared shitless when they were about to be grilled by the cops?

"Okay," she said in a small voice. She stood up, tugging at the bottom of her T-shirt to ensure it reached her jeans and didn't expose any skin. Then she followed Milo into the hallway.

"Hello, Shannon."

*Well, what do you know,* Milo thought. *Kline actually has a soft side to her.*

She smiled at the teenage girl and spoke in a conversational, rather than a confrontational, tone. "I'm Detective Kline, and this is Detective Bogart."

"Hi, Shannon," Bogart said, also smiling.

Shannon looked from one of them to the other. "Please don't make me go home," she burst out. "My parents know I'm here…with Julie. Just ask them."

"We did," Bogart assured her. "They gave us permission to talk to you. And they're fine about you spending time with Ms. Forman. So we're not here to take you home."

"Then why are you here?" She spread out her hands, palms up in question.

"We wanted to talk to you about Jim Robbins."

Shannon's eyes widened. "Did you find him?"

*Good girl*, Milo thought. *Turn your panic into concern for Jim.*

"Unfortunately, no," Bogart said. "When was the last time you saw him?"

Shannon's lips quivered, and her hand instinctively went to her shoulder. "I haven't really seen anyone since the accident. My old life was over. I couldn't deal with facing what might have been if I hadn't…" Tears welled up in her eyes.

Detective Kline stepped forward and squeezed Shannon's hand reassuringly. "We understand. Just one more question. Do you know anyone who might want to hurt Jim?"

"Hurt him?" Shannon stared. "Is that what you think happened?"

"We honestly don't know. He could have left town, but why would he?"

"I can't think of any reason. He was an awesome trainer. Everyone respected him. I don't really know why he'd leave, or why anybody would do something to him."

"Did Julie Forman know him?" Detective Bogart asked.

"Julie?" Shannon didn't have to fake her confusion. "Yes, they saw each other at Apex—that's the Olympic Center I trained in. Julie used to come and watch me practice. So she and Jim talked. But I think it was only about me and my future…my old future…" Tears slid down Shannon's cheeks, and she wiped them away with the backs of her hands.

Bogart shut his notebook. "I think we have everything we need. Thank you both for your time."

Casey was upstairs in her galley kitchen, sipping a cup of coffee and waiting for Hutch, when Lisa phoned. The call was expected, since three other calls had preceded it—the first two from Patrick, one telling Casey when the Chicago detectives showed up and the other when they left. The third call was from

Miles, about thirty seconds later.

Casey had been seriously concerned when Patrick told her what was going on. Even if Miles managed to get through an interrogation, Shannon wasn't anywhere near equipped to do the same—especially not without warning or preparation.

So Miles' report had been a real relief. Not only had he and Shannon come through with flying colors but Casey now had a good handle on where the cops' heads were. They were still uncomfortable with the Miles/Julie coincidences, but, more importantly, they were looking for leads on the Jim Robbins disappearance.

After listening to Miles, Casey had spoken briefly to Shannon, giving her a big bravo and then instructing her to make an immediate and succinct call to Lisa. Lisa's job would be even harder than theirs had been, given that she was not really Julie and had no knowledge whatsoever about Julie's verbal exchanges with Jim. Therefore, it was imperative that she be prepped before the cops could show up at Excalibur—to know how and when Julie and Jim had interacted, how their conversations had pertained only to Shannon, and, therefore, how casually she'd known him. And obviously, just as Shannon had never mentioned her final run-in with Jim, Lisa knew full well not to mention Julie's final findings in Jim's office. All hints at the PED distribution were off-limits.

Casey listened to Lisa's recounting of her interview. Thankfully, she'd followed instructions to a tee and held it together. The detectives' questions had gone in precisely the direction Casey had expected. And it sounded like Lisa's and Shannon's answers had been believably alike.

So Detective Kline and Detective Bogart had walked away with whatever suspicions were still nagging at them, but without any facts.

"I don't understand," Lisa said in that high, thin, nervous voice. "I thought the Montclair police might show up at Excalibur again, just to see if Milo and I were still here, to kind of check up on us. But an official visit from detectives who came here all the way from Chicago? Why?"

"Because a man is missing." Casey took a sip of her coffee. "The whole Miles-Lisa-Julie angle is a fishing expedition at this point. Kline and Bogart have done all the digging they can and turned up nothing. They were probably hoping that Miles would say something inflammatory to reignite their case—but he didn't. So forget the Barnes murder. Now it's all about locating Jim Robbins, or his remains."

"What if they do?"

"We'll worry about that if it happens. But I don't believe it will. I believe we'll uncover Robbins' whereabouts long before they do."

The brownstone's front door buzzer sounded, and Casey glanced down at her watch. It had to be Hutch.

"Lisa, I have to run," she said into the burner phone. "The FBI contact I told you about is at the door. I have a lot to review with him. I'll check in with you later." She paused. "We're getting there. So try to relax."

"I will," Lisa answered, this time sounding a little better and very relieved by the fact that another FI-caliber case solver might be on his way into the mix. "Thanks."

"No problem."

Making her way down the four flights of steps, Casey heard Emma's front-door greeting and Yoda's simultaneous announcement: "Supervisory Special Agent Hutchinson has arrived."

"Hi, Emma. Hi, Yoda," Hutch responded, having long

since accustomed himself to Ryan's omniscient creation.

"Good evening," Yoda responded. "The temperature in the brownstone is seventy-two degrees."

Hutch chuckled. Yoda always informed him of the indoor temperature, ever since the first time Hutch had commented that it was a cold night and he was keeping his coat on.

"Not to worry, Yoda. I'm not wearing a jacket."

"A wise idea," Yoda responded. "Emma often turns up the thermostat against my better judgement. I specifically keep it at the correct level."

Emma made an irritated sound. "I sit near the door, Yoda. I'm the one who gets blasted with drafts." She glanced up as Casey reached the bottom step. "Thank goodness. Maybe you can tell Yoda to stop pestering me."

"I don't pester, Emma. I state facts."

Casey grinned. "Can't argue with that one. But, Yoda, it's fine. I can attest to the fact that Agent Hutchinson is warm enough." She shot Hutch a teasing grin.

"On that note, I'm going home." Emma went back to her desk and gathered her things. "You two have fun."

"We're working," Casey responded with a frown. Emma was too young and too new at FI to overstep her bounds.

Emma heard the note of disapproval in her boss's voice and immediately dropped the subject. "Then good luck with your work. Night." She headed out the door.

Casey turned to Hutch. "Hey." She smiled at him—that soft, intimate smile that no one else ever saw.

"Hey back." The look in his eyes said he'd rather take her to bed than to work, but he was resigned to the fact that he'd have to wait. "Where do you want to work?"

"Let's go up to my apartment. I have everything spread out in the kitchen, along with my humming laptop."

"Lead the way."

Fifteen minutes later, Hutch was studying Claire's drawings, his forehead creased in concentration.

"I haven't worked the organized crime squads," he said. "But a couple of my buddies have. These are definitely Russian gang symbols."

"I looked up the meanings," Casey replied, pointing at her computer monitor. "The birds flying over the horizon are a symbol of freedom. The sailing ship on the shooter's right forearm means he's a roamer. And the bull is a sign of cruelty and rage."

"Not just cruelty and rage. The bull's the symbol of a hitman, the guy who does all the dirty work." Hutch angled his head toward Casey. "Are you sure you don't want to tell me what this case is about? Confidentiality or not, it sounds too dangerous. You're talking about major criminal enterprise here."

Casey sighed. "I wish I could. This case is snowballing into something much bigger than I ever anticipated. But all I can share with you is a theoretical overview. And not just because of FI's confidentiality agreement, since I'm fairly sure our clients are desperate enough to have me expand the role of our discreet FBI agent to help solve this thing."

"Then let me guess. You're going to be weaving in and out of what's legal to get this case solved." Hutch rubbed the back of his neck, scowling as he did. "That's what worries me here, Case. And that's not my ethical integrity talking. It's my fear for your safety. If you're dealing with the Russian mob, you're in way over your heads. Marc is the only one of your team members who's remotely trained to handle this."

Casey couldn't deny what Hutch was saying. She played the situation out in her mind and came to a decision.

"I'm going to take two steps toward containing this. First,

I'm going to get our clients' permission to more fully open up to you. I won't tell you any of the details of our investigation that would compromise you or force you to cross a line. Second, I will tell you now that this whole Russian crime angle just came into the picture today. If it turns out to be a key factor in the puzzle, I'll have Patrick arrange for security detail for each of us. I won't put my team in danger."

"Not just your team. You."

Casey smiled, reaching out to entwine her fingers with Hutch's. "I'm part of the team. So, yes, me, too. Don't worry. You and I are finally creating an 'us.' It's the wrong time to put my life in jeopardy."

That last part didn't please Hutch at all. "There's never a right time to put your life in jeopardy."

"I'll remind you of that when it's your ass on the line, Agent Hutchinson."

Hutch didn't contradict Casey, but the look in his eyes was pure guard dog. "Touché. Then I guess we'll have to keep each other in line."

## CHAPTER TWENTY-SIX

Patrick was at his home watching TV with Adele when his phone rang.

He glanced at the number and then answered the call ASAP. "Something happening, John?"

John Nickels was one of the best and most trusted security guards Patrick hired to assist him. He had a solid bunch of guys he contacted on an ongoing basis. They consisted of retired FBI agents and police officers, all experts in their field, all selected by Patrick, all of whom reported directly to him.

Tonight, John was the security detail watching Shannon, and Joseph Buzak, another of Patrick's A-plus guys, was watching Lisa and Miles.

"Shannon's at the Upper Montclair Starbucks," John said without preamble. "There's additional activity in the area. Not the usual sedan that follows her around. A new van that smacks of more than just surveillance. I don't know what they've got in there, but I'm getting a bad feeling."

Patrick's spine straightened. "Then move in and have a cup of coffee with her. Keep her calm, keep her safe. I'm on my way."

*Chicago, Illinois*

Ryan had parked on a side street where he could monitor Otter's progress. Marc was perched beside him in the back of the van, watching as Ryan's program superimposed the cell phone tower signal strength data on a Google map of the downtown Chicago business district. The program drew three intersecting circles on the map.

"You might be a genius, but I know what that is," Marc said. "A Venn diagram. I learned it in grade school. You were still in diapers."

Ryan rolled his eyes. "Except I'm doing this with formulas and algorithms, not chalk and erasers." He continued to watch and concentrate.

A few minutes later, he punched the air in mock salute, yelling, "Yes!" at the same time.

That didn't particularly impress Marc—not yet. He'd seen and heard this ritual many times from Ryan. Sometimes it was a major breakthrough, and other times it was just ego celebration.

"So, what does your primal chest-thumping mean this time?"

"It means I've tracked Jim's key contact to within half a block, and, judging by the buildings I can see in Google Earth, it's down to one building. Number one twenty-five South Wacker, near West Adams St. Let me see what Google has on the building."

Ryan entered some information. A few minutes later, he asked, "Hey, Marc, you speak Russian. What does all this stuff mean?"

Marc leaned forward, read through the stuff, and started chuckling.

"What's so funny?" Ryan demanded.

"Seems like this building has a Russian software company as a major tenant. They hire hot, young female software engineers straight from Russia and have them sell software projects to male engineers. It's a simple but effective sales model. The building has other tenants, mostly Russian companies. The coffee bar in the lobby is standing room only in the morning. I guess girl watching is a universal sport."

A corner of Ryan's mouth lifted. "A nice perk for us. Early-morning field trip tomorrow?"

*Starbucks*
*Upper Montclair, New Jersey*

Shannon was sipping her vanilla latte and nibbling on her brownie, trying to relax on her first solo excursion outside the apartment. She'd begged for this little bit of space, wholeheartedly agreeing to have one of Patrick's men watching her every move as she walked the bustling suburban streets of Upper Montclair. Being holed up in Lisa's small apartment, besieged by her worsened panic—now that Julie wasn't Julie and Upper Montclair wasn't the safe haven she'd run to—was worse than being holed up in her house in Chicago. Lisa's apartment was small, claustrophobic, and more than Shannon could bear. She was suffocating, and the isolation was only making things worse. She needed to breathe.

The walk had helped. So had being a part of humanity again.

Setting down her drink, she took a bite of her brownie and glanced around. People watching was always cool and usually distracting. That helped, too. It also made her a little homesick. Quickly, she sent another reassuring text to her mom, promising her that everything was fine, including her health.

She started when a tall, broad-shouldered man in his midfifties with thick graying hair and a neatly trimmed beard, dressed in a black sports jacket and slacks, sat down across from her, a cup of hot coffee in his hand. She knew who he was. John Nickels. Patrick Lynch had introduced him when he'd started being her security guard. But the two of them had never talked beyond that first meeting, and he always kept his distance.

"Mr. Nickels?" she asked in confusion.

"Hi, Shannon." John gave her a paternal smile. "I need you to act like I'm your father or your uncle—someone close and caring, definitely not a predator who's trying to pick up a sixteen-year-old girl."

Bewildered or not, Shannon giggled.

"Good girl," he said. "Now I want you to keep drinking your latte and munching on that delicious-looking brownie while you listen to what I'm saying, without looking scared. Remember that I'm here to protect you, and that keeping you safe is my number one priority. Nothing is going to happen to you while you're under my protection."

"Okay." Shannon paled a bit, but she stayed put and took another fierce bite of brownie. "Is someone watching us?"

John frowned, torn between candor and making sure Shannon didn't lose control, blow his cover, and endanger her life.

"I think so, yes," he replied carefully. "But you know you're going to be all right with me."

A tiny nod was her response.

It was reassuring enough to make him continue—not that there was any other choice. John had to get Shannon out of here and safely back to Lisa's apartment.

"There's a van parked in the municipal lot behind us that looks suspicious to me," he said. "It showed up shortly after you did. It hasn't moved in an hour, and the only sign of activity I've seen, other than the fact that the car is still idling, is the burly thug who's feeding the meter. He alone sets off warning bells in my head. I could be wrong, but my instincts say otherwise. Just to be on the safe side, you're going to leave here with me and go directly back to the apartment. I'll walk you inside and check out the place. Then I'll stand outside the door, just in case. Mr. Lynch will be arriving shortly thereafter, and he'll keep an eye on the building and make sure the van isn't hanging around. If it is, he'll take care of it. Does all that make sense?"

"Yes," Shannon managed, trying hard not to break down. "Do you think they're here to kill me?"

"I think they're here because they're scared. You talked to the Chicago Police. They want to know what was said and how much the cops know. So they're on high alert."

John's gaze darted quickly around to make sure they weren't being overheard. But the loud chatter and the even louder music ensured that they weren't. "I'm not trying to alarm you," he said. "I just want you to realize how serious this might be, and stay close beside me when we walk to my car. Again, act as if I'm your dad or your uncle. Chat about how much you're enjoying spending time with Julie. Tell me how cool her gym is, and how Miles is helping you with your homework. We'll be in the car in three minutes, and on our way."

Shannon couldn't eat another bite. She pushed aside her brownie and picked up her latte with a trembling hand. "What if they follow us?"

"Then we'll know that I'm right. But they won't get near you—not with me accompanying you. I don't think they'll even make an attempt." John shot her a lighthearted smile. "I'm a pretty scary-looking guy when I want to be."

And I'm armed, he thought silently. They'll see that, if need be.

Shannon took a last gulp of latte—as if that alone would give her the guts she needed to pull this off—and set down the empty cup.

"Should we go now?" she asked. "Or is it better if we stay awhile?"

John glanced briefly toward the rear of the coffee shop, mentally gauging the path they'd take once they walked around back. He then looked back at Shannon. "Slowly, wrap up the rest of your brownie," he instructed. "We'll toss our cups and head out front, walking at a brisk pace around back. My car is a dark blue sedan, parked four rows back. The van is gray, and it's two rows and several parking spaces closer to Starbucks. When I headed into the building, it was idling. Let's see if it still is, and what they do when they see me escorting you out. Just take my lead. Walk with me to my car, talking the way I said, and get in. Don't even glance their way. Lock your door manually. I'll take care of the rest."

With shaking hands, Shannon wrapped her brownie up in four napkins. She could have asked for another pastry bag, but her legs felt like water, and just getting from here to Mr. Nickels' car would take all her reserves. She'd have to rev herself up, force herself to be upbeat and chatty.

Right now, that felt impossible.

"Come on." John's big smile helped, as he rose and took the brownie from her. "I'll carry this. I promise not to take a bite."

A small smile curved her lips. "I trust you."

"Good. Remember that." He took her arm in a paternal fashion, guided her toward the door, and pushed it open. "So how's that world history assignment going?" he asked as they began the endless walk around back of the building. "Comparing today's family unit with the dynamics of the post-World War II family sounds pretty overwhelming to me."

Shannon looked up at him in surprise. "You have kids," she murmured in surprise.

"Besides you?" John replied quietly, reminding her of their play-acting roles. "Two in high school and one in college. I'm not just great at my job. I'm a super dad, too." He squeezed her arm. "Now get back in character. Answer what I asked you."

Shannon blinked as she processed the fact that Mr. Nickels was a real person. He had a life. He even had kids. Somehow that made this a little easier.

"Shannon?" he prompted her in a normal tone. "Please don't tell me that your silence means you haven't touched the assignment."

"I'm halfway through it," Shannon improvised. "I've been doing a lot of online research so I can really impress my tutor, Ms. Cosner. Julie's friend, Miles, is helping me. He's a computer genius."

All that was true, which made this charade much easier. "Ms. Cosner wasn't very happy with my decision to take a few weeks off from school. But she understood how messed up I was after my accident and the surgery."

Gently, John touched Shannon's shoulder. "How's the pain today?"

She shrugged. "Sometimes it hurts a lot. Sometimes it's okay. I'll get back on track with my physical therapy again soon, I promise."

"Good." John nodded in approval. "In the meantime, your mother made your next cardiologist appointment." Deep concern laced his tone. "Have you been taking your meds and eating healthfully? A brownie for breakfast doesn't exactly thrill me."

"I always take my meds," Shannon answered truthfully. "And the brownie was a one-time thing. Julie keeps on top of me about that. I eat the same good-for-me foods I did when I was training, plus I go through the exercise routine Dr. Schyler prescribed every day." She swallowed. "He made it perfectly clear that it's the only way I'm going to lead a normal life."

"I'm so sorry, honey." John's pained response wasn't staged. It was real. "But we'll tackle this as a family, and we'll win."

He sounded so much like her own father that tears filled Shannon's eyes. At this point, pretending was easy. "Thanks, Dad," she managed. "I know we will."

"We're almost there," Mr. Nickels muttered, his words yanking Shannon back to reality. "And I don't see anyone watching us on foot. So my guess is they're both still in the van." He guided her around the bend and toward the parking lot. "You're doing great.

"I want to hear about Julie's gym while we drive," he said aloud. "From what you told us on the phone, it sounds pretty amazing."

"It is." The parking lot was busy, with lots of Starbucks patrons jumping in and out of their cars, arriving and departing. But Shannon spotted the gray van in her peripheral vision. It was still idling. She had to force herself not to peer inside to see if she recognized the thugs Mr. Nickels had described.

"The car's over here," John said, pointing. "We can call Mom on our way home. She'd love that."

"Sure." It was all Shannon could manage. Playing house was over. Now she was face-to-face with her worst fears. Other than idling, the van was totally devoid of activity. What were its occupants doing? What were they planning on doing?

Abruptly, the reality of it hit. *They didn't want to watch her. They wanted to take her.*

She froze. "They're here to kidnap me," she said in a voice filled with paralyzed terror. "It's the only way they're going to get their answers."

John said nothing. He just gripped Shannon's arm tightly and nearly dragged her the few remaining steps to the car.

Thirty seconds later, she was in the passenger seat, door locked, and Mr. Nickels was sliding into the driver's seat. He immediately pressed the lock button, and they were sealed inside.

"Kidnapping is a possibility." He didn't insult Shannon by waving away her fears. He just responded in a straightforward but soothing tone. "We don't know for sure. On the other hand, they could just be low-level lookout, rather than strong-armers, which means they might have no clue what they're going to do next. Remember, not every criminal is a brain surgeon. In fact, few of them are."

That calmed her down a bit. "I guess."

"Regardless, our step one is complete," Mr. Nickels said. "You did an A-plus job, Shannon." He took out his cell phone and snapped a few pictures of the van. Then, he turned on the ignition, shifted the car into drive, and began heading out of the lot. "Let's see what they do next."

The answer to that came quickly.

As John reached the street and signaled right, the van shifted into drive and began creeping out of its spot, keeping a respectable distance between themselves and John's car.

"Okay, it looks as if we're going to have company on the way home," John told Shannon as he casually adjusted the rear-view mirror. "Don't turn around. Just face front." He made the turn and began cruising down the suburban street.

"Lisa's apartment is only a few blocks away." Shannon was freaking out again. "What happens when we get there?"

"The same thing that happened on our way out of Starbucks. I park. We walk. We chat. We go inside."

"What if they follow us? What if they try to grab me? What if we can't get away?" Shannon tried to catch her breath.

"I'll take care of things, no matter what. They won't lay a hand on you. I promise." John studied Shannon in his peripheral vision. "Please, Shannon. You have to trust me. Don't go to pieces on me now."

"I do. I won't." Shannon clasped her hands tightly in her lap and waited.

Despite the pedestrian traffic, they reached the apartment in eight minutes. John took an assigned parking spot right beside the building.

"Whose parking space is this?" Shannon asked.

John shrugged. "Someone who's not home." He was watching the van pull into the lot behind them. "They've got more balls than I thought," he muttered under his breath.

"What?" Shannon hadn't heard John's words, but she did see the expression on his face. "Where are they?"

"Behind us. Waiting." He reached under his jacket and pulled his pistol out of its shoulder holster.

Shannon glanced over and went sheet white. "You have a gun?" A pause. "Of course you do."

"Hopefully, I won't need to use it," John replied. "Remember, keep it together, wait for my signal, then walk beside me, and we'll be safely inside in two minutes." He paused, watching Shannon's eyes, still fixed on the pistol. "It's okay, Shannon. I'm coming around to get you now. Don't unlock your side until I'm there."

Before he could yank open his car door, the van swerved around and rammed into the driver's side, effectively trapping John inside.

Realizing the game plan, John kept his eyes on the van's

occupants and ordered Shannon, "Keep your head down and your door locked."

Instantly, she complied.

The van's passenger door flew open, and the thug who'd been feeding the meter at Starbucks jumped out, whipping out his gun in an obvious attempt to blow John away and kidnap Shannon. The driver remained at the wheel, ready for a quick getaway.

Neither happened.

In a heartbeat, John lowered his window and aimed his pistol at the thug's chest. The first shot would clearly be his—and it would be fatal.

Seeing this, the would-be kidnapper panicked. He leapt back into the van and slammed the door.

"Go, go!" he yelled to the driver.

The guy at the wheel jolted into reverse. He screeched backwards, then slammed into drive and took off like a bat out of hell.

John watched them until they disappeared from view. Then he turned to Shannon. "Are you okay?"

Her head still down, she nodded.

"They're gone. Let's get you inside ASAP."

He shoved at his car door until it opened, then raced around and ushered Shannon out of the car and into the apartment.

Patrick was five minutes away when he heard from John. He listened closely, then immediately began scrutinizing the highway on the off-chance that the van was somewhere nearby.

There was no sign of it.

"Are you with Shannon?" he asked John. "Good. Wait for me. I'll be right there and I'm coming up."

Shannon was still trembling when he arrived. John let him in. He'd obviously been guarding the door. Miles was in the kitchen, making Shannon a hot chocolate.

She glanced up fearfully as Patrick entered. Quickly, he shut and locked the door behind him.

"It's just me, Shannon," he said quietly. "I checked all around the apartment and the neighborhood. There's no sign of them."

"But what if they come back?" she asked.

"They won't. Not after they saw Mr. Nickels and his pistol."

He and John exchanged a look as Miles returned with the hot chocolate—a look that Miles intercepted.

"Hey, if you two need to go over details, I'm here with Shannon," he said.

"But you won't leave?" Shannon pleaded.

"We're not going anywhere," Patrick assured her. "I just want a full report on what happened."

He turned to John, and the two men walked into the living room, out of earshot.

The first thing John did was to hand Patrick a slip of paper. "The license plate number, make, and model of the van," he said. "I also took pictures of the perp who fed the meter and had the gun, and a bunch more of the van. The pictures won't be stellar, but they'll work. I'll text them to you."

Patrick nodded, sliding the paper into his pocket.

"I can give you a more detailed description of the perps. Like I told you on the phone, I only saw the armed one. Short, dark hair. Solid build. Thick eyebrows. Crooked nose, probably broken more than once. The bottom of a tattoo sticking out of his jacket. I couldn't make out what it was of; there wasn't enough of it visible. The driver never got out of the car, and I couldn't see much, except that he was male with no visible hair, a high forehead, and narrow shoulders—which makes me think he was probably on the thin side."

Again, Patrick nodded. "My concern is that you pulled your gun on them, which means they know Shannon's not here on some innocent visit. She's carrying incriminating information, and she's being protected from being hurt or killed."

John frowned. "If I'd had a choice…"

"You didn't. Clearly, they were planning on killing you and grabbing Shannon. That tells me their boss is worried enough to take risks." Folding his arms across his chest, Patrick said, "I'm doubling security, and not just on Shannon. On Lisa and Miles, too. Whoever's at the helm of this drug ring will realize that anything Shannon knows, they know, as well. They've all become targets now."

## CHAPTER TWENTY-SEVEN

*Chicago, Illinois*

The office building was contemporary and pristine—ten floors of white, chrome, and glass. The lobby was the same, accented with gleaming marble floors and white walls, with a granite reception desk, a blonde receptionist sitting behind it, and two uniformed security guards flanking it.

Quite the place, Ryan thought as he walked over to one of the plush chairs that lined the wall between the lobby and the adjoining coffee shop. He'd grabbed a cup of black coffee first, selected this perfect seat facing the entranceway, and was now ready for his surveillance a good half hour before the business day began.

He settled in, propping his iPad on his lap and angling himself to check out every person who entered the building. His earbuds were in place so that he and Marc could communicate.

This new role of his was way cool.

There were two reasons Marc had opted to send Ryan in today, rather than following his usual strategy of handling inside intel himself, with Ryan as the outside recipient.

One was that—after a lot of tweaking for the pocket-protector look, and even more bitching and moaning about having to downplay his appearance in order to achieve the necessary stereotype—Ryan had pulled it off. Marc, on the other hand, smacked of the military and of the Bureau. Not a good combo in a place potentially filled with experienced gangsters.

And the second reason for Ryan being the inside guy was that Marc knew that there was always the chance someone had been watching him when he walked into or out of Jim Robbins' apartment the other night, when he'd grabbed a few personal items for Claire. The last thing FI needed was for him to be recognized and for the team to be made.

Ryan was an unknown commodity. He was definitely the way to go. And since Ryan was convinced that Marc always had all the fun, he was thrilled to play the role of James Bond.

Now, he glanced up every minute or two, taking everything in as he pretended to be working on something uber-important on his iPad. Other people exited the coffee shop and sat down around him, all busily texting or talking on their cell phones. A few of them were beautiful women worth looking at, most of them Russian.

Now was not the time for a pickup, and oddly, Ryan didn't want one.

His gaze shifted to his right. The magazine rack situated there was filled with Russian-language periodicals and newspapers. No doubt as to who they were catering to.

It was eight twenty-five, and the building's employees started to arrive for work. Ryan blew a cloud of steam off his coffee and watched them.

There was definitely a stark contrast between the male and female populations. Most of the females were as stunning as the women sitting in the lobby. They looked like a stream of Russian fashion models—tall, straight-from-the-gym toned, hair done in the trendiest styles—definitely eye candy. The men, on the other hand, looked like Russian nerds or bruisers.

Interestingly, all those fashion-model types walked to the rear of the lobby and took the far bank of elevators. Ryan gave a quick glance at the photo he'd taken of the building directory. It indicated that they were headed to the multi-level Russian software company.

The businessmen and women were divided in their destinations. Some took the same bank of elevators as the Russian babes did, and some took the front bank of elevators. Those were obviously meant for people working for other companies in the building.

Those companies weren't employing the hot Russian women.

Marc interrupted Ryan's observations as his voice came through the earbud.

"Hey, seems like your program has tracked the cell phone to within our central zone," he informed Ryan. "Our guy should be walking through the front door soon."

Ryan returned to his iPad, appeared to be reading, but instead was preparing to snap pictures of anyone entering.

The first person who walked through the door was a definite dork. Ryan shuddered to think that, right now, he probably resembled him. He took the loser's picture just in case, but that wasn't their guy. Next came a tall, thirty-ish woman with long black hair and a curve-hugging pantsuit. Ryan gave her an A-minus, then took her picture. Probably just a formality. She didn't fit Marc's profile.

Finally, in walked a tough Slavic guy in an expensive Italian business suit, who looked less like a business exec than he did like a bloodthirsty fighter in an underground cage-fighting match.

Bingo.

Ryan kept snapping pictures.

As it turned out, he didn't have to rush. Bruiser bought himself a cup of coffee and reentered the lobby, scanning the area. His eye settled on a long-legged brunette stunner who was smiling to herself as she texted someone. Seeing the chair beside her was empty, the big guy made his way over and claimed it.

He leaned toward her and said something in Russian that had to be a come-on line, judging from his tone and body language. The woman laughed, tossing back her hair and responding in an equally friendly manner.

*Money talks*, Ryan mused silently, as he took more photos. Bruiser looked like Boris to her Natasha, definitely not a hot stud who would turn a girl on. But he smacked of cash, and that was clearly enough. Good. That gave Ryan plenty of time to study the guy and take pictures. He'd learned enough from Casey to lock in on certain behavioral signs. Bruiser had an eye for the ladies, a big-ass ego, and an aggressiveness about him that Ryan guessed went from the bedroom to the boardroom.

Eventually, the woman glanced at her watch and reluctantly stood up. She punched something quickly into her cell phone, speaking in rapid Russian as she did, and nodded her head toward the phone peeking out of Bruiser's pocket. He plucked it out, glanced down at the screen, and a wide smile split his face.

*Okay, that was a no-brainer*, Ryan thought. *She just texted him her phone number.*

After that, she hurried off to—no surprise—the far bank of elevators.

Bruiser rose, still smiling as he drank his coffee, and headed to the bank of elevators closest to where Ryan was seated. Ryan watched the elevator doors shut behind him, and the numerals as they ascended. Seventh floor and the elevator stopped. Once again, Ryan consulted his photo of the building directory. There were six companies on that floor.

It was up to him and Marc to figure out which was the right one.

Back at the hotel, Ryan and Marc set up shop to figure out who their mystery man was and where he worked. They did the initial checking on Marc's computer, so they could keep Ryan's open for all in-depth research.

"Of the six companies on the seventh floor, four are Russian businesses," Marc noted. "Those are the ones we concentrate on."

It didn't take them long to zero in on the likely suspect.

"RusChem," Ryan said, pointing at Marc's computer screen. "It's a Russian-owned biochemical manufacturer, with a sole production facility in Akron, Ohio, and sales offices strategically positioned across the globe to service regional customers."

Marc nodded, reading rapidly and noting the key points of information.

RusChem's Chicago office was one of their three US sales locations, along with Los Angeles and New York. Internationally, they were represented in Frankfurt, Germany, Sao Paolo, Brazil, and Shanghai, China.

The next section on the *About Us* page was even more interesting—and pertinent.

RusChem manufactured enzymes, coenzymes, monoclonal/polyclonal antibodies, recombinant proteins, and high purity chemical reagents. Their customers included leading companies in the IVD, API, life science and nutraceutical markets.

"This has to be the company we're looking for," Marc said. "Time to dig."

"I'm already on it." Ryan was clicking as fast as his fingers could fly across the keyboard. His frown deepened as the long minutes turned into an hour.

He leaned back, staring from his screen to Marc and back.

"All information on RusChem points back to Moscow. But the ownership information is either buried in bureaucracy or intentionally hidden. I've tried it from every different angle. Nothing. This is going to take long hours and a lot of patience."

Marc acknowledged that thoughtfully. "My guess is that we're going to find out that this supposedly legitimate company is nothing more than a front for criminal enterprise distributing PEDs throughout the world."

"Okay, but run by who? Marc, we've got a shitload of players here. Who factors in where?"

Ticking off on his fingers, Marc replied, "Shannon was unknowingly taking PEDs. Jim Robbins was the conduit. Robbins was connected to—what did you call him?—Bruiser. Bruiser is connected to RusChem. That's a hell of a lot of A equals B and B equals Cs. We need to figure out who Bruiser is. That'll be the key to answering all our questions and ending the threat to our clients' lives."

"Sounds simple." Ryan scowled. "Now how the hell do you propose we do that? I can dig up dirt on anyone. But I need something to go on."

"Then let's get you that something." Marc picked up his cell phone and punched in Casey's number.

"Hey," she answered. "I was just wondering how your spy cam operation was going."

Tersely, Marc recounted the situation. "I need Emma here now," he concluded. "Put her on the next plane to O'Hare. And tell her to pack the shortest, sexiest dress she owns."

## CHAPTER TWENTY-EIGHT

*Chicago, Illinois*

Slava was in one hell of a mood when he blasted into his office building the next morning. He didn't do his usual lobby scanning of the beautiful women he'd like to screw. He just strode directly into the coffee shop, pitying whoever waited on him today if the asshole didn't know that he took his coffee black. In Russia, he always drank black tea, but the black tea in this country sucked. If the server asked him if he wanted "room" in his cup, he'd probably choke the life out of the guy and enjoy doing it.

He ordered his drink and loomed at the counter, waiting, his jaw clenched as he recalled the phone call to Max yesterday. The lunatic had gone ballistic when he'd heard about Alexei's and Vitaliy's screw-up. No argument about the fact that it had been a big one—one that was going to cost them their lives. Slava had already verbally castrated them, even as he decided who he'd move up to be their replacements once they were six feet under.

But Max? The guy had reacted like a raging psychopath, screaming about his research being compromised, about killing everyone who threatened it, and about slitting the throats of his own people if need be. Half of it had been in English and half in

Russian, but, more than once, Slava had heard his name shouted with an expletive attached to it.

He didn't take well to being threatened. And if Max didn't calm down, it would be his throat that would be slit.

Slava's jaw clenched as he reached the counter and barked out a command for coffee. Fortunately, the coffee shop employee gave him the right drink, looking like a timid mouse as he did. Slava snatched the steaming cup from his hand, threw a crumpled five on the counter, and walked out. He stood in the lobby, loosening his tie and ignoring the scalding in his throat as he took a huge gulp of the hot liquid. A redheaded Russian woman with long, shapely legs gave him a coy smile. He ignored it. She wasn't his current type, and he wasn't in the mood.

He half scanned the room and was about to veer toward the elevator when a flash of blonde hair caught his eye. It belonged to a beautiful young woman he'd never seen here before. She was seated directly across from him and was studying him as intently as he was her. Exquisite, he thought. Natural blonde hair, loose and just brushing her shoulders. Huge blue eyes like the sky. The face of an angel. The body of sin. She was wearing a tight black dress that hugged every inch of her and that barely covered the tops of her thighs. One shapely leg was crossed over the other—legs that were surprisingly long, given her diminutive size, and that looked even longer thanks to the four-inch heels on her designer shoes.

When she moistened her full red lips with her tongue and then smiled at him, gesturing toward the seat beside her, he was lost.

He re-knotted his tie and made his way over, stopping to lower himself into the chair she'd designated.

"Hi," she said breathlessly, her voice as bewitching as the rest of her.

"You're American," he noted in a thick Russian accent.

"Is that a problem?"

"With a woman as beautiful as you? Never."

She gave him a more melting smile, and he could feel his erection pounding against his clothes.

"I am Slava. And you are…?"

"Isabella." She breathed the word in a soft, ethereal cloud.

"A lovely name." He watched as she took a sip of her coffee, frowning as she looked down.

"A beautiful face like yours should never wear a frown," Slava said. He sized up the problem instantly. "Let me buy you another cup."

Her smile returned, reaching her eyes. "Thank you so much."

"My pleasure." He rose. "How do you like it?"

A teasing spark flickered in her eyes. "Many ways. I'm adventurous. Surprise me."

He caught his breath. "I'd enjoy doing that very much." He nearly knocked over the businesspeople arriving for their workday, and was in and out of the coffee shop in record time, a fine sheen of sweat on his brow.

"With cream and sugar," he said, handing her the cup. "Just like you."

Their fingers brushed, and Slava literally caught his breath.

"Thank you," she said. "You're a gentleman. Such a rarity these days."

"Not always such a gentleman." He chuckled. "Did you just start work here? I would have noticed you." He shifted in his chair so that his trouser leg brushed up against her bare calf.

"I'm just in town on business," she answered ruefully. "I have to fly back to LA tonight."

Slava felt his erection deflate. "Can't you take the…" He searched his mind for the right phrase. "Late night to morning…"

"The red-eye," she supplied. She bit her lip thoughtfully. "I can try." She looked as eager as he did, which raised his spirits and his appropriate body part. He watched as she put down her coffee and pulled out her phone. "What's your cell number?" she asked.

"I text it to you. You give me yours." He, too, took out his cell.

She rattled off a number that he very much wanted in his contact information. He punched it in, sent her a text message from his unrestricted phone, and then waited to hear her message chime.

"I'll call you," she said when it arrived, rising and retrieving her coffee cup. "I have a lot of juggling to do—meeting and flight time changes—and arrangements with my hotel." Another seductive smile. "I'll make this happen, Slava. I want it as much as you do."

"That I doubt." He came to his feet, as well, lifting her fingers to his lips. "My evening is open to you, Isabella."

"Until then." With one last bone-melting smile, she turned and walked out the door.

Once out of view, Emma shuddered, wiping the fingers he'd kissed on her dress before she gingerly gulped down the rest of her coffee—being careful to only touch the rim—and slipped the empty cup into a Ziploc, which she then deposited in her purse. "I've got it," she said into the tiny microphone clipped to her bra. "And I think I'm going to puke."

"You missed your calling, Isabella," Ryan teased into her earbud. "Bruiser was about to come in his pants."

"Not funny. I'm pretty sure his eyes drilled a hole in my dress on the way out. And FYI, he's repulsive." She was already walking toward the curb, arm raised. "I'm taking a cab to the hotel. No way I'm walking on these shoes for another minute."

Cruising through the streets of Chicago was a bittersweet experience for Emma. She stared out the window of the taxi, flashes of memories popping into her mind like nostalgic photos. The just-like-in-the-movies suburban house with a white picket fence and rows of tulips that came up every year. Doing cartwheels on the lawn. Learning to ride a bike with training wheels and pedals she could barely reach. Her dad tinkering in the garage. Her mom cooking Sunday dinner. Her first day of kindergarten. Her sixth birthday party and the red velvet cupcakes with the heaps of white frosting her mom had baked for her and her twenty school friends. She and her parents going to the movies. Buying a deep-dish pizza and having her dad dangle a piece of mozzarella over her mouth, teasing her until she jumped up and chomped it between her teeth.

Emma blinked back tears. All of that was in the past, treasured memories that she'd stored away and that were only now resurfacing because of her first return trip home. The dark memories followed close behind. Her family moving to New York. Her parents dying in that horrible crash. Foster care. Life on the streets.

She'd become a different person since then—harder, street-smart, a seasoned pickpocket who had only now turned her life around.

She swallowed hard. She had to concentrate on business or she'd lose it entirely. But, despite her best efforts, long-suppressed tears slid down her cheeks.

Fifteen minutes later, under control with her emotions back in check, Emma knocked on the hotel room door. Marc swung it open, and Emma walked past him and directly over to a chair. She dropped down into it, groaning as she yanked off her shoes.

"Thank God." She massaged one aching foot. "I'm glad I'm too short to be a model." With that, she dug into her purse and handed the Ziploc to Marc. "Here's your evidence. I got Bruiser sweating like a pig in heat. He's as good as caught."

"You did a great job, Emma." Marc, with his keen sense of observation, noted the tears on her lashes and the strained look on her face. "I realize this must have been difficult for you. But you pushed past it and got even more than we hoped for. A name, a phone number, and the touch DNA we needed. You've moved up the FI team ladder."

That brought a small smile to her lips. "Thanks. I aim to please."

"Okay," Ryan announced from his spot at the computer. "I took care of the cell phone problem. All calls to Isabella will be routed to voice mail on an untraceable number. And since Emma gave Bruiser—aka Slava—nothing else to go on, we're in the clear. Slava, on the other hand, won't be too happy. He'll go to bed with a hard-on and never find his mystery woman. Tough break for him."

"My heart bleeds." Marc was shrugging on his jacket and snapping shut his suitcase. "Ready to hit the road?"

"Damn straight," Ryan replied. "At top speed. We'll brief Casey as we drive. I want to get back ASAP so I can have access to all my technological resources. Meanwhile, I'll be in the back of the van, subtly hacking into Homeland Security."

"To see if there's more on Slava," Marc stated.

"Yup. The DNA needs to go to a crime lab. But the partial name, the photos... Who knows what our government agencies have on him. So if not Homeland Security, there's the NSA, the DMV…"

"I get it."

Ryan grinned. "By the time I'm done, we'll know everything about Slava, including his jock size." A quick glance at Emma. "Hey, brat, are you all set?"

Emma inhaled sharply and shook off the rest of her nostalgia. "Not until I change into normal clothes and wash this crap off my face. She grabbed her backpack and a towel and headed for the bathroom. "Give me five."

*Burlington, Vermont*

Max sat in his study, his hands clenched tightly on the desk in front of him. His rage from yesterday had been eclipsed by reality and the difficult decisions he had to make. The attempt at kidnapping Shannon Barker had not only been unsuccessful, it had opened the door to major questions, complications, and the potential for dire consequences.

The episode itself would have been salvageable if the Barker girl had merely seen she was being followed and taken off. At worst, she would have taken her suspicions—and that's all they would have been—to the police, who would have shooed her off like an annoying fly. After all, she'd just been interviewed by two Chicago cops. She'd clearly given them nothing and doubtlessly come across as a traumatized teenager. So resurfacing again, claiming she was the target of some dire act, would come across as an overactive imagination.

But that wasn't what had happened. The fact that someone was after Shannon Barker had been validated and the kidnapping attempt foiled by some private security guy—a guy who was clearly safeguarding her and who carried a gun.

That raised the red flag question. Why did Shannon Barker have an armed bodyguard? She must have convinced someone her life was in danger. And that meant she knew something, provable or not. It also meant that, whatever she knew, she'd passed along to Julie Forman and her friend, Miles Parker. Did they also have a security detail watching them?

And who was orchestrating all this? It had to be professionals. Which made the threat to Max even more problematic.

This was a ticking time bomb. And when it exploded— well, Max couldn't risk any of the burning embers raining down on him.

He picked up his cell phone and pressed the familiar number.

Slava answered in Russian, respectful, if still pissed off by yesterday's reaming out. "Yes."

"Time to do damage control," Max told him. "And you're in charge of it all—in person. Not just the cleanup. The arrangements. The execution. Hire only the best you know to assist you. No more assholes who make costly mistakes."

That appealed to Slava and his ego, and the edge in his tone vanished.

"Alexei and Vitaliy—you want me to take care of them?" It was more of a suggestion than a question.

"Immediately," Max replied. "The bodyguard can identify them. He'll have taken pictures, run license plates, and questioned car rental places. They're a major liability."

"Don't worry. I made sure nothing leads back to you," Slava assured him. "But you're right. I'll fly out to Jersey and take care of them today. Their bodies—or what's left of them—won't ever be found." A pause. "Do you want me to take care of the Barker girl, too?"

"No. We can't risk it. But we need eyes on her, Julie Forman, and Miles Parker. They obviously know something. They have to be contained—but not killed. Keeping a low profile is paramount at this point. I have to figure out what they know and who's in charge of protecting them."

"And if they make a move to do something before you figure all that out?"

"Then there'll be no choice but to kill them."

# CHAPTER TWENTY-NINE

*Tribeca, New York*
*Office of Forensic Instincts*

Casey waited until everyone had gathered around the conference room table. No one got coffee. No one joked or talked. Tension crackled in the air since everyone had important information to share in the debriefing. Even Hero picked up on the strained atmosphere. His head was raised, as if he were ready to leap into action at a moment's provocation.

Hard copies of Patrick's report on Shannon's attempted kidnapping were waiting for each of them at their seats. Conversely, Ryan's notes were scribbled on pages that only he had, as they were filled with too much undecipherable, complex information for the average layperson to make sense of. But he was visibly chomping at the bit. So was Emma, who was proud of her role in uncovering a major facet of the case.

Claire was quiet, dark circles under her eyes, but she, too, had a lot to share.

And Casey, who'd already been briefed across the board, had her own information to impart.

"Damn." Marc was skimming Patrick's report. "This is a

direct attack, no attempt at subterfuge. Something really scared these guys—probably the Chicago cops showing up." He read on. "Talk about desperate," he muttered. "This whole operation fell apart after they saw John pull his gun. The whole point was to leave with Shannon no matter what. They should have been prepared for anything."

"Their desperation is what worries me the most," Patrick said. "So I've doubled security on Shannon and on Lisa and Miles." He glanced quizzically at Casey. "How much have you told Hutch?... Never mind," he said, waving away his own question. "There's no way we can ask him to run the license plates and do some facial recognition work for us."

"I wish we could, but we can't," Marc agreed. "This isn't an FBI case. It's ours, and, as you better than anyone realize, it walks a very fine line between legal and illegal."

"True." Patrick frowned. He hated that reminder. Even after all this time as an FI team member, working outside the law was still like fingernails scraping across a chalkboard to him.

"I'll take care of it, Patrick," Ryan told him. "You don't have to hear how."

Patrick looked relieved.

"To answer your question," Casey said, "I've told Hutch very little. But, at Lisa's and Miles' consent, he did some research on the tattoos Claire visualized on the shooter's arm. He feels we're dealing with Russian criminal enterprise."

Ryan sat up straighter. "You mentioned the Russian part when we talked. But what tattoos?" he demanded, looking at Claire.

In a strained monotone, Claire fully explained what she'd picked up off Julie's personal items. As she spoke, Casey emailed each team member photos of all the sketches Claire had drawn, plus the link to Hutch's explorations.

"That fits with what Marc and I came up with." Ryan's gaze found Casey. "May I?"

"Go ahead," she said with a nod.

Like a proud father, Ryan held up a picture of Otter and proceeded to describe his creation's technical capabilities.

"Ryan," Casey interrupted. "None of us understands a word of what you just said. I'm glad your new gizmo is doing its job. Please just get to the bottom line and tell the team what you found."

Only slightly deflated, Ryan put down the photo and scanned his notes.

"We embedded Otter in U.S. Cellular's downtown Chicago facility. Otter fed us precisely the data I needed to triangulate the primary location where Jim Robbins' most frequent contacts received his calls. It turned out to be an office building where a Russian-backed software company had its operations. Several smaller companies, also Russian, rented space there as well. So Marc and I positioned ourselves in the lobby to spot just who Jim's contact was. Once we connected our tracked cell phone to the right person, we had our man. We just had no idea who he was."

"That's where I came in." Emma couldn't contain herself anymore. "Seems this creeper has an eye for women, especially ones with headbands for skirts and Louboutins. So I brought my hottest bodycon dress, hopped a plane to Chi-Town, and put on an award-winning sex kitten act. I walked out with his name, and my coffee cup with his sweaty fingerprints. Now I'll let Ryan finish the geek speak."

Ryan ignored her sarcasm. "On the ride home, I made a few discreet 'inquiries' into our government agencies' servers, which gave me what I needed to identify Bruiser as Slava Petrovich." Once again, he glanced down at his notes. "He works for

RusChem, a Russian biochemical manufacturer. They have a manufacturing plant here in the US and sales offices all over the world. Chicago is one of several sales offices in the US. I still have more investigative work to do into the company, its operations, and its management. All roads lead back to Moscow, but whoever owns the company is a big question mark."

"Nice work." Casey pursed her lips, her wheels turning. "But these findings I am going to mention to Hutch, at least the parts that don't involve 'talking to' our government's servers. I'm hoping he can discreetly see if RusChem is on anyone's radar. He's already aware that we're dealing with organized crime here. And we know we're dealing with killers. If RusChem is the mothership, it's time to find out. I'd like to know if we're walking into a potential buzz saw before it's too late."

"Let's cover both convention and unconventional avenues," Marc suggested quietly.

"Meaning?"

"Meaning we also need lab results on the DNA evidence, plus as much unofficial info on RusChem as we can get," Marc replied. "Hutch can only go so far. He has to work within boundaries. We know someone who doesn't."

"Aidan?" Casey guessed. She was referring to Marc's older brother, who graduated from Annapolis three years ahead of Marc, and who was a former Marine—a hybrid intelligence officer and communications officer. Aidan was now a troubleshooter for Heckman Flax, the investment bank of all investment banks. He was in charge of all their trading platforms worldwide, and he travelled globally to put out fires on a moment's notice.

His connections, both corporate and military, were beyond extensive, spanning the highest levels of business and political circles.

"Yes, Aidan," Marc confirmed. "If anyone can ferret out

who controls RusChem, he can. I'll also ask him to find out what-ever he can on Slava Petrovich, including suggesting the right lab to run his DNA."

"Is Aidan abroad now or home?" Casey asked.

Marc shrugged. "Doesn't matter. What we need from him can be done from anywhere."

"He was in Manhattan yesterday," Ryan piped up. "We're putting the finishing touches on your bachelor party. Ten days to go. You're getting married in less than three weeks, remember?"

"Believe me, I remember." That softer smile touched Marc's lips—the one that always accompanied any mention of Madeleine. "I'm more than ready."

"Find Aidan and fill him in," Casey told Marc. "Anything we can get, from Hutch and/or Aidan, will be welcome. Especial-ly if we're dealing with a corporation that's a front for killers."

"Done." Marc was all business again.

Up until now, Claire had remained quiet. Now, she folded her hands on the table and said, "While we're on the subject of killers, Jim Robbins is dead. He's buried someplace rural. There are acres of land, a manor, and a body of water nearby. It's a very deep grave. I don't know exactly where the location is yet."

Ryan's eyes narrowed quizzically. Claire sounded discon-nected, factual rather than empathetic—very un-Claire-like giv-en that she was describing a murder. He glanced at Casey, whose expression was unreadable.

"That reminds me…" Marc reached into his case and pulled out two baggies: one with a man's hairbrush in it and one with a training medal inside. "I got these from Jim Robbins' apartment." He passed them over to Claire. "They were as per-sonal as I could find. Maybe they'll help give you more details about Robbins."

For a long moment, Claire just stared at the items, making no move to touch them or pick them up. "I'll take them home with me after our meeting," she said at last. "I need to be alone when I interact with them. My connection with Jim Robbins seems to be very strong. I'd rather not explore it in public."

That did it. "Claire-voyant, what the hell is going on?" Ryan demanded. He was being totally unprofessional, and he knew it. He was also pushing Casey, who was scowling at him. But he couldn't seem to help himself.

"You're acting weird," he pressed. "Something obviously happened when you figured out Jim Robbins was dead. What was it?"

Claire raised her head and met Ryan's gaze. She didn't look surprised. She looked weary and almost nakedly exposed. It twisted something inside Ryan to see her like that.

"I didn't 'figure out' Jim Robbins was dead," she responded in a robotic tone. "I lived it, not the murder, but the death itself. It was a first for me, and I'm a little shaken. I'll get over it. It won't keep me from delving further. I just need some personal space." She eyed the objects Marc had brought. "These should help. Maybe I can get some background on Robbins, or motivation for why he was killed. Or even a more specific location for his body."

Ryan's brow was furrowed in confusion. But this time he took Casey's cue and shut his mouth.

"Jim Robbins' job at Apex hasn't been filled, either," Casey reported. "Shannon made a phone call to her friend Jessica. There's an assistant trainer standing in for him who is set to stay on in the event that Jim doesn't return. So far, she hasn't offered either Jessica or Billy any supplements. My guess is that she won't. Slava—or whoever runs RusChem—wants this channel permanently closed so it doesn't lead back to him."

Casey paused, shaking her head. "This whole scenario

feels odd. We've got Russian mobsters, PED trafficking, and murder. That's big-time stuff. Yet there's an elite personal aspect to all this that just doesn't fit. Handpicked trainers. Handpicked athletes. None of whom are replaced when they're out of the picture."

"Couldn't whoever's running this drug ring have shut down the Apex connection and taken it elsewhere?" Emma asked. "There are plenty of competitive athletes and trainers out there."

"Not at the Olympic level," Casey replied. "And that's where they obviously want to be. Again, elitism. This is still conjecture on my part, but I'd say that this isn't just about peddling drugs. It's about who they're peddling them to—subjects who can attain a grandiose goal. If personal recognition factors into this, that's not your typical drug ring or your typical organized crime scenario."

"Based on your theory, there's another inconsistency." Marc rubbed his jaw thoughtfully. "After they killed off Julie Forman and Jim Robbins, we're seeing more surveillance than action. They're dancing around our clients. There should have been hits put out on them, not increased surveillance or kidnapping attempts. Drug rings wipe out threats; they don't watch them. And they also don't stand still. They branch out and grow. This one is very insular. It's almost as if protecting their privacy trumps moneymaking. I see where you're headed, and I agree with you. There's something else going on here. We don't have the answer yet."

*East Village, New York*

Claire was sitting on her living room rug in lotus position, the two Ziplocs Marc had given her lying, untouched, beside her. She knew what she had to do—and she was working herself up to do it.

She was just about to reach for the first bag when her doorbell rang. A wave of relief swept through her. She didn't care who it was. It meant a temporary reprieve.

She stood up and walked over to the door, peering through the peephole.

Ryan.

Turning the lock, she let him in. "Hi."

"Hey." He stepped inside the apartment.

"Aren't you supposed to be hacking systems and figuring out who owns RusChem?" Claire asked.

Ryan nodded. "And I will—in a few hours. Marc and Casey are still talking to Aidan and Hutch." He angled his head, openly scrutinizing her—not sexually but with puzzled concern. "You look like hell."

"Thank you," Claire said sarcastically, shutting the door behind him. "It's good to see you, too."

"That's not what I meant."

"I know." Claire walked into the kitchen. "Do you want something to drink?" She was already pulling out a bottle of water. That was Ryan's usual choice, at least in her place. He wasn't exactly an herbal tea kind of guy.

She handed it to him.

He placed it on the counter.

"Thanks." Instead of making himself comfortable, he was still watching her. "After you told us about your visions and the way you reacted to them, I decided to check on you."

Claire gave a faint smile. "You just saw me at the office."

"I meant personally check on you."

Her brows rose slightly. "In bed or out?"

Ryan responded to her attempt at humor by giving her

that drop-dead grin that defined the word sex. "Now that you mention it, both. The second would be more chivalrous, but the first would be mind-blowing."

"Since when are you known for your chivalry?"

"I guess since now."

That was a huge admission coming from Ryan McKay. Slowly, over the past few months, he'd changed, started to allow a bit of his soul to peek through. And, God help her, that change made him all the hotter.

Claire didn't want to think anymore. He was here, she was hurting, and he could make it go away—for a little while.

She closed the gap between them, pressing her fists against the hard wall of his chest, as if trying to push away the ghosts. "I don't want chivalry. I want you. In bed. And I want that now." She gripped his shirt and fitted her body to his. "Please," she whispered.

"Shit." Ryan's breath hissed out from between his teeth. He dragged Claire even closer, tangling his hands in her hair and tilting her head back so he could ravage her mouth. "Are you sure?" he managed.

"Very sure."

All words ceased.

Ryan continued his onslaught, devouring Claire as he backed her into the bedroom, stripping her as he walked. The back of her legs hit the bed, and she tumbled down onto the mattress. While Ryan tore off his shirt and jeans, Claire wriggled out of her thong and tossed it aside. Ryan kicked off his boxer briefs and leaned over, pulling Claire higher up on the bed.

Then he was on her, and in her, and their world became pure physical sensation.

It wasn't slow and sensual—not this time. It was hard, fast, and frantic.

Claire cried out as Ryan pushed into her, once, twice, and then in a steady rhythm that made her back arch so she could take him deeper each time. Ryan made a raw, rough sound, his hands clenching into fists on either side of the pillow as his motions quickened.

The rest was a wild, sweaty explosion of the senses.

They both came with a vengeance, their bodies in that rare total sync that was theirs.

Neither of them moved. They just lay there, collapsed into the mattress, dragging air into their lungs.

Claire was abruptly jerked back to reality when she felt tears sliding down her cheeks and onto Ryan's shoulder. She froze, more mortified than stunned. Yes, her feelings for Ryan were complicated. But she didn't cry—not this way, like a weepy teenager. Not in front of anyone, much less Ryan. She sure as hell wouldn't be doing an about-face to that rule after sex, no matter how shattering.

No, the emotional tidal wave building up inside her had nothing to do with Ryan. It was the release of raw, pent-up feelings caused by unthinkable revelations… images…internalization…

Fighting back the dam that was about to break, Claire knew the moment Ryan became aware of the moisture on his shoulder. He tensed up, turning his head so his lips were at her ear. "Everything all right?" he asked, sounding bewildered.

Claire nodded, then shook her head, then nodded again. "Fine," she managed to say in a thoroughly unconvincing tone. "It's not what you think." To her dismay, new tears began to slide from beneath her lids, and her whole body began to tremble.

Ryan shoved himself up on his elbows, now clearly alarmed. "Did I hurt you?"

"No. But you'd better go."

"Go?" He blinked, beads of sweat still dotting his forehead, his own body still shuddering in the wake of his climax. "Claire, what the hell is going on?"

"I'm about to lose it," she whispered. "And I don't want you here when I do."

"I'm not going anywhere." He pushed his hips against hers, reminding her that their bodies were still intimately joined. "So let's go for option two. Talk to me."

Talk to him? That was a first. Ryan wasn't big on touchy-feely conversations. And he was the last person she could share this with. He had no faith in her gift—or, in this case, her curse.

"I can't. I'm too… You don't understand…"

"Maybe not." Ryan's knuckles caressed her cheek. "But I'll try."

That did it.

Claire began to openly sob, turning her face into the side of Ryan's neck. "It won't go away," she wept.

"What won't?"

"The aura of death…underground…buried…" The words were just tumbling out, uncensored, and Claire had no control over them. "I'm always inside the head and emotions of whoever I'm connecting with, experiencing what they're experiencing. It drains me, horrifies me, affects me. But when the pain is gone, when they die, it's over. The connection is severed."

"Okay." Ryan didn't come back with any jibes. He just listened.

"Like with Julie." Claire swallowed, still fighting for self-control, and still losing the fight. But at least she was somewhat coherent now. "I felt the impact of the bullet, the pain, the dying. But once she was gone, so was the vision. I've never actually felt a dead person before. But now I am. And the experience of death, it won't go away. It's living inside me. I'm living inside it. I can't concentrate on anything else. I guess that just now when we…when I…"

"Came apart in my arms?" Ryan supplied, trying to help Claire in the only way he knew how.

It worked.

"Yes." Claire could feel Ryan's gentle teasing flow through her, start to ease back the pain. Her crying slowed, then ceased. "It was like one giant release. The proverbial floodgates opened."

"That's pure skill on my part," Ryan said. "I'm the provider of giant releases."

Claire leaned back, her face still drenched with tears, blinking at Ryan's audacious statement and smug expression. In spite of herself, she started to laugh. And the laughter felt good, oh so good.

"You arrogant ass." She punched his shoulder, touched by the lingering concern she saw on his face. "But, in all fairness, I guess I needed that. So I should be thanking you, huh?"

"Definitely." His body hardened inside hers, and his dark blue eyes got even darker.

"Okay, you're right," Claire said with a straight face. "Thank you, Ryan. You were a great listener."

His crestfallen expression was priceless. "That's not the kind of thanks I was hoping for."

"Really? I'm shocked."

Picking up on her humor, realizing she wanted exactly the kind of thanks he did, Ryan gave a relieved groan. He rolled onto his back, taking Claire with him. "Let's do this again," he murmured. "This time slow. I want you to feel me, only me, every second. No dark visions." He took her mouth in a hot, devouring kiss, tangling his hands in her disheveled blonde hair. "And no crying this time. It sucks for my ego."

"Your ego is beyond fine." Claire kissed her way down his throat and his chest, tasting the salt of his skin. She raised her head and met his smoldering gaze. "But instead of crying, how about if I just make you beg?"

A chuckle vibrated through him as he stretched his arms over his head. "Go for it, Claire-voyant. I'm all yours."

## CHAPTER THIRTY

Aidan answered his cell on the fifth ring, and, even then, he dropped it with a clatter to the floor. There were some groping sounds, and then Aidan's voice.

"You are a huge pain in the ass," he informed Marc. He sounded like he'd been running a marathon, and definitely like it was a bad time.

That could only mean one thing.

Marc's lips curved into a smile as he settled himself on his and Maddy's living room sofa. "Busy?" he inquired.

"Not funny."

"Gee, I haven't even asked for the favor yet, and I'm already on your shit list."

"I don't know what favor you're talking about, but you're sure as hell on my shit list."

"I'm guessing it's not because you're in bed with some new hottie."

"Yeah. Right. Abby has made sure I have no sex life. And, thanks to you, she's found new ways to torment me."

"Thanks to me?" This time Marc chuckled.

Abby was Aidan's just-turned-four-year-old daughter—the daughter Aidan never even knew he had until Social Services placed her in his arms. She was the product of a torrid affair that had ended eight months before Abby was born. Right after Abby's birth, her mother was killed in a car crash. Which left Aidan as her sole surviving parent.

Taking on a baby meant throwing Aidan's world into chaos. Who he was, what he did—a baby just didn't factor into any of that. He was faced with two choices. Either man up and take care of his daughter or place her in the foster care system.

To Aidan, a Marine to the core, there really was no choice to make. Reluctant or not, he'd accepted fatherhood with grave responsibility.

And then he'd fallen in love with his precious little infant.

The truth was, Marc was crazy about her, too. She had him wrapped around her little finger.

"Abby? Your precious little princess? Driving you crazy?" he asked with mock surprise. "Well, now, that's a surprise."

Marc's sarcasm was well earned. While other little girls her age were having tea parties, Abby was climbing to the highest rung on the monkey bars in the park and swinging upside down, or using Aidan's sensitive documents to line the cage of the gerbil she was hosting for her preschool class. She was a creative little tyrant, with a personality as big as her mind.

Just picturing his niece made Marc smile. "I'm still unclear as to how Abby's tormenting you is my fault."

"Because she's in the process of trying on her flower girl dress for the seventh time. I've counted, because each time she tries it on, she gets distracted by some must-do activity. And every one of those activities means ripping, staining, or somehow destroying that damned dress. Plus, every fifteen minutes, she wants to know when she gets to wear it. Three weeks doesn't work for her. Couldn't you and Madeline push up the wedding to, say, tomorrow?"

Marc burst out laughing. "I'd love to, for Abby's sake and for mine. But this wedding has taken on a life of its own. So I can't help you there. What I can do is to grab Maddy and come over tomorrow night. Between the two of us, we'll help Abby expend some energy and get you some peace. How's that?"

"In exchange for…?" Aidan's mind was a steel trap. "I seem to recall you mentioning something about a favor."

"I had a feeling that would register at some point." Marc reached for the beer he'd been drinking. "It's work and it's important. Will Abby let you talk?"

"Only if she talks to you first."

"My pleasure. Put her on."

"Princess?" Aidan called out. "Uncle Marc wants to say hi."

"Is he here?" Marc heard Abby's deceptively innocent little voice reply eagerly.

"He and Aunt Maddy will be here tomorrow night. But he's on the phone, and he wants to say good night to you."

Running footsteps, and then Abby was on the line.

"Hi, Uncle Marc. Are you going to sleep now?" She sounded puzzled. "It's so early."

Marc bit back his laughter. "I think it's you who's going to sleep, cutie pie."

"I'm not tired. I'm trying on my dress. Daddy says I'm 'stroying it. It's only got three rips. One is big. I got it 'cause I wouldn't let Daddy help me put it on. It's pretty clean. But the magic marker won't wash out." She lowered her voice conspiratorially. "Daddy doesn't want you to know, but he bought me another dress to save for the wedding. It's the same, only not ripped or dirty. Daddy hid it, but I know where it is. It's on the top shelf of his closet in a pink bag with a zipper."

Marc heard Aidan groan in the background. His own shoulders were shaking with laughter. "That was a good idea on your daddy's part. So let's not spoil things for him. Don't tell him you know about the dress, and let it sleep in his closet until the wedding."

"Okay, but that's still ten plus eight more days away. I counted on the calendar."

"Ten plus eight more is eighteen," Marc responded to her glum little voice. "That's less than twenty. Remember when it was lots longer?"

"Uh-huh. But it's still long."

"How about if you and Aunt Maddy make a special flower girl calendar tomorrow night? You can draw a picture on each day, and decorate it with glitter and sparkles. Then, Aunt Maddy can help you think of a flower girl job for each day, something to make the wedding even more special. Being a flower girl is really important."

"Yay!" The glumness evaporated as quickly as it had come. Abby's voice was filled with joy, and Marc could almost see her jumping up and down. "Can we start before dinner?"

"Of course we can. But you have to get some sleep now. Otherwise, you'll be tired and Aunt Maddy will have to do the whole thing herself."

"Night, Uncle Marc. I love you."

The phone clunked to a table or a desk, and Abby was off, racing to her room. "Daddy, I want to sleep in my dress," she called as she ran. "I'll brush my teeth. Can you read me a story?"

"Only if you take off the dress and put on your nightgown," Aidan called back. "I'll be in by the time you're done." He picked up the phone. "You've got five minutes," he informed Marc.

Marc didn't waste one of them. "I need you to do some recon for us," he said. He then swiftly filled Aidan in on what they knew and what they needed to know. "Can you do it?" he concluded.

"Of course I can do it. Marines rule." Aidan never got tired of their rivalry over the Marines versus the Navy SEALs.

"How did I know that was coming?"

"Because you're pretty smart—for a SEAL."

"Daddy, are you coming?" Abby's voice drifted down the hall from her bedroom. "I want to show you my purple glitter. I tried it on the wall and it looks really nice."

"I'm going to kill you," Aidan told Marc between gritted teeth. "You're getting a never-ending parade of strippers and lap dancers at your bachelor party."

"Thanks for the warning."

"Email me everything you've got. Bring the cup that has this Slava Petrovich's DNA with you tomorrow night. I'll have something for you within a few days. Now I've got to get some rags to wipe the wall with. Good night."

*Office of Forensic Instincts*

Downstairs in his lair, Ryan munched on another handful of trail mix and studied his computer screen, waiting for his results. When they came, his lips curved into a self-satisfied smile, and he pumped the air with his fist.

"Oh, yeah, Yoda. I'm good."

"I know that, Ryan," Yoda replied. "You do exceptional work."

Ryan chuckled. "I'm so glad I programmed you with all the right answers."

He continued to stare at the screen, his ebullience fading as intense concentration replaced it. He clicked a few more times and delved deeper into his findings.

He hated big companies—except when he loved big companies. Big companies had the resources to do big things. And, in the case of Facebook, that meant successfully working on using facial recognition software and technology for social media purposes. Precisely what Ryan had needed to work his magic. It would be Facebook-specific, precluding his extending the search to the broader Net, but that was okay by him. Facebook was ginormous.

Armed with the photos John Nickels had taken at the Montclair Starbucks, Ryan had spent the past two hours deftly poking around, using Facebook's capability to search for the two thugs who'd attempted to kidnap Shannon. Not that he believed they'd have Facebook profiles—that would be ridiculous, not to mention way too easy for him. But their girlfriends? Friends? Family members? Ryan had gone under the absolute assumption that any or all of them had Facebook profiles, and Ryan would be able to exploit the social media giant's data for FI's benefit.

He'd started out by hacking into Facebook's skunkworks and finding their facial recognition project. He'd then downloaded a copy of it, tweaked it for his own purposes, and let it loose against Facebook's live database. His program hadn't let him down. He'd just gotten an email with a URL pointing to the picture and the name of the Facebook profile in which it was found. One click and he'd seen the profile picture, along with the name associated with it.

Thanks to a squishy family reunion photo posted by the sister of Thug Number One, Ryan had just identified him as Alexei Kozlov. Not only had the facial recognition software identified him but Kozlov's bare arm was completely exposed in the photo. His tattoos were clear as a bell and exactly as Claire had described them.

This was the scumbag who had not only attempted to snatch Shannon Barker but who had killed Julie Forman.

Well, now the fucker would get his.

On to Thug Number Two, which was a lot trickier. No

one had actually seen him. John had gotten a half-visible shot of him through the van window. Ryan had enhanced and enhanced the photo until he got a telltale marker—a jagged scar on his right cheek. Also, his head was shaved. Nice—not thrilling, but nice. There'd still be no identifying him from this scratchy shot.

But Ryan got lucky. In Alexei's photo, his sister had named everyone present. Sure enough, right in there with the group clench was their dear friend, Vitaliy Bolshov, who looked just like the blurry picture John had taken, right down to his bald head and the jagged scar on his face.

Vitaliy's left arm was slung over the shoulder of one of Alexei's cousins, and his right arm was gripping a slutty-looking woman who was pressed up against him and who he might as well be screwing on screen. The good news was that, thanks to Vitaliy's arm-baring stance, Ryan could see that he had a few ominous-looking tattoos of his own. The better news was that Vitaliy's girlfriend, Olga Dubova, was tagged, her name in blue, which meant she had a Facebook profile.

Ryan lined up his cursor and clicked on Olga's name.

Up came her profile, complete with intimate poses of her and Vitaliy, some of them downright gross and some of them just what Ryan needed—camera-facing, clear-as-a-bell face shots.

No doubt that Ryan had his man. He saved all the photos and the two profiles to his hard drive, with the intention of running these new tattoos by Hutch.

With both killers identified, Ryan went for gold.

"Let's try one last thing, Yoda," he said aloud. "Let's see what we can come up with using Slava Petrovich's photos. I'm sure he's a hell of a lot smarter than the other two morons. But you never know. Maybe, just maybe, we'll get lucky again."

This one was a bear. No girlfriends, friends, or family members with Facebook profiles linking to Slava.

Ryan wasn't about to give up. He picked out the best front-on shot of Slava he'd taken as Bruiser walked into the Rus-Chem office building. Using that as a base, Ryan fine-tuned it until you could practically count the guy's nose hairs. Then, he uploaded that into his program and let loose.

Long minutes ticked by. And then it happened. A telltale bing. Ryan had an email. And the email had a link.

Clicking on it, Ryan waited—and the photo came up.

He'd hit the jackpot.

The profile belonged to some girl named Delores Lamb. She was a twenty-eight-year-old paralegal at a Chicago law firm. Ryan focused on the specific photo he'd been directed to. Evidently, Delores and her friends had gone to a club for a TGIF night out. The picture showed them, gathered together in a group pose, while some bartender—given credit in the comment beneath the picture—had taken the shot.

Ryan barely glanced at the group of women. What his gaze was narrowed on was the trio of lowlives sitting together with their "dates" at a nearby table.

In the background or not, Ryan could see with utter certainty that he was looking at Slava, Alexei, and Vitaliy—each one wrapped around a woman who had to be a prostitute, based on the cash Slava was shoving into their hands.

He had his link. Slava Petrovich was connected to the two killers who'd murdered Julie Forman.

Saving and printing everything, Ryan grabbed his cell phone.

His chair was still swiveling as he raced out the door.

## CHAPTER THIRTY-ONE

It was after eight that night when Hutch reached the FI brownstone. He was beat. He was really enjoying his job at the New York Field Office, but it was new and it was intense. So his days were swallowed up by briefings, phone calls, and observation of fieldwork. Today he'd also tracked down his buddy who worked the Eurasian Criminal Enterprise squad, and reviewed all the tattoos Casey had forwarded him—the original three and now the three new ones that Ryan had uncovered. There were no surprises to the conversation. The tattoos and what they represented were exactly as Hutch had researched them. It was what they implied that worried him.

He punched in the dummy Hirsch pad code he'd been issued by FI and stepped inside.

"Good evening, Supervisory Special Agent Hutchinson," Yoda greeted him politely.

"Hey, Yoda." Hutch shrugged out of his jacket. "I need to see Casey right away."

"Certainly. She's on the second floor in the main conference room with Ryan."

"Thanks." Hutch loped up the stairs and knocked on the half-opened conference room door. "It's me."

"Come on in," Casey called. She gave Hutch a half-smile as he walked in. He wasn't fooled. Her chin was set, her brow was furrowed, and she was in work-solution mode.

Ryan was pacing around the room, arms clasped behind his back, looking as intense as Casey did. He paused to shoot Hutch a wave, then continued pacing.

"Grab a cup of coffee and join us," Casey said.

Hutch nodded, heading over and pouring himself a cup of much-needed caffeine, then perched his hip against the credenza. He had a feeling this investigation of FI's was getting more and more complex. Well, he wasn't about to make things any easier.

"I ran everything you sent me," he told Ryan without preamble. "It was pretty straightforward. Nothing, I'm sure, you didn't pull off the web. The cobweb on your criminal's shoulder indicates he's a drug addict. The cat on his forearm is the mark of a thief. And the dagger through his neck is—no shocker—the sign of a murderer. The six drops of blood dripping from it mean he's killed six people."

"Yeah." Ryan nodded. "That's what I got online. Did you talk to your friend?"

"Sure did. He verified my suspicions. The KGB was known to use this particular Russian mob offshoot to do 'special projects.' In other words, you're dealing with hard-core criminals here, not street gang members. These pigs go way back. They've done major time in prison. They've murdered people in cold blood. They're scary, and the people they work for are even scarier. They're well-connected, including now, through corrupt channels in the FSB."

"Dammit," Casey muttered.

Hutch could read her thoughts. She'd heard him loud and clear. She was well aware that the FSB—the Federal Security Service of the Russian Federation—was the main successor agency to the former KGB. And she was beginning to realize just how shark-infested the waters were that her team was wading in.

"Are you going to tell me what this investigation is about or not?" Hutch demanded. "Because I know you, Case. Even though you feel ultimately responsible for the safety of your team, you feel equally responsible for resolving things for your clients. You have no intention of backing away. Well, I'm sure as hell not sitting around while you put your life in danger—again."

Hutch's emphasis was clear. While Casey was very protective when it came to the lives of her team, she sucked when it came to safeguarding her own life.

"Point taken," she replied, chewing her lip as she weighed her options. "I'm caught between a rock and a hard place. You know I can't divulge anything without talking to our clients. And they know less than you do about this whole organized crime thing. If they knew, they'd freak, and that would blow our entire investigation. We need them to keep it together."

"You're obliged to tell them everything," Hutch reminded her.

"I realize that." Casey dragged a frustrated hand through her hair. "And I will. Just not as explicitly as we're discussing here. Our job is to solve their case and to keep them in one piece." A brief pause. "I also have another responsibility, and that's to watch your back. Which means keeping the things I share with you on the straight and narrow. I'm sure our clients would welcome you with open arms. But I have to make sure I don't violate your ethics or your responsibility to the Bureau."

A corner of Hutch's mouth lifted. "I appreciate you looking out for me, sweetheart. But I've gone out on a limb before. When it comes to your safety, my loyalties seem to run a little murky."

"A little?" Ryan looked distinctly amused. "I'd say a lot. But, hey, that works for me. I want you on board."

"I'm waiting for some additional information from another source," Casey said. "That should complete the picture. Once I have it, I'll get our clients' permission to bring you fully into the loop."

"Get their permission now," Hutch responded. "That way we'll be good to go the minute your other source comes through." He met Casey's gaze with insightful certainty. "Aidan works as quickly as I do."

Casey's lips twitched. "Duly noted, Agent Hutchinson. I'll call them now."

*Burlington, Vermont*

Max was in a meeting with Dmitry discussing the accommodations and various regimens for their new training arrivals when the call came through.

The only reason Max even acknowledged the ring tone was because it came in on his private line. Only a few people had that number. And given that Slava was now orchestrating a major initiative, he had to be mindful of everything.

"Do you want me to answer it?" Dmitry asked.

Max glanced down at the phone, unsurprised to see that the number was blocked. No one who had this number wanted to be recognized. And Max was adamant that it stay just that way.

"I'll take the call." He punched on the phone and put it to his ear. "Yes?" he said, purposely not reverting to Russian until he knew who and what he was dealing with.

"Hello, Max."

The voice at the other end spoke Russian, even though he

also spoke perfect English, as well. It was Ilya Andropov, Max's mole in the Ministry of Economic Development of the Russian Federation. Ilya was an essential asset, protecting the anonymity of Max's ownership in RusChem. He reported back to Max on all inquiries that were made regarding the company, swiftly identifying any and all problems or potential infiltrations. In return, he was extremely well compensated—as well he should be.

Whatever this phone call was about, it was important.

"What is it, Ilya?" Max asked, switching to Russian himself.

"A red flag. It seems there have been some inquiries into RusChem. The inquirers were sent on a wild goose chase, but I wanted to advise you of the situation immediately."

"Who made these inquiries?" Max demanded. "And what, specifically, did they pertain to?"

"I wasn't privy to the information, although I haven't given up trying. I do know that they were made anonymously. That means it's someone with internal connections. I don't think anything was divulged. That doesn't mean the avenue wasn't pursued."

"Son of a bitch." Max gritted his teeth. Whoever was in charge of protecting Shannon Barker was delving deep—and they had the connections to do so. "Find out whatever you can. I want to know every detail that transpires."

He slammed down the phone.

"What is it?" Dmitry asked.

"RusChem. Someone's probing into it. Ilya doesn't know who, and he's having trouble finding out."

"Does Ilya know what it is that they're looking for?" Dmitry asked.

"Not yet." Max rose and began stalking around the room, trying to displace his agitation. "This is bad, Dmitry. It's more than just a police investigation, and it extends way beyond the protection of one Olympic hopeful. This is being run by a well-connected adversary. And it's a direct threat to my re-search—and to me." A dark scowl. "From this point on, anyone is expendable."

*East Village, New York*

It was nearly midnight, and Claire knew she'd procras-tinated long enough. Burying her head in the sand was an un-familiar reaction for her; one she disliked intensely. She wasn't a coward, certainly not when it came to her gift. She'd long ago accepted that there were times to embrace it and times to rue its existence. But it was always her responsibility to use it as it was needed.

And that time was now. FI's clients were counting on her. FI was counting on her. And she wasn't ducking this new and deeper aspect of her gift any longer. Whatever came of the next few minutes, she'd stay with it and stay strong.

Quietly, she settled herself on her thickly cushioned sofa, Jim Robbins' hairbrush and training medal neatly laid out on the coffee table in front of her. Automatically, she folded her legs un-der her in lotus position, which always brought her a soothing sense of calm.

She glanced at the two objects and felt a stronger pull to the medal. Picking it up, she shut her eyes, holding it in a secure but not crushing grip. She couldn't drag out the images; they had to come to her.

Unfortunately—or fortunately—it rarely took long for that to happen when it came to Jim Robbins. Even in death he seemed to reach out to her, and she somehow knew that his soul was neither dark nor light but more of a muddied gray. He'd been a foolish, greedy man, but he hadn't been evil, and he certainly hadn't deserved to die in such a violent manner.

Violent…agonizingly violent.

Poison.

That was the first certainty that crystalized in Claire's mind. Along with it, she felt shooting pains rip through her gut, cutting off her very breath.

She refused to give in and release the medal. She was going with this, come hell or high water. The images were clear, and she was living inside them. Jim…writhing on the floor of an elegant room with a long, polished table. He was contorted in pain, animal groans emanating from his throat, foam frothing at his mouth. The torture went on and on, until with a final shudder that racked his body, he went still.

Death…death…

Claire gasped, fighting her way to the surface. She was drenched in sweat, shaking so violently she could hardly hold on to the medal. But she wasn't letting go. Nor was she losing her focus.

Now she was outside Jim's lifeless body, aware of his immediate surroundings as she hovered over him.

Gleaming hardwood floors. Burgundy velvet drapes hanging at the windows. And the mahogany table—it was a dining room. A dining room in the mansion she'd pictured. Mountains in the distance. Rippling water. Acres of untouched land. Green. Green. New England.

The awareness of the location popped into her head just as the vision vanished.

Another took its place.

Someone was standing in the dining room. He'd watched Jim die with a dark and hollow soul.

A man. Tall. Lean. Cast in shadows. Faceless. Nameless.

The leader. The killer.

Claire tried to force something more tangible, but it

wouldn't come. He was shrouded by anonymity, a cold-blooded monster, and he was central to FI's investigation. Yet she couldn't see him, couldn't perceive more.

Except for one thing.

He'd kill again unless they stopped him. And it would be one of them who died.

## CHAPTER THIRTY-TWO

*Office of Forensic Instincts*

No member of the Forensic Instincts team was surprised to see Hutch sitting at the conference table when they filed in. They'd all been briefed that Casey had spoken with their clients and that Lisa and Miles had been thrilled that FI could convince their FBI contact to play a more comprehensive role in their case. All of them, particularly Shannon, were badly shaken by the attempted kidnapping, and, extra security or not, they rarely ventured out of the apartment or the gym. The overwhelming fear and anxiety were wearing on them, and Casey could sense that a meltdown was imminent.

All the more reason to include Hutch in the mix.

"Hey, guys," Hutch greeted the team.

They all responded in kind.

"Another play-by-the-rules guy—I feel less lonely already," Patrick said, settling himself in his chair, coffee mug in hand. His banter was light, but his mouth was drawn, and there were dark circles under his eyes. He was worried and exhausted from his long hours of safeguarding their clients—and less than optimistic about the odds of no further violent attempts being made. He took a belt of coffee. "Although somehow I doubt that either one of us will be playing within the confines of those rules."

"I'd say that's a safe bet." Hutch spoke with his customary candor. "But, as usual, you guys make it impossible for me to mind my own business and stay honest."

He folded his arms across his chest and leaned back in his chair, waiting patiently until everyone was caffeine-fixed and seated. Then he addressed the group.

"I want to set some ground rules, just so we're clear, not only about this case, but about my overall role here. Yes, I've moved to the Big Apple, but I'm not a member of Forensic Instincts. I work for the FBI. That being said, I happen to be in love with Casey. So my loyalties are sometimes divided. But that doesn't mean I'll be compromising myself, or you and your commitment to client confidentiality, on a regular basis. That's precisely why I rented Marc's apartment rather than moving in here. Your firm and I need our separate space. I'm sure that, at times, we'll call on each other for help. But I'm trying to keep some sort of line, however blurry, in the sand. I already know where Patrick, and obviously Casey, stands. I hope the rest of you are on board with this."

"*You'll* call on *us*?" Emma leaned forward, eyes sparkling. "Does that mean we'll be some kind of confidential informants on your cases?"

Hutch's lips twitched. "You never know."

"Well, I'm certainly cool with that."

"No problems here," Ryan said.

"Not with me, either." Marc met Hutch's gaze. "Aidan emailed me a few hours ago and said he'd be calling soon with solid information. Once he does, I'm sure we'll need your help."

"And you'll have it."

"I'm on board with everything Hutch said," Claire put in. This time there was strength in her voice, and she was the old Claire again. But, rather than a lost, faraway look in her eyes, there was genuine fear. "I also have some new information of my own."

Everyone looked at her.

"Last night I sat down with the training medal Marc brought me from Jim Robbins' apartment. Once again, I got some clear images. They were nightmarish. I saw Jim Robbins poisoned to death. And I saw a veiled image of the killer as he watched him die. Robbins was killed in this man's home—the manor I told you about last time. The death was prolonged and agonizing." She shuddered.

"You *saw* the killer?" Casey was all over that one. "What did he look like? Is he Russian? Did you sense that he owns Rus-Chem?"

"I wish I could answer those questions." Claire sighed. "The truth is, I just don't know. He was only a shadowy figure. I couldn't make out any of his features. All I can tell you is that he's tall and lean."

"That's not Slava," Emma said at once. "He's built like a Humvee."

"True," Marc concurred. "Anything else?"

"One new thing. This time, when I saw all that green acreage and the surrounding mountains, I got a general location. New England. I know it's not much."

"It's more than we had before," Casey replied.

"It makes sense." That idea clicked with Hutch. "There are tons of rural places in New England where someone can stay invisible." His forehead creased in a frown. "I just wish we could narrow it down further."

"Hopefully we'll get some help from Aidan on that." Casey's gaze was narrowed on Claire, and she studied the apprehension in her eyes. "There's obviously more. What is it?"

Claire wet her lips with the tip of her tongue. "The killer is feeling threatened. *We're* making him feel threatened. He's going to come after us. And right now…all my instincts are screaming that one of us is in danger of dying."

A heavy silence greeted Claire's ominous premonition.

"Shit," Ryan muttered at last.

Along with that expletive, Marc's cell phone rang.

"It's Aidan," he announced. He punched on the phone. "You have everything now? Good. We're all here. I'll put you on speakerphone."

He pressed the speakerphone button and placed the iPhone in the center of the conference table. "You're on, Aidan."

"This one was tricky," Aidan began. "I got what you needed, but my sources seem to feel that our probing didn't go unnoticed."

"So RusChem knows we're checking into them?"

"Yup. I don't think they know who's doing the probing—not yet. But that's only a matter of time. And given what I'm about to tell you, we're all going to have to watch our backs."

"Go on," Casey said.

"RusChem's owner is a scientific genius named Maxim Lubinov," Aidan reported. "You can Google the guy to get his public persona, including a photo and bio. Harvard pedigree—college and medical school. He's now a foremost expert in microbiology and stem cell research. He's basically reclusive and doesn't make many public appearances, but he did recently speak at the Marriott Marquis on scientific advances in increasing cell energy production. You can read the summary of his presentation yourselves."

Ryan was already on his computer, calling up the readily available data.

"And his private persona?" Casey asked.

"Father's a high-ranking military officer. I'm sure that's provided his son with necessary contacts throughout the Russian Federation. Lubinov's initial career was as a research scientist—a fact that's conveniently missing from his bio because he pushed ethical boundaries to the point where he resigned before the company could fire him."

"What's the company name?" Ryan asked, his fingers still flying.

Aidan supplied it but then said, "You won't find much there, and I wouldn't waste my time. What's more important is that Lubinov used the opportunity to fly solo. He developed a series of health supplements and sold them to Osen Pharmaceuticals in a lucrative deal."

"Osen Pharmaceuticals is huge," Marc murmured. "Lubinov must have scored a bundle."

"He did," Aidan replied. "More important still is what he did with his newly acquired financial gains and stream of income."

"He launched RusChem," Casey guessed.

"Right. And he's gone to great lengths to keep all details of the company under wraps, including who they are and what they do."

"All this is a smoke screen for cashing in on some PED distribution?" Patrick asked, brows raised. "No way. This is much too elaborate a setup for just that."

"You're right," Aidan agreed. "Lubinov's goals are much loftier than cash for drugs. From what I was able to gather, he's heading up some kind of grandiose research project involving über-PEDs. He's secreted himself away at a private estate in Burlington, Vermont, where he converted a massive, twelve-thousand-foot home into a boutique sports medicine and training facility. His employees are few and unconditionally loyal. He says jump, and they say how high. Clearly, there's a lot more going on in that mansion than I'm privy to. But he's obviously on the verge of coming up with a breakthrough formula that he believes will rock the world."

That important chunk of information sank in for a minute.

"Burlington," Claire murmured. "That's in the Green Mountains. And Lake Champlain is nearby. That's the place I was seeing."

"I'll give you the coordinates, Ryan," Aidan said.

"Good." Ryan scribbled down the information Aidan provided him with.

"Hi, Aidan, it's Hutch." Hutch knew Aidan through his friendship with Marc, a friendship that dated back to Marc's FBI days.

"Hey, I didn't know they let you in," Aidan returned dryly.

"Just lucky, I guess." Hutch was simultaneously processing what Aidan was saying and pondering another, equally important offshoot of Lubinov's work. "I've got a good handle on Maxim Lubinov. What I want to know is, where does Eurasian Criminal Enterprise fit into this? Is Lubinov hiring mob members to act as RusChem employees, as well as to eliminate any potential threat to his work?"

"Absolutely. He needs them for both. This way, his name isn't associated with RusChem, and he doesn't have to get his hands dirty protecting his interests. He's got Slava Petrovich—that guy you asked me to look into—doing both. Petrovich is Lubinov's cleaner, as well as his front man for RusChem. Petrovich hires the right people to kill off the wrong ones, and takes care of the bigger jobs himself."

"Maxim Lubinov is a hands-on killer when he has to be," Claire amended. "He's poisoned someone himself."

"Oh, I have no doubt that's true," Aidan replied. "Lubinov will do anything to protect his venture. If murder is necessary, so be it. He's not a guy with a conscience."

There was a brief pause and the sound of Aidan turning a page. "Getting back to Slava Petrovich, I checked with my former FSB contacts about his background. He's one terrifying SOB. His nickname is Slava the Slayer, and he was known in the FSB for taking care of problems using whatever means necessary. No further explanation required. But, guys, this bastard is dangerous, and he has skills, so you'd better be careful." A pause. "On the other hand, I don't see how you can avoid tangling with him if you want to get to Lubinov. This is an ugly situation all ways around. Are you sure you don't want to cut your losses on this one?"

"Not happening," Casey replied firmly. "We're going to stop Maxim Lubinov and secure our clients' safety."

"The hell you are," Hutch shot back in a no-bullshit tone. "You and Forensic Instincts aren't immortal. Nor are you expendable. You're not becoming collateral damage."

"Okay, this is where I hang up," Aidan said. "I've given you everything I know. What you do with it is up to you. But, for the record, I agree with Hutch. Not to mention that Madeleine, and especially Abby, would kill me if anything happened to Marc."

"Nothing's going to happen to me, Aidan," Marc replied.

"Good. Because I've spent a hell of a lot of time with Ryan planning your bachelor party. You're going to be there to endure every embarrassing minute."

"Good-bye, leatherneck." Marc's middle finger was already on the cell phone button.

Hutch pulled over a laptop the minute Aidan hung up.

"I want to read Lubinov's bio, the public details of his life, and the transcription of his conference speech firsthand. No offense, Ryan."

"None taken. You're the profiling expert. Do what you need to." Ryan was staring at his own computer screen. "I'm concentrating on the coordinates Aidan gave me so I can zero in on Lubinov's estate."

The reasons for Ryan's actions were obvious. Still, he stopped short of voicing them aloud. Hutch didn't need to hear something compromising, even though he knew damned well what FI was planning.

His disapproving stare bored into Ryan, who just kept his gaze fixed on his computer screen. A weighty silence filled the room.

With a muttered oath, Hutch went back to his analysis.

The team exchanged glances. There was no doubt in their minds that Hutch was going to stand in their way. And maybe he was right to do so. This case had spiraled out of control. What they were now facing was really scary stuff, extending far beyond the scope of their expertise. Former KGB agents now employed by Organized Crime, a megalomaniac who killed on a whim... This was the stuff meant for the FBI. But how could they involve the Bureau when all the proof they had had been illegally obtained? What the hell were they going to do?

Abruptly, Hutch sat back in his chair. "Okay, you wanted my professional assessment, so here it is. Based on everything Aidan said and on what I'm reading here, my belief is that Lubinov suffers from narcissistic personality disorder." Hutch ticked off the telltale traits on his fingers. "He's arrogant, haughty, and consumed with his own importance. He expects to be treated in a superior fashion. He only respects those he feels are his equal, and that includes pretty much no one. He's obsessed with his own brilliance and his indisputable path to success. He is unwilling to recognize the needs and feelings of anyone else and will take advantage of whoever he has to in order to achieve his goals."

"Isn't that like a megalomaniac?" Emma asked.

Hutch nodded, still deep in thought. "Megalomania is the term that was once used to describe this disorder." He frowned, clearly not finished with his assessment. "But I think there's more to Lubinov than just that. In my opinion—again, based on everything I'm hearing and reading—he's also ruthless enough to have antisocial personality disorder." Once again, Hutch elaborated. "He has a disregard for right or wrong. Rules and laws don't apply to him; they're for others. Based on Claire's vision, there's evidence of hostility, aggression, and violence—plus, he displays a total lack of empathy for others and lack of remorse about harming them."

"A.k.a. wack job," Emma muttered.

"No." Hutch shook his head. "Understand that personality disorders are not mental illnesses. Lubinov isn't crazy. He's fully functional and can strategize and carry out whatever plans he devises."

"In some ways, that makes him even more dangerous," Casey noted aloud.

"You bet," Marc said. His gaze was sober as it found Casey's, and he spoke to her as only her right-hand man could. "I totally agree with what Hutch is saying. Which means I strongly suggest that, once Ryan figures out where Lubinov's estate is, you squelch his urge to go all GI Joe on the place. Anything we might or might not contemplate doing will take the same level of strategizing and implementing as Lubinov is capable of."

"Absolutely." Casey didn't bat a lash.

"Gee, why doesn't that make me feel better?" Hutch asked.

Casey turned to him, decisiveness written all over her face. "You've been more than wonderful. Thank you so much for your help. It was invaluable. But you need to leave now."

He arched a brow at her. "Why? So you can plan an illegal invasion of Maxim Lubinov's compound—one that will put all your lives at risk? I'm not going anywhere."

"Hutch, we've already put you in an untenable position," Casey replied quietly. "Whatever we do from this point on, you can't be involved."

"She's right, Hutch. This is where you get off." Patrick's words were few, but the look he gave Hutch conveyed it all. Hutch had given them the analysis they'd asked him for. He hadn't crossed any indelible lines—not yet. All he had was supposition. If he walked away now, he'd be clean. If he hung around, he'd be blatantly violating his obligations to the Bureau.

"I'll take things from here," Patrick added, still holding Hutch's gaze.

"Son of a bitch." Hutch slammed his fist down on the desk. He read Patrick perfectly. He knew—and hated—the fact that he was right. He also knew that, no matter what he himself did now—and what he'd said earlier—ultimately, he wasn't going to be able to keep his promises—not to Casey and not to the Bureau.

He pushed back his chair and rose. "I won't sit in on this official meeting," he said. "But that doesn't mean I won't be watching every move you make. If I get the slightest inkling that you're about to do something stupid, or if I manage to dig up my own solid evidence, I'm bringing the FBI on board. I'll give you the courtesy of letting you know, so you can alert your clients and cover your asses. But that's where my promises end. We're now talking about a criminal enterprise operation involving murder, mass production and distribution of illegal drugs, and the involvement of Eurasian organized crime."

"We have no solid evidence, Hutch." Casey was visibly displeased but not surprised. She couldn't argue with his rationale; it was sound. "I brought you into this case on a minimal and confidential basis. Please don't violate my trust. If we find solid proof, then we can talk about involving the FBI. Otherwise, this case belongs to Forensic Instincts."

Hutch's jaw set. "We'll see." Setting down his coffee mug, he shoved back his chair and strode out of the room.

The echo of the door shutting—hard—reverberated off the walls and made Hero pick up his head and growl.

"He's right, Casey." Patrick spoke up at once. "We all know we're in way over our heads. I'm aware that we have no solid evidence. But we'd better get some fast, and then we'd better involve law enforcement."

"Don't you think I realize that?" Casey fired back. "But this case is far more complicated than Hutch is privy to. Up until now, keeping Lisa's identity and everything she witnessed a secret was paramount to keeping her, Miles, and Shannon safe. That's no longer enough. I get it. I also get that we've broken every law in the book to acquire the information we have. We have nothing legitimate to give to the FBI to elicit their help." Casey turned up her palms in question. "So tell me how we're going to come up with this magical evidence fast enough to stop Maxim Lubinov—before he and his Russian mob kill our clients?"

"Hey." Ryan sat up straight, no longer hunched over his laptop. "We don't need evidence. I know where Lubinov's compound is."

"Cut it out, Ryan," Patrick replied sharply. "We do need evidence."

"Well, we don't have it. What we do have is the information I just dug up."

"Fine," Patrick countered. "So let's arrange for an anonymous tip to the Bureau. They'll send in SWAT teams to handle the job."

"Yeah, and we'll all go to jail," Marc reminded him. "What Casey said is true. Our evidence was all illegally obtained. And this wouldn't be a little anonymous call, like a tip-off to an impending bank robbery. The accusations made would require explanation and elaboration, things that only professionals—in this case *us*—would know. We'd be screwed."

"Marc..." Patrick began.

"I don't like it any more than you do, Patrick," Marc cut him off. "But we've got to do this ourselves. Not like crazed superheroes." He shot Ryan a pointed look. "But like seasoned pros. We need a well-thought-out plan and the perfect strategy with which to implement it."

"Then let's come up with one," Casey said. "Now."

## CHAPTER THIRTY-THREE

Emma walked through Little Italy, finishing up the twenty-minute trek from Tribeca to her small but airy apartment on Mulberry Street in Chinatown. Hopefully, her two roommates wouldn't be home. It wasn't that they were a problem to live with; they weren't. Nikki was a nursing student who spent most of her time at NYU. And Kelly was an editorial assistant at a small publishing house in Midtown. Both girls were a little on the boring side. But they were basically cool—and they made paying the rent feasible. So living with them was okay. Except for days like today, which had been so intense that all Emma wanted was some downtime alone.

And she wouldn't get much.

The FI team was pulling an all-nighter to lock in on the right plan of attack. Each of them was getting a few hours off to shower, nap, and get their asses back to the office and to the brainstorming session. Casey had arranged it so their downtime was staggered. This way, the strategic wheels kept on turning.

As it turned out, Emma would never get her downtime—but not because of FI or her roomies.

Just as Emma opened the apartment door, she felt her

pocket vibrate, signifying the ring of her burner phone. Feeling totally wrung out, she groaned, even as she wriggled the phone out of her pocket and answered it.

"Hello?"

"It's Lisa."

"Everything okay?"

"I guess." Lisa sounded as if she were wound tight as a drum. "I just wanted to talk to you. I know Forensic Instincts is doing everything to solve our case, including asking more of your FBI contact. And I'm really grateful. But I'm still scared. And, frankly, I'm losing my mind. I feel like I'm in jail. So I need to know exactly what's going on. My gut tells me I'm getting half answers."

Emma shut the door, dropped her stuff on the hall table, and headed for the kitchen. She was suddenly very awake and very unhappy. Fielding Lisa's questions was way out of her league—especially when her mouth always acted before her brain. How much could she say? How much would Casey permit her to say?

She was in deep shit.

"I wasn't there when Casey talked to you, but I'm sure she was completely up front," she tried, hoping that she was doing the proper amount of tightrope walking. "Casey is a straight shooter. She's honest with our clients and protects them with everything she's got. That's why she's leaving no stone unturned."

"What stones? I don't know any more than I did a week ago—except that Shannon was almost kidnapped and that Patrick's men are practically living with us. What aren't I being told?"

Emma was half tempted to put Lisa on hold and call Casey for advice. But that would only tip Lisa off to the fact that her fears were justified. No, Emma would have to do this on her own.

"There are no secrets, Lisa. What you're probably sensing is that we have to protect our confidential informants and their sources." Emma opened the refrigerator door and tried to buy herself some time to compose her answers. She had to rely on her street smarts. They were the best ammo in her arsenal.

"Listen, I just got home and I'm starved," she announced, cradling the phone between her shoulder and her ear. "So, while we're talking, you get to listen to my microwave reheat last night's pasta. Then you get to hear me stuff it in my mouth."

"No problem." The normalcy of Emma's conversation definitely took Lisa down a notch, just as Emma had hoped. Lisa, Miles, and Shannon were living like terrified trapped mice. A little normalcy was what was needed.

That gave Emma an idea—one that would give her the opportunity to develop the right game plan and one that would also give Lisa a much-needed diversion.

Popping her pasta in the microwave and setting the cook time for two minutes, Emma stepped out on the proverbial limb and prayed Casey wouldn't kill her.

"How about if I come out there tomorrow?" she suggested. "I could spend a little time with you guys, clarify what Casey told you, and maybe even take a spin class."

"That would be awesome." No surprise that Lisa jumped at the chance. "Do you have time?"

"I'll make time." This part came easily, because it was fact. "Besides, I like spending time with you. We're kind of kindred spirits."

"Yes. We are." Lisa's entire mood was lighter. "What time can you get here?"

"How about ten-ish? I can go straight to the gym and meet you there. Then we'll head back to the apartment so I can talk to Shannon."

"That would be perfect. The poor kid needs some cheering up. If anyone can make her laugh, it's you. And, frankly, I could use some of your perkiness about now. So I'll see you at the gym around ten. And not to worry—I'll set up a spin class just for you."

Emma called Casey with a sick feeling in the pit of her stomach. The minute she answered, Emma launched into the details of what had just happened and what her plans were for tomorrow.

"Oh, Emma." Casey sounded more frustrated than angry. The team had been spinning in neutral for hours, and she was stressed to the hilt. "The last thing we need right now are more complications."

"I know." Emma rushed on to explain. "But, Casey, you didn't hear Lisa's voice. She's not only about to shatter but she's beginning to think we're keeping things from her. Which, obviously, we are. I know it's for all the right, necessary reasons, but Lisa wouldn't understand that. We've got to tell her something. And we've got to keep her grounded, especially now with things coming to a head. The same goes for Shannon. Miles is different. He thinks like a computer. So he'll be okay with us, as long as Ryan is in the IT driver's seat."

Emma paused only to suck in a breath before plunging on. "I figured this would give me time tonight to pick your brain and get your instructions on what to say and what not to say. You guys could keep working on your plan while I provide diversionary tactics with our clients. I'm sorry if I screwed up, but it was all I could think of when Lisa started grilling me."

To Emma's surprise, Casey began to laugh. "In some convoluted, Emma-like way, that actually makes sense and is a good idea," she said. "Plus, you were really put on the spot, and you thought on your feet like a pro. You're a handful, Emma Stirling, but I'm proud of you."

Emma blinked. That was the last thing she'd expected. But she'd take it. Casey's approval meant the world to her.

"I'd rather do this training session in person," Casey continued. "We're all here, so you'll have comprehensive prep. Can you come back to the brownstone now? I realize you're operating on empty."

"No problem. I'll just swallow my pasta, throw on my running gear, and jog over."

Slava's flight landed late, thanks to the usual delays at O'Hare. That fucking airport had one of the worst stopover ratings in the country, which sucked, since everyone and his brother flew in and out on a minute-by-minute basis. Plus, the weather had been foul, and the drenching rains had delayed the flights even further.

Normally, he would have been jumping out of his skin. But this time, he'd used the hours to think and to plan. He'd already contacted Alexei and Vitaliy and arranged to meet them in a deserted area of Newark down by the Passaic River at five a.m. Thanks to the positive tone he'd taken, the assholes assumed this was an important follow-up meeting that had to be held in private. Just as well. Their misconception would make Slava's job that much easier. He'd just bring the physical tools he needed. He already had the skills. For years, he'd used them. But, at this point in his life, his role as a cleaner was only accessed on rare occasions, primarily because he wasn't operating with the backing of the Russian government. If he were caught, he'd be on his own. So hiring others to do the killing was a far better option.

Still, he missed the days when he was the one doing the fieldwork.

He'd have his chance now. Once he'd finished his role as the cleaner, he'd take Alexei's and Vitaliy's newly repainted and re-license-plated van and be on his way. They sure as hell wouldn't be needing it. He'd drive straight to Upper Montclair. He'd scope out the apartment and the gym, subtly and expertly, and see what kind of security was on his targets. He could smell an operative, be it CIA, FBI, police, or a spy, a mile away. The KGB had trained him in how to spot them and, if need be, how to neutralize them. He'd take photos and have Max run them. They'd know who they were dealing with in short time.

All threats would be eliminated.

All the lights in the Forensic Instincts brownstone were shining brightly as the team wrapped up their Emma prepping.

Scribbling furiously on her third sheet of paper, Emma finally finished taking notes. She put down her pen and sank back in the conference room chair, gazing around the table at the team. They all looked like hell. After countless hours of brainstorming—with countless more to come—they were physically exhausted and mentally spent, and yet they'd taken two hours with her to lay out her dos and don'ts.

"Wow. I feel like I've been prepped for battle," she said, glancing down at her pages.

"That's because you have," Casey responded frankly. "We're reaching the end goal here. Everything we do has to go as perfectly as possible, or lives could be lost."

Claire shifted uneasily in her chair. "I can't shake the feeling that that's true," she murmured. "And every time you bring it up, the aura gets stronger. I know we're moving toward converging on Maxim Lubinov. He and his fortress conjure up an overwhelming sensation of death. Whatever plan we come up with has to be flawless."

"That's the goal." Patrick rubbed the back of his neck, trying to ease the taut muscles that were screaming for a hot shower.

"We won't be leaving this room until we do," Marc added. He was holding up better than the others. His days as a SEAL had trained him for this kind of sleepless, pressure-filled work. His gaze was still alert, and his stance was still taut. A few forehead creases were the only signs he showed of the frustration he was feeling over not yet having come up with the ideal plan.

"I feel guilty going home to sleep," Emma said.

"Don't be." Casey waved that thought away. "You need some rest. You have to be on all day tomorrow. And you have to inspire confidence in our clients. If you look like something the cat dragged in, they're going to assume there's trouble. They might take off, which would create a lot more of a mess out of all this."

"Yeah," Ryan agreed. "Casey's right. You have to handle Lisa and Shannon and keep them calm. And remember what I said: tell them to have Miles call me with any questions, worries, or whatever that he has. I'll make them go away."

Emma nodded.

Claire reached over and took Emma's hand. "Stop feeling guilty. You're doing your job, the same way we are. Yours starts in the morning. Ours continues tonight. So preserve your strength. You'll need it."

"You can feel a little guilty if you want," Ryan amended. He was indisputably the crankiest member of the FI team when he sacrificed his sleep. "The only two team members who get any shut-eye tonight are you and Hero."

Hearing his name, Hero picked up his head and woofed.

"You said it, boy." Ryan gave the bloodhound a sage nod.

"The difference is that, when Hero doesn't sleep, he takes it like a man," Marc noted dryly.

"Very funny."

"Not meant to be."

"Enough, guys." Casey was in no mood for their ornery banter. Right now, she was totally focused on Emma. "Let me hear the overall premise you need to convey tomorrow," she instructed her. "Make it frank and direct."

Emma didn't even glance at her notes. She just interlaced her fingers on the table and met Casey's gaze.

"I'm explaining to Lisa that we now believe that Shannon was part of a big medical experiment involving numerous targets and designer PEDs. Shannon was just one of many. We're on the brink of figuring out who's at the helm and who that person has working for him or her, doing things like the attempted kidnapping, the surveillance, etc. It'll only be a matter of days. Then it will all be over and they'll be safe."

"Good girl." Casey gave her a supportive smile. "Concise. Optimistic. Honest. And with just enough new information to satisfy their need to feel included. You'll do great."

"Casey," Patrick inserted, "if you can spare me for a few hours, I can personally drive Emma to Upper Montclair, keep an eye on her, and then drive her back."

"No way." Emma didn't wait for Casey's response. She just blurted out her words—and then thought better of it when she saw the expression on Casey's face.

"I'm sorry," she said, looking from Casey to Patrick. "That sounded awful. Patrick, you're awesome. But, with all due respect, that idea is a mistake. Whoever's watching our clients—seeing me roll up in a car with New York plates, driven by a guy who smacks of FBI, and who acts as my babysitter? I'm supposed to be a friend and a fellow gym rat. I've got to keep up that image, not raise red flags."

"She's not wrong, Patrick." Ryan lent her some support. "Now that Lubinov knows we're on to RusChem, he's bound to have his best guys on the surveillance beat. Emma's got to look like a regular person. If they suspect she's a PI or any other kind of threat, she'll be in more danger than she will be going this alone."

Patrick frowned, clearly torn between instincts and logic.

"You can assign one of your security guys to watch me when I'm in Upper Montclair," Emma suggested.

"I'll do better than that." Patrick leaned back and folded his arms across his chest. He wasn't backing down. "I'll have my guy ride the same trains as you. He'll keep his distance. But he'll also keep you in his sights."

"I like that idea." Casey rose, going over to pour herself another cup of coffee. "That's how we'll do it."

"But…" Emma began.

"No arguments." Casey shot Emma a no-nonsense look as she returned to her chair at the head of the table. "You're not winging this alone. It's Patrick's way or no way."

"Fine." Emma slumped in her seat, but she didn't push Casey any further.

Casey resettled herself, taking two long sips of hot, black coffee, which shot the ongoing and essential burst of caffeine into her system. "And while we're addressing the rules, remember, I want you back at the office by four o'clock, before the serious rush hour traffic begins. That's more than enough time to spend with Lisa and Shannon. We need you here."

"I have to make a few calls," Patrick told Emma. "But I'll text you the name, specs, and photo of the security guy I assign to you. You'll have the information within the hour. Memorize it—especially the photo—and call on him if anything seems off or if you feel like you're being watched. No foolish heroics."

"I promise," Emma replied. She might be irked by the restrictions, but the flipside was nice. She now had a new family who actually cared about her.

# CHAPTER THIRTY-FOUR

Vitaliy and Alexei were cut up into pieces and dissolved in acid before Slava returned to his hotel to check out and head to Upper Montclair. No more sloppy bullshit burials, like the one he'd done with Jim Robbins. Max was too fucking worried about extreme, time-consuming measures translating into capture. The truth was that acid eliminated evidence. Exhumed bodies told secrets. But Max had no experience with this kind of thing. Beneath his self-imposed ruthless exterior, he was nothing more than an inventor. Slava was a born killer.

The Passaic River had washed the last of Vitaliy's and Alexei's blood off his hands and arms. He'd yanked off his red-splattered T-shirt and soaked it in the river, as well. Then, he'd pulled on a casual sweater. His jeans were dark, so any trace of blood he'd missed would blend in with the denim and never be noticed.

He'd climbed into the van and driven back to his hotel, where he'd carefully showered away any last vestiges of the murders. He packed the sweater, T-shirt, and jeans in a plastic bag, which he shoved into his suitcase, donning a store-bought business suit before checking out. He scowled down at himself. The clothing wasn't his taste. Everything he wore was custom-made, with style and flair. But it was imperative that he blend in with the crowd. And wearing this boring gray thing with its equally boring striped tie would ensure that no one remembered him.

He reached West Orange, New Jersey, as planned, making a few phone calls along the way to issue orders and ensure that his replacements for Alexei and Vitaliy were already stationed and doing active surveillance. Everything was in order. He'd expected no less. This time, he'd done the hiring. And the men he'd hired were skilled and hard-core. They didn't make mistakes.

He checked into the Best Western he'd preselected using a pseudonym and the corresponding fake credit card. The place was as close to Upper Montclair as he could get without upgrading to a fancier hotel. It was about twenty minutes away by car and was large enough and populated enough for him to fly under the radar. He normally preferred first-class accommodations, but he wasn't here for a vacation.

Traveling light—one suitcase and a suit bag—he got to his room and put out the Do Not Disturb sign before flipping the deadbolt. Carefully, he hung up his suit bag. His suitcase he simply tossed onto one of the double beds. He was tired and he was hungry. It was barely eight o'clock. His men were in place. He had time for a power nap and a big breakfast.

Then it would be time to get to work.

The train slowed and then finally pulled into the Upper Montclair station.

Emma rose and slung her gym bag over her arm. She was relieved to be here but a little nervous about the job ahead. She was a hell of an actress, but this was the real deal, not some con job. Like Casey said, there were lives at stake.

Patrick's linebacker security guy, Brian Mason, had already closed his iPad, tucked it under his arm, and was ready to exit the train behind her. He'd been her shadow from the time she'd boarded the subway at Grand Street in Chinatown to the time she'd arrived at Penn Station and hopped the Montclair-Boonton line to Upper Montclair, to now, when she was about to disembark. He'd seated himself several rows back and diagonally across from her—a respectable distance away but one that could be spanned in a matter of seconds if need be. For the forty-plus minutes that they'd been on the train, he'd barely moved a muscle, ostensibly scrolling through something on his iPad throughout the trip. Emma wasn't fooled. Every ounce of his attention had been focused on her. No one else would ever pick up on it; he was just that subtle.

Patrick never hired anyone but the best.

Emma stepped off the platform and gave a causal glance behind her to ensure that Brian was there. Of course, he was. She then began her short stroll, skirting around Bellevue Plaza until she hit the main drag and making her way the couple of blocks to Excalibur.

Lisa was wrapping up an aerobics class when Emma walked in. Still, she spotted Emma immediately, and her whole face lit up. She couldn't finish her group's cooldown stretches fast enough.

Emma grinned at her, then perched at the desk and waited. Brian was somewhere right outside the building. Idly, Emma wondered if he was wearing a Lycra outfit under his polo shirt and slacks, all prepped to burst into Excalibur and participate, if need be. The image almost made her dissolve into giggles. She knew he'd stay outside and watch the gym like a hawk. Still, the vision amused her enough to ease some of the tension from her body.

While she waited, she looked around the bustling gym,

taking in the extensive and pricy equipment, inviting décor, and diverse activities going on—not to mention the dozens of members filling the place. Lisa and Miles had gone all out with Julie's inheritance. This place was incredible. Kudos to them.

"Hey." Lisa appeared at Emma's side, greeting her as she wiped her face and neck with a towel. As casual as her motions were, the tension emanating from her body was palpable—as was her relief regarding Emma's presence. There were stress lines etched across her forehead and dark circles under her eyes.

"Hi," Emma replied, giving her a quick hug. "I love your gym. It's awesome."

"Thanks." A hint of a smile. "We busted our asses to make it the go-to place in Upper Montclair. I'm proud of the outcome." Lisa sucked in her breath. Clearly, the virtues of Excalibur were not the main thing on her mind right now. "Spin class starts in twenty minutes. Can we grab a couple of bottles of water and hang out in my office till then?"

"Great." Emma was glad to be getting Lisa alone for a while—but not for the same reasons Lisa had in mind. No heavy conversation. Not now. The poor woman was a wreck. It was time for some nonsensical girl talk, a little bit of information and words of reassurance, and the promise that they'd get into an in-depth update when they got back to the apartment, so that Miles and Shannon could be in on the talk, as well.

Mentally, Emma reviewed the notes she'd taken, along with Casey's instructions. Provide enough details to ensure peace of mind. The process would be like peeling back the layers of an onion. Start with the topical stuff. Pare slowly down to the heavier-duty data. And stop when your eyes started watering. Never forget that this was a need-to-know mission. Nothing about Maxim Lubinov or RusChem or the magnitude of the threat to their lives could be mentioned. Only the broader, more general realities, accompanied by a slightly more in-depth explanation.

Girding her loins, Emma took the bottle of water Lisa hand-ed her and followed her into the back room that was her office.

"Sit." Lisa shut the door behind her and gestured at one of the soothing-toned aqua chairs positioned across from her desk. She took the adjacent chair, rather than using the one behind her desk. Clearly, she was opting to talk without the barrier of a large, solid object between them. It was hard enough to have a normal conversation with the combined sounds of blasting music and pounding feet emanating from outside her office walls. No point in adding distance and formality.

Emma sat down, grinning as she sank into the buttery soft leather. "Wow. These are awesome. But comfort? In a gym? I thought we were supposed to suffer, nonstop."

Lisa managed a small smile. "Not at Excalibur. The ex-perience is supposed to be adrenaline-pumping—and, yeah, somewhat body-pushing—but upbeat and addictive. My goal is always for clients to leave feeling great about themselves and the world." Her smile vanished. "Maybe it's my way of giving them a feeling I'm totally lacking these days."

Emma felt a pang of sympathy and of admiration. Talk about coping with a positive spin. "It's going to be okay, Lisa." With a quick glance around, she amended, "Julie."

Grimacing, Lisa uncapped her bottle and took a gulp of water. "At this point, I don't even know who I am. I only know I'm caught in some terrifying trap, and I don't know how to escape."

"It's not your job to escape," Emma replied. "It's our job to give you back your freedom. And we will. We've got our FBI contact fully on board now. He's a get-it-done guy, just like the rest of us. I can't get into his exact role, because we owe him the same confidentiality we owe you. But he's got skills, contacts, and experience. Trust me—he's the best."

Emma stopped to take a healthy swallow of her own water, using that time to regroup. The outer layer of the onion had just been peeled away.

It was enough for now.

No surprise that Lisa had other ideas.

"Can you tell me *something* about this FBI agent and what he's doing on our case?" she asked, spreading her arms wide, palms turned up in frustration.

"Like I said, there's not much I'm at liberty to say." Emma shifted in her seat, gazing through the glass pane that separated Lisa's office from the rest of the gym. "Plus, I don't think we should get into anything heavy while we're here. Not only is our privacy limited but we only have fifteen minutes. I'd rather just hang out and then have some fun with you and this spin class. Afterwards, we can grab some takeout, head back to your apartment, and get into your concerns when we're all together. I promise I'll tell you everything I can. Okay?"

"I guess that works." Lisa sounded reluctant but resigned. "There's a great Chinese place a block away if you like Chinese."

"Like it? I'd kill for some General Tso's chicken. Add some great house special fried rice, an egg roll, and a super-hot guy to pay for it, and my life is complete."

Lisa began to laugh, and Emma gave herself a pat on the back. She knew that when she turned on her whole youthful enthusiasm thing, it was infectious. It also humanized her and inspired trust. She could already sense that Lisa's paranoia about being kept out of the loop was abating. Emma had to capitalize on that, not only with Lisa but with Shannon, as well.

"Oh, Emma, you're such a breath of fresh air," Lisa said. "I can't tell you how much this visit means to me."

"Enough to pay for General Tso's?" Emma's eyes were twinkling.

"I'm not a super-hot guy," Lisa reminded her.

"Oh, well. You can't have everything."

"No, you can't."

"But, hey, I'll settle for a free meal anytime."

A pained expression crossed Lisa's face, and Emma recognized it immediately. She herself had worn it many times, and it had nothing to do with the investigation. "It never completely goes away, does it?" Lisa murmured.

"The memory of being on the streets and grabbing anything you can because you're afraid it won't come around again—including something to fill your belly and make that horrible gnawing pain disappear?" Emma was right there with Lisa, connecting in a way that few others could. "No, it doesn't."

Lisa fidgeted with her water bottle. "Julie paid for my lunch the day I met her. She watched me wolf down a burger and fries like some kind of wild animal, and she knew my whole resume was bullshit. What's worse, I knew that she knew, but I didn't care. I was just so hungry." Glancing up, Lisa met Emma's damp-eyed gaze. "She was very good to me, better than anyone had been in a long time. I relive that day, and the day she was killed, and I feel guilty all the time."

Emma reached over and squeezed Lisa's hand. "But now you know her death wasn't your fault. No one was after you. They were after her."

"I know." A pause, and Emma got the feeling that Lisa was about to say something she'd thought long and hard about.

Her next words proved Emma right. But their content stunned the hell out of her.

"When all this is over, I'm going to do the right thing." Lisa's tone was firm. "I'm not going to run. Neither is Milo. I'm going to give Julie back her identity, and all the respect that goes with it. Shannon isn't the only one who cared for her. Her other students, maybe a bunch of friends—they all did, too. She deserves to be mourned, not resented for taking off without a word. And, once Forensic Instincts exposes whoever's running this PED operation, Julie can be acknowledged for the brave and heroic woman she was."

Emma blinked. "Lisa," she blurted out. "You understand what that means for you, right? Leaving the scene of a crime is a felony. So is identity theft, stealing someone's inheritance..."

"And I'll probably go to jail for it all," Lisa interrupted to finish Emma's thought. "I know. But I won't go on living a lie. And I won't let the world keep thinking the worst of Julie. She didn't take off. She was murdered."

Before Emma could respond, a buzzer went off on Lisa's iPhone, and she rose from her chair. "Spin class time," she said, striving for a lighter tone. "Time for me to see what you've got."

## CHAPTER THIRTY-FIVE

Slava had found a dirt alcove diagonally across from Julie Forman's apartment building, where he'd parked the van. The area was concealed by trees and scarcely noticeable. He settled himself behind the wheel and opened a newspaper, looking as if he were hanging out waiting for someone—which, in fact, he was.

He had three quarries: Julie Forman, Shannon Barker, and whatever security team was keeping an eye on them. His own new hires were hovering around the gym. They'd informed him that the Forman woman was inside. Now they'd wait, advising him immediately if she left.

So for now it was the Barker girl and the bodyguards he was looking for—more the latter than the former. He doubted the Barker kid would be coming out anytime soon. After nearly being kidnapped, she was probably quaking inside Forman's place. Plus, she probably didn't have any great insight into what she was being protected from. Feds, cops, and PIs weren't in the habit of briefing teenagers on anything more than the basics. At least one of them had to be armed and stationed either right outside or inside the apartment unit. There'd be another couple of them in or around the parking lot, keeping a watchful eye.

Not a challenge for Slava. He'd spot them. Analyze them. Pick out the weakest link. Then he'd wait until the guy was heading off for a break. He'd drag him into the van and use whatever methods of torture were necessary until he got his answers.

After that, he'd slit the guard's throat and take care of his body before reporting back to Max.

He hunched down in his seat and waited.

Forty-five minutes later, his plans changed.

A phone call from his guys told him that the Forman woman was on her way home. And she had a friend with her.

Surveilling the guards could wait. Something better was being delivered right into his hands. This was going to be one hell of a party.

Lisa was actually laughing as she and Emma approached the apartment. They were carrying bags of tantalizing-smelling Chinese food, and Emma had her backpack slung over her arm. She was telling Lisa a story about when she was a kid and had bitten into one end of an eggroll, squirting its contents all over the waiter.

"I'd never tasted an eggroll before," she was saying. "How did I know it was filled with so much stuff, or that the shell was so breakable?" She wrinkled her nose. "It blew out of the back end like a cannonball. The waiter stumbled backwards, then slipped and fell. He was okay—he got up in one piece—but he was gritting his teeth and spitting out words in Chinese. I'm sure he was swearing at me. Anyway, my parents didn't punish me, but we never went back to that place again. I guess we weren't welcome."

"Yeah, I'd guess not," Lisa agreed.

Both women dissolved into giggles as they walked through the parking lot and into the apartment building.

*That fucking, fucking bitch.*

Slava's entire body was coiled with rage. It pounded through his body, coursed through his blood. He could barely see past it.

But he'd seen enough.

He'd known her the instant he saw her, even in her workout clothes, carrying that ridiculous backpack. And that voice—how could he forget it? It had haunted his dreams and heated his loins since she'd promised to call him, walked out of the building, and disappeared off the grid.

No one deceived him like this. No one. He was too smart to be taken in by a slut who was really a cop. But he'd been thinking with his dick, not his brain. He'd bought her coffee. She'd walked out with the cup and probably his DNA. She knew who he was and what he was.

Well, he was about to know a hell of a lot more than her name.

Fuck the surveillance. Fuck the Forman woman and the Barker girl. Fuck all his strategic plans.

He was getting his hands on *Isabella.*


The Chinese food was consumed in record time.

As they ate, Emma explained to Lisa, Miles, and Shannon where things stood on the case—precisely the way Casey had told her to. She started with the fact that Shannon was part of a big medical experiment involving designer PEDs and a whole bunch of targets. Quickly, she reassured them that FI was on the brink of uncovering the mastermind who was orchestrating the whole operation, along with whoever he had working for him—and that included not just Shannon's attempted kidnappers and those surveilling them but the Jim Robbinses all over the country, who were the reapers of this medical experiment.

Emma finished her update by giving her word to Lisa, Miles, and Shannon that this nightmare would be over in days, not weeks, after which they'd all be safe.

Of course they had questions. They wanted details about the monster running the show, about precisely how Forensic Instincts planned on bringing him down, and about how their mysterious FBI contact fit into the picture.

Emma deflected the questions by stressing the sensitivity of the situation and the need to keep them safe by telling them as little as possible.

"Trust me," she said with her customary frankness. "I've never lied to you, steered you wrong, or placated you—and I'm not doing any of that now. I'm helping my team put an end to this. Please, let us do our job. Once it's over and you're safe, I'll personally tell you every single outstanding detail."

"Emma, you know how I feel about you." Lisa shoved aside her empty plate and shook her head. "I trust you implicitly. But it's *our* lives that are at stake. We have the right to know everything—*now*, not later."

"Leave it, Lis." Miles surprised Emma by stepping in and helping her cause. He looked deeply pensive, staring at Emma as if focusing in on her thoughts and succeeding in reading them. "Forensic Instincts is afraid that, if we know the whos and the whats of the situation, we'll jump in and do something stupid that could jeopardize their entire plan. And, given our mental states, they're probably right."

He turned to meet Lisa's frightened gaze. "Think about it." He put a soothing hand on her arm. "Can you swear that if you knew who all the players were you'd just sit still and stay put? I know I couldn't."

Lisa's gaze faltered. "I... No," she admitted. "I couldn't make that promise." She squeezed her eyes shut, and there were tears shimmering on her lashes when she opened them. "I just want this to be over."

"And it will be." Emma was speaking to Lisa. But she was watching Shannon in her peripheral vision. The young girl was openly weeping, her body trembling with fear.

Instinctively, Emma reached over and gripped Shannon's hands. "Don't be afraid, Shannon. No one will hurt you again. You're safe here. And soon you'll be able to stop living like a prisoner. I promise."

"I just want to go home." Shannon's choked words reminded them all that, despite her maturity and bravado, she was still a sixteen-year-old girl who had been pushed beyond her limits. "I miss my family. I miss my friends. I want to be normal again." A sob escaped her. "As normal as I can be with the damage that's been done to my body and the stuff I've gone through."

"You'll go back to seeing that great therapist you said you were visiting right after your accident—the one Julie referred you to," Lisa said, her attention shifting from her own unease to Shannon's. "Dr. Hawke, right? She was helping you a lot. She'll help you now. You'll get through this. We all will."

"I guess." Shannon took a huge shuddering breath.

"We have a bond, Shannon, one that's formed by going through a life crisis together." Lisa reached over to tuck a hair behind Shannon's ear, giving her a small smile. "That's not going away. Miles and I are your friends for life."

Shannon managed a smile in return. She dashed away her tears and even finished the last of her fried rice.

"Okay, enough drama. Subject closed." Emma popped up and began clearing the table. "I came here today for two reasons—one, to fill you in, which I just did. And, two, to spend some fun time together." She pointed at her backpack. "I brought some mindless DVDs with me. Plus I just downloaded some new apps on my iPad—games we can play against each other." She arched a brow in Miles' direction. "I expect you to cut us some slack. If you start winning every game, I'm taking away your iPad and tossing your iPhone out the window."

A broad grin spread across Miles' face. "As long as you pre-acknowledge my superiority, I'll agree to that."

Emma rolled her eyes, turning off the kitchen faucet. "You sound just like Ryan; it's nauseating." That made her remember Ryan's offer. "By the way, while this big reveal is going on, Ryan said you could contact him with any questions you have. I guess he figures great minds should stick together."

Miles looked relieved and pleased. "Thanks, Emma—for the offer and the compliment. It's good to know that Ryan's got my back."

"We all do." Emma picked up her backpack and dumped out the DVDs. "Okay, Shannon, you get first pick."


Across the street from the building, Slava stared at the apartment window, his eyes still blazing. If anything, his rage had intensified as the couple of hours had passed.

It had taken him about ten minutes to figure out who the security detail was on Isabella. The guy had been following her and the Forman woman—a respectable distance away—as they arrived at the apartment building. And he'd been perched on a nearby bench ever since—talking on his cell phone, working on his tablet, scrolling through some fascinating material. All amateur bullshit to Slava. The guy reeked of law enforcement. When the time came, Slava would have to put him out of commission. Temporary, permanent—it didn't matter. Whatever was quicker. Screw the interrogations. Screw his orders from Max. He was burning to get his hands around that fucking bitch's throat.

Her throat and a whole lot more.

It was after three o'clock, and Emma remembered her promise to Casey. Be back at four. *Gotcha, boss.*

With hugs all around, she shoved all the things she'd brought into her backpack, gave her promise to call the second things were over, and headed out.

She said a quick good-bye to Patrick's security detail, posted just inside and outside of the apartment, and left the building. She trekked through the parking lot, spotting Brian casually reading on the sidewalk bench. She had no doubt he was totally aware of her and of the time. He'd wait for her to cross the street and then follow her to the train station and back to the Forensic Instincts brownstone.

Without so much as glancing in his direction, she looked to the left and to the right. The street was empty. No traffic. Great.

She stepped into the road.

Slava had turned the van's ignition key the instant he'd spotted her leaving the building. Now he remained, hunched down, waiting for the exact moment he needed.

There it was.

Isabella was three-quarters of the way across the street. Her guard had risen to follow. Slava eased the van out of its alcove. The guy took one step. Then two. Then he was off the sidewalk and into the street. Three steps more and he was too far from the curb to jump back to safety.

Slava floored the gas.

He saw the stunned expression on the man's face as the van plowed into him, sending his body crashing into the windshield and then careening off to the roadside, where he lay, unmoving.

Isabella spun around, her backpack toppling to the sidewalk as her hands flew up to her face and she let out a voiceless scream.

The rest happened in a burst of activity.

Slava swerved the van over and leapt out. Grabbing Isabella around the waist, he clamped his big hand over her mouth. He flung her into the van, shoved her aside as he jumped back into the driver's seat, and screeched off.

He watched her struggle to a sitting position, his expression smug as he waited for her to see who her kidnapper was.

Recognition was immediate.

Her eyes found him, and they grew round with shock and fear.

Slava's smile was pure evil, his Russian accent thick. "Hello, Isabella. It is time for that date we never had."

## CHAPTER THIRTY-SIX

Marc and Ryan were arguing over strategy, and Claire was fidgeting in her seat with some inner growing agitation when Patrick's cell phone rang.

"Yes, John," he answered. Frowning, he covered his other ear with his palm. "Speak up. I can barely hear you, it's so loud. What the hell is going on there?" A pause, and Patrick lurched off the chair, firing questions into the phone. "Mowed down? What's his condition? What about... He took her? Did you get the van's license plate? Is there anything left on the scene but the backpack?" Another pause. "I'm assuming Mountainside Hospital? I'm leaving now. I'll meet you there. If there's a medical assessment before I show up, find out when he'll be up to talking." All eyes were on Patrick as he slammed down his phone.

"Slava Petrovich got to Emma," he said, his expression grim. "He ran down Brian and took Emma right off the street. Brian's in an ambulance on his way to the local hospital. And Emma is...gone."

"Oh my God." Claire's hands flew up to her face. "I knew it. I felt it."

"How do you know for certain it was Slava?" Ryan demanded.

"John witnessed the scene from inside the apartment. He heard the screech of tires and got to the window in time to see a man matching Slava's description grab Emma, shove her into a van, and speed off. Brian was bleeding in the road. John called 911 and got down to the street ASAP. Brian was breathing but unconscious. John is in the ambulance with him now. The EMTs are working on him. And Emma…" Patrick rubbed a palm over his jaw, looking as if he were going to be sick.

"Shit." Marc's mind was racing. "Slava must have been scoping out the area near the apartment. Emma probably walked there from the gym with Lisa. Slava would have made Emma as Isabella the minute he saw her."

"And that will make him go crazy," Claire whispered. "He won't care about any orders he's received. He won't even care about Lisa and Miles anymore. He'll be irrational. His rage will take over." Tears had already formed in Claire's eyes. She steepled her icy fingers together and looked directly at Casey. "Slava will torture her, Casey. He'll…" Her voice trailed off. She and Casey had both been there. They knew what brutal assailants did to their victims. And a former KGB agent? God only knew what he was capable of.

"We're heading up to Vermont." Casey was already on her feet, her customarily steady demeanor gone. Her voice was quavering, and her body language screamed fear. "We're getting into Maxim Lubinov's compound. Screw the legalities."

"Casey, wait." Marc reached out and grabbed her arm. "Let's take a rational breath. We don't even know for sure that Slava took Emma to Burlington. He might be keeping her local while he reaches out to his boss. They might be discussing using her as a bargaining chip to get to whoever she's working with—us."

"'Might' doesn't cut it, Marc."

"I agree. That's why we need to divide and conquer, not

all jump in the van and race up to New England. Rescuing Emma is all that matters. We have to cover all our bases to do that."

He waited until Casey regained a modicum of control and gave him a tight nod. "What do you suggest? I'm not rational on this one," she said.

"Like I said, I suggest we divide up and close off Slava's options." Marc understood that Casey was asking him to run the show, something she rarely did. But he was her go-to guy, and she was a mess. Right now, she needed his level head.

He naturally assumed the command and control that was pure Marc, the former Navy SEAL. "You, Claire, and Patrick will stay behind," he instructed. "Your various skills are needed here." He angled his head in Patrick's direction. "You deal with the situation in Upper Montclair—the cops, John, Brian, the hospital—until you get some answers and, hopefully, find out if Slava is holding Emma nearby."

"Consider it done," Patrick replied.

"Bring Hero with you when you go to Upper Montclair," Casey added. "He'll be an asset."

Hero's head came up, and he scrambled to his feet, as if knowing he was being called upon.

Reflexively, Casey stroked his head. "He knows Emma's scent. We have more than enough of her things for me to make scent pads. Whatever trail turns up, Hero will follow—with God's help, directly to Emma."

"Excellent idea." Patrick gave Hero the hand gesture to follow him. "I'll make the scent pads. I'll be in constant contact with all of you."

"Make sure of that," Casey said. She watched them leave, her wheels turning and her leadership skills kicking in. She knew what Marc was about to say, and she knew he was right. So she said it for him.

"I'm calling Hutch right now and getting the FBI ball rolling. We needed proof? Now we have it. And Claire..." A quick glance in her direction. "Do anything you can to pick up on Emma's energy. Use it to figure out where she is."

Claire rose. "I'll find a way. I have to. I need to go downstairs and get a few personal items out of her desk. Then I'll hole up in my yoga room, where I have the serenity and clarity of mind to focus completely on Emma." Emanating determination, Claire was off on her mission.

"Am I missing anything?" Casey asked Marc.

"Nope. We're set." He was now in SEAL mode. "Let's go, Ryan. I'm getting my gear together, and we're leaving for Vermont. Bring whatever techno-stuff is necessary. And I'm calling Aidan from the road. We need him on this."

Ryan was shutting down his computer and gathering up the equipment that went with it. "The rest of what I need is in my lair. I'll grab it and meet you at the van." He paused, visibly bugged by something.

"What is it?" Casey demanded.

"Don't call Hutch. The last thing we need is a SWAT team bursting into Lubinov's compound and screwing everything up. We can pull this one off fast and clean, without FBI interference."

"Forget it, Ryan," Casey responded in a tone that told him it wasn't happening his way. "I'm calling Hutch now. He can reach out to the appropriate field office and put them on standby. As soon as we have confirmation that Emma's in Lubinov's manor, SWAT can go in. I want you to work with them. No vigilante bullshit. I want Emma in one piece and Lubinov's entire crime ring put away."

"And if we get there first and somehow figure out she's inside—before the FBI's red tape has allowed them to act?"

"We'll cross that bridge when we come to it."

Anyone standing in the lobby of the Best Western would have pegged Slava as an ardent lover rather than a kidnapper and a killer. He guided Emma along, keeping her slightly in front of him, one of his arms wrapped intimately around her shoulders, the other arm tucked subtly behind her, hidden from view. The sharp blade of his knife was pressed into the small of her back, ensuring that she didn't make a sound.

He kept up the charade until he'd maneuvered her up the stairs, down the hall, and safely into his hotel room. Once he'd double-locked the door, everything changed.

He put down the knife. Whirling Emma around, he grabbed a handful of her hair and used it to yank her head back—so hard that tears came to her eyes and her mouth dropped open. Before she could cry out, Slava snatched one of the linen napkins folded near the takeout menu on the side table and crammed it into her mouth. With one huge hand, he locked her wrists behind her back and dragged her across the room to the bed. He backhanded her across the face, first once, then twice, sending her toppling onto the bed, red bruises already forming on her cheeks.

Before she could recover, Slava had pushed her high enough up on the bed to accomplish his goal. He yanked off his belt and bound her wrist to one of the bedposts. He used a pillowcase to do the same to her other wrist. He spread her legs wide, shoving each foot between the bed frame and the bed, wedging them in so tightly that there was no wrenching them free.

Emma was weeping now, choked sobs that were stifled by the gag. Her eyes were huge, filled with dread, and her breasts were rising and falling with the force of her breath. Her stare was on Slava, and there must have been a plea in her gaze, because his next words crushed it to bits.

"Save your tears, dear *Isabella*." His broken English

was more than adequate for what he had in mind. His lips twisted into a cruel, triumphant smile as he stood back to admire his handiwork and revel in Emma's primal fear. "We've just gotten started."

He walked over and retrieved his knife, returning to kneel between her legs. He leaned forward, holding the blade to her throat. Ever so slightly, he nicked the delicate skin there and was rewarded with a few drops of blood and a muffled whimper.

He captured the blood with his fingertips, holding it up for Emma to see. Then he reached down to wipe the droplets across her lips, first her upper one and then her lower one.

"Gag is coming out," he said. "Taste blood. Answer questions. If you scream or talk, except to answer me, I'll slit your throat and you bleed to death. Nod if you understand."

Emma nodded.

"Good." He reached into her mouth and yanked out the gag.

Emma winced as the gag was torn from her mouth. She stayed rigid and didn't make a sound, unsure of what to do—or not to do—to avoid retaliation. Her heart was pounding so hard it hurt. So did the skin at her throat, where Slava had pricked it. She had never known white-hot panic like this. Then again, she fully realized what this animal had planned. What would come first? The torture? The rape? The murder would be last, after he'd dragged as much information out of her as he could.

She should tell him nothing except to go fuck himself. She should spit in his face. She should be the ballsy girl she always was.

She couldn't do or be any of those things.

She was so scared. Of all of it. Most of all, she didn't want to die. Oh, God, she didn't want to die.

"Lick your lips," Slava ordered her. "Taste blood."

Emma obeyed, gagging at the iodine flavor and praying for a miracle she knew wasn't coming. Brian could be dead. No one knew where Slava had taken her. Even FI had no starting point from which to initiate a trace. They couldn't find her.

It was over.

She flinched as Slava rose from between her legs, her gaze following him over to the nightstand, where he poured a glass of water and shoved it against her mouth. "Drink so you can talk."

Emma hesitated. She wasn't sure she could get down the water, much less hold it down.

"Drink or I hold your nose and pour it down your throat until you choke."

She had to do this.

Closing her lips around the rim of the glass, Emma took a few tentative sips and finally what she prayed would be an acceptable swallow. She forced the water down past the lump in her throat. Then, she lay back and waited.

"Good." Slava set down the glass and returned to his kneeling position between her legs. His eyes were black with rage, their depths empty, devoid of humanity.

"Your name," he commanded. "Your *real* name."

"Emma." Was that gravelly sound really her voice?

"Emma what?"

"Emma Stirling."

"Well, Emma Stirling, you picked wrong person to fuck with. No, maybe not in all ways," he amended, considering his choice of words. The look in his eyes changed to lust, as he sat back and studied her body, taking in every inch of her.

Emma's insides turned to ice. She knew the customary Lycra workout clothes she was wearing clung to her figure—all she wanted now was to be swallowed up by an oversized T-shirt and baggy sweatpants.

"Nice," Slava commented, his lips twisting into a cruel smile. "Very nice. Maybe I put the gag back in for now. Talk can wait."

Emma gritted her teeth as he reached for it, locking her mouth shut. Simultaneously, she tugged frantically at the bonds around her wrists. Her primal instinct was to fight. She knew it wouldn't help. It would probably make things worse. But she couldn't help it. She was fighting for her life.

"Lie still." Slava pressed an elbow into her stomach until her head rolled with pain and she went still. "Now open your mouth or I open it for you." The massive fists at his sides told Emma there'd be no contest.

She obeyed his order.

"Good. Now, first I take what you offered in Chicago. But different. No pleasure. Pleasure would have been for Isabella. Pain is for Emma Stirling." Another cruel smile. "But much pleasure for me."

He stuffed the napkin back into her mouth. Flourishing the knife, he began to cut her Lycra top and sports bra, starting just above her breasts and slicing downward until he'd reached her waist. Then, he peeled back the layers and stared at her naked breasts.

"Beautiful," he said, ignoring the way Emma shrunk as far into the mattress as she could. "Just like I knew." He cupped both breasts in his huge palms, and Emma swallowed back her vomit.

He bent to take a nipple in his mouth. Emma cringed, squeezing her eyes shut.

Slava's cell phone rang. He ignored it, lowering his head until Emma could feel his hot breath against her skin.

The phone kept ringing, over and over, stopping only to start ringing again.

Slava angled his head to see the caller ID and then leaned over to grope at the nightstand, muttering a few choice words in his native tongue. Emma didn't have to know Russian to know he was swearing.

A temporary reprieve.

Bless whoever was on the other end of that call.

## CHAPTER THIRTY-SEVEN

Slava kept one of his hands clamped on Emma's breast, furious that Max was calling right now. All he needed was an hour, *one hour*, with this gorgeous bitch, and he'd be sated. He'd have taken all her body had to offer and then some. He'd have punished her in ways that excited him even further. And he'd have oozed every ounce of pleasure out of his body and every ounce of life out of hers.

One fucking hour.

Why was Max calling? He knew that Slava had landed, checked into his hotel, and was surveying the necessary areas in Upper Montclair. He also knew that Slava didn't like—or need—anyone to check up on him. So what the hell did he want?

Snatching up the cell phone, he answered in Russian, his voice rough, gravelly, and pissed. "I'm busy."

"Whatever you're doing to her, it stops now," Max commanded.

"How...?"

"One of your new flunkies called me. He was trying to reach you for further instructions. He saw you take the girl, and he assumed you were on your way up here, which is exactly where you should be."

"I'll leave soon."

"You'll leave *now*. My private jet's already on its way. It'll land in Morristown, New Jersey in less than an hour. Get yourself to the airport and get on that plane—*with* the girl, who'd better be intact."

"She's one of them."

"I assumed so. Which is the only thing that turns your blatant disregard for my orders into something I can live with. She's crucial to safeguarding my work and to ensuring my freedom *and* yours. So stop thinking with your dick, and think with your brain. We need to know everything she knows—and we need it before she's too traumatized to provide it. I'll do the interrogating. You'll provide the incentive. That part should entice you."

"Maybe." Slava's anger waned a bit. But not enough. He wanted absolute control over Emma Stirling's body and her life. "Let's say I do what you're asking and you get what you need. Then what?"

"Then she's yours. Do with her as you please. I don't give a damn. But for now, I need her alive, healthy, and talking. So get your hands and your instruments off of her. Tie her up, throw her in the van, and drive to the airport. Your reward will be as sweet as you want it to be."

Cupping Emma's breast, Slava pondered Max's promise and then reluctantly withdrew his hand. "Fine. But don't forget what I'm owed, or I'll be happy to remind you."

Hutch was beyond frustrated.

He'd been in solution mode since Casey had called and blurted out the details of the crisis with Emma. He'd burned up the phone lines, setting the process in motion by appealing to his ASAC, who'd called the ASAC in the Albany Division—the division that handled Vermont. As shit luck would have it, their SWAT team was out of town training. The SWAT supervisor was willing to call them back, brief them, and devise a tactical plan. Then, given that the United States district attorney would be prepping the warrants, they would travel to Lubinov's compound and be ready to move in. Hutch had stressed that this was exigent, but he knew that SWAT wouldn't budge without those warrants.

So, despite all his hard work, he was facing a brick wall that he knew Casey would refuse to accept.

It was time for a blowout with his stubborn, reckless girlfriend.

Casey answered on the first ring. "Finally," she said in greeting. "What do you have for me?"

"We're screwed on the make-it-happen-now front," Hutch stated bluntly. He went on to explain the dilemma they were facing. "So the wheels are in motion, but we're going to need some time."

"We don't have time," Casey countered. "Emma's life is on the line."

"You're not even sure she's in Burlington."

"I know the odds are good."

"You're waiting until the Bureau can get there."

"The hell I am."

Hutch slammed down his fist. "Dammit, Casey, you can't just—"

"Watch me. Marc and Ryan are already en route. That means they're hours ahead of the FBI. I'm giving them the go-ahead. If the SWAT team shows up first, they'll back down. If not, they're going in."

The line went dead before Hutch could respond.

Marc's conversation with Casey was a minute long.

With a terse sign-off, he disconnected the call and turned to Ryan, relaying Casey's orders.

Ryan nodded, flooring the gas just a tad more than he already was and speeding up the highway.

"Don't get a ticket," Marc instructed. "We can't afford the time, and we can't give an explanation."

"I've got my eye out for cops," Ryan replied. "But we've got to push it as much as we can."

Marc didn't argue. Instead, he picked up his iPhone and pressed a private number.

"Yup," Aidan answered. Abby's voice in the background told Marc that his brother was working at home.

"Black Hawk." Marc uttered the two words tersely.

There was a long pause at the other end. "Are you drunk?" Aidan finally asked.

"Not even a little."

"Black Hawk? Marc, we haven't played that game since we were kids."

The game in question was a Special Forces battle that two like-minded brothers had reveled in. Yes, it was fictional, but to them it was real, with hand-to-hand combat, military warfare, amphibious attacks, and tactical strategy that was pretty sophisticated for two boys of eight and eleven. Back then, they didn't know it would be their futures. They only knew that they loved playing it. When one of them said "Black Hawk," the game was on.

"Yes, I know," Marc replied. "But I need you to fast-forward it and come through for me now. It's urgent."

"Okay, I'm listening."

Marc laid out the entire situation to Aidan: Emma, her life-threatening circumstances, and the FBI's time constraints.

"The SWAT team won't reach her in time," he concluded. "So we have to. Ryan's with me. He'll pinpoint our targets. But it'll take the two of us—you and me—to pull this off."

Aidan's wheels were turning. "I'll need to get in touch with a Marine buddy of mine and call in a favor."

"Then do it. If we don't get to Emma in time, she'll be tortured, raped, and dead. You and I did military cross-training. We're in sync. I'll follow your lead. Just make this happen."

Aidan swore under his breath, and Marc knew exactly what he was thinking.

"We'll get it done before SWAT arrives," Marc said quietly. "Abby won't be caught in the crossfire of you being prosecuted. And capture is out of the question. You know how good we are. I promise you that Abby will never be left alone."

Aidan blew out a breath. "I'm all she has, Marc. She's my world—and I'm hers. You can't promise me shit." A pause. "Goddammit. I can't let Emma die. And you and Ryan can't do this without me."

"Exactly."

"This is the first and only time, Marc. Understood? Never again, and only because it's Emma."

"Heard loud and clear."

"I want Madeleine to stay with Abby. How soon can she get here?"

"I'm calling her now. She'll be there by the time you pack up your gear. She won't leave Abby's side until you walk back through your front door."

Aidan didn't doubt that. Madeleine was amazing with Abby, and his little princess adored her. "Okay," he said. "Let's do this."

"You know the coordinates of where we're headed," Marc said. "We're already an hour ahead of you, with four more to go.

We've got one stop to make in Burlington. Get on the road as soon as Maddy arrives. And let me know our meeting place after you make your phone calls."

Claire had been holed up in her yoga room for over two hours.

No matter how hard she tried, she couldn't seem to calm down enough to channel her energies where they needed to go.

She'd set the stage perfectly, shutting the blinds and turning on the room's low, soothing lights. She'd then seated herself in lotus position on her mat, placed Emma's things in front of her, and begun taking deep, cleansing breaths. She had to make this happen. But she also knew that what she was striving for couldn't be forced.

Finally, her mind shifted into that wide-open, ethereal place where white light dominated her being, and she knew she was ready.

Eyes closed, she allowed the energy to flow. She reached out, and her fingers found Emma's "emergency-hot-guy bag"—a faux suede pouch that held all the essentials Emma felt were necessary if a last-minute date opportunity arose.

Unzipping the pouch, Claire removed the shimmery pale peach lip gloss that Emma claimed went with everything. She unscrewed the top and pulled out the wand with the soft tip that was moistened with gloss.

Slowly, she slid the pad of her finger over it, feeling the sticky substance coat her skin.

Emma.

Her image slid into Claire's head and immediately took shape. Emma. Bound. Gagged. Crumpled on a leather seat. Crying. Hurting. Her body trying to curl into fetal position. Bruises on her face and at her wrists and ankles, where she was bound.

And the terror. It was overwhelming. Thoughts of torture and sexual assault and dying all crashing into Claire at once.

Oh, God, poor Emma. How much of that had happened already and how much was yet to be?

Claire shifted her concentration to Emma's surroundings—the tan leather seat and the tightly enclosed quarters.

It wasn't a room. It was small and contained. A cabin. Filled with noise. A loud, thrumming sound that pounded inside Claire's head. A motor? No, an engine.

Emma was on a plane—a plane bound for Burlington, Vermont.

She'd be there soon.

It was making its descent now—Claire could feel the pressure build in Emma's ears, see the tops of the lush green trees draw nearer. She didn't need to call on her gift to know that Emma was being taken to Maxim Lubinov's compound.

Marc and Ryan didn't have much time.

It was after nine o'clock on a moonless night when the FI van arrived in Burlington, and Marc and Ryan broke into the Department of Land Records in City Hall.

Quickly and efficiently, they used their flashlights to rifle through the file cabinets. Ryan's search of the tax records revealed the lot and block number of Lubinov's estate: Block 026-4, Lot 001. Quickly, they pulled the architectural plans for the buildings that made up Max's compound, spread the sheets out across a tabletop, and took pictures in rapid fire.

"We've got more than enough," Ryan said at last. "Let's get the hell out of here."

Marc nodded, already returning things to their proper spots and shutting the drawers and cabinets.

He and Ryan left the building, easing the door shut behind them until they heard the telltale click that signified it was locked. Then, they jumped into the van. Marc checked in with Aidan for the third time in the past few hours and carefully explained the plan to Ryan as he drove.

"Are you listening to me?" he demanded, seeing that Ryan was studying the photos.

"I'm listening. I've got my part down pat. No worries." A pause, as Ryan continued to pore over the diagrams. "The master bedroom suite is in the northwest corner of the manor," he murmured. "By the time you and Aidan are ready to move in, my guess is that that's where Lubinov will be."

"Which means our point of entry should be in the living quarters, not the sleeping quarters. Now we just need to figure out the most desolate area, and the one closest to the lake."

"Yup. That's why I'll be covering all our bases and leaving as little to chance as possible."

"Meaning?"

"Meaning I'm going to get as accurate a handle on where the most security is located before I let you two loose."

"And how do you plan to do that?"

"You'll see when we get there."

"Get where?" Marc's head snapped around. "We're meeting Aidan at the warehouse he instructed us to. Not on Lubinov's grounds. Remember?"

"I remember. But you and I are making a quick stop on Lubinov's turf. We've got the time. Aidan hasn't even gotten to Burlington yet. And I have some of my own recon to do. So when we get to the fork in the road about a mile down, veer left."

## CHAPTER THIRTY-EIGHT

The expansive grounds surrounding Lubinov's mansion were utterly dark and equally still. The house was secreted behind groves and groves of trees, set so far back from the road that it would be invisible to a passerby.

A perfect place for top-secret experimentation.

Marc maneuvered the van just inside the property line and into a hidden recess in the wooded area that was a considerable distance from the dwellings.

"Okay, Ryan, this is as far as we go. Whatever it is you have in mind, it better be fast, and it better be from here. I've indulged you because you swore you'd get crucial data for us. But this is where I draw the line."

"No sweat. I'll go the rest of the way by foot." Ryan had climbed into the back of the van and was rummaging around in his duffel bag. "Here," he announced.

Before Marc could continue his tirade, Ryan pulled out a bird-like drone with a broad wingspan and a brown underside.

"Is that an owl?" Marc asked.

"Sure is." Ryan grinned. "Meet Hooter—Bee's big brother in flight."

"Give me a break." Marc shook his head. "Only you

would think of naming your drone Hooter."

"Hey. Show some respect. Hooter is going to surveil Lubinov's property and take videos that will provide us with a map you and Aidan need to follow. He's a nighttime drone—no moon, no problem. And he has infrared video camera capability."

Ryan continued, as if Marc weren't thoroughly familiar with infrared technology from his night vision training.

"Infrared detects warm objects relative to their surroundings," he explained. "So humans and animals outside the house will show up as bright spots. Buildings, assuming they're warmer than their surroundings—pretty much a given at this time of night—will show up, as well. Most important, so will security guards, who, obviously, need to be avoided. Like I said, no moon, no problem."

"Thanks for the brush up course. Still, I have to admit I'm impressed with what you've built with your owl drone. Except for one caveat—distance. How close do you need to get for Hooter to do his job? Because, like I said, we're not moving in. We have no idea how much security is stationed on the grounds. Lubinov's not going to situate himself in such an isolated locale and then leave the place unguarded. If we thought he would, then Aidan and I wouldn't have devised such an elaborate plan to get inside the house. We'd just kick the door down and walk in."

"I won't have to get close to the buildings," Ryan replied. "Just close enough to use Hooter. Unlike Bee, he flies from a distance. Not to worry." He gathered up the drone and its controls. "He'll only have a few passes before he's noticed. So it's a good thing I made him as accurate as I did. Be back in a few minutes."

"I'm going with you," Marc said, unfastening his seat belt.

"That's not necessary."

"Yeah, it's necessary. You may be a tech genius, but you're an arrogant asshole. I'm a former Navy SEAL. SEAL outranks ego. You're only getting a little wiggle room. My lead. Our getting killed won't do Emma any good."

"Killed." Just tasting the word on his tongue seemed to give Ryan a cold dose of reality.

"Yes, Ryan, killed." Marc's jaw set. "Did you think we were watching some thriller movie? This is real. Now stop yammering, and let's get this done."

They stayed low to the ground and only went as far as Marc would allow.

Fortunately, it was far enough. Hooter soared over the mansion twice, did his job, and, ten minutes later, Ryan and Marc were back in the van and off the property.

Marc drove a half mile closer to where they were meeting Aidan, pulled over, and turned off the engine. Then, he and Ryan climbed into the back of the van and reviewed the videos. From what they saw, they drew a rough map of the property that was closest in proximity to the mansion—a map that included buildings and their estimated sizes.

The stable complex, situated about five hundred feet behind and to the side of the manor, was enormous. The infrared had picked up quite a bit of human and animal activity going on in that immediate area. Horses were being tended to in a corral, and a cluster of guards was posted at all the doors.

"Clearly, that's not just a bunch of stables, offices, and a veterinary clinic," Marc muttered, studying the massive rear buildings. "For security to be so tight, that's got to be where the PED experimentation is going on."

Ryan nodded. "The good part is that the manor itself has fewer guards than the stables do. It's obvious where Lubinov's focus is—on his work. That should make it a little easier for you and Aidan to get inside. They have to be holding her in a section of the place that's nowhere near where the real work occurs."

"We'll enter here." Marc pointed at the unguarded study located in the manor's living quarters, farthest from the activity and closest to Lake Champlain. "We'll go room to room. And we won't walk out until Emma is with us."

As he spoke, his iPhone vibrated. "Talk to me," he said to Aidan.

"I'm here," his brother replied.

"Good. We're a few miles away. See you in five."

Marc punched off. "Let's move," he told Ryan.

The warehouse Aidan had gotten his Marine buddy to lend him was right on Lake Champlain, five miles across from the Lubinov compound.

Marc pulled the van up to the wide steel doors and waited.

Aidan heard the sound of their approaching tires. He verified it was them and then pressed the necessary controls to roll up the steel door.

He gestured for them to pull in.

Marc did as instructed, parking the van next to Aidan's SUV and turning off the ignition. He and Ryan jumped out—Marc carrying a large duffel filled with his waterproof bag, wetsuit, and diving gear, and Ryan gripping the maps.

After reflexively glancing outside to ascertain that the three of them were secure, Aidan rolled down the warehouse door and joined the other two men.

"We got closeup videos of the manor and drew you and Marc a map," Ryan began by announcing.

"You did *what*?" Aidan glared from Marc to Ryan and back. "You were on Lubinov's property? Are you both completely insane?"

"Easy," Marc said. "You're right. But it was worth it. Take a look." He took the map out of Ryan's hands and showed it to Aidan. "Now we know our point of entry."

"The ground-floor study," Aidan muttered. "Yeah, okay, this helps. But you're still assholes—especially you, Marc. Ryan's a civilian. You're a fucking Navy SEAL. Since when did you become so careless?"

"It's called taking a risk. And it got us what we needed, Raider," Marc shot back, referring to the Raiders of the elite Commando Units of MARSOC—the Marine Corps Forces Special Operations Command—in which Aidan had been a plank holder—one of the original members to train.

"Hey." Ryan held up both his hands, as if to break up a brawl. "You can beat the shit out of each other later. For the record, this was my fault. But Marc's right. We got what we needed. So let's use it."

Still muttering under his breath, Aidan unzipped his bag and pulled out all his scuba equipment and a waterproof gear bag. Inside the bag were night vision goggles and his weapons— KA-BAR knife, 9 mm SIG Sauer pistol, and M4 carbine, which was short and compact but with lots of fire power.

Marc had the same, except that, instead of the M4 carbine, he carried a 9 mm H&K MP5, a submachine gun that was, up until recently, standard issue for the FBI.

Both men began pulling on their wetsuits.

"Where's the boat?" Ryan asked.

"Over there by the dock." Aidan pointed. "You said you've handled one before, right?"

Ryan rolled his eyes. "It's a little powerboat, Aidan. I've taken more girls out in those than—"

"Fine, never mind." Aidan waved away what he knew was coming. "You have your iPhone on you?"

"Always." Ryan didn't let him interrupt. "And my signal to move in is when you text me the word: 'Success.' Very original."

Aidan didn't smile. "It's not meant to be original. It's meant to get the message across."

The small, quiet powerboat glided through the waters of Lake Champlain—the perfect spot from which Aidan and Marc could make their amphibious infiltration.

They were about a mile from shore when Aidan said, "Stop."

Ryan cut the motor and clutched his flashlight with the red lens over it.

"Wait for the text," Marc reminded him, putting on his night goggles.

Looking a whole lot less cocky and whole lot more worried, Ryan said, "Be safe."

"We plan to be."

Marc rolled into the water alongside Aidan and adjusted his snorkel. Then, getting the thumbs-up from Aidan, he gave a hard nod, and the two men began to scuba in.

They reached shore, removing only their fins and breathing apparatus, staying in their wetsuits, and leaving on their scuba boots, night goggles, and hoods. Moving quickly, they made their way to the mansion. The first thing they did was to cut the spark plug wires on the diesel generator. Then they manually engaged the transfer switch, which cut off the utility power and caused the diesel engine to continuously crank without starting.

The entire house went dark. A commotion ensued inside—lots of yelling back and forth and pounding footsteps.

Marc and Aidan used the chaos to their advantage. Capable of seeing through their specialized goggles, they crept up to the study window, jimmied it open, and climbed through. Pistols raised, they made their way from room to room, moving rapidly alongside the walls, dodging cell phone flashlights when necessary and, as a result, bypassing the guards in their search for Emma.

Avoiding the master suite, they headed toward the basement.

"Hey!" A guard was posted outside the closed door. He reached for his gun as he spotted their moving forms.

In one swift move, Aidan had the guard in a choke hold, and Marc used the butt of his gun to knock him unconscious.

"There must be something—or someone—down there worth keeping hidden," Aidan muttered.

Marc nodded, yanking open the door and descending the long flight of steps.

Aidan was right behind him.

The basement was musty, mostly a storage pit, with no activity or people in view, and lit by battery-operated incandescent wall sconces. So no one down here would be tipped off to the fact that there was a blackout.

"There." Marc nudged Aidan with his elbow and pointed to a corridor off to the right.

Footsteps emanated from the hallway. A couple of security guys walked out, carrying Styrofoam cups of coffee. They talked as they drew near, probably headed for their break—and a whole-house blackout they didn't even know existed.

Marc and Aidan each took one of them, dispatching them the way they had their colleague.

The guards crumpled to the hard concrete floor.

"Their replacements will be on their way," Aidan said. "They'll find their friend at the top of the stairs and blast down here."

"There's another set of basement stairs at the opposite

end of that corridor," Marc replied. "I remember them from the map. We'll take those up once we have Emma. Come on."

The corridor was short, with a bunch of storage closets and only one room. The unyielding handle told them that it was locked from the inside.

Aidan planted one foot on the ground and used his other foot to deliver a front kick near where the door latch was. The door fell open on its hinges. Aidan and Marc then burst inside.

The room was devoid of furniture but for a four-poster bed, a few chairs and side tables, and more wall sconces.

On the bed lay Emma.

Marc and Aidan were greeted by her haunted, terrified gaze. She'd been stripped naked, bound, and gagged, each of her limbs tied to a bedframe post. There was dried blood and bruising on her body, but there wasn't time to evaluate the extent of her injuries now.

Slava was kneeling beside her, unzipping his fly, several knives sitting on the bedside table, and an evil sneer on his face.

He whipped around at the commotion, his smile fading, and he leapt to his feet, groping for the gun that was still clipped to his belt.

He didn't stand a chance.

Before his fingers had closed around the weapon, Marc squeezed the trigger of his raised SIG Sauer and delivered one lethal head shot right between Slava's eyes.

The impact sent Slava crashing backward, blood oozing from his forehead. His body shattered the side table, then rolled onto the floor in a lifeless heap.

Stepping over him, Marc grabbed a blanket from the foot of the bed and wrapped it around Emma as Aidan sliced the ropes binding her.

"It's Marc," he said as he removed her gag, aware of the fact that she couldn't see him or make out his identity through his scuba gear. "Aidan's with me. We're getting you out of here. Hold on."

Emma's teeth immediately began chattering, and she whimpered, the expression in her eyes almost painful to see.

"Easy," Marc murmured, as, very gently, he lifted her blanketed body into his arms. "We're almost home free."

Aidan was already in the shattered doorway, scanning the corridor. "We're clear," he announced. "You lead. You know where the staircase is."

They took off.

As they rounded the bend at the opposite end of the corridor, they could hear racing footsteps approaching the now-empty room.

They ascended the steps two at a time, and Marc kicked open the door at the landing hard enough to knock over the guard on the other side.

Waiting to hear his grunt of pain as he fell over, Marc shoved open the door, and he and Aidan bolted for the study.

Even carrying Emma, Marc shot through the window in one smooth motion, with Aidan right behind him. They squatted down, using their powerful quadriceps to hustle them across the grounds.

"I've got you," Marc murmured to Emma, who was shaking violently and making agonized sobbing sounds. "You're safe."

Aidan was texting Ryan as he moved.

As they neared the lake, the red beam pierced the sky like the Bat signal.

The powerboat reached shore, and Marc waded out, placing Emma on the boat. Then, he climbed in, Aidan alongside. Ryan turned the boat and sped away from shore.

Behind them, they could make out a convoy of trucks pulling up to the Lubinov mansion and a blur of figures swarming inside.

"Looks like SWAT," Aidan noted.

Marc turned around to see. "Yeah, I'm guessing it's Albany SWAT. Hutch must have made this happen. Good. They'll finish up where we left off. So much for Lubinov. I hope he rots in hell."

Ryan glanced over, seeing that Marc was still cradling Emma, rocking her like a baby in distress.

"How is she?" he asked.

"Not good," was Marc's blunt reply. He reached over to grab the bottled water that Ryan had just uncapped and was handing him, along with the couple of extra blankets they'd brought on board. "Time to rehydrate," Marc told Emma.

"Okay...but Marc." She stopped him with a painfully devastated expression. "I tried not to say anything or to answer Lubinov's questions. I tried. But those instruments he let Slava use...they hurt. I was scared. After a while...I told them I worked for Forensic Instincts. Not about Lisa's identity switch, but about FI. I'm sorry."

"Stop it." Marc put down the water long enough to wrap the extra blankets tightly around Emma, easing both her internal and external chill. "You were a trooper. Now sip slowly." He held the bottle up to her lips.

She complied, coughing at first but then gradually swallowing small amounts of fluid.

"Damn straight you were a trooper," Ryan said. "We're so proud of you. Besides, it doesn't matter anymore. The FBI has Lubinov by now, along with all the psychos working for him, and those poor athletes who won't even understand why they're being taken in."

"They won't be charged. But they'll make ideal witnesses. They'll help put the scumbags away." While he was speaking, Marc was studying Emma's bruised and swollen face. He remembered the rivulets of blood on her body, along with additional bruising around her ribs. "We've got to get you to a hospital."

"No." Emma blanched. "I just want to go home." Tears were spilling from her eyes. "He didn't rape me, Marc, not yet. You stopped him. My cuts sting, but they're not that bad. Please. Just get me home."

Marc's jaw tightened. She needed medical care, and she needed it now.

"Listen to me, Emma," Marc said, soothing her as best he could. "You can't travel all the way home in the condition you're in. You have to go to a local hospital, just to get checked out and receive whatever treatment is necessary. You'll be released in no time." *After the police and the FBI grill the hell out of you*, he thought grimly.

"Ryan," he said, recalling his teammate's attention.

Still steering the boat, Ryan peered over his shoulder, brows raised in question.

"We have to figure out a way to work this."

"I hear you."

"From here on in, it'll just be the two of us," Marc continued. "Aidan's going home."

Aidan frowned, visibly bothered by leaving Emma in her condition and by off-loading all the responsibility onto Marc and Ryan.

"Marc…" he began.

"No." Marc sliced the air with his palm, effectively cutting his brother off. "That was great teamwork, Black Hawk. Now it's time to grab your SUV from the warehouse and head back to the city and to Abby. We got it from here."

Knowing where he belonged, Aidan nodded.

"I don't give a shit about discovery," Ryan said. "I'll carry Emma into the hospital myself."

"That's not an option." Part of Marc was totally on board with what Ryan was saying. He hated having to let Emma handle any part of this on her own. But he also knew the ramifications of them admitting her. They'd have to provide their identities, their explanations—everything that would ultimately expose them and FI to criminal charges.

"The University of Vermont Medical Center isn't far from here," Marc said. "We'll pick up our van at the warehouse, and you'll drive us to the ER entrance. I'll carry Emma inside and make sure she's in a wheelchair or on a gurney before I—"

"No." This time it was Emma who interrupted. Her voice was weak, but her resolve was strong—as if she were reading Marc's mind and understood what had to be done. "You'll be noticed. You can't help but be. Just leave me near the outside ER door. I'll cry out for a doctor the minute you drive away."

"And how are you going to explain why you're alone on their doorstep, naked and injured?" Ryan demanded.

"I'll say I was attacked near the hospital grounds and that I got away."

"That's all she needs to say," Marc agreed. "The staff will be concentrating on treating her, not interrogating her. That part will come later. And, by then, we'll be there to run the show."

He tucked a lock of disheveled hair behind Emma's ear. "Listen to me," he said. "Ryan and I will be watching the ER door to make sure someone helps you in. Don't try to be stoic like you usually do. Be an emotional wreck. Beg them to call Ryan. They'll do it ASAP. That call will be our cue."

"Cue for what?" Emma asked.

"To start counting." Marc knew that Emma was far more

panicky than she was letting on. "We won't have left the hospital grounds. We'll wait two hours—enough time for us to have flown from Manhattan to Burlington—and then rush in. I need you to hold it together for that long, okay?"

Emma gave a tentative nod. "What about the cops? How do I answer their questions?"

"Act too freaked out to talk. Let them wait. Get hysterical if you need to. Just let the doctors fix you up. We'll handle law enforcement when we get there."

"I can do that." Emma was talking as much to herself as she was to Marc.

"I know you can. Meanwhile, I'll call Casey. She'll want to fly up here. The whole team will."

"And call Lisa," Emma whispered. "Tell her that she, Miles, and Shannon are safe. It's finally over."

## EPILOGUE

*Offices of Forensic Instincts*
*Two weeks later*

The whole FI team—plus Hutch, Aidan, and Madeline—was gathered around the main conference room table.

Casey carried in the cake, which was chocolate frosted, decorated with yellow buttercream flowers signifying friendship, and bearing the scripted words: *Welcome Home, Emma.*

Not welcome *back.* Welcome *home.*

Casey placed the cake in the center of the table, which was decorated with a bright yellow tablecloth, napkins, plates, hot cups, and plastic silverware, along with an enormous urn of freshly brewed coffee and a large cake slicer.

"This one's all yours, Emma," Casey told her. "You can share or eat the whole thing yourself. We're so happy to have you back we'll all forfeit our pieces, right, guys?"

There was a chorus of enthusiastic agreements.

Emma stared from the cake to her teammates, and tears filled her eyes—eyes that were no longer swollen or haunted but had yet to boast that Emma sparkle. "Thank you," she murmured. "Of course I'll share. What all of you have done for me—it means more than I can say."

"*You* mean more than *we* can say," Claire replied, gently squeezing Emma's hand.

"Yeah, we missed your mouthy quips," Ryan informed her. "It was way too dull around here."

"I'll remind you of that when I'm myself," Emma responded, her lips curving into a smile that hadn't come for two weeks.

The welts on her face had gone down, the cuts on her body were rapidly disappearing, and her bruised ribs were healing. She was sore and shaky but physically on the mend. Emotionally, she was, and would be, going for counseling for months, dealing with the deep-seated scars of her trauma.

Still, little by little, Emma was starting to be Emma again.

Over the past two weeks, the team had taken turns sitting with her at her apartment, helping her through her recuperation period—a period that had been ordered by Emma's doctor and by Casey. Madeleine had visited, too, both as a friend and as a nurse, checking out Emma's wounds and refreshing her bandages as needed.

The FBI, of course, had come to interview her, both at the University of Vermont Medical Center and here in New York. With the help of Marc's coaching, she'd told them everything— except the identities of her rescuers. To that question, all she said was that the two men who saved her were dressed totally in black with night goggles and hoods, and that they hadn't spoken to her, only brought her to the hospital and vanished. She assumed they were heroic FBI agents.

No one at the Bureau had countered that.

"Are you up to cake slicing?" Casey asked now, gazing uncomfortably at the knife. "Or do you want me to do the honors?"

For a moment, Emma eyed the slicer. Then, she said, "I'll do it." With a determined look, she stepped forward and cut generous helpings for everyone, her hands steadier than expected. "Go for it, gang," she urged.

They all complied, beaming as they watched Emma scarf down her piece of cake and cut a second. Finally, her appetite was returning.

"This is the absolute last thing I'm eating until the wedding," she declared. "It's only a few days away. I have to fit into my dress."

"Why does every woman say that?" Patrick asked, shaking his head in bewilderment. "I've heard Adele utter those same words a thousand times over the past thirty-five years. And she's never had a problem fitting into anything."

Casey laughed. "It's a female thing."

"Yeah, Marc," Ryan said cheerfully as he polished off another forkful of cake. "Get used to it. You're about to enlist for life."

Marc put down his plate and wrapped his arm around Maddy's waist. "I'm a willing recruit."

"Even if you have to give up lap dances?" Maddy's eyes danced, as she reminded Marc of the unexpected and unappreciated part of his bachelor party—a part that he'd been bitching about all week.

"No comment." Marc glared from Aidan to Ryan to Hutch.

"Kudos to us, Aidan," Ryan said. "He's still pissed off.

"Yeah, the arrangements did have their benefits. Which reminds me…" Aidan dug around in his shirt pocket and produced a slip of paper. "The lovely Yvonne—lap dancer number one—asked me to give you this." He offered the paper to Marc. "It's her cell phone number. She said that anytime you get bored, give her a call, and she'll give you more than a lap dance."

Maddy reached over and snatched the scrap of paper, tearing it into a dozen pieces and tossing it into the trash. "Problem solved."

Everyone burst out laughing.

"Pardon me, Casey." Yoda's voice echoed through the room. "My data scanner has just alerted me to a national press conference that's about to air on all major networks. It's being held by the FBI and pertains to Maxim Lubinov. Shall I display it for you?"

"By all means." Casey's brows rose in interest. "Put it up on all screens."

"Of course."

An instant later, a visual appeared on the enormous, centrally located conference room TV, as well as the panorama of screens surrounding it, providing a perfect view from every angle.

*Breaking News* flashed in red at the bottom, along with the caption: *FBI and local authorities break up national drug trafficking operation.*

Three official-looking law enforcement representatives in suits stood there—a stocky gray-haired man and a slim blonde woman positioned on either side of the dais, and a broad-shouldered African-American man, who was up at the podium. On the front panel of the podium was the customary imposing seal that read: *Department of Justice, Federal Bureau of Investigation.*

The authoritative spokesman at the podium stepped closer to the microphone and addressed the TV audience.

"Good afternoon. I'm Special Agent in Charge Rodney Bloom of the FBI Albany Division. With me today is United States Assistant District Attorney Roberta Elden and Captain of the Chicago Police Department William Regis. We are here to announce the results of an extensive, ongoing multi-law enforcement operation that has led to the indictment of Dr. Maxim Lubinov, a renowned Russian-born microbiologist, who is formally being charged with drug trafficking, manufacturing and distribution of illegal PEDs, kidnapping, murder, and attempted murder.

"In addition, the Department of Justice, along with the

Albany division of the FBI and the Chicago Police Department, has evidence tying the above crimes to the murder investigation of a young woman, Julie Forman, who was allegedly killed as a result of uncovering incriminating information on Lubinov's drug ring. On Lubinov's property was found the body of James Robbins, an employee of Lubinov's, who'd been missing from his Chicago home for over four weeks."

The SAC went on to detail the part that Russian Organized Crime played in the cartel, and then went on to name names, including all of Lubinov's employees.

The list was endless.

No mention of Emma, Lisa, Miles, Shannon, or any outside investigative source was made.

Casey glanced around the table and raised her coffee cup. "Good news all around. The FBI and DOJ get the credit, we get to stay clean, and we have the pleasure of making yet another ADA's career skyrocket."

"That should be easy with Lubinov representing himself in court, the arrogant bastard." Marc rolled his eyes in disgust.

"An ugly combination of narcissistic personality disorder and antisocial personality disorder." Hutch reiterated his earlier evaluation. "Good thing he'll be locked up for good."

"That scene he made prior to his Grand Jury hearing was a media circus, with Lubinov raving on the front steps of the courthouse about his research and about how one day the world would recognize his genius." Marc gave a humorless laugh. "He really believes the courts will value his scientific advances over his crimes, and that he'll be exonerated. And that's even knowing that his assistant, Dmitry Gorev, is cooperating with the authorities. It seems the kid finally grew a conscience."

"Better late than never," Patrick pointed out. "It'll help the ADA's case."

"True." Marc nodded.

"I wonder what the government will do with Lubinov's research," Ryan mused aloud. "Will they destroy it or have their pharmaceutical resources alter the formula until it's safe for use?"

"We'll probably never know," Casey replied. "But I can live with that. The important things have all been resolved, including keeping our clients safe and giving them back their lives. Case closed."

"Giving them back their lives how?" Emma asked. "You said you were working on legal options to keep Lisa and Miles out of jail."

"And we did," Casey replied. "We've had talks with the right attorneys, who have subsequently made the right deals. And, before you ask, yes, our clients are totally on board with everything. Documents have been signed and dated. In fact..." She glanced at her watch. "Lisa and Miles should be arriving at the brownstone any time now, just to see you. Shannon is back in Chicago with her parents, but she sends you her love and the promise to stay in touch."

"All of that sounds awesome." Emma sighed in relief. She shot Casey a quizzical look. "What does 'right attorneys' mean?"

"It means a few top-notch lawyers with whom we have good and mutually beneficial relationships," Casey clarified. "They've been able to work out a deal whereby Lisa's and Miles's jail time will be converted into one year of stringent community service—providing that Lisa repays Julie's inheritance and testifies at her murder trial. Since Julie has no living relatives, Lisa chose to pay back the inheritance by converting the vacant building a block down from Excalibur into a gym and café for foster kids."

"What a great idea," Emma exclaimed. "That way, Julie's dream stays alive in Excalibur, and Lisa's dream to help other foster kids is realized."

"Yup." Casey nodded. "The deal is contingent, of course, on Shannon's testimony, which she's ready and eager to give. So stop worrying. It's all going to be fine."

"This time," Hutch qualified. Despite the celebratory mood, he was less than thrilled with the team. "Look, I ran the necessary interference with the Bureau regarding Emma's capture. I backed up her story, and I kept my mouth shut about FI involvement. But, Casey, you gave Marc and Ryan the go-ahead to act without law enforcement, knowing that SWAT was on its way. In turn, they went ahead and put themselves in a life-threatening situation."

"If they hadn't, I might not be alive today," Emma reminded him. "Every second mattered."

Hutch couldn't argue that one, and he didn't even try—especially because it would make him an utter hypocrite, given the rules he'd broken in the past to save Casey's life. "I know, Emma. And I'm more than grateful that you're okay. But this constant vigilante stuff worries the hell out of me. One of these days, FI might not be so lucky. And I couldn't live with myself if any of you was hurt—or worse."

"It won't come to that, Hutch." Casey gave him a tender look, fully aware of how torn he was—and why. "We're the best there is at what we do. You know that. And you also know that we always stay within the confines of the law—unless we can't." Her wink was playful. "But thank you. Your concerns have been duly noted."

"Yeah, right, and you'll take them under advisement." Hutch rolled his eyes. "You're going to make me old before my time."

"I'll keep you young, I promise."

Hutch couldn't help but thaw. "I'll hold you to that."

Maddy gave him a sympathetic look. "Our job, it seems, is to love them and live with them—but not always happily."

"I'll take the job," Hutch replied. "God help me, but sign me up."

*****

## ACKNOWLEDGEMENTS

I'm fortunate enough to work with an amazing, dedicated group of people who are the best consultants any author could ask for. They possess not only specialized knowledge and experience that make them the experts that they are, but also the generosity of spirit to share that expertise with me and help me create the best book possible.

Specifically, I want to thank:

Angela Bell, Public Affairs Specialist, FBI Office of Public Affairs, who quite simply defines the word "awesome."

SSA James McNamara, FBI Behavioral Analysis Unit, retired, Behavioral Criminology International, former Captain United States Marine Corps, whose vast knowledge of criminal human behavior is a fascinating counterpart to his firsthand knowledge of the skills and character of a US Marine.

Debbie D'Alessio, Personal Trainer, who spent hours teaching me everything from professional training techniques to the basics of using state-of-the-art training equipment.

Shannon Wojnar, who introduced me to the world of competitive gymnastics.

"JP" and "his daughter", who brought Chicago to life for me, and gave me an insider's view of the city and its surrounding suburbs.

Dr. Paul Sedlacek, who combines extraordinary veterinary expertise with overall medical knowledge (along with a dash of creativity) to lend understanding to the human/animal anatomical similarities and differences.


As always I want to thank the following:

My readers, who inspire me, cheer me on, and love my characters as much as I do.

And to my family, who are my heart and my champions—I feel eternally blessed to have you. I love you, always.